Born in Izmir, Turkey, ASLI PERKER is a writer and journalist. Her novels include *The Scent of the Others* and *The Executioner's Graveyard*. A bestseller in Turkey, *Soufflé* is her first novel to be translated into English. She lives in Istanbul.

www.asliperker.com

'A modern Turkish writer with the subtle, steady gaze of Balzac. With quiet brilliance, Aslı Perker shows how couples and families from Paris to the Philippines cope with sudden catastrophic loss. And at the heart of the book, balancing loss, there is always food: warming, adding flavour, expressing love and celebration.'
Maggie Gee OBE

D1113640

Aslı Perker

Soufflé

TELEGRAM

First published 2013 in Turkish as *Sufle* by Dogan Egmont Publishing
This English edition published 2013 by Telegram

1

Copyright © 2013 Aslı Perker / Kalem Agency
Translation © Aslı Perker

ISBN 978 1 84659 144 0
EISBN 978 1 84659 145 7

A full cip record for this book is available
from the British Library.

Printed and bound by CPI Group
(UK) Ltd, Croydon, CR0 4YY

TELEGRAM
26 Westbourne Grove, London W2 5RH
www.telegrambooks.com

For Rukhsana

'Given the choice between the experience of pain and nothing, I would choose pain.'

William Faulkner

One

Lilia knew something was wrong as soon as she turned her head to the right as she stepped out of her room, just as she did every morning. Even though Arnie devoted long hours to keeping his room in order, and locked the door before leaving for work so that his wife couldn't mess it up, he had not once realised that he always slid the kilim rug lying in front of his bedroom door slightly to the left. Maybe that was because Lilia fixed it with the tip of her clog every morning, after he left for work.

Over the last few years of their marriage, which they'd managed to keep going for more than thirty years now, they had come to an easy understanding that the smartest thing to do was to have separate bedrooms. They found a way to live in the same house without touching each other's lives. The only thing that suggested they had once been lovers was the small, elegant and understated kiss that Arnie planted on Lilia's lips every night when he came home. In the minutes that followed they would usually sit on the stools placed around the counter in the middle of the kitchen to eat the delicious meal Lilia had prepared, while watching the news presented by Jim Lehrer on Channel Thirteen. Although Lilia had turned into an American in the last thirty-seven years she had lived in the United States, her almond-shaped eyes set in her dark complexion like beautiful jet stones and the ginger taste she added to every meal kept her Filipino roots alive.

Ever the gentleman, Arnie would always compliment Lilia on her cooking before washing his own dish and asking to be excused to go to his room. And so after a forty-five minute interruption, Lilia would go back to her own life. She'd either spend some time in front of the computer in a closet space she'd arranged for herself as a study or take a look at the newspapers her husband had brought home. Every night at ten o'clock she'd hear the sound of Ed's footsteps, and once the tall, blonde man had appeared at the kitchen door she'd remind him to be quiet. Although this retired fifty-five-year-old police officer had been living on the second floor of their two-storey house for the last ten years, most of the time Lilia needed to force herself to remember he existed. Ever since he'd started working night shifts as a security guard at a shopping mall, he had got into the habit of coming downstairs every night at the same time and this added a new element to Lilia's routines. After sitting on one of those stools for fifteen minutes to have his late supper, Ed would respond to Lilia's curious looks by saying he really liked the food, and then he'd feel good about himself for filling a tiny part of the huge emptiness in the life of this sixty-two-year-old woman.

But that's as far as it went. Living in the same house could only bring them so close together. Lilia could never find the courage to ask this man, who had become almost a part of their family, where he disappeared to at the weekend.

Fortunately she had been smart enough to include the food in the $400 rent Ed had been paying each month, so that they had an excuse to talk. Otherwise Ed would fade away into a ghost, eating only peanut butter and jam squeezed between two slices of toast, like all Americans did.

It was because of these small routines in her life that Lilia realised something was amiss that morning. The small kilim in front of Arnie's door – which was a present from a Turkish lady who had stayed with them once – remained perfectly in its place. That could only mean one thing: Arnie had not left his room. Still, Lilia knocked on the door a couple of times before taking the liberty to enter. When she didn't hear any response, she walked into the room to find her husband collapsed on the floor right next to his bed. He had his pyjamas on, so she couldn't figure out how long he had been in that position, but instead of screaming or panicking she picked up the phone and dialled 9-1-1. While the person on the other end of the line was asking questions, she realised that her husband was still alive from the weak pulse she felt at her fingertips.

Before long the loud wailing of the ambulance could be heard in their quiet neighbourhood. Lilia had not left her husband alone until that moment and tears welled up in her eyes for the first time as she walked down the stairs. What really made her heart ache was the thought that Arnie had probably tried to be quiet as he fell. Why couldn't he just collapse loudly like other men? Why did he have to try to hold onto the edge of the bed? Lilia was sure that her husband had fallen like that for the sake of quietness: the damned absolute quietness of their house.

11

After she had opened the door and sent the paramedics upstairs she turned her wet eyes towards the other houses in the neighbourhood. No, there was no one standing outside the doors. The curtains hadn't even been pulled ajar. Instead of admitting that nobody cared, Lilia preferred to think that their neighbours were at work or had taken their kids to school. How had she broken away from the explosive life she had once been a part of and fallen into this state of placidity? How had she come to accept living like this? Still, she couldn't bring herself to get mad, not at her neighbours, not at her husband and not at her own indifference. When had her anger – which she thought would never cease in her youth – faded away? In her crowded family, fights had been as common as hugs and happiness. During their short times together the place would echo with both yelling and laughter. Parties would turn into fights, then back into parties, then into drunken meetings and fury fests, but they were always great fun in the end. There was always someone to complain about in her loud family. There was always someone to get angry at, or be proud of, or to kick out of the family only to be taken back in later.

In Arnie's muted world, on the other hand, Lilia's family was little more than a circus, entertaining and interesting at the beginning, and becoming too loud and cheap with time. For Arnie, what could be better entertainment than a nice Sunday afternoon spent watching baseball, quiet dinners where nothing could be heard but the clinking of silverware and his intelligent but rarely made jokes? What sanctuary could replace Arnie's safe, clean and tidy room, which was filled with the most essential newspaper cuttings filed carefully in a ring binder? What Filipino folk song could give the same joy as the calm, self-confident voices of the PBS presenters? And how about those old tales of fairies and spirits that his wife and her family told after every Christmas dinner? These people had lived in the States for years and benefitted from all kinds of technology and medicine, and even drove the latest models of cars, but they still believed in some mysterious creatures who lived in trees. What's more, they thought it was a great idea to pass these stories down from one generation to another. Arnie found this unacceptable and he certainly hadn't allowed his kids to be brought up with this kind of nonsense. He had turned a blind eye to the stories that were told in front of them once a year, but ultimately he had managed to implant a love of tranquillity and peace in his children. In fact, he'd been so successful that now they rarely called, hardly ever came for dinner and when they did – only on special occasions – they stayed for barely an hour. They had never once asked them to take care of their grandchildren. Even though they weren't his biological son and daughter, they'd inherited or learned his habits 100 per cent.

Lilia, on the other hand was heartbroken at having to spend all that time alone in her room, but she never got angry at them. She had given and done everything she could for those children whom she hadn't carried in her womb for nine months. She'd managed to bring them over from Vietnam despite all the bureaucratic difficulties, spent a lot of money on making them healthy and sent them to the best schools. More importantly, she'd given up her life for theirs. During the early years of their marriage they had lived in

Manhattan, and Lilia's exotic beauty, her creativity and the way she stood out from all the other women around her had helped them enter social circles and made the vibrant young couple guests of honour at every party. She'd been able to show her paintings to important people at these parties, and had put on art shows at galleries that were normally unapproachable. She'd enjoyed being right at the heart of this intellectual and bohemian world. Moving out of the city to a big house with a lot of rooms and a garden after they had adopted the children was, of course, Arnie's idea. It was what was supposed to be done, just like all American families with children always did. Besides, these kids who had been exposed to so much trauma needed a quiet, calm and peaceful place, and he shouldn't have had to tell her that Manhattan was as far away from that ideal as you could get. As always, Lilia complied.

In the end, they'd been left alone in this huge house with seven rooms, who-knows-how-many closets and four bathrooms, which they'd bought for the sake of the children. Since she'd never been able to do all the cleaning herself, and the Mexican lady she had hired had always done a sloppy job, dust covered every inch of the house and it was almost impossible to see the garden through the thick layer on the windows. And now, the children they had raised with such great care wouldn't bring their own children over, not even for an hour, complaining that the house was too dirty.

The sounds coming from the walkie-talkies brought Lilia back into the present. After the paramedics carried sixty-year-old Arnie out to the ambulance on a stretcher, Lilia climbed up as well and sat beside him, holding his hand. They drove to the hospital accompanied by wailing sirens which echoed through the desolate streets of New York suburbia. Lilia didn't find the silence in the ambulance uncomfortable, she had had many years of practice in the art of silence.

♥

At the same time, only six hours ahead, Marc was opening the door to his apartment with a small cake box in his hand. He left his gallery to come home early every Friday. He always bought a couple of desserts from the pâtisserie, which was on the right-hand side of the street as he entered Rue Monge, and walked a little faster so that he would be reunited sooner with the love of his life, Clara, his wife of twenty-two years. Once he reached the stairs, he would wait impatiently for the smell of coffee that escaped through the gaps around the door of their first floor apartment. They had discovered the filter coffee years ago on a trip to New York, and since then they had put aside Europe's most valued espresso and become addicted to vanilla coffee.

They had been living in the same apartment ever since they got married. The only spacious element in this one-bedroom home was the kitchen. Since Clara had always loved cooking from an early age, it had become the place where she spent most of her time. It wouldn't be wrong to say that it was the most inviting room in the apartment, with its flowers, plants, accessories, the table in the middle and a small TV in a corner. Their living room had become a library, filled with books carefully placed on the shelves, and they usually sat in the kitchen to read the books they picked. Marc never complained about any of this and happily followed his wife to their bedroom at the end of every night, getting drowsy as he smelled her perfume mixed with the aroma of food that she left behind her. He wouldn't trade this pleasure for anything in the world.

At the beginning of their marriage, they had talked about moving to a bigger apartment when they had children. They would need at least two bedrooms. They even speculated about the chances of finding a big kitchen like this one again. In the end they never needed to look for another apartment. They tried to have children for a long time, without giving up or giving into despair. When it came to the point of using medication or hormone shots, they finally gave up. They didn't listen to the advice they received from their friends about adopting. They never told anybody, but what Clara wanted was a little Marc, and what Marc wanted was a little Clara. An adopted child wouldn't fit that description. Instead, they found happiness in each other and themselves became children who never grew up. Their list of routines got longer over the years and they grew happier with each passing day. While Clara was getting better in the kitchen on a daily basis, Marc took refuge in her warmth as he sat in the corner reading his comics: *Fluid Glacial, l'Echo des Savanes, Psikopat, BoDoii.*

It was impossible for Clara to teach Marc the names of vegetables or the smells of spices. After the first couple of times she had sent him to the farmers' market ended in disaster, she decided to leave him alone and learned to accept him as her most loyal customer. She thought of Marc's insistence on getting a little something from the pâtisserie on Fridays as a childish notion, yet she loved it. She surrendered to having a real dessert from the outside world once a week and it grieved her deeply that her treats still weren't as good. She rolled the cream in her mouth, pasting it to her palate and feeling the scent of it behind her nose, and tried to figure out what went wrong with her own baking.

They went on a lot of trips to many different countries over the years. Clara came back with recipes and Marc brought with him newspapers, books and comics. Neither of them could ever forget the taste of the stuffed pepper they'd had in Istanbul. Once, on a trip to Greece, Marc said that the stuffed pepper tasted just like the one in Istanbul, and Clara objected fiercely. Even though she tried many times, she was never able to cook it the same way. When she also tried and failed to stuff mussels with rice like the Turks did, she started planning a new holiday to the Aegean region of Turkey. Marc never opposed anything Clara wanted or planned. He loved to give himself fully to the rhythm of her life. Happiness overflowed in their sixteen-square-metre kitchen and settled in his bones.

He was also very happy in his gallery, right across the Seine. He sold original artwork by the artists of every comic book he had ever loved since he was a little boy. He had everything: the inked pages of *Lucky Luke*, the sketches of *Asterix* and pages from *The Adventures of Tintin*. His gallery had become so famous in time that enthusiasts came from all over Europe to visit him. The reality was that he was making a lot of money. Despite this fact, Clara still mentioned how little every meal she cooked cost and how much they saved by eating at home instead of at a restaurant and this made Marc laugh every time. They could eat out at the best restaurants every day if they wanted, but even suggesting this would be a huge blow to Clara's reason to live. At least he had managed to convince her not to give him a lunch box to take to work with him. Marc locked the door of his gallery every day at noon and went to his favourite comic book shops after grabbing a quick bite to eat. He tried to follow every new book and artist. During their New York trip, he was astonished by how big the industry was and they had to establish the rule of going to one restaurant for every comic book shop they visited. When he saw how many issues came out every month, he was at a loss to understand how the readers managed to follow everything. He even toyed with the idea of moving to this chaotic city as he walked among the shelves, admiring the books he saw. Towards the end of their fifteen-day trip though, Clara had started complaining about how small the farmers' markets were, how the yolks of the eggs were too pale and how weird the milk tasted. It looked as if the only thing this Paris gourmet liked the taste of in New York was the coffee. And, of course, as always, he was ready to do whatever she wished.

Marc waited outside the door for a couple of minutes with the keys hanging in his hand. He realised the smell of coffee was missing, however much he tried to sniff it with his nose lifted in the air. He checked his watch; it was ten past three, just like every other Friday. It was impossible for Clara not to have made the coffee. It was also not possible that she had left for some urgent matter without letting him know.

Clara always let him know. Even when he had to leave his gallery to go somewhere at short notice, she would always call at just the right moment to be informed about any change of plan. He felt a tingling sensation in his hand, which was holding the cake box. Nervously, he turned the key in the lock. When he stepped into the hallway he heard the sound of the TV show, *Des chiffres et des lettres*, the numbers and the letters. Clara would never miss the show, not unless she had something absolutely crucial to do, and would always try to reach the designated number with the numbers given as quickly as the contestants did. Marc walked into the kitchen hoping to find his wife struggling with the numbers, forgetting about the whole world. Instead, Clara lay collapsed on her side right in front of the kitchen counter. The coffee jar she had been holding before she fell had broken into pieces on the floor. Marc could smell the vanilla coffee now. Almost choked by sobs, he pressed two fingers against his wife's incredibly slender wrist. She had no pulse. Then he touched her precious neck. There was no pulse. After he had made the necessary phone call he lay down next to his wife and held on to the smell she had left behind.

When the phone rang at ten past four, one hour ahead of Paris time, Ferda looked at the clock on the wall and smiled. She was glad that steam had just come out of the pressure cooker, and she had turned the heat down low and set the alarm for twenty minutes' time. This way she could talk to her daughter freely. Öykü lived in Paris and called her every Friday at the same time, just before leaving work. She said talking to her mum at the end of the week always bode well for a very happy weekend. She would ask Ferda about everyone, every incident that took place, almost requesting a detailed report of everything she was missing by not being there. How was her aunt, was her uncle well, did the cousins who had a fight make up, did her other uncle still live in that house or had he moved to another place; she wanted to know everything. She would sometimes ask about the price of honey at the deli across the street, or whether the branches of the tree in front of their building had been trimmed, and sometimes she asked how Ferda marinated her celery root dish.

Ferda didn't understand why her daughter, who had been living in Paris for the last six years, was interested in the price of honey or the branches of a tree, but she never asked for an explanation. She was happy to talk to her for as long as she could. Besides, this way she felt as if they lived in close vicinity still and shared the same concerns and delights and this helped her not to go crazy missing her baby girl. Her daughter always said the same thing: 'It's only a three-hour flight, why don't you jump on a plane and come over whenever you want? I come to Istanbul all the time. You can come for breakfast and go back for dinner if you like, you know.' Ferda couldn't tell her daughter why jumping on a plane simply didn't work. Being a mother wasn't like that. She wanted her daughter to live downstairs or across the hall. She wanted to go to her place for a cup of Turkish coffee in the morning, or cook for her so that she wouldn't have to do anything after coming home tired from work. She was a great help to her son and daughter-in-law. She took care of her grandchildren, and cooked for them. They just had to stop by at the end of the day and grab their Tupperware filled with food. Thanks to her, they'd never had a problem with low blood sugar. She could never say these things to her daughter, though. If she did, God forbid, her daughter might move even further away, out of fear of getting stuck in a lifelong trap.

She actually understood why Öykü had moved to Europe. The first time she visited Paris to see her daughter, she silently wished that she had been born there herself. It was a beautiful city. Every street, every corner was an artwork. The transport system was easy, as was walking from place to place. Öykü had taken her to farmers' markets and searched in her mother's eyes for approval of how striking they looked. Ferda had thought they were beautiful, too. The whole thing looked like a French movie, refined and elegant; but it could never replace the farmers' market in Feneryolu, thought Ferda. The farmers' markets in Paris were only one-tenth of the size of the ones in Istanbul, but she couldn't deny that she enjoyed the cheese stands here. She had to confess that being proud of Cyprus cheese, Izmir tulum, kasseri or braid cheese was silly after seeing the variety of cheese available in France.

While she made her daughter's favourite dish – stuffed vine leaves – in that tiny Parisian kitchen, Öykü showed her some samples of French cuisine. Ferda thanked God that her daughter was good in the kitchen. They were able to talk in the same language that way. What if she had been a girl who didn't know the difference between dill and parsley? She knew a lot of young women like that. Whenever her daughter called her to ask for a recipe she felt proud. She told her friends how Öykü loved cooking, how she tried even the most difficult recipes. She wanted to say to them, 'She's not going to be one of those new housewives who can't put food on their husbands' tables,' but she didn't since she had no idea whether the man her daughter was going to marry would care about that at all. Öykü didn't care much for Turkish men. Ferda knew from the films she'd seen that French men had as much of an appetite as Turkish men, but the difference was that they cooked themselves. They didn't think women should do all the cooking in a household; they came from a different culture. Öykü's beautiful gift was going to be wasted, but this would be the least of her concerns if her daughter married a French man.

Ferda answered the phone feeling excited about their weekly conversation, which she was looking forward to so much.

'Öykü ...'

'Mrs Ferda?'

'Yes, it's me.'

'This is Sema, your mother's next-door neighbour.'

Since Sema was both her mother's next-door neighbour and her landlady, Ferda couldn't decide what this phone call was about. It had been a couple of days since she had wired the rent; maybe there had been an unexpected problem. Or could it have been time to raise the rent and Ferda had forgotten about it? The reason for this forgetfulness was a lack of vitamin B, she was sure of it.

'Sorry, Mrs Sema. My daughter always calls from Paris at this time, that's why ... sorry again. What's the problem?'

'I think you should come here as soon as possible. Your mother fell; I think she's broken a bone. I heard her screams and thank God I have the keys to her apartment. I had to go in, I apologise for that. Anyway, we called the ambulance; I think it'll be here pretty soon. You should come here or maybe go straight to the hospital, I don't know …'

Ferda hung up the phone saying she would be there soon. After turning off the stove, she ran out the door. She kept repeating to herself: 'I hope it's not her hip.' Everybody knew what a broken hip meant at the age of eighty-two.

Fortunately they lived very close to each other. When her brother decided to get married and hinted that he wasn't going to move out of the house he had shared with his mother for years, Ferda got smart and rented a small place for her mother very close to hers. Thanks to that decision, she was there in a flash now, and arrived at the same time as the ambulance. Her mother, Mrs Nesibe, loved to exaggerate even the smallest kind of pain, and now she was moaning almost in pleasure to show the world how much it hurt. Ferda knew that what she had been most afraid of had finally happened. Her mother would have to move in with them. Who knew for how long? And she understood at that moment that the hardest time of her life had just begun.

Two

The green garment caught Lilia's eye in the whiteness of the hospital. Calmly, she waited for the doctor to approach her. The emotional turbulence she had gone through before leaving the house had already disappeared in the ambulance, and it had left a strange, peaceful feeling in its place. She knew that she could stand up strong and serenely if they told her that her husband had passed away. In fact, she didn't even mind admitting to herself that deep down it was what she wanted. Lilia felt tired. The sentimental fatigue she had been experiencing for years had surfaced all of a sudden. She wanted this unofficial loneliness to come to an end, so that the world would know she was alone. Arnie, who had seemed to exist in her life for the last thirty years, had actually withdrawn into his clamshell around twenty years ago, condemning her to a graceful solitude.

True, they had felt like a family for the first few years after the children had come along, and they had lived their lives accordingly. All the same, this active way of living had eventually burnt itself out after about ten years. When the children arrived, one of them was eight and the other was nine years old. They had both had more than their share of life's sorrows; so much so that neither Lilia or Arnie had been able to reach them. It didn't help that they couldn't speak the same language, either. So, while the children were learning English, Lilia and Arnie started studying Vietnamese. The four of them would walk around the house with dictionaries in their hands, working hard on something that was new to all of them. In the end, they had simply got used to being silent all the time, so that even when the children started speaking fluent English they had nothing to say to each other any more. Gestures and facial expressions had already replaced words. Anyway, not long after that – only nine years after moving to the United States – Giang, who was a year older than his biological sister, started university, and Dung followed him a year later. Instead of sharing their lives as a family, ten years after adopting the children Lilia and Arnie ended up simply paying tuition fees and all of the other expenses, and had to accept the fact that they wouldn't be spending Thanksgivings and Christmases together any more.

The number of visits dropped dramatically and the rare phone conversations they had usually revolved around how much money the children needed. Once the Internet came into their lives, the phone conversations became emails. This way, the rare sounds that Lilia had got used to left her life, too. Arnie didn't care about any of these things. He thought this was exactly what other parents went through with their kids. It would take him a long time to figure out that these changes had all been part of a message that the children were trying to send them. However, even this wouldn't teach him to trust Lilia's instincts.

Years later, Lilia had broached the subject over coffee and pumpkin pie after a Thanksgiving dinner. She had mentioned how important she thought Thanksgiving was and commented that people expected to be appreciated once in a while. The children understood where this was going right away. They had been waiting for this opportunity for years. Dung started speaking, cutting to the chase. She had always been more ferocious and quick-tempered than her brother. She accused Lilia and Arnie of making money out of them. As she announced that they knew how people who had adopted children from Vietnam received a contribution from the government, her face took on a look of complete defiance. With the government's help, Lilia had never had to work, wasn't that right? Giang showed his approval by constantly nodding his head. The moment she heard this accusation, Lilia felt that she had finally lost the sense of happiness that always rose and danced somewhere inside her despite every challenge she faced. Her fierce confidence in human kindness had been proved wrong. All the same, she didn't offer to show them the hospital receipts from their early medical treatments, which Arnie had filed religiously, or the monthly payments on their house, which had been bought for their sake, or the pile of payment slips for their university expenses. She didn't try to convince them that the money from the government wouldn't even cover one-third of what they had spent over the years. Instead, she nursed her broken heart that night as she fell asleep.

Arnie kissed them on their cheeks as he saw them out later that evening. He didn't say: 'You were unfair to us, and you broke Lilia's heart.' Instead, he continued to send them and their newborn children cheques for modest sums every holiday and birthday over the following years. The two of them never talked about this afterwards. Lilia never knew if Arnie felt like he had wasted time, money and emotions on those children, as she did. And once they had moved into separate bedrooms, this issue was buried along with all the others.

Now Lilia wanted to be really alone. She wanted some divine power to cut this bond between her and her husband, which she couldn't break herself and which would torture her for as long as it existed. She wanted life to present her with everything she had put off or been afraid to do on a silver platter. She was thinking of what she would do if her wish came true. First of all, she should go on holiday. She wanted to go to Italy, where she had been once as a young woman, so that she could breathe in the Roman air one last time. She was dying to go back to experiencing everything she had once cut short but could still remember. She had been generous to life and to people, and now she wanted them to return the favour. She had to sell that huge, dull, dusty old house at once and move back to Manhattan. Just like in the old days. She had to see every movie, go to all the Broadway shows and walk around museums all day long. It still wasn't too late for picnics in Central Park, or bicycle rides through the city. Visiting the Statue of Liberty was at the top of her list – to remind her why she had come to this country and this city in the first place.

She had come to this city to shine, to blossom, to paint and to breathe life in. At the age of sixty-two, and especially at this particular moment, she didn't feel old at all. She was healthy; her skin was still beautiful. Her jet black hair still resisted turning grey. It was almost as if God had given her a strong body so that she could enjoy life to the fullest. She might have lost her faith in people but not in herself. She had to call her siblings and arrange a trip with them. She had to speak more Filipino and learn to look at America from a tourist's point of view. Lilia felt proud of her energy and her hopefulness. A smile, which looked good on her broad cheeks, spread across her face. She stood up and greeted the doctor with a look of happiness, caused by the private wishes she had just discovered. The doctor misinterpreted the joy on Lilia's face. He smiled and said:

'Your husband is stable now. A minor cerebrovascular incident took place in his brain, which caused a paresis. Fortunately, it stopped before it could do too much damage. His left side is weak. We can't be certain how long he'll be in this state or if he'll get his mobility back. Still, I'll write down the names you'll need for physical and psychological therapy, which he should start right away. There are some tough days ahead of you. For both of you. I'm sure you'll need some psychological help, too. We'll talk about this in more detail later. That's it for now. It'd be a good idea to go home and get some rest. You'll have a lot to do once he's released.'

The smile froze on Lilia's face. She kept on staring into space for a while after the doctor left. She was still trying to recover from the 'his left side is weak' comment. She sat back down on the chair behind her and felt as if the energy that had been flowing through her body half a minute ago was draining out through her fingertips, leaving her feeling like an empty sack. The number 'sixty-two' was throbbing in her brain now. She felt old, too old. She wasn't sure which of the children she should call first. Although Dung was the more aggressive of the two, she had never tried to hide the fact that she felt closer to Arnie. She directed most of the anger she felt towards Lilia and treated Arnie like one of the victims in this story, as if he had nothing to do with any of the decisions they had made. Maybe she was simply exercising her natural right to hate her mother, like all girls did at some point in their lives. If she had been Lilia's biological daughter, she'd have found some other reason to confront her.

Lilia picked up her phone and looked at it reluctantly for a few minutes. She didn't have her reading glasses with her since she'd left in such a hurry, so she stretched her hand out in front of her to try to make out the names on the screen. She wished she was one of those mothers who knew their daughters' numbers off by heart. The love she had wanted to give for years had been hemmed up inside her and had blossomed into a deep sense of sadness. Finally she found the number and pressed the call button, nervously. Dung had put such a distance between them that she didn't even want to make this phone call, even though it was completely to her advantage. Knowing that she was about to hear her daughter's irritated voice on the other end of the line, she almost felt her heart failing. That's why Lilia felt considerably relieved when Dung didn't answer the call. She knew perfectly well that the young woman never went out without her phone and the only reason she hadn't answered was because the caller's name had appeared on the screen and she didn't have time for her so-called mother. When she heard her daughter's voicemail greeting, Lilia thought it would be punishment enough not to leave any message. She knew that Dung would call back if she thought the subject was important enough. Lilia was sure that the hot-blooded young lady was going to yell at her later for not leaving such an important message, but she chose to call Giang instead. After several rings, she heard her son's tired voice answer the phone, clearly unwilling to utter a single word. 'Hi Lilia, how are you?' he asked. Lilia now regretted letting her children call her by her first name during their teenage years. Back then she hadn't expected to fill their mother's place, and so she had never approached the subject. Besides, since she was responsible for her own name, Lilia – the name of her favourite flower – she liked as many people to call her that as possible. The more people called her Lilia, the more she felt like a Lilia.

The name that was given to her when she was born was Manggagaway: the goddess of sickness. This was the goddess who healed the sick, mended wounds and brought people together; she was the negotiator and held a very respected place in Pagan culture. Some people said she merely disguised herself as a healer while she actually spread sickness, but Lilia refused to even listen to this interpretation. Lilia liked Manggagaway, and as a little girl she had even had a go at healing people whenever they felt some sort of pain, closing her eyes tightly and putting her hands on the spot that hurt. Unfortunately, this was an impossible name for Americans. They tried to abbreviate it, but by doing so they destroyed it and changed the meaning completely. So she chose her own name instead. Later on, at the parties she went to, she learned about the E. M. Forster character named Lilia in *Where Angels Fear to Tread*. The intellectual types she met at those parties always asked whether her name came from one of the characters in the novel. She read the book in a heartbeat and was scared by the meaning it gave to the name. The Lilia in the book was a free-spirited woman who went to Italy and fell in love with both the country and a younger man. Sadly, she died during childbirth at a very young age, which meant that she faded unseasonably, just like the lily.

Along with all of her ancestors, Lilia believed that the meanings of names affected the destinies of people, but she got rid of this fear by convincing herself that this belief only applied to the name given at birth. All the same, she couldn't help thinking about this superstition during a couple of phases in her life. Wasn't her life just like the lilies? Wasn't she fading a little bit more year in, year out? And hadn't she brought this unhappiness upon herself by toying with her own faith? When the children first came to the United States, she and Arnie had also tried to Americanise their names, but since they hadn't been able to explain what they meant during that silent era they had given up and continued calling them by their original names. They thought they would change their own names one day when the time was right. However, the children turned out to be more loyal to their origins than she had been. Maybe it was because their names were the only things left over from their previous lives. 'Giang' was the name of a river in Vietnam and 'Dung' meant beauty. Both children were very firm about making people say their names correctly. Lilia sometimes felt that Dung looked down on her on this issue as well as many others. And she was not completely wrong in thinking that Dung saw her as someone who had betrayed her own identity.

'Hi, Giang, I have some bad news. Arnie is sick. He had … uhm … a clot … burst in his brain and he had a kind of a stroke. He's in intensive care now. We're at St Joseph's.'

'God! When did this happen?'

'I found him at ten past nine this morning. He had the bleeding earlier, or whatever it was.'

'Why didn't you call before?'

'I'm sorry. I didn't have time. I just got myself together.'

'OK, I'll come after work today. Does Dung know?'

'I called her but there was no reply.'

'I'll let her know. I'm not sure if she can come over today. Her in-laws are coming for dinner tonight. But I'll definitely stop by.'

As she hung up, Lilia wished she had never called him. One of things that saddened her the most was the fact that the children spoke to each other every single day. They knew about each other's schedules. They even bought houses close to one another. They only had this distant relationship with her and Arnie. Her beloved son had informed her that he was going to stop by after work. In actual fact, he worked as an executive at an insurance company, thanks to the money they had spent on his education. He could leave his office whenever he wanted, especially at a time like this. But he could only stop by after work. And he still had the nerve to question her. He had asked why she hadn't called earlier and she had answered as sheepishly as ever, saying she was sorry. She shoved the phone into the pocket of her dress, her hands shaking. The tears she had been expecting for a while now stood at the edges of her eyelashes, caused by pure anger. She stood up and walked to the exit, wobbling in the blurry corridor. She wanted to go home and get rid of the terrible hospital food that was circulating in her system as soon as possible. She had a craving for *nilaga*, just like every other time she had felt unhappy or tired since her childhood. That cabbage soup with potatoes, meat and fish sauce was just what she needed right now.

Getting out of the taxi in front of their house, she walked to the side door, which opened directly onto the kitchen, instead of heading to the front door. As soon as she stepped into the house, the familiar smell of her kitchen wrapped and soothed her without wasting any time. It took her in its arms, ready to heal all her wounds in just a little while.

Marc was standing in front of Clara's wardrobe, trying to pick one of her outfits. The minute he opened its doors, his wife's scent slapped him in the face and shook awake all of the feelings he'd thought he had under control. He didn't even know how much he had cried, how long he had slept or what he had been doing since they'd taken Clara's lifeless body away the day before. He vaguely remembered what people had been saying around him, and knew that a funeral home had been arranged to take care of everything. He also remembered taking two pills with a glass of water, and he hadn't noticed when everybody went home and he was left alone. The only thing he knew for sure was that he had to pick an outfit and take it to the funeral home.

Marc had always found it strange to see dead bodies exhibited in open coffins. As a matter of fact, whenever he and Clara had gone to funerals they had always talked about this afterwards and promised each other not to let it happen to them. Neither of them had known that this day would come so early. They had always thought that they would die one after the other in their old age, and they'd based all their principles on that idea.

On the contrary, Marc had suddenly found himself alone with Clara's cold body. He was only fifty-five and Clara was fifty-two. Before he could shake off the effect of the antidepressants he had taken, all the arrangements had already been made. How could he explain this to Clara? Death wasn't rational or practical like they'd thought. The shock shook you to the bone. The person left behind wanted to see the face of the woman he loved one more time. It simply wasn't possible to say goodbye that quickly.

Now he was standing in front of the shelves, thinking. What would Clara want to put on? Which of her outfits would she like to be wearing when they said farewell? He looked at her dresses hanging in a row. His wife had carried on wearing dresses while all the women in the world tried squeezing their bodies into trousers. She preferred short-sleeved ones both in summer and winter and would put on one of her many coloured cashmere cardigans whenever she felt cold. He finally decided on a brown dress. As for the cardigan, he picked the blue one, which warmed his heart whenever he saw it. Unfortunately, he had never said this to his wife. He took it in his hands and held it to his nose. Maybe Clara had put the cardigan in the wardrobe without washing it and left her scent on it as a gift to her husband. He didn't fight the tears; he let them dry on the soft wool. When he found the strength to go on, he picked a pair of Clara's tiny ballet pumps and put everything in a bag. He stumbled towards the front door. He couldn't find the courage to look towards the kitchen. He hadn't eaten anything since the day before, and he had only drunk some water from the bathroom sink. He went out, pulled the door shut and left behind an apartment that was silent and colourless as it had never been before.

He usually walked or took the metro wherever he went. Now he neither had the energy to walk or the heart to see the Place Monge farmers' market, which was right next to the metro station. Place Monge was only a hundred metres away from their apartment and Clara went there three times a week to do all her fruit and vegetable shopping. Everybody at the market knew her. At Christmas she'd come home with gift baskets from the farmers filled with clementines, apples and quinces, and in return she'd take them her most delicious cakes and savouries wrapped beautifully with ribbons. Marc knew that the farmers were going to wonder where Clara was that day. They were used to her letting them know whenever she was going to be away for a while, even when she went on holiday. Marc knew only too well that their eyes would also be searching for the bright face of his Clara on this grey day.

He walked away from the market and got into one of the taxis that were waiting at the stop. He gave the address of the funeral home to the driver and closed his eyes. He didn't even want to see daylight. He still couldn't believe the reality of what was happening, or the possibility that life could change that rapidly. He remembered that he hadn't called the gallery to let his assistant, Amou, know what was happening. The idea left his mind again as quickly as it had arrived. Nothing else mattered, and this had no importance, either. Amou loved his job as much as Marc did. They sometimes saw each other at various comic book shops during their lunch breaks, but after a brief nod to each other they would just carry on browsing. Amou was as isolated from social life as Marc was and he wanted to share all his time with the thing he liked most: comic books. Marc had got lucky when he married Clara. He knew everybody around him because of her. Everybody was fond of him and thought of him as a friend for the sake of his lovely wife. Clara had established and secured his friendships and made sure they would last for ever. If his apartment had been filled with people and friends the day before, his wife was the only reason for that. Everybody in their lives knew that he was Clara's baby and that's why they were going to take care of him just like they would with an orphan. Marc wished in his heart that Amou would one day be as lucky as he had been. He wished that someone would love Amou as much as he had been loved.

When the taxi driver stopped in front of the funeral home, he shook his head sympathetically. He took Marc's money with a gentle but serious look and held out his hand with the change. Marc had already closed the door behind him. His hand was holding the bag tightly and wasn't expecting any money back. He felt dizzy. He hoped that someone would see him from inside the building and come out to take the bag from him so that he could run away from this place. At that moment he suddenly understood how hard it was going to be to come here the next day and say goodbye to Clara. He forced himself to go inside and hand over the bag, giving his name to the first person he saw before leaving as quickly as he went in. He couldn't bring himself to say,

36

'These clothes belong to Clara Bellard.' He wasn't ready to say his wife's name. He hopped into a taxi again and said, 'Rue Monge, l'Hôtel des Arènes.'

Des Arènes was one of the hotels on their street. It was just some place he saw almost every day as he walked to his gallery. He asked the receptionist to give him the darkest room on the remotest floor, if possible. The receptionist immediately understood that this man with red eyes and no bag was not a tourist but a troubled Parisian, so she filled in the form as quickly as possible, made him sign it and sent him to the most unloved and unappreciated room in the hotel. When Marc entered the room, he didn't even bother to open the curtains. He was sure that the window faced a wall. He switched off the table lamp that had turned itself on automatically when the door opened and let himself fall onto the bed. Before long he had slid into a deep sleep from which he wouldn't wake up until the next day: a sleep without dreams and without memories.

When he opened his eyes the next day, he had a hard time remembering where he was for the first couple of minutes. In the pitch darkness of the room he couldn't tell what time it was. He followed the fluorescent hands of his wristwatch through his half-opened eyelids. It showed twelve o'clock. When he looked at the tiny spot which magnified the date to see which day it was, he suddenly realised that he was about to miss Clara's funeral. The wake was going to start at half past one and they were going to the Cimetière du Montparnasse for the burial at a quarter past two. He got up and left. While he was trying to mend his broken heart with a twenty-two-hour sleep, all hell had broken loose outside. All his distant relatives and friends had been looking everywhere for him for hours. They had already called all the hospitals and asked the police for information on suicide incidents that day and the day before. Everybody was waiting nervously for him to reappear. Marc hadn't thought about this, but once he got home he realised how worried everyone had been. All the same, he was in no condition to feel ashamed of his irresponsible behaviour. Right now he could only deal with one feeling and he expected everyone to understand that. Without saying a word he went straight to his room and changed into a suit.

When he went into the bathroom to shave, he sat on the toilet with the electric razor in his hand and closed his eyes so he wouldn't have to see anything that belonged to Clara. He shaved with his eyes shut. He wouldn't be able to stand seeing his wife's shampoo at that moment. Or her anti-wrinkle eye cream. He wasn't going to touch Clara's brush or one of her rings that she'd left on the basin, next to the soap. When he went back to the living room to join the other people, one of Clara's oldest friends, Odette, came up to him and brushed some hair from his collar. She took his face in her hands and looked him in the eyes. Her face was swollen from so much crying and her nose and mouth had almost changed shape. Marc waited in vain for her to say something extraordinary to ease his pain. He looked at her with pleading eyes, because he didn't know how to deal with all this alone. Instead, Odette asked if he'd had anything to eat. Marc realised that he hadn't touched any food for the last two days, so he answered with a shake of his head. Whenever he'd got sick or felt a little down before, Clara would make him *jardinière de légumes*. She would collect some seasonal vegetables, cook them just the right way and then, after she was sure he had eaten the whole thing, she would hold him tight. She would say, 'You're going to be OK now', and add, 'Don't worry, my hugs and *jardinière de légumes* will work their magic in a couple of minutes.'

After helping him to sit down, Odette went to the kitchen. It was hard for her to enter this room, too. Clara's whole existence had settled on each tile, plate and fork, and even on the messy table. She was sure that there would be something to eat in her friend's fridge. She opened the door, squatted down and examined its contents for a while. She took out one of two small containers and heated it up in the microwave. Odette knew that she couldn't bring Marc into the kitchen, so she brought the food to him on a tray.

'Everybody is going to come to our place after the funeral. I've hired a very nice catering service. I'm sure Clara would appreciate it. You'll come too, right?'

Marc nodded, approvingly.

'You can stay with us for a while if you want. I'll rearrange everything here if you like and … clean it up … '

Marc knew what Odette meant by cleaning it up. Clearing the fridge, tidying up the kitchen and making everything that belonged to Clara disappear. He knew that he couldn't do any of those things, so he nodded again. He only had one objection.

'I'm going to stay at a hotel. I'll pack a small bag and leave tonight.'

'The hotel you stayed at last night?'

'Yes.'

'May I ask which one?'

'Des Arènes.'

'OK. If you change your mind you can always come to our place. You know that.'

'Yes.'

Odette didn't feel completely comfortable leaving Marc alone. She had no idea whether he was one of those suicidal types. She was only beginning to realise now that she'd never really tried to get to know this man. He had chosen to live his life under Clara's wings and seemed happy to live just like the moon: the world's satellite. So much so, in fact, that in order to know him you only had to know Clara. Marc had lived his life as one of her extensions: the most important one, probably. The peace he had found in his wife's presence was obvious to their friends and they had always been surprised by this kind of total surrender. Odette had thought about their relationship sometimes and been jealous of it. She had comforted herself by thinking that this kind of intimacy, which she hadn't experienced with her own husband, was the result of not having any children. She was grateful to God for her kids. Thanks to them, she would never experience this kind of absolute loneliness. She looked at Marc again; he seemed to be having a hard time swallowing his food. If they could only have had a child, he would have got over this pain much more quickly. He would have been forced to, because the well-being of the child would have been more important than anything else. Marc, on the other hand, was probably going to recover by getting married again. Odette was surprised to see how angry it made her even to think about this probability. She knew it was ridiculous to feel that her friend had already been betrayed, but still she couldn't help throwing Marc a look of hatred. She felt sure that after only five or six months, Marc was going to come and tell them that he was with someone new and then he would get remarried. He was going to be another woman's satellite. He was one of those men who couldn't survive without a woman by his side. He hadn't even managed to feed himself over the last two days. How long could he survive like this?

Completely ignorant of the plans being made for him, Marc struggled to swallow his last mouthfuls of food. The couple of hours ahead felt like a heavy weight that he had to carry on his shoulders. He already longed for the hotel room he was going to afterwards and the hours he would spend there sleeping. He wanted to get away from this apartment, from the smell of Clara, from all these faces that reminded him of her, and especially from himself. The one thing that reminded him of her the most was himself. Clara had been the blanket he pulled over his body for years. Now she was gone and he was left shivering with cold. Some nights, lying face to face under the covers, they used to talk about whether they could live with someone else after all these years. Both of them would say, 'Not possible.' Marc would always say it a little bit louder. And then they would go to sleep, happy in the knowledge that their love was eternal. Marc remembered those nights now as he looked around him. He looked at the other women in the apartment: his friends. He thought once again, 'Not possible', and then saw the harsh look on Odette's face.

While her mother screamed at the top of her lungs in the hospital, making sure that everyone heard her, Ferda kept apologising to people for the inconvenience they were causing. She knew very well how much it hurt to break a bone since she had broken both of her arms on different occasions. At the same time, she also knew it wasn't necessary to scream quite that much. Mrs Nesibe, of course, was going to make sure she did this kind of pain justice. She had always been good at exaggerating any kind of discomfort or emotion and was generally very successful at getting people to work tirelessly for her. When the sound of her voice finally faded away, Ferda guessed they must have anaesthetised her ready for the operation.

Hours later, the doctor left the operating room covered in sweat. Mrs Nesibe had been one of the most difficult patients he had ever encountered. When he came out to talk to Ferda he took a deep breath before getting started. 'The operation went well,' he said, then added, 'Well, we had a hard time putting her to sleep. You know, her hip didn't break when she fell. She fell because the bone broke by itself as it couldn't carry the weight.' Ferda listened to the doctor with an expression that was meant to show that she understood him perfectly. 'We've inserted the prosthesis. Now the most important thing is to start the physiotherapy in no less than two or three days. It's very important for her to keep moving. Now, Mrs Nesibe's pain threshold is very low ...' Ferda accidentally snorted at this point, and then tried to turn it into a more reasonable smile. 'Her pain threshold is low? Or rather, her exaggerating threshold is really high,' she said to herself, but she decided not to share this thought with the doctor. Still, he continued with a smile, as if he knew just what she was thinking: 'So, even if she screams like she did before, you still have to make her move.' Ferda nodded energetically, which was supposed to mean, 'Of course.' She kept the thought of all the hardships she was going to have to suffer with her mother to herself. She knew perfectly well that they were standing at the beginning of a road, and that road led to the end of Mrs Nesibe. Ignoring the doctor standing right in front of her, she closed her eyes for a minute and prayed to God for help. Maybe she would need to do more yoga, which she had started recently. There was no way she could handle this kind of burden without the help of some kind of spiritual aid. She knew that most old people died within a year of breaking their hips. It was called the embolus, which led to heart failure. Despite this, she also knew that some people lived for many more years after this kind of an injury and deep down she felt sure that her mother wouldn't die of a failing heart. It would have to be something more glamorous than that. Besides, hadn't she lived a very healthy life so far, despite all her imaginary illnesses?

Her mother had been 'sick' for as long as Ferda could remember. Mrs Nesibe had a habit of fainting very frequently and when she didn't faint, she slept heavily as a result of the antidepressants she took. Passiflora – the drug, not the passion flower – was her best friend, and the lemon cologne she used with its eighty-five per cent alcohol content was her second best. Whenever she encountered the slightest bit of disobedience from her children, she would threaten to jump out of the window or, if she wanted to be a little more subtle, she would fall noisily onto the tiles of the kitchen floor. Everything she experienced was exaggerated: her happiness, her sadness, her nervousness, her illnesses and, especially, her pains. Her suffering was so great that it sometimes seemed as if the whole world was one of her limbs. And yet, despite all of these so-called pains, none of the tests that had been taken throughout the years ever showed anything serious. In fact, she was in better shape than many of her peers.

A couple of days after the operation, Mrs Nesibe left the hospital moaning and groaning and tossing her head wildly from left to right, but with no actual tears in her eyes. Just like every other time when something like this had happened, she couldn't help saying her daughter's name every two minutes, making Ferda feel the same despair she had felt all her life. Getting her mother into the tiny lift to go upstairs to her daughter's apartment was going to be something else altogether. Ferda had no doubt in her mind that her mother would have a fit. She had spent some time at home getting her mother's room ready before she was discharged, and she had also tried to prepare Sinan for what awaited them in the near future. Sinan had known Mrs Nesibe since he was a little boy – long before he had married Ferda thirty-five years ago – and he knew all of her habits as if she was his own mother. His mother-in-law had also been famous for her fainting fits back in the day. Just like every other child on their street, he knew that he had to go and let Ferda know if Aunt Nesibe – which was a way of addressing older women – fainted on the street. Unlike all the other children, whenever he saw Ferda at the door his heart started beating so quickly that he stuttered and couldn't say what he had come for, and in the end the poor girl had to work out what had happened without his help. When Ferda reached her mother in a case like this, she would see that the fruit seller on the corner, the man from the deli or the woman from the variety shop was already rubbing Mrs Nesibe's wrists with the lemon cologne she always carried in her bag to bring her back to life. And when her mother recovered, Ferda would take the bags from her hands and let her mother lean on her as she helped her walk back to their house. She always knew that everybody on that street – including the ones who had helped Mrs Nesibe to recover – was laughing behind their backs, except for Sinan.

When Sinan told his family that he wanted to marry Ferda, he knew perfectly well what he was getting into. When his brothers asked him, 'Are you sure?' they were only referring to Mrs Nesibe. They didn't have any doubts about Ferda. The whole neighbourhood was in love with her. That poor girl had been born a saint, and on top of that she was beautiful. She was the wife and daughter-in-law everybody wanted to have. However, nobody in the neighbourhood wanted Mrs Nesibe as an in-law. Mrs Saniye did her best to make her son change his mind, telling him that this would affect the whole family, but Sinan wouldn't listen. In the end, they had no choice but to go with Sinan to ask for Ferda's hand in marriage. Unfortunately, Ferda's father had not lived to see this happy day: he had died of cerebral bleeding at a very young age which, according to many people, was the result of a very unfortunate marriage to Mrs Nesibe.

When Sinan's family came to see Mrs Nesibe to ask for permission for Ferda to marry their son, as was the custom, it was the happiest day of Mrs Nesibe's life. As it turned out, she didn't faint once from that day until the wedding. She didn't feel tired at all, and even though she took care of almost everything she never once said she was exhausted. The neighbours welcomed this new behaviour, but at the same time they were a bit surprised. 'Weddings bring miracles,' their ancestors had said, and maybe they were right. Unfortunately, everything went back to the way it had been as soon as Ferda was married. Mrs Nesibe suddenly realised how tired she was. She didn't know which bed to sleep in and the Passiflora was never enough. When the neighbours came to congratulate her after the wedding, she complained about how hard it was to clean the whole house by herself, how hard it was to deal with her son and how Ferda had already forgotten all about her. Just like that, Sinan began his marriage to his mother-in-law as well as to his wife.

Now, when Ferda told him that her mother was going to be living with them for a while and that it was probably going to be very tough, he didn't even react. When had it ever been easy to live with Mrs Nesibe and why would he expect it to get easier now? It didn't matter to him. On the other hand, he knew that his wife was going to lose it. The only advantage they'd had so far was the fact that his mother-in-law lived in another apartment. True, there had been times when she had stayed with them for a couple of days or they'd gone on summer holidays together, and Sinan didn't have any good memories of those times. They'd both almost had nervous breakdowns but they'd dealt with it easily enough, knowing that she would soon be going back to her own place. This time was different as she was going to be around for a while, but by now he was too old to care. He was almost sixty and when he wasn't at work he spent most of his time watching TV or reading. Nevertheless, it was unsettling to think that Ferda was going to be spending so much quality time with her mother.

When Mrs Nesibe was finally brought home, she felt so tired that she couldn't even tell Sinan off for not coming to visit her at the hospital. Her face looked very pale and her body was genuinely weak for the first time in her life. Ferda saw all this, and for the first time she also believed that her mother was really in pain. The room she had arranged for her was small but very clean and tidy. She had remembered to put a small TV on a chest of drawers and had made Sinan line up all the channels her mother liked to watch. The bathroom was right next door, so getting there wouldn't be a problem. At the hospital they had shown Mrs Nesibe how to sit up in bed and move around using a walker. It was very important for her to put some effort into getting up and about again with the help of a physiotherapist. Ferda had already made Sinan buy the best walker they could find, and she had put it in a corner of her mother's room. She was going to do everything in her power to help Mrs Nesibe recover and return home as soon as possible.

As it turned out, that was nothing but wishful thinking. They realised it wasn't going to be that easy just a couple of hours after Mrs Nesibe came home. Even when she really needed to go to the bathroom, there was no way of convincing her that she could move by herself if she wanted to. She had already spent the whole recuperation period in the hospital and her doctor had told her that she could get up and walk as soon as she got home. He had advised her not to be scared of moving. In fact, it was very important for her to start walking right away. Despite all that talk, Mrs Nesibe kept on crying and saying that she couldn't do any of those things. How could she possibly stand up and walk when she couldn't even sit up in bed? She begged them to wait for a couple of days until her pain went away. After a while, Ferda told Sinan to go to the living room and do whatever he wanted to do. It was going to be a waste of time for both of them if they tried to do this together. Besides, she didn't want them both to lose their minds.

Trying to ignore the screams coming from the small bedroom, Sinan sat on his rocking chair opposite the TV. It didn't matter how high he raised the volume of the show he wanted to watch: he could still hear the noises coming from his mother-in-law's room. For the first time he regretted agreeing to remove the living room door. Then, the moaning slowly faded away. His wife had closed the door of her mother's room. From then on she was going to battle it out alone behind that closed door, begging her mother not to scream.

Ferda had thought that with the help of the physiotherapist her mother would begin to change her mind and slowly get used to walking again. However, Mrs Nesibe managed to frustrate the therapist on her first day. She wouldn't even let the therapist move her legs while she lay in bed, let alone get up and move around. When Ferda got embarrassed by her mother's constant yelling and went to apologise to the neighbours, she gathered that they had indeed heard everything that was being said in her apartment. Not one of them put her out of her misery by saying that they hadn't heard a thing. A whole week had passed and Mrs Nesibe still moaned and howled and said that her pain wasn't getting any better and pleaded with Ferda even louder, ignoring her warnings that everybody in the building could hear her. 'Do you want to kill me? I'm going to faint from the pain. Please, let's wait for a little bit longer, my darling,' she said, deliberately using the 'darling' she never said. Ferda was sure she was going to faint. She didn't know how her mother did it, but she was a master of fainting whenever she wanted to. In the end, she caved in and agreed to take a break from trying to get Mrs Nesibe to move. She also thought that her mother might really be in pain this time. The therapist had pulled all kinds of faces to show how little she approved of this decision when Ferda told her, and said: 'I'm sorry to say this, but if we can't get her to move now, she isn't going to be able to move later even if she wants to. Let's take a break if you want, but we have to get those legs moving soon.' Ferda knew what the therapist was trying to say. She was saying that if she didn't want her mother to be confined to bed for the rest of her life she had to make her get up, whatever it took. Still, the therapist didn't know the first thing about her mother. If she didn't want to get up, there was no way to make her do it. On top of everything, Ferda needed a break. The whole dynamics of her home had changed in the last week and her mother's presence had turned their calm lives upside down. And so, they stopped.

She helped her mother with her toilet situation a couple of times a day and did her best not to vomit as she carried the bedpan to the bathroom. Mrs Nesibe also called out for her once or twice a night after they went to sleep, either because she needed to use the bedpan or because she needed some more painkillers. Sinan also woke up every time she yelled 'Ferda!' and usually neither of them could get back to sleep afterwards. Whenever Sinan finally fell asleep again, he usually had to wake up to go to work almost immediately after that, and so dark circles had been growing around his eyes. The lack of sleep had also triggered Ferda's migraine and she had got used to getting on with her daily chores with a constant pain twisting inside her skull. Meanwhile, people were coming non-stop to pay their respects to her mother, and since Ferda always wanted to serve her guests the best possible homemade treats she had to spend all her spare time in the kitchen preparing food. Still, she managed to get things done as successfully as ever.

Ferda had enjoyed trying different recipes, making everything at home and watching people's reactions as they ate her food ever since she was a little girl. She had always baked her own birthday cakes for her husband and children, had never succumbed to buying pre-seasoned chicken from the supermarket and had never used ready-made tomato paste in her life. She always made her own jam by exposing all kinds of berries to the heat of the sun on her balcony and she always dried her baby aubergines just as she had learned from Mrs Mahide, who was from Antep, a beautiful city in eastern Turkey. Sometimes Sinan took her with him on his business trips to various cities in Anatolia. Whenever they went together they were always invited to dinners made by the local people and Ferda always came home with recipes, which she tried out religiously as soon as they got back. She never stopped cooking the same thing over and over until she had developed a real sense of it. That was how she had become a master of Circassian chicken, palm meatloaf and *habenisk*, which was a type of lentil dish. She had never had much of an appetite though, which was why she still only weighed fifty kilos at the age of fifty-eight. This was also why she didn't have a comfort food, but instead had a comfort drink. Whenever she felt weak, depressed or frustrated, she would make herself a glass of *salep*, a drink made from wild orchid roots which Öykü said tasted exactly like chai latte, and then she would sprinkle it with cinnamon to calm her nerves. Sinan found it strange that she could drink this hot beverage even at the height of summer, but he knew all about the sacred bond between his wife and this drink and so he never said a word about it.

Now, after two weeks of constant battling with her mother and all that extra work, she had finally found some time to sit down and relax. Her mother must have also been tired out after all those visitors as she was still sleeping soundly. Ferda had been craving *salep* for some time now, and so she made herself a particularly creamy one. The first sip was especially heavenly. She artfully wiped away the cinnamon that was stuck to her upper lip, added this taste to the one already on her palate and felt warm again deep inside. She was thankful that winter had finally arrived after a hot and humid summer in Istanbul. She liked hearing the sound of steam coming from the heaters. Somehow it cheered her up. One of the reasons why Ferda was so happy about Mrs Nesibe's deep sleep was because now she would finally have time for the phone call she was about to receive from Öykü. She had already spoken to her daughter once during the week to tell her about her grandmother's condition, but she had left the details for their longer conversation. She knew that the phone was going to ring in a couple of minutes. Before it did, she poured herself another cup of *salep* so that she could enjoy the limited time she had to spend with her daughter to the fullest. She had forgotten to get the cordless phone mended so she had to talk on the fixed one in the hallway, which was right next to her mother's room. If she didn't want the noise to wake her mother up she would have to move quickly and grab the receiver the second it rang. She took a chair with her, went to the hallway and waited with her mug in one hand and the other glued to the receiver. She picked it up on the first ring.

'Mum?'

'How are you, sweetie?'

'I'm good. More importantly, how are you? How's the nutcase doing?'

'Thank goodness she can't hear you. She's the same as always. What would your grandmother do if she didn't moan? She's sleeping now, that's why I can't really talk. But you can hear me, right? I have to whisper. She won't let us close her door. She says the room suffocates her when the door's closed. We never thought about this when we decided to take the doors out of the living room and kitchen and now it's come back to haunt us. She's all ears, she listens to everything. She asks about every little thing, you wouldn't believe it. Who called? What did she say? Why did you say that?'

'So the legs aren't working, but the brain is.'

'Exactly. She even drove the therapist crazy. She had to yell at her in the end. She told her she was acting like a baby. She doesn't know the half of it. What a baby she can be!'

'Does she get up at all?'

'Are you kidding? She's making my life a misery. She says it hurts and she can't take it. I don't know, sweetie. I told the therapist not to come for a while. I thought maybe we can take a break. I don't know. It might really be hurting her. I can't decide whether I should push her or not. She's very old.'

'Mum! Push her! You have to. Because if not you'll have to take care of her.'

'Don't say it like that, sweetheart. She's my mum, what can I do? Don't worry though. I'm going to make her walk. She'll have to do it in the end.'

Their conversation would have gone on for longer if Mrs Nesibe hadn't chosen that moment to interrupt it.

'Ferda! Are you talking to Öykü?'

'Yes, mum. (See, she hears everything.)'

'I want to talk to my baby girl. Why doesn't she call her grandma?'

Ferda wasn't too happy that one of her favourite things in the world had been cut short, but still she extended the cord into her mother's room and handed her the receiver. If there had been a whole pot of *salep*, she seriously would have drunk it all. And then Mrs Nesibe picked up on the smell, too. Covering the speaker with her hand she called out to Ferda: couldn't she have a cup of *salep*? While her mother chirped away on the phone to her granddaughter, Ferda got to work boiling some more of her favourite drink.

Three

Marc had shut himself away inside a hotel room, leaving the rest of the world outside its door. He had just wanted to be alone in that dark room which looked out onto a wall and hadn't set foot outside once since he'd gone in. He had been at Des Arènes for exactly ten days and hadn't seen anybody but the hotel employees who brought him food. He didn't know that Odette had called the hotel a couple of times to ask after him, and he would never have guessed it himself.

Odette was told that Marc had hardly eaten anything. The people who worked at the front desk couldn't tell her anything else because they hadn't seen their guest at all since he checked in. Since they were also curious, they had asked the room service people about him and learned that he spent all his time sleeping. Normally they wouldn't have shared this information about their guests with anyone, but Odette had explained the situation and said she was worried that he might hurt himself. After this comment the hotel staff nervously tried to keep an eye on him throughout his stay, and when they saw him coming downstairs with his small bag at the end of the tenth day they were relieved. The last thing they wanted was to have to walk into a room with a dead man inside it.

Marc's beard and moustache had grown and his eyes were swollen from so much sleeping. When he opened his mouth to speak, even he was startled by the sound of his voice: a wheezy sound that came from deep inside his chest. Without needing to say much, he handed over the money and left, followed by the pitying gazes of the hotel staff – especially the female employees. The weather was colder than it had been ten days ago, and even though it was only four o'clock it was already almost dark. Rue Monge was bustling with people on their way home from work and the lights were twinkling in the shop windows. As he looked around, he remembered once again why he hadn't wanted to go out for days. There was the bookshop Clara adored, right across the street. She would go there once a month to buy four books to read, and she always criticised Marc for shopping in big stores like Fnac, even though she admired their founding principles. The neighbourhood was like a family to her, especially after living in the same place for as long as they had. Right next to the bookshop was the fishmonger's which Clara always went to. Whenever Pierre – with his dirty apron wrapped around his belly – saw Clara, he'd wink at her flirtatiously and insist on giving her whatever was freshest. She would usually go into the shop craving a certain kind of fish and leave carrying something completely different. And right next to that was the florist's where Clara would stop by almost every day to say hi to the owner. In the summer Madame Paulette would always offer her some Benedictine liqueur, and in the winter they would raise their small glasses of cognac to toast each other's health.

How was Marc going to carry on living here? How was he going to be able to walk past these shops every day? As he kept his eyes fixed on his shoes and started to walk home, he didn't realise that all those people from all those shops were following him with their eyes and asking themselves the same question. How were they going to get used to Clara's absence, after she'd become a part of their lives? Even worse, how were they going to stand seeing this man's misery? Marc didn't realise that Françis had already seen him from afar while smoking a cigarette outside his *boulangerie*, which was just a few steps away from their building, or that he had been waiting for him. That was why he almost jumped out of his skin when he felt a hand take hold of his arm. Without saying anything, Françis gave Marc a bag, and Marc carried on walking after he'd taken it without saying a word; without being able to say a word. He entered the code for his building, hoping he wouldn't see anyone else, and ran upstairs to the first floor, relieved to find the hall empty. By the time he got to his door he was out of breath. Trying not to make any noise so that the neighbours wouldn't hear him, he slowly opened the front door.

He knew only too well that if Clara had been left behind instead of him she would have found consolation in the warmth of her neighbours and her neighbourhood, and would have let herself be mended in their safe arms. He, on the other hand, was practically running away from his own shadow. The truth was, he knew no other way of dealing with what was happening. He had thought about leaving the country during some of his nightmarish sleeping sessions at the hotel. He wanted to go to a country where people spoke another language. He had thought about leaving the life he had behind him, but he knew he couldn't do it. He turned his head away as he passed the kitchen, which stood on the right-hand side of the door. He left the bag Françis had given him on the living room table and threw his jacket down on one of the armchairs. After standing in the middle of the room for a while, he realised that he needed to hear a human voice: a voice that would help him shed the weight of every piece of furniture in this apartment. They didn't have a TV in their living room and Clara's small radio was still in its place on the kitchen window sill. He went to their bedroom and turned on the alarm clock radio. All of a sudden, the sound of 'Non, Je Ne Regrette Rien' by Edith Piaf filled the room. This finally made Marc think of something other than his wife. How was it that people's lives never changed? As far as he could remember, he was seven years old when he first heard this song. He had been reading the same comic books and magazines for years. The same TV shows with almost the same guests had been on for years. Even the news and the issues talked about by intellectuals had always been the same. Only the decor of the studio had changed. The same group of people met at the same square of the same street every Sunday and danced to the same tune. This was a city that had history pouring down from its walls and it never let anybody forget the past. How was he going to forget Clara when he was chained to a city like this? How was he going to remove her from his life when nothing was ever allowed to be removed?

He turned on the lamp on the bedside table and sat down on the bed. When he looked around the room, he suddenly realised that the traces of Clara on the vanity table had been erased. He lifted up the bedspread just a little and looked inside. The sheet and the pillowcases had been changed. He stood up now and pulled back the bedspread completely. The pillows had been puffed up and the wrinkles on the pillowcases, which had given Clara lines on her face every morning, had been ironed out. He rushed to the bathroom in a panic. He opened the cabinet doors and checked inside. His wife's lotions weren't there; neither were her bottles of nail polish or her nail polish remover. Her hairpins and deodorant were all gone. Only her brush had been left behind. He examined it in vain for several minutes to see if he could find a single hair. He felt a lump in his throat. He opened the lid of the dirty laundry basket next to the washing machine and looked inside. It was empty. Now he ran back to their bedroom and stood in front of the wardrobe. With his heart in his throat, he opened the doors. Tears started falling as he came face to face with the empty racks. He opened the drawers; they were empty. Her socks, her handkerchiefs and everything else that belonged to her were all gone. Nothing with his wife's smell on it was left. He wanted to call Odette and scream in her ear, asking how she could deny him Clara's memory. How could she steal his wife from him? How could she wipe everything away without asking him? He sat back down on the bed. With his elbows on his knees and his head in his hands, he began to sob. All kinds of feelings had poured down upon him and they weren't going to go away. He needed his wife; he needed something that had been left behind.

Then, suddenly, he looked up; his tears froze on his cheeks as he stood up and walked briskly to the kitchen. After standing at its door in the dark for a while, he gathered the courage to turn on the light. It looked neater than it had ever looked before. Even when he searched for the familiar smells, he couldn't find them. The vase on the table was empty. The scattered cookbooks had been picked up and put back on the shelves. Even the radio antenna had been taken down and had settled into the hole that had been waiting for it for years. Marc walked to the drawers next to the oven and stood in front of them for a while. After a couple of minutes, he opened the second one from the top. The oven glove with the embroidered cockerel on it was still there, where Clara had left it. Nervously, he reached his hand out towards it. After caressing the cockerel embroidery with his fingertips, he raised it to his nose and breathed in the familiar smell of all kinds of food that had blended together there over the years. He still held the glove in his hands as he sat in the chair, on his side of the table, forgetting to close the open drawer. After some time had passed, he finally put it on his right hand, slowly and carefully. Despite how hard he tried, he couldn't feel her. He leaned over the table, rested his head on his arm and started crying again. Until he fell asleep.

When he opened his eyes hours later, his arm had gone to sleep and he felt hungry for the first time in days. It was a little after eleven o'clock at night. With a strange feeling of guilt, he took off the glove and laid it gently on the table, almost not wanting to hurt it. He stood up in the middle of the kitchen and looked around him. There had been times when he'd had to take care of himself in this apartment before. He'd stayed behind for a couple of days when Clara had gone to visit her aunt who lived in the South. Luckily, Clara would always leave some food stocked in various containers and write a note explaining what should be eaten first. She would even put some cheese on some slices of bread and wrap them in cling film, so that Marc would only have to put them in the oven for three or four minutes. Now, the empty shelves in the fridge only emphasised the fact that Clara wasn't there any more. He knew he wouldn't find anywhere open at this time of night. Maybe he could walk to Mouffetard and eat a Turkish kebab in one of those places which mainly stayed open for bar hoppers. He had done that with Clara from time to time. Some days they would let themselves eat as much as they liked, even though they knew they would suffer for it at the end of the night. Marc remembered those days of adventure with a smile that reflected his sorrow. This was not one of those days. Then he remembered the bag Françis had given him on his way home. There must be something inside he could eat. He went to the living room, picked up the bag and came back to the kitchen. Not that day, but some day in the future, he would realise that this kitchen, which he was so scared of right now, was the only place that could mend his wounds, slowly yet gently. He had to surrender himself to it, just as people surrender themselves to the warm arms of loved ones whenever they feel down. Everything in that kitchen would have to cover him like a warm quilt and blow on his hands to heat them up.

He opened the box and clumsily cut himself a slice of quiche Lorraine. He turned on the TV as he picked up the crumbs that fell on the sideboard with the wet tip of his finger. The late night news was talking about the long-awaited Jean Giraud comic album. They were describing how people had queued for hours the night before to buy one and how it had sold one million copies on its first day alone. Marc stared at the TV, amazed. He had been waiting for years for that day to come. When he turned to look at the calendar on the wall, he saw the note Clara had written on the day in red pen: '*Un grand jour pour Marc et JG!*' A big day for Marc and JG! The legendary French artist had been working on this album for years and the whole comic world knew that the book was going to be released at midnight that day. On the news they were explaining how thousands of fans had gone to shops in almost every city in France, waiting for hours despite the cold weather to get hold of a copy, and how no other comic book had received this much attention in years. If everything had gone according to plan, Marc would have been in that queue the night before, too. Clara was going to make him sandwiches and that long wait was going to turn into a cheerful little picnic. Marc had been dreaming for years about holding that book in his hands the day it came out. He had been planning to come home with it and lose himself in its pages, peacefully sipping his coffee. And he had forgotten all about it. He had completely forgotten that *that* day was the day before. He was looking at the TV screen without even blinking and when they showed the cover of the book at the end of the news he almost choked on his food. He looked at his watch; it was almost midnight, but he couldn't stop himself from calling Amou. He was sure that Amou would have been in that queue the night before and that he was holding the book in his hands right at that moment.

'Marc?'

'Hi, Amou. I'm sorry I couldn't call before, but I just couldn't.'

'I know, don't worry. Everything's good at the gallery.'

Amou was having trouble hiding the excitement in his voice. He wanted to tell Marc that the book in his hands was a masterpiece, but he didn't know if it was a good time.

'Did you buy Moebius?'

'Yes! I waited in the queue all night long and I bought it just before dawn. Marc, it's really good. Words aren't enough to describe it. It's extraordinary. There were queues outside every bookshop in the city and they only sold one book per person. Luckily I managed to convince a friend to stand in the queue for you and we bought one for you, too.'

Marc couldn't breathe. He started crying against his will as he pressed the receiver hard against his ear. Amou waited silently at the other end of the line, without mentioning that he'd had to pay his friend to stand in that queue. A minute or so passed before Marc could finally speak again.

'Thank you … thank you. I'll see you tomorrow at work. For everything. Thank you for everything.'

He carried on crying after he'd hung up the phone. He didn't know why. He didn't understand that the pain was trying to drain itself out of his body, but he felt unbelievably tired. It felt as if the roads he'd been walking for years and the hours he'd spent without sleep had finally caught up with him, and were collapsing on top of him. The tears weighed a ton; his whole body was heavy. He put the box of quiche in the fridge and went to the bedroom. He slipped in between the cool sheets and turned his back to the emptiness Clara had left behind her. Despite how much his heart kept throbbing with pain, his eyes simply shut down. The second before he fell asleep he realised that he wanted to wake up the next morning. And that life was going to move on.

While her husband was still in the hospital, Lilia had rearranged their house to fit the new circumstances of their lives. There was no way that Arnie could stay in his room on the first floor any more. As he was going to be depending on Lilia for most of his daily needs, she had to carry his things to the room closest to where she spent her days, which was the small dining room right next to the kitchen. The dining room had become a much livelier and cosier place than it had ever been thanks to Arnie's bookshelves, personal belongings and desk. Of course, when Arnie came home he didn't agree in the slightest. He hated the idea of living so close to the kitchen. First of all, he couldn't stand the smell of food and secretly wished that his wife was one of those women who only cooked microwave dinners. Although he'd never said a word about it, he had never got used to Lilia's food, which was far too rich for his taste. Her cooking – which everybody else raved about – meant nothing to him. True, she was good at Italian food, but that wasn't the kind of thing they were supposed be eating at their age anyway. Besides, a simple sandwich was much easier, not to mention cleaner and cheaper.

Retiring to his room early wasn't only a way of escaping the smell of food. It also meant that he didn't have to listen to Lilia's unnecessary phone conversations with her siblings, acknowledge the tense silence between them or endure the possibility of running into Ed. Not that he had anything against him; it was just that they had nothing in common to talk about. He didn't have much in common with anyone, as a matter of fact, so he always preferred to be alone. Even when his friends from work came round for dinner from time to time, he would go to his room for fifteen minutes to collect his thoughts before joining the conversation again after this short break. But now it looked as if he'd lost his privacy for good. He knew that he needed Lilia to help him move around and even to go to the bathroom for a while at least, but he'd still much rather be alone when he was done. Hiring a nurse was out of the question, unfortunately. The hospital fees had been obscenely high and their insurance covered so little that they'd already spent most of their savings. They also had to find a way of dealing with the expenses from then on. He was sure that the rest of their savings would be gone in no time. He was going to start receiving his pension every month, but that money couldn't possibly meet all of their needs. He also knew that Lilia was too old to be acting as a full-time nurse. However healthy she was, it wouldn't be fair to expect her to climb up to the first floor several times a day. Under these circumstances, he had no choice but to stay on the ground floor until he got better – and he firmly believed that he was going to get better.

Since Lilia thought she had done a great job in such a small space of time, she was annoyed to see the total lack of appreciation on Arnie's face. She knew what a private man he was but he couldn't possibly expect her to walk up and down those stairs all day long. It was bad enough that she had to take care of a half-paralysed man at her age; she didn't feel that she could do much more. The ideal thing would be to hire help for Arnie, but they both knew that was impossible. Their insurance wasn't even going to fully pay for the physiotherapist who was going to come three times a week. She had been thinking about this for days now, trying to come up with a solution. There was only one thing they could do as far as she could tell and that was to rent the four rooms which had been left empty for years. Their house was very close to a school that taught English to foreigners, which meant it would be very easy to find lodgers. She could even include food in the rent like she did for Ed to make the offer more inviting. She already cooked every day; all she had to do was to increase the amount. This way she could keep the tenants away from the kitchen, too; at least when it came to cooking. The day Arnie came home, Lilia decided to broach the subject. While she was a little reluctant to bring it up, she wasn't overly worried as she knew that she held complete power over the household for the first time in their marriage. The last thing Arnie wanted in the house was more people and more noise, especially with this new living arrangement. All the same, although he explained this to his wife, he also knew that they didn't have any other choice. For the first time in his life he wished they'd saved the money they'd spent on the kids. Dung and Giang had only visited him once in the hospital and even then they'd left early, saying that they needed to pick up their children. He hadn't expected them to stay all day, but all the same it hadn't been easy to see how little they cared for him. Even for someone who knew how to control his feelings and was proud of his ability to hide any resentment, it hurt. After all, he was the one who was having to put up with having strangers in his house in return for offering his children such luxurious lifestyles.

He accepted the offer out of pure necessity. Lilia would go to the school the next day to put up flyers. The small smile that escaped at the edge of her lips hinted that she liked the idea. Lilia wasn't about to say anything to Arnie, but she wasn't exactly devastated by this change in their situation. She was going to enjoy seeing some activity in this house at last; it would be so nice to see people coming and going and be able to say a few words to somebody else every now and again. She had been alone and quiet for far too long.

On his first day at home, Arnie realised just how much he was going to need Lilia's help. It was one thing not to be able to go to the bathroom on his own, but another altogether that it took them twenty minutes to walk there, even though it was only forty feet away. Lilia was very patient, as she always had been. She didn't lose her temper and always tried to help her husband as best she could. Arnie appreciated that, but he still couldn't control his own anger and found himself yelling at her a couple of times. Why did she have to stand on his right side instead of his left? Couldn't she see that it was his left side that was weak? Why hadn't she thought of opening the bathroom door before they went there, so that he wouldn't have to stand and wait while she struggled with it? He knew this was the first time his wife had ever encountered a problem like this, and she was doing the best she could. She was going to learn and improve, but still he couldn't stop himself from vomiting out the anger he felt towards his own life and fate, using any little mistake as an excuse. He realised that he'd exhausted his wife over the course of the day. Lilia certainly felt very tired by the time they had dinner, and she went to her room early. She didn't forget to give her husband a good night kiss before going upstairs. She also remembered to turn on the baby monitor she had bought to keep an ear open for Arnie, so that she'd be able to hear if he needed anything in the middle of the night. She climbed up the stairs feeling very aware of each creak that came from the wooden staircase under her feet. After slowly washing her face, she examined it closely in the mirror. She had still felt young up until ten days ago, but now she was trapped with an ill and unhappy man in a creaky house in a boring suburb. To top it all, she didn't know how long this was going to go on for. An uncertain future lay ahead of her. She wanted to leave everything behind and just go. Instead of falling into a troubled sleep, she wanted to get into a cab and drive far away. She lay down on the bed and closed her eyes. She spread her arms out to her sides and started saying one of the prayers from her childhood which she thought she'd forgotten a long time ago. When she was a little girl, she and her friends would do a kind of a tribal dance to help them to achieve happiness. Even though they didn't know exactly what they were doing, they would go into a trance towards the end and come out of it feeling completely rejuvenated. Whether it was true or not, Lilia strongly believed that this ritual brought her some kind of internal strength. When they first moved here she had wanted to do the dance in their garden just once, but Arnie had stopped her. He had explained that white Anglo-Saxons didn't even drink tea in their gardens, let alone dance. He'd gone on to say that if she wanted to be respected in this community, it would be better if she didn't spend a lot of time outdoors. That's why she'd had to get a driver's licence. She had always liked walking, but it wasn't appropriate to walk in this neighbourhood; it was frowned upon.

It had taken Lilia years to come to terms with this way of living: owning beautiful front gardens but not enjoying them, putting stylish white chaise longues out on the porches but not sitting on them once. And she had become one of them, despite her dark skin. Now she saw how meaningless everything she had been forced to do really was. Maybe she had gained the respect of her neighbours by not doing the things she liked, but after all these years she didn't even know who those neighbours were. After all this time they still only said 'hi' from a distance. She fell asleep struggling with these thoughts again, as she did every once in a while. She hated herself for being weak and living her life according to what other people wanted from her. That's why her brows were knitted together as she closed her eyes.

When she heard Arnie's voice on the baby monitor, it was half past six in the morning. The tone that reached her through those tiny holes told her that her husband was mad at something. Lilia jumped out of bed and ran downstairs, even though her aching kneecaps tried to stop her. She found Arnie at his door, leaning on his walker as if he was about to faint. Despite all the years they had spent together and the situation they were in right now, she realised that she was still afraid of her husband in some ways, and she asked him hesitantly what he was doing up by himself. Arnie roared in her face that he needed to go to the bathroom. While Lilia was trying to explain that she might not have heard him because she was very tired and that she was sorry, Arnie cut her off sharply once again and said he had only called out to her once and then decided to try to go by himself. Without saying another word, Lilia helped her husband back to his room. It was obvious that he couldn't stand up any longer in his current state. She had to convince Arnie to pee in a plastic cup they had bought at the hospital and then clean him up before going back to her own room to change. Over the coming days and months she would begin to understand just how tough her life was going to get. She was going to go to bed every night hoping that the next day would be a better one, but find herself even more worn out the next morning. She was going to sleep less and less, and when she did it would be stilted and filled with nightmares. Some nights she was going to turn down the volume of the baby monitor and simply stop caring about all the insults Arnie would hurl at her.

Despite all the difficulties she was going through, Lilia had managed to go to the language school and had found four tenants for her four rooms. They had all agreed to have meals included in the rent. With tenants arriving day in, day out, the house started getting noisier. Even though Lilia warned them about it from time to time, she didn't ask them to be absolutely quiet. She had changed her lifestyle for Arnie and lived the way he wanted for years. Maybe it was his turn now. She listened to her husband's complaints about not being able to sleep at night because of the sounds coming from upstairs with a smile on her face, and stored all of his whining in a corner of her brain, just like some dirty laundry that was never going to be washed. She spent even longer hours in the kitchen now, without forcing herself to turn down the volume of the TV. She listened to the recipes given on some shows and wrote them down. With the new faces in the house, her cooking had also become more varied and colourful. Some spices and vegetables she had never used before now made their way into her food. Although she was sick and tired of taking care of Arnie, she couldn't help thinking that his illness had been the best thing that had happened to them in a long time. While in the past the TV presenters had been their only dinner guests, the evening meal had now become a small festivity every night and Lilia really looked forward to it during the day. Since they were students, her tenants stopped by the house at all different hours of the day, chatted with Lilia around the kitchen counter while she cooked and even helped her with small chores. None of them tried to get to know Arnie, and they all assumed that his bad temper was a result of his condition. Lilia didn't mention that Arnie had always been a very private, quiet and, in fact, a boring man. Even Ed had started coming to the kitchen a little more often thanks to this new energy in the house. Of course, it didn't escape Lilia's attention that one tenant in particular had played a role in this sudden change in Ed's habits.

Ulla was a beauty, the result of an African father and a Swiss mother. She had been born and raised in Switzerland, studied in France and then went back to her native country and started working there. Taking some time off from her job, she had come to New York to improve her English, which she needed for work. Her mother tongue, Romansh, was one reason why everybody was interested in her. She was very happy with all this attention and didn't shy away from reading poems in this strange mixture of a language. When Ulla came home in the middle of the day and asked Lilia '*Co vai?*' Lilia knew that Ulla wanted to know how she was.

Similarly, when her Japanese tenant, Kano, stuck his head around the kitchen door and said '*Nanika atta?*' she knew he meant 'What's up?' She was happy just to know the answer to this question – '*Genki desu*', 'I'm fine' – as it was enough to make her feel more or less accomplished. Kano was a twenty-eight-year-old graphic designer, and like all Japanese people he was stylish, polite and hardworking. Even though his lessons started in the afternoon, Lilia found him meditating in the garden every day very early in the morning and this gave her some of the strength she needed to start her daily battle. Kano wasn't a Buddhist like many of his Japanese – and even American, British, Australian, Swedish or French – peers; instead, he believed in Shinto. His religion didn't have a prophet or a sacred book; he prayed to trees, the sun, rocks and even to sounds. Early in the morning, Kano would sit on the dewy lawn and murmur something with his face turned to the sky as a prayer. Then he would come inside, complete this ritual with a cup of miso soup and return from the eighth century to the modern age. Lilia and Ulla, who had accepted Buddhism when she was sixteen years old, made him tell them all about his faith and were very surprised that a man of his age should want to hold on to those old rituals.

Now that Kano had entered her life, another world famous food had made its way onto Lilia's menu: sushi. She searched online for hours to find the easiest recipes to follow and watched a lot of videos to see how it was done. Arnie had never understood how his wife could include strangers in her life this quickly. It was almost like she had no boundaries; she didn't have any principles or rules. It had been less than a month since these people had moved into their house and she already knew all about their favourite foods and, what's more, she even cooked them. The conversations grew longer with each passing night and sounds of astonishment, joy and curiosity rose from the kitchen. Arnie, on the other hand, insisted on keeping his door closed at all times. He had told Lilia that he wanted to eat in silence before everybody else came down to the kitchen if possible, and that he wanted to keep his door closed afterwards. That wasn't all: he also asked if they could be a bit quieter and suggested that maybe the tenants could eat in their rooms. Lilia didn't even listen to the last two requests. She wasn't about to ask people to have their dinner in their rooms. She wasn't going to ask them to eat in silence, either, or walk on tiptoes. She could get him earplugs from the pharmacy if he liked, or they could plug headphones with a long cord into the television.

Arnie resisted both of these suggestions without really understanding why, and almost out of spite preferred to let himself be irritated by others. It was partly because he wanted to annoy Lilia as much as she annoyed him. He didn't want her to enjoy anything at all. He had begun to realise that the anger his wife had been building up for years was finally surfacing. He had noticed before how Lilia had been repressing many parts of her personality for a long time now and had become very unhappy, especially in recent years, but he had thought that if he turned a blind eye they would never have to deal with it. Now it looked as if his wife was taking her revenge on him while he lay there, helpless. He knew that he couldn't fight back. His hands were tied. He couldn't accuse Lilia of not taking care of him, but it was obvious that she didn't take him seriously any more.

Lilia, on the other hand, found it much easier to take care of Arnie with this vibrant new spirit in the house. In the mornings she opened her eyes feeling happier at the thought that she was going to see Kano praying in the garden. She loved having a cup of Turkish coffee with her Georgian tenant, Natalie, after taking care of the morning chores, and she especially looked forward to seeing Flavio, who always woke up the latest but had a sophisticated look in his sleepy eyes. Unlike the other Spanish people Lilia had come to know in her life, Flavio had light blonde hair, blue eyes and freckles, which looked like they'd been sprinkled over his face. Lilia had mentioned this the first time she met him and Flavio had fed her a line he had clearly been working on for some time: 'I'm a Spanish albino.' Lilia didn't tell him that he couldn't say that kind of thing – even as a joke – in the United States.

Flavio was a forty-two-year-old philosophy teacher. Now that he had reached middle age, he had wanted to get away from the place where he'd lived all his life and had decided to come to New York, as he'd been there once before and loved it. Since he couldn't afford a place in Manhattan, he had found Lilia's advert inviting. The ad had said that the house was in walking distance of the town's train station and that the train ride to Manhattan only took twenty-five minutes. He also liked the idea of having someone to cook for him. He had just got divorced and didn't even know how to scramble eggs. There were thousands of books and articles to read and a lot to think about, and cooking interfered with both of those activities. Lilia had felt the magnetic effect which Flavio created around him the first moment she saw him. He wasn't handsome or ugly, and he wasn't the most sociable man in the world, and yet his polite composure instantly grabbed women's attention. He talked about the most ordinary things in such a poetic way and understood every little detail so deeply that his audience couldn't help being drawn to him – just as an average-looking man can turn into a handsome, charismatic rock star when put on a stage with lights and music. Whenever Flavio talked, his hair got wavier and his eyes grew deeper. While the other women in the house were all ears whenever he was talking and always went out of their way to catch a glimpse of him, Lilia seemed to be the most excited of all whenever he turned his gaze in her direction. She felt some kind of secret bond between them that was hard to describe, but didn't know what to do with this feeling. Whenever Flavio's blue eyes met hers she had the urge to stir the food in the pan or look for some unnecessary spice in the cupboards. She found these unexpected emotions inconvenient to say the least, but she was happy to be finally feeling things with every cell of her body. She wondered if her husband could sense how the energy in the kitchen was changing day by day, and how much of those feelings seeped into his room from under the closed door.

All of these events also helped Lilia to forget about their children's complete lack of interest in their lives. Although it still upset her that they never called and she thought about it some nights right before she went to sleep, her tired eyes closed before she could think any further, and the next day was always a little more hectic, leaving no time to think. The physiotherapist who came three days a week had also started becoming a part of the household. She could never resist the biscuits Lilia served with coffee in the kitchen after her sessions with Arnie, and they always helped her tense body to relax after dealing with such an uptight patient. She was curious about how a woman like Lilia had managed to stay married to a man like Arnie for such a long time. She asked whether Arnie had become the man he was now after he got sick. Lilia replied to this question in a whisper, after making sure that Arnie's door was securely closed:

'Arnie has always been a very private person. Of course, we had some good times when we were young and we did some travelling, but Arnie has always wanted some alone time during the day. Even before we moved to separate bedrooms he still spent a lot of time in his study.'

'But he wasn't as angry as he is now ...'

'Well, I made sure that I didn't create the kind of environment that made him angry. I did everything the way he liked it. I never made a peep in the house after he went to his bedroom at night. Can you imagine, he used to say he could hear sounds coming from the kitchen in his room, which was on the first floor. Is that even possible? But I never complained. I lived on my tiptoes in this house for years.'

'What about now? Isn't it very hard for him to live in the next room? Besides, he's not very stable, psychologically speaking.'

'Yes, but I'm not that healthy any more, either. I'm sixty-two years old and I have tons to do every day. If I tried to do everything the way he likes it on top of everything else I'd lose my mind. I don't know who'd take care of us then.'

'He also complains about the tenants. He says they're too loud.'

'There's nothing we can do about that. Maybe he's just realising it now, but this is how normal people live. They speak, they shuffle, they slurp, they laugh, they talk about their days, they flush the toilet without worrying about making a noise. They don't take five minutes to close the fridge door so that they can do it quietly. This is the normal way to live. Not living behind closed doors, or trying to hide from your own shadow. We lived like that for years and what happened to us? He had a seizure. Maybe he'll get better if we start living loudly.'

'Don't you have any children?'

'We do. Two. Adopted.'

'The ones in the pictures in Arnie's room?'

'Yes. Dung and Giang.'

Lilia said the names in such an angry way that the therapist couldn't find the courage to probe any further. Instead, she asked about the food Lilia was preparing.

'*Khachapuri*.'

'What?'

'*Khachapuri*. It's a Georgian dish. One of our tenants is a young Georgian woman. This is the first time I've ever tried to make this type of food. I found the recipe online. We'll see how it turns out.'

'What are those small pieces of dough you've got there?'

'Well, first you make small pieces of dough, and then you roll them out into thin circles and fill them with cheese mixed with black-eyed peas. They actually have a special type of cheese for this, but since I couldn't find it I'm using feta, instead. I added some salt, too. After you deep-fry them, you serve them with boiled chicken marinated in garlic. I'm curious about whether the others will like it.'

'Where are the others from?'

'One of them is Swiss, one of them is Japanese and the other one is Spanish.'

Lilia realised that even saying the word 'Spanish' made her knead the dough a little harder. She was trying to hide the fact that she thought about Flavio more than anybody or anything else for most of the day, even from herself. Was he going to come home early that night? Was he going to be home for dinner? Was he going to talk about the book he was reading? Was he going to like the food she had made? Lilia looked forward to the nights. On the days when Flavio came home late she'd put his plate away with cling film on top and watch TV in the kitchen until he came back. If he came home really late she'd go to bed feeling a little heartbroken, hoping that she'd see him the next morning. She didn't question herself yet to see if she was embarrassed by these thoughts. It was enough to know that these feelings warmed her heart.

It had already been more than two weeks since her mother had moved in with them and Ferda had managed to adjust herself to the new pace of their lives. She usually woke up a couple of times during the night to look after her mother and got up very early in the morning. After she had fed Sinan and sent him to work, she helped her mother with the bedpan. Mrs Nesibe was still refusing to go to the bathroom and said she didn't even have the strength to use the bedpan. If Ferda was only a couple of minutes late in the mornings, her mother complained about the pain in her kidneys and moaned loudly. While Ferda used her once-broken wrists to help her mother sit up, Mrs Nesibe would curse her sad fate. Life had never been kind to her, she said: she had become a widow at a very young age, her only son had turned out to be ungrateful, her body had betrayed her and she had lived in pain all her life. And now she was an invalid. She had always known that this was going to happen sooner or later, that she was going to have to throw herself on the mercy of others. She didn't even think about what was happening to her daughter.

Ferda's whole body ached. She could feel every disc on her spinal cord. Even though she had tried to tell her mother that she didn't need to be confined to bed for the rest of her life, she understood perfectly well that her mother's goal was not to solve the problem: it was to exaggerate it. They had finally stopped the physiotherapy after Mrs Nesibe had made no effort whatsoever. When Ferda tried to move her mother's legs in the bed, every groan pricked Ferda's skin like a needle. All the same, Mrs Nesibe's strong body gave her a healthy look and her appetite was just perfect. She told Ferda what she felt like almost every day, and when she was served she wolfed it down. She had a craving for courgette pâté one day and lamb ribs the next. Her mother had always had a good appetite, but the way she wanted to eat now made Ferda suspicious. Sometimes she wondered if these were the last requests of a dying woman. Since she had always been good at feeling guilty, she usually found herself in the kitchen cooking whatever food her mother had requested. When Mrs Nesibe wanted lamb neck pudding and found out that her daughter didn't know how to make it, she looked at her with glaring disappointment.

'You're saying you've never made neck pudding?'

'No … yes … I mean, I've never tried it.'

'Even though it's Sinan's favourite dessert?'

Sinan had never liked this pudding, which was made of lamb's neck with orange and cinnamon. What's more, he had never really understood the point of it, but he'd never told his mother-in-law the truth and always pretended that he loved it. Whenever he was served this dessert with a cinnamon stick stuck in it he was afraid he was going to throw up, but he always lost the feeling of nausea after the first bite. Despite these feelings, he had always complimented his mother-in-law profusely every time she made her speciality, and so Mrs Nesibe believed that this was her son-in-law's favourite dessert and made a habit of cooking it every Ramadan Eid.

Suddenly Ferda had the feeling that her mother was going to get up, put an apron on, go to the kitchen and start making the dessert out of love for her son-in-law. Instead, Mrs Nesibe realised at the last moment that she had almost been sitting up in bed, leaning on her left elbow as if she was about to stand up any moment, and so she fell back onto the bed and cursed her destiny once again. '*Oy vey*, Mrs Nesibe, how did this happen to you? How did a woman like you end up in this state? If I was the old me I'd make the dessert right away, but I can't even move any more,' she said, as tears rolled down her luminous cheeks. Although Ferda felt some sort of compassion for her mother, she couldn't bring herself to worry about those tears since she knew this was just another act in her mother's lifelong drama. She went to the kitchen and came back with a piece of paper and a pencil. She sat down on the carpet next to her mother's bed and held her hand. She said: 'It's OK, mum. You give me the recipe and I'll make it.'

Mrs Nesibe started to describe the dessert, her face still wet with tears: 'First you're going to boil the lamb's neck, until it becomes really tender and starts falling to pieces. Then you'll need to boil it a couple more times, with fresh water each time. Then you're going to shred it ... no, tear it into pieces like this, and then put it back in the pot again. Add some water, sugar, a little lemon zest and some orange zest. And some cinnamon and cloves. Then cook it until there's no more water left in the pan. Then add raisins, dried plum, dried apricot and some more cinnamon, and cook them together again. Make sure you don't burn it, though. When it's all cooked, sprinkle some almonds, pine nuts and cinnamon sticks on top and serve it warm.'

Without asking how much sugar, cinnamon or apricots she needed, Ferda scribbled the recipe down on the paper. She knew that her mother could tell her how much of each ingredient she'd need if she asked her; her memory was still in very good shape. Nevertheless, Ferda wanted to challenge her own ability to capture the taste of every food without knowing every last detail. She was a master of this particular art. In the meantime, her mother had calmed down and her tears had finally stopped. From the way she was moving her dentures in her mouth, Ferda could tell she was getting hungry – maybe at the thought of the neck pudding. She asked her if she wanted some green beans sautéed in onion, garlic, tomato sauce and olive oil. 'Sure,' Mrs Nesibe said, and added: 'Ferda? Do you have any yoghurt? If you do, can you put some yoghurt on the side?' Mrs Nesibe would never just settle with what was there. There was always one more thing to ask for. If she wanted beans, she wanted them with yoghurt. If she wanted yoghurt, she wanted some sugar in it. If she was eating sugar, she'd ask if there were any strawberries. And so the list went on, endlessly, and Ferda started going back and forth between the kitchen and her mother's room several times a day without a break. She talked to her friends on the phone once in a while when her mother took her incredibly short naps and so at least she was able to tell them how she was doing. She was always very careful though, because most of the time her mother woke up in the middle of the conversation and asked who that was on the phone. She would insist on talking to them if it was anyone she knew, and wouldn't stop talking until she was certain that they were convinced she was about to die and felt genuinely sorry for her.

Under normal circumstances, Ferda had a very active social life. She would go out more than twice almost every day, help everybody with their chores, meet with a big group of friends every two weeks and go to the parents' meeting at her grandchildren's school if needed. Now she felt secluded from all these events. As if it wasn't enough that she spent all her time with her mother during the day, she couldn't even enjoy a chat with her husband at night, since they were always interrupted by Mrs Nesibe's demands. Her mother always apologised half-heartedly for the inconvenience and for interrupting her time with her husband – but could she please give her legs a massage? They were really aching, even though they were supposedly paralysed. Did that mean it was going to rain? Or was there going to be unseasonable snow? They had also had to take a break from their regular film nights, which had become a habit in recent years. Ferda would make a note of the films her daughter suggested and would go to see them with her husband once a week. If Sinan didn't want to go, she'd see them by herself during the day. Films had become one of the things Ferda and Öykü always discussed in their weekly phone calls. Unfortunately, this had changed, too.

Ferda didn't like the fact that she kept talking about her mother, just like new mothers who only want to talk about their babies. While life continued outside, her own life had been squeezed into four walls. Since she couldn't go to see her grandchildren any more, her son brought them over to her after school some days. As Ferda showered them with hugs and kisses, she heard her mother reproaching her own grandson for not visiting his grandma often enough. Having said this, there was no such thing as 'enough' in her vocabulary. Anybody who didn't spend at least two hours a day with her was good for nothing, as far as she was concerned. During those brief hours when Ferda was reunited with her grandchildren, she tried to make them happy and put the pound cakes she had hurriedly mixed in the oven. Strangely, it was always Mrs Nesibe who smelled the cake in the air before anybody else. It seemed like everything always worked in her favour. Ferda promised herself that she wasn't going to be like her mother when she was older. She tried to ignore the fact that all women became their mothers sooner or later. All women were going to have the same illnesses that their mothers suffered. They were all going to end up with the same expression on their faces and act in the same way. But this wasn't going to happen to her; she wasn't going to become Mrs Nesibe. She was going to make sure to cut the wires of that time bomb ticking inside her before it finally detonated.

Going to the farmers' market meant something special to Ferda. Going from one stand to another was like taking short trips to those small villages she had never visited. She'd find whatever she was looking for by following the smell that lingered on the tip of her nose and she was always inspired by the colours of the fruit and vegetables. As far as she was concerned, a plate had to be as well planned as a still life painting. The stuffed vine leaves had to shine as if they'd been polished; the parsley had to look vigorous and strong. The harmony of tastes, on the other hand, should resemble a unique symphony. No ingredient should casually enter a plate of food. They all had to serve a purpose. The tomatoes should complement the bitter taste of the aubergine and the subtle taste of cinnamon in the meat was there to calm people's nerves, which were strained throughout the day. The cumin in the meatball wasn't only there for its taste; just the perfect amount had to be sprinkled on the minced beef to help the stomach digest the food. Too much tomato paste in the dish would be like too much make-up on a beautiful face. If too much was added, the food would look as cheap as lipstick used instead of a blusher. No, there was no extra ingredient in the bread Ferda baked; her friends were wrong about that. The delicious taste came from the organic wholemeal flour she used, which wasn't purchased from the supermarket but came straight from the countryside. Her *tarhana* soup smelled different, of course, because the pepper she used in it had come from Urfa, one of the Eastern cities. What made her meat stew more delicious than other people's was the lime tree leaf she always added to it. Anyone who ate this stew relaxed instantly and then went on to discover the love in their souls.

Ferda tried to escape from the unhappiness her mother had brought to her home by going to the farmers' market whenever she found the time. She couldn't go to all the different ones in the different neighbourhoods to buy the freshest items like she used to do before, but even a short trip to the closest one helped her to ease her mind and breathe freely again. She knew that if she told anybody that the flower of a courgette gave her a sense of peace they would just laugh at her, and so she kept the depth of her feelings to herself. The thing that made her happiest was to cook her loved ones' favourite dishes. Cooking artichoke for Cem, vine leaves for Öykü, or moussaka for Sinan filled her heart with love as much as they did. Whenever Öykü told them she was coming home, Ferda would become as clumsy as an inexperienced lover and sometimes she would even burn the food.

She remembered trying to make the biscuits her mother loved, even as a very young child. Her relationship with food reflected how much she wanted to make people happy. That was why she was going to do her best to make that neck pudding for her mother now, no matter how angry she was. And so, she found herself pleading with the butcher after her trip to the farmers' market. If they didn't have a freshly butchered lamb, couldn't they do it the next day? Her mother was on her sick bed and was craving neck pudding. Even the butcher, who literally lived with the smell of meat inside his nose, found this dessert strange. He grimaced at the image of it, which he then tried to forget immediately. 'Dessert made with lamb meat?' he said, almost with disgust, but still he confirmed that he would have the fresh lamb by Friday. Ferda was an old customer. Even though she had reduced the amount of meat they consumed recently because of her husband's heart problems, she was still a valuable customer. She wasn't an easy one either, and certainly didn't shy away from giving very specific instructions. Unfortunately, she was the only person who would ask for veal rib instead of lamb, and that upset him. He had a problem with people who didn't know how to eat everything properly, but there was nothing he could do about it.

When Ferda came home from the market two hours later, a surprise was waiting for her, and it wasn't a pleasant one. Mrs Nesibe greeted her daughter from her bed with eyes that were almost crimson with tears. Ferda understood what had happened by the way her mother's legs were lying in the bed, with her kneecaps slightly touching. She tried not to look at the empty bedpan right next to the bed, as she found the sight of it extremely irritating. She knew that her mother could have reached it if she'd wanted to, and if she only tried a little harder they wouldn't have to go through all this. Still, no matter what else she was feeling, it broke her heart to know that her mother had cried that hard. Before she did anything else, she went straight to her mother and hugged her. She wanted to say, 'Don't worry, these things happen, we'll get over this together,' but she couldn't. What stopped her was the fact that she didn't believe a word of it. Still, she wrapped her arms around Mrs Nesibe, tightly. After staying like that for a while, she went to the bathroom and came back with a roll of toilet paper, a large bowl of soapy water and a cloth. She lifted up her mother's gown and started cleaning away the dark spots on her legs. She only thought of opening the windows when the smell became overwhelming. Meanwhile, Mrs Nesibe's shyness hadn't lasted long. After keeping quiet for a couple of minutes she had started telling her daughter how they had exchanged roles. Once she had been the one who'd cleaned Ferda, and now it was her daughter's turn to clean her, wasn't that right? Ferda looked at her mother, stunned by this remark. Was there any way to make her understand that they didn't have to live like this? Was it actually possible that her mother, to whom she had always given credit for being extremely smart, believed the absurd lie that her mind had created? That was so typical of her mother, though. As always, she had decided what she wanted and had started acting accordingly, no matter how important and irreversible the outcome might be. She didn't even realise that she was dragging herself, her daughter and her whole family towards a disastrous ending.

When Ferda stood up after she had finished cleaning, she felt the pain intensify in her left knee, which had been bothering her for weeks. She knew it was because she'd taken a long break from yoga. It was at the top of the list of things that kept her so energetic at her age. Those exercises, which she regretted having learned so late in life, cleansed her thoughts, cooled her heart and kept her body in shape. At first she had thought that yoga would help her to deal with these difficult days, but now she realised that there was no time for anything else but her mother. Ferda walked to the bathroom with the bowl in her hand, still trying to stretch her leg. After dumping the dirty water in the toilet, she put it in the bathtub and began to fill it with hot water, so that she could clean it. As she listened to the running water, she kneeled down and pressed her arms against the cool edge of the bathtub. She tried in vain to stop the tears from rolling down her cheeks. She wished she was with Öykü now; she wished they were baking a cake.

Marc woke up before dawn every morning and walked quickly so that he could get away from his empty apartment as soon as possible. Since nothing was open and there were no familiar faces on the streets at that time of the day, he was able to walk to his gallery in peace. Even though Amou – who had originally opened the gallery every morning – was surprised to find the doors open on the first couple of days, he had got used to it in no time. Marc kept the doors open very late now as an excuse not to go home, which was not only something new for him but for the customers, too. After all, they had grown accustomed to finding the gallery closed at the most unusual hours of the day.

Marc ate his dinners out and only went home after he was sure that all the shops in his neighbourhood were closed and there was no one else around. After having dinner somewhere in the Odéon district every night, he sometimes watched a film and sometimes went to a bar. Since he had always found more peace at home than anywhere else, being outside for long hours at a time exhausted him. The clamour of the restaurants, the music at the bars and the cold cinema seats became overwhelming after a while. He was also bored with fancy restaurant food, which was generally very good quality and extremely extravagant, and he missed the simple tastes of their own kitchen. His stomach, which felt heavier every day, must have been reacting to all the different ingredients that were used in those places. When he was at home, he only ever went to the kitchen for a couple of minutes and spent most of his time either sleeping or leafing through the books in the living room. He had refused to go to any of the dinner parties he'd been invited to so far. He couldn't find the courage to socialise with friends yet. Whenever one of them stopped by the gallery, he kept the conversation short and prayed that they would leave soon. He had never been a very sociable man, but he had also never been rude or cold to their friends before. What's more, he had never been the sort of unloving creature who would turn his back on the friendship they offered. Before Clara died, the sincerity of the conversations around the dining table had always warmed his heart. Now, he couldn't even imagine himself sitting among them. He felt that there were no more words left inside him. It was impossible for him to look anybody in the eye. He often found himself looking anywhere else but at the face of the person he was speaking to. He didn't even know what he was talking about most of the time; he would mumble something about a film he had seen or a customer who had come into the store.

The closer it came to Christmas, the more desperate Marc became. He would close his eyes as he walked the streets if he could. He took the long way home using a different route just so he wouldn't have to pass the corner shop where they bought their Christmas tree every year. He had closed the curtains on the front windows of his apartment so that he wouldn't have to see the family living on the first floor across the street. For years they had watched each other's Christmas preparations and sent Merry Christmas messages by signalling to each other with the fairy lights on the windows. Before, whenever Marc entered their apartment during those happiest weeks of the year, he would always drink in the smell of vanilla, ginger and chocolate chip biscuits so that he wouldn't forget it until the next year, and that sweet smell had always made him happy. This year he didn't take out the Christmas ornaments, which stayed in a bag under the bed. He didn't stick the paper snowflakes, which he liked to scratch off with his short fingernails at the end of the holidays, onto the windows. Some days he sat down and cried because he missed drinking hot chocolate with whipped cream on top. He wanted to go to Montmartre to pray at the Sacré-Cœur and then go to a café for profiteroles afterwards, like they always used to do, but he couldn't find the strength to do any of those things.

The whole city was a prison to him. Wherever he went, he couldn't get rid of the heaviness in his heart and the sorrow dug deeper and deeper. The continuous pain he felt on the bridge of his nose had become a headache now and he always carried painkillers in his pockets.

On the twenty-fifth morning of every December they would always go into the living room with their pyjamas on and open their gifts under the tree, just like two little children. Although they always felt sad when Christmas was over, the thought of the approaching New Year would cheer them up again. This Christmas morning Marc went into the kitchen without a gift and sat down at the table. Since he knew that nowhere was going to be open that day, he had bought a couple of things to eat the day before and was prepared to spend the whole day at home. After he had eaten his breakfast out of a brown paper bag, he took two of the sleeping pills he had started taking after Clara's death. Before long he felt tired again. He stopped staring at the TV, turned it off and shuffled back to the bedroom. He had disconnected the landline and hadn't even turned on his mobile phone so he wouldn't have to hear any kind wishes from friends. He went back to his messy bed and pulled the quilt up over his head. He slept through most of the day, until the shaking bed finally woke him up.

Odette had called Marc over and over again, and when she couldn't reach him she had hopped in a cab and made her way to Rue Monge, leaving all the Christmas dinner preparations to her husband and friends. When everybody's children had got older and started celebrating holidays with their own families, Odette, Sylvie, Clara and Suzanne had started the tradition of celebrating Christmas together, as a group of old friends, at one of their apartments. Odette had called Marc days ago to let him know that they were going to be eating at their place this year. Her husband, Henri, had also stopped by the gallery one day and told Marc that they really wanted him to come. Marc hadn't told them that he wasn't going to attend, but they had all more or less guessed that he wouldn't show up. That's why Odette had decided to go and fetch him while they were getting ready for dinner. When Marc opened his eyes, Odette was still holding his arms and shaking him wildly.

'Did you take something? Tell me!'

'Just sleeping pills.'

'How many? Tell me how many!'

'Two.'

Odette calmed down when she heard the number.

'I've been trying to wake you up for the last ten minutes. I knew you'd taken something, but I didn't know how many of what, so I got worried. I almost called an ambulance.'

'It's not that I don't think of killing myself sometimes, but I can't even do that without Clara.'

This was the first full sentence which made any sense that Odette had heard from Marc in months. She looked at him in surprise and with some degree of satisfaction. At least he'd managed to say something relating to his feelings. That couldn't be bad. She looked around her: this apartment, which had been full of happiness back in the day, looked dark and lifeless now. Marc's loneliness had settled in every corner. The despair of this man, who lay under the covers and slept on Christmas Day, was even reflected in the mirrors.

'Get up, let's go.'

'I'm very tired.'

'You're not tired. You're depressed. I'll be waiting for you in the living room. Get dressed up. I have tons of things to do at home. If anything happens to my *Bûche de Noël*, I'll hold you responsible.'

Marc didn't tell Odette how much it hurt to hear the name of this dessert, and got dressed without any protest. He couldn't help seeing an image of Clara on a Christmas morning a couple of years ago. He remembered as if it were yesterday how she had swayed to the rhythm of the song coming from the radio while she made her *Bûche de Noël* before everybody arrived and started drinking cocktails. While she used her left hand to pat the small sieve she held in her right, she sang as she watched vanilla powder snowing onto the cake: 'Let it snow, let it snow, let it snow.' After putting some clothes on, he followed Odette unwillingly out of the door. That line of the song had already buried itself in his brain for the rest of the day.

A couple of days before New Year's Eve, Marc felt as if his body had gone numb with pain and he didn't think he could take much more of this. Only a few months earlier, when Clara was still with them, they had planned to spend New Year's Eve in Normandy, at a big house that had already been paid for with the same group of friends. Although Clara's death had changed Marc's plans, the others were leaving in a couple of days. They had insisted on him coming along too, but he was not about to be convinced on this one. All the same, he understood that at least their friends had to get used to the loss and get the sadness out of their system. It looked as if 31 December was going to be the hardest day of the year for Marc. This was going to be the first New Year's Eve he'd ever spent alone. Despite this fact, he was really looking forward to it. Maybe he could finally get on with his life when these festivities had ended; maybe he could find a way not to think about Clara every minute of the day. Perhaps his life could finally become a little more normal. He had been playing hide and seek in his own neighbourhood for months. He went out at the most ridiculous times of the day and took the most absurd ways to get to wherever he needed to go, just so that he wouldn't bump into anybody he knew. He had stopped going to their old deli when he needed something. Instead, he went to the Muslim deli three streets down. He could hear people's voices – especially those of Arabs calling their relatives far away – coming from the small phone booths in the shop. He had also gone into one of them from time to time and stood in front of the phone, wondering if he had a long distance call to make. He couldn't think of anybody else other than Clara's aunt, but he had nothing to say to Yvette. At those moments he understood how narrow the borders of his life had been. This fact, which he had never thought about until Clara passed away, often came to his mind now. Sometimes he sat on the stool that had been placed there for the customers and looked out at the street. He knew that the people who worked at the shop thought there was something wrong with him and this made them treat him extra nicely. He used this to his advantage and didn't feel like giving any explanation. Maybe they would think he was crazy, but he didn't care about that either. He paid for whatever he bought and only left when someone else needed to make use of that small space. The Arab owner of the shop usually acted as if Marc had only been there for a few minutes and thankfully never asked any questions.

Although Marc was running away from the whole world, he felt at peace when he was with Amou. Maybe it was because he was the one who knew Clara the least. Marc didn't feel like he had to talk about his wife when he was with him. He didn't have to remember how perfect, kind, beautiful, understanding and sweet she was. They could look at an original page of a graphic novel for minutes on end without uttering a word and could walk to opposite ends of the shop without feeling the need to make any comment whatsoever. Amou had no clue about the social world either, and was just as alone as Marc was. He was equally indifferent to the beautiful women who passed by the large windows of their gallery. Marc knew there was a chance that Amou might also experience the same kind of pain one day.

On the other hand, the anguish Marc suffered reached such a climax over time that he wasn't even sure he wanted to get rid of it any more. There was a kind of philosophy in this feeling that gave him strength: a person who had experienced absolute happiness might choose to look for infinite sorrow, to avoid settling in the middle. When one day he stopped in front of the sign pointing towards the pilgrimage route which ended at the Cathedral of Santiago de Compostela in Spain, he felt as if he could walk for miles thanks to all the pain he was feeling. Maybe then, when he reached the rite of communion at the end of that road, he could start life all over again. As it happens, instead of following the Way of St James, Marc decided to follow another path that emerged from within. A path that would heal him with time and help him to see life's beauties once again.

Four

Before Ulla came to New York from Switzerland, she never would have dreamed she'd be staying in a house that smelled like medicine. She'd imagined living in a trendy neighbourhood in Manhattan, in a chic apartment just like the ones she'd seen in films, but this house was much cheaper and closer to the school she went to, and so she'd chosen to rent a room here. Of course, the flyer hadn't mentioned that a half-paralysed, difficult man would also be living in the house. Although she'd originally planned to move somewhere else after a month, she had soon changed her mind once she'd got to know the place better. The crowded household, which consisted of up to seven people including the other tenants, was not only much more fun but also more exciting than her usual family of three. Besides, she believed that an extraordinary bond was being built between her and her landlady. There was a special charm about her that she couldn't quite figure out, but she was irresistibly drawn to it. It could be some kind of mystical power. Ulla had been looking for that mystical presence in another person all her life, and so her adoration of Lilia grew stronger every day. Hearing the answers to her questions about life from an older woman confirmed her belief in wisdom. She'd been looking for this wise woman ever since she was a little girl, confident that she would find her one day. Once she'd even thought it was the Turkish hairdresser she used to go to in Switzerland. Now, she was sure that it was Lilia. With the help of her landlady, she began to understand the importance of food in people's lives. She understood that every bite that passed through her throat would become a piece of her identity and that it was possible to give and receive messages through food. Maybe that was why she'd come all the way to New York: her real learning was going to take place in this house.

Lilia was at the supermarket when Ulla found Arnie collapsed on the floor. Even though Lilia had taken care of his every need before leaving the house and had told him not to get out of bed, Arnie had been on his way to the kitchen to try to catch the ringing phone when he had a dizzy spell and fell to the floor with the sound of Dung's voice leaving a voice message ringing in his ears. Ulla had called 9-1-1 as soon as she saw him lying on the kitchen floor. While she tried to make him lie down on his back, she also tried to help the operator on the phone by telling him everything she knew about this man.

Lilia's phone rang just when it was her turn to pay at the cashier. While she tried to find her mobile phone in her giant handbag, the girl at the cashier had already started reading the barcodes of the various items and was putting them in a bag. That meant that Lilia had to apologise a hundred times when she finally had to leave the store without taking any of those things with her. Since she couldn't explain her husband's condition to the cashier in a couple of minutes, she had to leave the young girl's sulking face and angry words behind her and went to stand in the queue for a taxi, feeling extremely irritated. She was about to explain her problem to the woman standing in front of her in the queue to see if she could take her taxi when the phone rang again. This time Ulla told her that the ambulance had already arrived and had taken Arnie to St Vincent's. In answer to Lilia's question, she said 'No, the paramedics didn't know what the problem was. Only the doctors could answer that one.' When their phone conversation ended Lilia saw that the woman in front of her had already put five of her many bags in the boot of the taxi and was now struggling with the rest. She had nothing else to do but wait. It probably didn't matter anyway, since the ambulance had already taken him to the hospital. Could Arnie's body take another blood clot? Lilia had learned from her earlier experience how wrong and unhelpful it was to make a guess.

After she'd given the cab driver the name of the hospital, she sank back into the big car seat and closed her eyes. At that moment she realised that whatever was happening or whatever time it was, she still thought about Flavio in every spare minute. She'd been trying to ignore the fact that she found herself daydreaming about this young man most of the time now and had interpreted her feelings as nothing more than a need for excitement in her unadventurous life. In actual fact, she'd finally become aware of her sexuality again in recent weeks for the first time in years, and she'd even started fantasising in front of a mirror again – something that she hadn't done in a very long time. She'd never once considered cheating on her husband, yet she couldn't help wondering whether Flavio would find the skin dangling from her arms as repulsive as she did if he ever saw them up close. One day she had put on her slimming corset – which had been buried inside a drawer for years – under one of her dresses and had been pleased with the result. Of course, she had almost ripped it off her body after a couple of hours when she was sure she was going to faint. She also couldn't deny that she'd found herself standing in front of the hair products in the supermarket more than once. The idea of having dark, chestnut hair certainly tempted her; she wasn't going to lie about it. It looked like it would go well with her dark complexion. She'd even tried putting on red lipstick before going downstairs a few times, and actually thought it really suited her. All the same, she'd wiped it off each time with a square of toilet paper out of fear that a sudden change like this might make Arnie suspicious.

That wasn't all. For the first time in a very long while she had brought one of her blank canvases up from the basement to her room and put it on the easel, which had been quietly waiting there for years. She hadn't started painting yet, but she drew images on it in her mind from where she lay on the bed. Eventually she'd got completely fed up with not being able to decide what she wanted to do, and so she'd procrastinated, using Arnie's voice coming from the baby monitor as an excuse. Could there be anything more satisfying than a legitimate excuse not to do something creative for someone who'd realised that they lacked any real talent? In the rare moments when Lilia found the courage to be honest with herself, she had admitted using the children as an excuse for exactly the same reason in the past. She'd be relieved to know that she wasn't the only person in the world who had a habit of blaming others for their own shortcomings.

When she arrived at the hospital, Lilia felt more curious than worried. She wanted to know which direction her life was going to take now. On her way up to the ninth floor she kept thinking how her whole life depended on what happened to another human being, and by the time she left the lift she felt really upset with herself. She went to the busy information desk and gave them her husband's name. It wasn't possible to guess anything from the face of the woman who was searching on the computer for Arnie's name and room number. Lilia waited patiently, wondering if the people who worked at the hospital became grumpy over time or if the hospitals simply hired grumpy people to work for them. After a couple of minutes the woman looked at Lilia over her reading glasses and told her that the doctor was still with the patient and that she would have to wait. Lilia sat on one of the many chairs lined up against the wall. She put on her reading glasses, which she'd hung around her neck so she'd be able to read the shopping list, and found Ulla's number. It was really refreshing to have someone whom she could call without having to hesitate. Since the doctor still hadn't appeared after the phone call, she leaned her head against the wall and closed her eyes. Before long, she had dozed off.

When she lifted her head, which had almost dropped onto the chair beside her, and opened her eyes with diffi-culty, she found the doctor standing in front of her. Arnie had suffered another minor cerebrovascular incident, but there was nothing to fear at the moment. There had been no change in the course of his illness. When she asked if it was still only his left side that was weak, the doctor said, 'Yes.' They weren't going to release him that day, as they wanted to monitor him for twenty-four hours, but she didn't have to stay there with him. Sadly, Lilia realised how little desire she had to see her husband. She was tired of looking at his gaunt face. Still, since it wouldn't be proper to leave without visiting him, she went to his room. Arnie looked as if he hadn't the strength to talk. He followed Lilia's movements with his eyes. Although he didn't show any sign of affection himself, he expected her to go to him and hold his hand. His wife was one of those people who always felt compassion for others. Even when her children had made her sad, she had always been gentle with them. Just as he'd imagined, Lilia walked towards him and kindly took his hand in her own, being very careful not to move the tube that was attached to it. All the same, there was no warmth in this touch. It was a learned gesture, a casual courtesy. Arnie looked carefully at his wife for the first time in years. She looked very well groomed and a little more beautiful than usual, considering how much she had let herself go in recent years. She had combed her hair to one side, just like she used to do when she was young, and this had revealed her high, round cheekbones. He tried to remember the exact moment when he had fallen in love with her, but his memory failed him. He'd never had anything to say to her, but when did his wife stop telling him things? She didn't even look him in the face now. She kept looking around the room, murmuring meaningless things. She said: 'You're going to get better; everything will be fine. You're not in pain, are you?' Arnie didn't know if he was going to get any better. He didn't like the fact that he couldn't guess how his life was going to turn out in the future. This was especially frustrating as he had always been proud of his ability to guess things, like the scores of baseball games, the results of presidential elections or the winners of tennis tournaments. He didn't even want to think that he might be in this state for the rest of his life. This was enslavement; he was enslaved to a house, to a room, to a woman and to this kind of a life. That's why he kept trying to move: so that he would be free again.

He knew that Lilia couldn't stand him any more, and he couldn't stand her either. Instead of appreciating everything she did for him he had started hating her, and asked for the most impossible things at the most impossible times of day and night just to give this hatred some kind of release. It was obvious that their marriage had failed a long time ago, but they had needed a tragedy like this to help them understand that they couldn't live together any more. He guessed that his wife was trying to stay sane in this nightmare by hiding behind those people she had only known for such a short time. He, on the other hand, had no other choice but to get better. He realised that he finally had a dream for the first time in his life. Arnie had never been someone with dreams, even as a young man. He had lived his life by following the example of people who had lived before him and had built it on the same template that had always been there, with just some small changes brought about by the times he'd lived in. Marrying a foreigner and adopting children from Vietnam were not the results of an open mind; that was simply the new template of those years. But now he finally had a dream:

to get well and live alone for the rest of his life. To live in peace in his 200-square-foot room.

After she had stayed with Arnie for fifteen minutes, Lilia excused herself and left to go home. She didn't know if Arnie hadn't replied to any of the things she'd said because he didn't want to talk, or because he couldn't talk. She didn't care any more, either. It was easier to bear each other's presence at home. At least there were other things around to distract them. They didn't have to look one another in the face in an empty, silent room like this one. Lilia tried to remember how her husband's eyes had looked when he was younger; they had got smaller and smaller behind his glasses over the years. What was it that had made her fall in love with him? She couldn't remember, no matter how hard she tried. She felt exhilarated as soon as she had left the hospital. The thought of being able to spend a night without Arnie in the house made her blissfully happy. She was free of his fretting and fuming. She wouldn't have to feel his existence every second behind the kitchen door, or try to control every word she said. She could have a big dinner with all the young people in the dining room. Spaghetti with meatballs, a large salad and some red wine, she thought. They could even light a fire in the fireplace. She hoped that everybody, and especially Flavio, would come home early that night. When she caught herself thinking about what she was going to wear, she blushed. In her mind she started looking through her dresses, which were all from charity shops. They were all very baggy and boring. She imagined herself in a plain, tight, long black dress. She hadn't put on anything remotely like that in years. There was no reason for her not to look good if she put on her slimming corset. Unfortunately, after she'd put on some weight and her body had lost its shape, she had stuffed all of her clothes – including a black dress – into a big rubbish bag and sold them to the Cancer Care charity shop for a small sum. Now the best she could hope for was to find a black blouse and a black skirt in that big pile of nothing in her wardrobe.

She was lucky; after making some quick phone calls she found out that everybody planned to come home early that night. The snow that had started falling in the late afternoon definitely helped. All of the tenants had learned how difficult it was to find a cab or wait on a train platform when the weather was bad. When she arrived home, instead of preparing the food for that night, she went straight to her room. Before taking a shower, she lay some of her outfits out on her bed so that she could see her options. When did she become this tasteless? Where had she found all these flowery shirts and mustard-coloured skirts? How did she manage to collect these horrible pieces when she'd thought she'd been having fun wandering around charity shops? The evidence of how pathetic her life had become was right there in front of her eyes. She couldn't even remember the last time she'd bought herself something new. She had turned into someone else, carrying around other people's tastes. In the end she'd become an unappealing, unhappy, unremarkable, moody, classic American woman. She pulled the only wearable dress from the ugly mess on the bed. It wasn't black, as she'd imagined. It wasn't tight either. But at least it was plain and brown. She piled all the others in a corner of the bedroom so she could throw them out afterwards, and went for a shower. She also wanted to get rid of the heavy smell of the vitamin B tablets she had started taking on the doctor's recommendation.

Before they sat down at the table, they removed all the canvases which had been leaning in front of the fireplace and prepared to light the wood, which had been stored in the basement for years. When everybody had taken their places, Lilia struck the match and they started eating, accompanied by the first light and crackling sounds of the fire. The conversation took its course naturally, as it always did. Lilia happily welcomed the compliments made to her hair and make-up and couldn't stop herself from looking towards Flavio. If someone had asked her, she couldn't have said what she expected. Even though she was very happy to be feeling energised again, Lilia didn't know if she would be able hold Flavio's hand if he were to offer it. Besides, she could still see the age difference when she stood next to someone young, despite how much younger she felt both physically and mentally. She didn't intend to think much about it that night, though. All she wanted was to be happy, without analysing things too much. If only everything had gone the way she'd planned it.

It was Natalie who first smelled the smoke spreading through the room. While they were trying to understand what was happening, the smoke that had kicked back from the chimney had already covered the fire and eventually spread through the whole room. Before long, they couldn't even see each other through the thick cloud of smoke. Lilia stood frozen, not knowing what to do. There was no fire to be extinguished, but the smoke had started spreading to the other rooms on the ground floor, too. Flavio had to grab hold of her by the shoulders and drag her outside. Meanwhile, he was yelling 'Everybody out!' in his strong accent and trying to tell Lilia that they had to call the fire department. Lilia kept saying that they didn't need the fire department. The chimney hadn't been cleaned in years; that must be it. Ed was the one who finally came downstairs and stopped the nonsense. He had smelled the smoke from his room on the second floor and had called the fire department without wasting any time, depending on his instincts, which had grown sharp after so many years as a security guard. Now he was shouting at Lilia, asking how she had dared to light that fireplace. That thing hadn't been used in years; didn't she know that it had to be cleaned? While Lilia stood with her eyes glued to the ground rather than facing him, just like a little girl, she was wondering what embarrassed her the most: Ed yelling at her, making such a big mistake or not inviting her oldest tenant to dinner. Truth be told, they hadn't used that fireplace once since moving to the house. Arnie had always seen it as an unnecessary luxury and expense and Lilia had never stood up to him.

This time it was the sound of the fire engines that interrupted the silence of the neighbourhood. The neighbours, who had never been seen in flesh and blood before, now started peeking out of their windows. It made sense for them to feel justified in interfering as long as the drama concerned their well-being, too. They needn't have worried; the firemen were done in no time. They opened all of the windows on the ground floor and told everyone to vent their rooms before going to bed. In the end, they all went back into the house, cleaned their plates quietly and headed up to their rooms. Lilia opened only one window in her bedroom, got under the blankets without changing her clothes and turned on the TV at the foot of her bed. She needed to hear somebody else speaking to drown out the sound of her own inner voice. If not, her heart was going to break into a thousand pieces and she would end up crying all night long.

Ferda proudly watched her eldest grandchild kneading the dough. Naz was only eight years old but she already liked to help her grandmother in the kitchen and was talented, too. Ferda wondered how her granddaughter was going to remember these days in the future. She didn't only want to spend time with Naz because she enjoyed her company, but also because she wanted to give her good memories. She hoped that one day her granddaughter would look back on their time together – at the hours spent baking and cooking – and would draw something useful from it to help better herself. Didn't she herself have happy memories of those short moments she had spent with her paternal grandmother in her youth? She had lost both of her grandmothers at a very young age, but still held on tightly to the memories they had made together. She could still see the shapes formed by the flour on her granny's apron while she made *katmer*. Or how she used to push the hair away from her forehead with the back of her hand. She had realised just how necessary that gesture was – which she'd thought was something only old women did – the first time she'd ever got her hands greasy. She noticed to her surprise that most of her fondest memories involved her mother complaining about her husband to Ferda's beloved late aunt around the kitchen table. For Ferda, every conversation that took place in the kitchen was delightful only because it had happened there. She even missed the fights that took place around the warmth of a stove. Didn't she feel like the days she had spent in her grandmother's kitchen gave her strength at the times when she felt the weakest? What a kitchen that was, too. It looked just like the vintage kitchens you saw in those interior design magazines nowadays, with its high counter in the middle, the oven in a corner and the copper pans hanging on the walls. Nowadays people spent a fortune on building kitchens like that one.

Re-tinning the copper cups had played an important part in their lives back then, too. She could still hear the voice of the local re-tinner, who walked around the streets pushing his cart and touting for work. Her father's mother also used to use this word to mean 'to scold someone'. She would say, 'I really re-tinned Mrs Leyla this time', and then she would go on to describe in detail how heartily she'd done it. Although Ferda loved this word, she had never once used it in that sense in her whole life. This made her wonder which words she was going to hand down to her only granddaughter. Which words would remind Naz of her grandmother in the years to come? What was her trademark? She searched for these words, but she couldn't find them. Why shouldn't she borrow 're-tinning' and pass it along to another generation? She used the word precisely at the right moment. Naz was telling her about a friend at school who had pushed her.

'You could have re-tinned her.'

'What could I do, grandma?'

'Re-tin her. It means scold her.'

Naz put her tiny hands on the counter and started giggling. Ferda smiled, feeling pleased with herself. She had done it. She was sure that she had passed the word down to the next generation.

'You're very funny, grandma. Is re-tinning kind of like re-timming?'

'No, honey, there's no such word as re-timming. There's re-timing, which means something completely different. Re-tinning can mean to reprimand. To … censure, angrily.'

'For example, our teacher yelled at Attila the other day. Uhm … because … uhm … he didn't know something. So, did she re-tin Attila?'

'Yes.'

'For example, the other day mum re-tinned dad.'

'Children carry the best news,' Ferda thought, as the old Turkish saying goes. She couldn't be sure whether she wanted to dig deeper into the matter or not. She was curious about what had happened in her son's relationship with his wife, but she thought it would be a bit low to try to get information from her eight-year-old granddaughter. So, she decided to let the subject drop. However, Naz was determined to use the new word in her vocabulary in all kinds of different sentences.

'Then dad re-tinned mum really bad, and mum carried on re-tinning dad. And me and Cenk were sitting there, so mum re-tinned us too and told us to go to our room. Then mum and dad re-tinned each other all night long.'

'Huh.'

Ferda couldn't say anything else. This meant something might be wrong with her son's marriage, but she still didn't want to drag Naz further into this conversation. Then she had a vision of Naz, a little girl, walking around and using this word all over the place, and she realised that people were going to find it very strange.

'Well, this word is kind of for older people, honey. You can use it when you get older, OK?'

'Why? I like it. From now on I'm going to re-tin people who push me at school.'

Ferda decided it would be best to change the subject and make her granddaughter forget all about it.

'Look, sweetie, I think this dough is a little soft now. It looks like it needs more flour. It's supposed to have the same consistency as your ear lobe.'

Naz wiped off the dough that was stuck to her fingers and held her own ear lobe. She carried on feeling the dough with her other hand. She shook her head, disapprovingly.

'We can put some more flour in here, grandma. It's not good yet.'

Just when they had started shaping the dough, they heard Mrs Nesibe's voice call out: 'Fusun!' Surprised, Ferda looked in the direction of her mother's room and dried her hands on the cloth hanging from the small pocket of her apron. Naz had got used to her nana calling out to her grandma all the time, but she was also confused by the name. She didn't know why, but her nana kept re-tinning her grandma.

'But your name isn't Fusun, grandma.'

'Yes, darling. I think your nana is a bit confused.'

Ferda tried not to show her granddaughter how shaken

she was. In fact, her body was trembling. Fusun was her mother's first baby. However, she'd got sick shortly after her birth and died before her first birthday, just like a lot of other babies back then. Mrs Nesibe would talk about Fusun once in a while and say how hard it was to lose a child. Each time she would add: 'I wouldn't even want God to punish my enemy like that.' But she had never called her second daughter Fusun by mistake before. It was a name that normally stayed in the past and was remembered every now and again. Although she had never seen her sister, Ferda had always carried the pain of losing a sibling somewhere in her heart. It might have been an extension of her mother's grief. Maybe her mother had just woken up from a dream about Fusun. Maybe she had held her little baby in her arms once again. With these possibilities on her mind, she left Naz alone in the kitchen and went to her mother's room.

'Fusun, can't you hear me?'

'I'm here, mum.'

'Good. I've been calling for you. Where were you? Is your dad home?'

'Mum, it's me, Ferda. I think you were dreaming. Maybe you're not fully awake yet. Let me get you some water.'

As she walked back to the kitchen she could still hear her mother talking about her father. She knew how easy it was to lose track of time and place sometimes, especially after a nap. Her mother's tired body mustn't have fully woken up yet. Just a couple of minutes later, she came back to the small bedroom with a glass of water in her hand. Mrs Nesibe looked Ferda straight in the face with her deep blue eyes, which hadn't lost anything of their glow.

'Fusun, what happened to me? Did I have a stroke?'

'Mum, it's me, Ferda. You broke your hip, remember? Then you came to live with us. You can't walk because you gave up walking. But you didn't have a stroke.'

'That husband of yours, that snake, he broke my leg.'

'Mum, what are you saying? Why would Sinan break your leg? Hold on. Drink this water. You're going to be fine. Come on, sit up.'

'That water is poisoned. I won't drink it. Where's Ferda?'

'God, mum, it's me, Ferda. Fusun was your other daughter, my sister. She died when she was a baby.'

'My mum killed her. She was jealous of our love.'

'Come on, mum, drink some water. You'll be fine.'

'I won't, it's poisoned.'

While she was trying to make her mother drink a sip of water, Ferda didn't realise that Naz had been standing by the door, watching them with wide eyes. She almost jumped out of her skin when she heard her granddaughter's voice:

'Grandma, why is nana calling you Fusun?'

'I don't know, honey. Go back to the kitchen. Have you finished the apple pockets yet?'

'No, I haven't filled them yet. Aren't you going to come?'

'I'm coming, my darling. Go ahead and start. You know how to do it. I'll give your nana some more water and then I'll be there.'

'Why does nana think the water is poisoned?'

'She's kidding, sweetie. Don't mind her. Come on, back to the kitchen now. Look, mum, your grandson's daughter is baking for you. Do you see how lucky you are? We'll make some tea, and you'll have some of the pastries when they're ready.'

Mrs Nesibe turned her gaze towards Naz now, and examined her carefully.

'Is this Fusun's daughter? She looks just like her.'

Ferda thought she was going to lose her mind for a second. She put the glass down on the bedside table and covered her face with her hands. It was almost as if somebody had pushed a button in Mrs Nesibe's mind and all the information there had got mixed up. Since she didn't know how to deal with the situation, she went back to the kitchen with Naz. She poured herself a glass of water and sat at the table. Naz sat right across from her.

'Grandma, has nana gone crazy?'

'No, of course not. She's a little confused, that's all. She's very old, you know.'

'But I'm not Fusun's daughter. I'm Esra's daughter.'

'Yes, honey, you are. I think your nana is just tired.'

'Is she going to die soon?'

'I don't know, darling. But you mustn't think about those things. She's very old, anyway. Don't worry, OK?'

'OK. You're not going to die soon, are you? You're still young.'

'Yes, my darling. But let's not think about these things now. Let's put the filling in our dough. Then we'll put them in the oven, so they'll be ready on time.'

While she folded down the sheets of dough filled with apple, cinnamon and walnuts, Ferda wondered what she was supposed to do. First of all she had to call Sinan and tell him to come home from wherever he was, pick Naz up and take her home. These were not the kind of things a child should hear. She didn't want her granddaughter to get any more anxious than she already was. She also made a mental note to call the doctor first thing on Monday morning. Could this be the beginning of dementia? Their upstairs neighbour from her childhood, Aunt Pakize, had recently gone through the same thing. Her daughter, Tulin, had told Ferda that she'd had a very hard time coping with it. She often said, 'I can't invite anyone home, she says the craziest things.'

After they'd filled the last pastries, she let Naz put the tray into the preheated oven. The oven gloves that came up to Naz's elbows looked very sweet on her. She was so talented, her little bunny. Having learned from previous times, Naz set the alarm for thirty-five minutes before her grandmother even opened her mouth.

'Thirty-five minutes, right, grandma?'

'Yes, my darling. Very good. Now do you want to watch the film I got for you? The bee thing.'

'Bee Movie!'

'Oh, so my little princess knows English, too!'

When Naz had started watching the film, she went back to her mother's room and immediately realised why she hadn't heard her voice at any point in the last fifteen minutes. Mrs Nesibe had gone back to sleep. She went to her bedroom and called Sinan from her mobile. When he didn't answer she dialled her son's number. Her son didn't usually answer all her calls, but it was a different story if one of the children was with her.

'Yes, mum?'

'Hi Cem. I called your father but I couldn't reach him. Can you come over in half an hour and pick Naz up?'

'What happened? Did she drive you crazy?'

'No, not at all, she's the sweetest thing. It's because of your grandmother. She said some weird things. I don't want Naz to be scared.'

'What do you mean, weird things?'

'She called me Fusun. She said that your father broke her leg. And when I wanted to give her some water, she wouldn't drink it. She was convinced it was poisoned.'

'Wow. So she finally lost it.'

'I don't know, Cem. I don't know anything yet. It all happened so suddenly. It started just after her nap. She asked if Naz was Fusun's daughter. I'm going to call the doctor on Monday. I hope it's not dementia. That's the last thing we need. Do you remember Aunt Pakize?'

'Yeah, the lady who lived upstairs from our old building. It happened to her, right?'

'Yes.'

'Mum, you're screwed.'

'We'll see. Maybe it wasn't anything serious.'

'Did you call my uncle?'

'Not yet. I'll call him today. I don't know how I'll manage, though. You know how she listens to every phone conversation. I can't use the mobile all the time. It's so expensive. Anyway, can you come and pick Naz up?'

'Sure, I'll be there as soon as I can.'

'Good. Listen, me and your daughter baked apple pastries. You'll have some, won't you?'

'Of course. See you then.'

After hanging up, Ferda slowly pushed open the door of the small room with her fingertips to see if her mother was still asleep. As far as she could tell in the dark, Mrs Nesibe was lying down with her eyes open. When she looked more carefully she saw that her mother was muttering something to herself and tears were dribbling down from the corners of her eyes to her chin. Ferda's heart ached. She felt so bad that she almost started crying herself. Just when she had turned around to leave, she heard her mother say, 'Ferda, is that you?'

'It's me, mum!' she chirped back, happily. She had come back, thank God.

'I saw your sister in my dream. Your father, too. I think they're calling for me. My time has come.'

'Don't talk like that. Only God knows if it's time or not. Just because you had a dream, you mustn't overdramatise things. You can't let yourself go like this, mum. Please. Think of me.'

'It's not under my control. What can I do? I can't even walk any more.'

Ferda didn't want to go there again. Whenever her mother claimed she was bedridden, Ferda couldn't help telling her that she was the one to blame for that and then it always turned into a big argument. She wasn't in any state to handle that right now.

'Naz and I baked some apple pockets for you, mum.'

'Oh, is that what I can smell? I think they're done. Go and check on them, they're almost burning.'

When the doctor came to visit Mrs Nesibe on Monday, her mind had never been clearer. She remembered what she'd had for lunch not only that day, but also a week ago. She named all of her relatives one by one, and even knew the dates of their births and deaths. She didn't remember anything that had happened last Saturday. What's more, she successfully completed the short test that the doctor had brought with him. He gave her ten words to memorise in ten minutes and when she was asked what they were, she remembered them in perfect order. Under those circumstances, there was nothing the doctor could do but tell Ferda that there could be some occasional slipping in her mother's memory from time to time. That might turn into dementia in the future, of course, but they would have to wait and see if it would. It might be a good idea to make a note of her daily behaviour in a diary. This way they could understand the case much better. 'Of course,' thought Ferda, 'that's just what we need, mum's mental diary.' All the same, she knew she was going to do whatever the doctor told her. Whenever she was given a task to carry out, she made sure that she saw to it, no matter what. When the doctor left, the first thing she did was to dig around in the cupboard for one of the Filofaxes that had been given to Sinan over the years. After cleaning the dust off the leather cover, she found the date inside it and wrote 'FIRST DAY.' The first couple of pages of that diary would be filled with fairly ordinary incidents; however, they were going to get stranger by the day and it would eventually become impossible for Ferda to understand them. She wasn't going to be able to work out how much of what her mother said was true and sometimes she would even doubt the facts that she knew herself. Eventually she was going to stop taking notes altogether, when she saw that it did nothing but hurt her. Her brother would be shocked for the first time when Mrs Nesibe told him that the father he knew wasn't really his father. Even though he wouldn't believe her, he would still take out all of the photographs that were kept in shoeboxes to see if there was really a family resemblance between himself and his father. He would finally relax when he saw the same eyes, the same nose and even the same bald head looking back at him. All the same, this wouldn't stop him from having nightmares in which he called other men 'dad'.

Her mother's evaporating mind wasn't Ferda's only problem. She was working really hard to keep her mother's body clean and stop it from getting bed sores from lying down all day. She turned Mrs Nesibe's body from one side to the other every couple of hours and massaged it with all sorts of ointments and lotions. The bedpan problem had reached such a level that in the end she had started putting nappies on her mother, at least at night. Whenever she wanted to open the windows to get rid of the strong mixture of smells in the room, they went through a major crisis. No, of course she didn't want to kill her. Who had ever died from the cold in five minutes? No, she hadn't turned off the heating in her room. If she wanted she could touch the radiator and see for herself. No, of course she wasn't mocking her, she wasn't trying to remind her she was crippled. She would finally be able to convince her mother that the heating was on by putting the muslin scarf that Mrs Nesibe wore around her neck at all times on top of the radiator and handing it back to her after five minutes. Every day meant another war for Ferda: with herself, with her mother, with the sheets and with the nappies. It was a never-ending struggle. There was only one shelter for her in this house where she was imprisoned, and that was the kitchen. She took refuge in the sponge cake in the pudding, the *orzo* in the *pilaf*, the dill sprinkled on the courgette and the summery smell of the unseasonable cucumber. Still, when she looked at the small containers filled with all kinds of food that she kept in her fridge, she didn't feel like eating any of them. Those foods and desserts which she knew how to make by heart didn't satisfy her any more. When was the last time she had cooked something using a recipe? How long had it been since she'd actually measured the sugar or flour for a cake? Why didn't she ever try the French recipes Öykü kept sending her? What did the Spanish eat? Or the Koreans? Was it true that people ate worms in New Zealand? Did the Cambodians really love eating fried spiders? When Ferda thought about this last delicacy she had to put her hands on her neck to get rid of the shiver she felt there. It might be a tough transition from roasted cauliflowers to fried insects, but she could bring change to her kitchen without being that radical. She didn't want to change her cooking habits because she actually craved different tastes, but because she just couldn't see any other way of escaping from the world she lived in.

This was the first Saturday morning in a long time when Marc hadn't woken up early. On the contrary, his body curled more tightly under the covers to the sound of the soothing voice of the rain. He carried months' worth of fatigue on his shoulders. He had spent most of his time outside since Clara's death. He had walked like he'd never done before and discovered places he had never seen before in Paris. He'd had no idea what had been hiding in this city where he'd been born and raised. For the first time in his life he went to the neighbourhoods where mostly Arab people lived, which he'd been scared to go to in the past. That area was every bit as bad as he'd imagined. While his own neighbourhood was always quiet after nine o'clock at night, those streets were very much alive, with people sitting out on the street in front of the buildings. He didn't feel safe around the young Arab men. He walked by them without looking at their faces, trying not to make it too obvious how scared he was of them. He'd always thought that the police were right to be afraid of entering those neighbourhoods. Burning cars had become almost a tradition for these people. After he'd had a closer look at where they lived, Marc understood what they were rebelling against. Still, didn't everybody live according to their own choices? During these tours, Marc realised that he had lived his whole life without ever looking at other people's experiences, without ever questioning what was happening. Now he saw that young people had a very different perspective on life these days, and especially on sex. And he'd thought that he and Clara had the free spirit of 1968. Marc was only fifteen back then and he'd been in the perfect position to follow the chaos created by that revolutionary wind as it swept through the world. It wasn't that he was interested in world politics or understood anything much about it; when the revolution came to him he had no choice but to join it. The most intense events of May 1968 had taken place in his own neighbourhood, at his own school. And the riots, which ended at the end of that month, had left a legacy of human rights, sexual freedom and drugs behind them. Marc had experienced a little bit of all of them, but when he saw how young people lived now he understood how naïve they'd been back then.

When he walked around those Arab quarters, he'd been mistaken a few times for a rich French man who was there to buy drugs. After that he'd realised that no other French men came to these neighbourhoods for any other reason. Still, he didn't run away. Instead, he went into one of the bars and listened to the beautiful, piercing voice of the violin. He had listened to the same music – the *malouf* – in Tunisia with Clara. The atmosphere there had been completely different. Walking through the back streets of Paris, he realised that they'd been treated as tourists who had gone to a circus in Tunisia. He had to walk around Paris to see the real North Africa.

He also went to the Pigalle quarter for the first time in years. It had been a long time since he'd last walked through the maroon-coloured curtains into one of those shadowy places and watched a woman putting on a show behind a thick layer of glass. He felt embarrassed when he bought a token from the man sitting in the booth; it almost felt like this was his next-door neighbour. As with many other men, he couldn't help getting aroused by the woman's provocative words and movements. When his fifteen minutes were finally up, he felt even worse than before and left with a feeling of nausea. He didn't know if it was the sight of another woman's naked body or the fact that he'd paid to see it that repulsed him so much. Maybe if he could stop thinking about what Clara would say for a minute he could relax and enjoy the experience a little.

The hardest thing for Marc to deal with was the dreams. He had never realised before how the realness of dreams had the power to drive people crazy. Dreaming was a simulation;

the experience was so real it hurt. On days when he woke up from one which his wife had been in, he couldn't get rid of the feeling all day long. It didn't only feel as if he'd touched her neck; he could even feel the softness of her skin on his fingertips. He'd look at his fingers after opening his eyes and for a long time he found it hard to believe that it had only been a dream.

Now, this Saturday morning he had finally let it all go. He didn't head out to the streets early in the morning and he didn't care about the pain the dreams caused him; he simply curled up under the covers. Today was the day that would change his world. He had to be brave; he had to fight first with himself, then with the city and then with all of his memories. He knew before he even left the bed that he was going to be a wreck by the end of the day, but he also knew that he couldn't run away from life any longer. He was tired of living like somebody else. At last, he opened his eyes just a crack at around ten o'clock and peered at the world outside from where he lay in his bed. The grey sky of Paris seaped in between the curtains. He should start the day with a good breakfast; maybe he'd buy a delicious croissant from Françis. After he'd filled his stomach he would have to get to work on what he'd decided. Marc was going to set up a new kitchen from scratch today. He was going to take out whatever there was in the cupboards, put it all in bags and take it to a second-hand store; then he was going to go to Tout le Marché and buy everything from scratch. He was going to build himself a new life with a new kitchen. He was going to learn how to cook. Truth be told, Marc was hungry. In fact, he'd been starving for months.

With music playing in the background, he started putting everything into bags: the burnt pans, cups without handles, boilers without tops, brand new saucepans, stylish steamers; everything. He had got used to the company of the voices on TV in Clara's absence over the last couple of months. In fact, his inspiration for doing all this was a show he'd seen several days ago, on late night TV. Two men hosted *Escapade Gourmande*, a show in which they travelled to various different countries and cities and cooked the local food. The programme originally aired in the afternoons, but it was also repeated after midnight. Marc first saw it while he was eating the sandwich he had bought from a fast food stand on his way home from a bar. At the end of the show, he realised that he was still sitting there watching it when the credits were rolling down on the screen. Then he found himself turning on the same channel the next night at around the same time, and after the third time he'd watched it he knew that he liked this programme.

It wasn't the recipes that attracted him; it was the way those two men understood the world through food. The salmon wasn't only a source of vitamin B, for example, or a fine dish for a dinner party; the salmon was wisdom. Salmon wasn't prepared with a berry sauce just to create a good-looking plate; according to Irish mythology, the salmon achieved wisdom by eating berries and with every bite, man gained wisdom, too. This fish, which travelled from the salty ocean to fresh water to spawn, represented the bond between the two worlds, according to the people of the North. Marc was surprised to find out how meaningful every bite he'd taken really was. *Escapade Gourmande* was the way out Marc had been looking for: a direction that could help him to escape his inner world and take the first steps into a new life.

After he'd finished with the big pieces, he started on the drawers. The grater, peeler, egg whisk, ice cream scoop, pastry bag, mozzarella slicer: whatever there was, he got rid of it all. Whenever he found himself holding on to a spatula for more than a minute, he had to force himself to drop it and put it next to the others. When he picked up the entangled beaters from the hand mixer, tears gathered in his eyes. He remembered the birthday cakes Clara had baked for him; but still, he didn't change his mind. The cloths and tea towels, which were washed, ironed and neatly folded, couldn't avoid their sad fate either, and were kicked out of the kitchen. Before tying the strings on the last bag, he picked up the oven glove, which had helped him to feel his wife's warmth on that first night, and added it to the load. He apologised to his wife as he did so. He begged, 'Please forgive me, my love, but I have to start somewhere.' When he stood at the kitchen door and looked back with the bags in his hands, he saw that even the napkin holder, which had always been on the table, wasn't there any more. He wished he'd written down the name of every object he'd thrown away. The items he thought he'd listed in his mind so that he could buy them later on were already slipping away. The only things he remembered for sure were the pans and the cloths. He had to leave right now before he forgot them, too. He took a cab to the second-hand shop at the corner of Rue Monge and Rue du Cardinal Lemoine and then continued on foot after dropping them off. He couldn't even remember the last time he'd been to Tout le Marché. Clara had taken care of every kind of household need. She was the one who always bought Marc's socks or the nails to hang things up with around the house. He hadn't even chosen the colour of the jumper he was wearing at that moment. He liked green, but he wasn't sure he would have picked this colour if he'd bought it himself.

It was a classic Saturday in Paris. Half of the city had filled the cafés, and the other half had filled Tout le Marché. After spending several minutes in front of the information board at the entrance, he finally found the department he was looking for and took the escalator up there. He never would have expected kitchenware to look so artistic. Now he realised that the influence of the past could be seen in kitchen utensils, too, as it could in all other art forms; he remembered every object he saw here from his grandmother's kitchen when he was a boy. The sparkle of the copper cups caught his eyes. While he was pushing his empty shopping trolley, he noticed a group of people standing in one corner of the store. They looked just like the art lovers who pushed each other out of the way to see the seventy-seven by fifty-three centimetre Mona Lisa at the Louvre. He joined the crowd after parking his trolley. The item that was attracting so much attention was the last masterpiece of the famous French chef, Michel Bras: a seven-piece knife set worth 2,000 euros. Every piece in the set had a different level of flexibility and a different handle. What's more, they were all handmade. This artwork, which had been a joint creation between the French chef and the famous Japanese knife master, Kai, was the perfect instrument for bringing together the delicacies of Japanese and French cuisine. As he observed the women who were gazing at the set with adoration, Marc realised that some of them considered these knives to be as valuable as any jewellery. He gulped, thinking of the knife set he'd given to the second-hand shop earlier that day. It had looked like a nice set, but he was only just beginning to realise that it might have been a lot more valuable than he'd thought. He walked towards the other shelves, leaving the knife crowd behind him. While he was trying to work out which knife was used for what purpose, he saw the three-piece beginner's set by Wüsthof. The set was sold with a small guide and cost only 120 euros. 'Perfect,' he said, without realising that he'd smiled without forcing himself for the first time in months. He felt both pleased and confident about his first choice. Sadly, he soon lost that feeling when he found himself standing in front of the shelf full of pans. At least thirty different pans hung right in front of him and he had no idea how they were different from one another. Just when he'd decided on one of them, he looked at the one next to it and changed his mind.

If one of the shop's employees, Sabina, hadn't come to help, he probably would have left without buying any of them. Sabina was a young woman with a very soft voice, who wore her hair tied back in a ponytail. She had decided to come to this man's rescue after she'd watched him from afar for a while and realised that he didn't have a clue what he was doing. Customers usually came here knowing exactly what they wanted and didn't need any help. Sometimes they even got angry when help was offered. Marc, on the other hand, almost cried with gratitude when Sabina asked him if he needed any help. He only told her what he was looking for after he'd thanked her many times and told her how utterly hopeless he was.

'OK, so what do you want the frying pan for?'

'Excuse me?'

'What are you going to cook in it?'

'Oh, I don't know. An omelette?'

'OK, that's good. It's easy. If you could also tell me what your budget is, then we can decide on one really quickly.'

'Budget?' Marc thought. It looked like having an interest in cooking wasn't cheap after all. He had thought a frying pan would cost about ten euros or fifteen tops, but the prices he saw here told a very different story.

'Uhm ... I don't know. Not very expensive, but something with a long lifespan.'

'OK. One more question. Steel or Teflon?'

When Sabina realised that her customer was on the point of giving up after that last question, she decided to take the matter in hand. It was obvious that this man didn't know anything about cooking. Looking at the knife set he'd chosen, she realised he was a complete beginner. This meant he would end up burning the omelette if he used a steel frying pan. She showed him a simple, reasonably priced but good quality Teflon pan and said, 'This is it.' Marc had no intention of questioning her. In fact, if she could help him with the rest of the shopping she would also be saving him from going crazy. After frying pans, they looked at pots, saucepans and cutting boards. Sabina couldn't help asking:

'Have you just moved to Paris?'

'No, why?'

'You're buying new kitchenware.'

'No ... no, but I'm going to start cooking for the first time.'

She looked at Marc, smiling. Even though she wanted to

know why, she decided not to ask. Instead, she carried on walking with him between the shelves. After they'd picked up a couple of small things from the cooking utensils section, Marc felt like he couldn't handle any more on one day. This had taken much longer than he'd expected, and it had been tiring. He wanted to have some strength left to cook his first meal later that night. And he had bought the most important thing for it – the colander – already. The rest wasn't that important.

After he'd thanked Sabina, he walked towards the cashier as she watched him from behind. When he saw an espresso machine on the way, however, he stopped one more time. He hadn't found the courage to use the coffee maker at home yet, and it didn't seem like he was ever going to be able to use it again. Maybe the love affair he'd had with American coffee had finally come to an end. Without looking at the price tag or even thinking twice, he put the espresso machine in his trolley and continued on his way. Sabina watched in a daze, wondering how this sad, strange man, who had queried the price of everything, had ending up buying one of the most expensive items in the store without even thinking?

After a bill of 1,300 euros and a short taxi ride, Marc found himself standing in front of his building carrying many different sizes of bags. He thought maybe he should have accepted the cashier's offer of a delivery option. He entered the code for the building, left one of the bags at the door and carried the others inside. Right when he was hoping that nobody would see him or offer any help, he saw Françis standing right beside him with his apron wrapped around his belly. Contrary to what Marc had expected, he didn't ask any questions, but simply helped his neighbour to put the bags inside the lift and then carry them to his apartment. The master of quiche knew enough about cooking to understand what was in those bags. Still, he didn't say a word. Just as he was turning around to get back in the lift, he saw Marc's hand stretched out to him. 'Thank you for the quiche, it was delicious,' he said. Françis accepted the thanks, which were long overdue, and squeezed his hand, firmly.

Five

Growing up in the Philippines inevitably meant being familiar with voodoo. Everybody experienced it at least once, in one way or another. In her childhood, Lilia had spent a lot of time sitting in people's kitchens where she listened to tales of the various kinds of spells that had been cast by all kinds of women. However, unlike other people, she had also watched how plants, bugs and weeds were mixed, crushed and cooked in big pots over a fire. She had never rejected, ignored or made fun of spells like some of her peers. They wouldn't have done so either if they'd known how many women married the men they loved or got rid of their enemies or helped their kids to survive deadly illnesses with the help of magic. Lilia's great aunt was one of the best-known witches in Siquijor, and this meant she'd been able to live a good life without ever having to work. She had never needed a man's protection, either. Even though she lived in a small house close to Cantabon Cave instead of in the town centre, people would bring bowls of food to her house; and when she was given more gifts than she could handle, Lilia had taken her share of the pie. Everybody knew that Lilia's aunt was very fond of her niece. They even said that she taught Lilia everything she knew, preparing her for the future. And so, when Lilia left her country at a very young age to emigrate to the United States, the women of her village had been gravely disappointed. She had been the only protégée of the mighty witch and was widely believed to be her only successor, who would one day be responsible for curing the village of all of its troubles. Lilia had known nothing about those expectations and certainly didn't know how much power she really held.

Her aunt hadn't exactly followed the advice of the Filipino saying: 'Be as smart as the devil and as peaceful as the dove.' She had never held back from casting bad spells as often as good ones. After all, she believed that if she'd been given that talent, it was because she was meant to use every part of it. Maybe that was what made her as powerful as she was in the village. Just as she'd never felt the need to explain herself to other people, she had never justified her actions to Lilia, either. What's more, she had never taught her anything at all. She knew that what her niece had seen over the years would be enough. If people thought there was a book for teaching voodoo, they were mistaken. Everything was simply filed away inside the human brain and translated into natural knowledge later on.

Lilia was surprised to find how naturally that knowledge came to her now. Sometimes when she was stirring something in a pot, she would suddenly remember a formula she had never used in her life; the mixture or prayer needed for different spells would form itself automatically in her mind. Some days she would even swear that she could smell the herbs from her aunt's kitchen. Her aunt, who never nagged, shared knowledge or showed any interest in improving other people's lives, had only once given Lilia a piece of advice: 'Use the talent you were given.' She didn't even have to try very hard. Planting a small ball of black pepper in the shrimp would do it; or adding a pinch of ash to the water for the rice. Who would detect a tiny quince seed stuffed inside a dark green cabbage? And who would suppose that sprinkling a recipe with prayers could sew the seed of love? Nobody could guess that molasses injected into a pomegranate seed would tar a person's insides for ever and drive him or her from one grief to another. They wouldn't understand that someone who is fed with basmati rice mixed with five seeds from five different figs glued together with egg white will die soon after that. Of course, not everybody could work magic. Only people who were born with this talent were able to use it. And the thing known as 'food' was the most important element of all. The centre of the earth was not a giant ball of iron; it was every kitchen of every home.

Lilia stirred the food on the stove one last time before covering it with a lid. Just as she was wiping the steam from her reading glasses with the bottom of her sweater, Flavio walked into the kitchen. They hadn't seen each other much since the night when the chimney kicked back. Flavio came home later at nights now, didn't eat the food Lilia left out for him and spent most of his time in his room whenever he was at home. It was impossible for Lilia not to sense the tension between them, but she couldn't figure out what had caused it. She said 'hi' in a slightly higher voice than she'd expected, as she wasn't able to restrain her excitement. The chirping sound of her own voice made her feel even more uncomfortable.

She was also surprised at how quickly she'd forgotten that Arnie was in the next room. How much did Arnie actually pick up on about what she was feeling? This question also made her realise how little she really understood about her own emotions. What she had been going through seemed to resemble love. How else could she explain how excited she felt when she saw him, how she thought about him every minute of the day, how she tried to cook his favourite things, or how disappointed she felt on the days when she couldn't see him? Flavio was growing inside her like a tumour, and in the end it was going to have to be removed.

'Are you hungry? There are some leftovers from yesterday. Or if you can wait a little longer, this will be done soon. Or I can make scrambled eggs.'

She had noticed Flavio's hand hanging in the air to interrupt her, but she still wanted to give him every possible option.

'I'm fasting today.'

'Fasting?'

'Yes, today is Ash Wednesday.'

'Oh, yes, I forgot.'

'I'm not going to eat anything at all until tonight. And then I can only eat a very small portion. And I can't eat meat. I was actually going to ask you about that. If you're making meat today, I'll get some takeaway food.'

Lilia looked at the pot. She could hear the bubbling of the pepper sauce which was covering the pork chops. She had chosen this dish especially, thinking how much Flavio had liked it when she'd made it before. It was going to be delicious, especially as it was going to rest now in the sauce until dinner. Before she could say anything, Natalie walked in.

'Happy Ash Wednesday.'

Lilia looked surprised.

'Are you fasting, too?'

'No! Are you?'

'No. Flavio is.'

'Oh, I'm not fasting but I'm going to church. Are you going, Flavio?'

'Yes, I'm going to Manhattan. I hear that one of the biggest cathedrals in the world is on 113th.'

'I'll come with you. If you don't mind, of course.'

'Sure, let's go together.'

Lilia detected a kind of chemistry between the two of them, which she'd thought she'd seen between Flavio and Ulla before. At the same time, she was sure that Flavio had feelings for her.

'You know, it's been a while since I last went to Manhattan. I don't know if I mentioned it already, but we used to live there before we had the kids. Yes, on 28th and Park Avenue South. And I used to go to the United Nations sometimes to do some translation work there. Actually, I can come with you guys today. Arnie's therapist will be here soon, so he isn't going to need me for a while.'

She called out to Arnie to see how much he had heard: 'Right, Arnie?' As usual, she was answered by silence instead of by her husband.

'Of course, I won't come to the church. I'll leave you guys at the station. There are a couple of books I want to get from Barnes & Noble. What time is it? Ten thirty. The next train is at ten fifty-seven. I'll be ready in five.'

As Lilia went to her room without waiting for a reply,

Flavio and Natalie sat on the stools and waited. Natalie whispered to Flavio, making sure Arnie wouldn't hear her, 'I think Lilia feels really suffocated in this environment. It's like she wants to get away. And she's right, too. It must be really hard having to spend your life with a sick man, especially someone like him.'

Even though Flavio knew exactly why Lilia wanted to come with them, he didn't say anything. Instead, he mumbled something that sounded like a 'yes' and then let it go. Lilia's interest in him, which at first he'd interpreted as the normal behaviour of a kind landlady, was now impossible to ignore. It had been particularly obvious on the night when they'd all had dinner together. Her affection wasn't particularly irritating or exaggerated, but it still made Flavio feel uncomfortable. He'd been trying to come home late or spend most of his time in his room ever since that night. He had hoped that this way she would give up on him or at least understand that he didn't feel the same way, but his strategy obviously wasn't working too well. This morning she'd looked at him with yearning eyes instead of sad ones. He hadn't known where to look to avoid meeting her gaze and was relieved when Natalie finally arrived. Now he only had to spend twenty-five minutes on the train with her, and he could do that easily. Lilia was an extraordinary woman; he had no doubt about that. He could also see that she'd been very beautiful when she was younger. Nevertheless, she had come into this world too soon. What's more, there was no denying how perfect she was in the kitchen. That food on the stove already smelled delicious at half past ten in the morning. The steam, which lifted the lid off the pot every once in a while, had escaped, found its way to his brain cells and made him feel instantly famished. He was scared he would eat some of it if he stayed in the kitchen any longer. Again, it was Natalie who made the first move:

'If we stay here much longer, I don't think you'll make it through to night-time.'

'Exactly. Let's wait outside,' he replied, gratefully.

As the train moved along the rails, Lilia told Natalie and Flavio about the legend of Sleepy Hollow. They'd both seen the film with the same name, but they'd had no idea that it was actually a small town on this line. They also would never have guessed that many people believed the legend, including Lilia. Just when she was showing them the spot where Johnny Depp rode his horse in the film, they heard the conductor asking for their tickets. Flavio, who was sitting by the aisle, stopped both ladies from getting their purses out and gave the man $40. Since he'd only been expecting one dollar in change, Flavio thought the conductor must have made a mistake when he was given back ten dollars and twenty-five cents. He told the conductor gently that there had been some mistake. Before Lilia could do anything to stop it, the conductor pointed at her and said, 'The lady's a senior, isn't she?' Lilia didn't feel like saying she was sixty-two, not sixty-five. Instead she nodded, approvingly. It wasn't going to help her to feel any less embarrassed, anyway. Flavio's face turned crimson. He didn't understand why he felt like he was in a relationship with this woman and was ashamed about it; but that was exactly how he felt. With a forced smile on his face, he lowered his hand – which had been hanging in the air for a couple of seconds – and put the money back in his wallet. Natalie quickly changed the subject.

'So, does Johnny Depp ride his horse on this road in the film?'

Grateful to the young woman, Lilia continued with her story. At the same time, she couldn't help repeating the conductor's words in some corner of her mind. What was she doing on this train, anyway? What strange instinct had made her decide to go to Manhattan all of a sudden? She also didn't know why she'd lied to all of her tenants by saying that she often went to Manhattan when she rented out the rooms. Whatever the reason, she certainly didn't want them to know that it had been at least three years since she'd last been to the city, and that instead she usually spent her free time strolling around the supermarkets or second-hand shops in their own suburb. Maybe she'd thought she could escape the reality of her boring life by lying to people about it. Was it that same boredom that made her feel the way she did towards this young man who was sitting across from her? What was it that made him so attractive anyway, when she looked carefully? Really, he was only as attractive as the women who were interested in him were desperate. He was a great person for a girl like Natalie to go to church with, but that should be it. What about Ulla? She probably wouldn't even want to go out for drinks with him. But still, when Lilia had suggested leaving them at the station, neither of them had protested. They hadn't said, 'Come with us, we'll have a coffee afterwards, or see a film.' As she resolved all of these issues in her head, she had also come to the end of the story. Now silence hung between them. They all looked out of the window and hoped for this strange union to come to an end. Just before they reached the station, Lilia asked Natalie:

'So, I take it you're not going to eat meat today either?'

'Yes, I won't eat meat, but don't worry, I'll eat out.'

'No … no, I'll just prepare something without meat.'

'Will you have time?'

'Of course.'

Looking at Flavio, she added: 'Just as it said in the flyer, food is included in the rent.'

Once she was alone, Lilia looked around her in that colossal station. When was the last time she'd seen so many people in one place? Since she didn't have a real plan, she decided to follow her pretend one. She went to one of the station's many exits and asked one of the men standing there if there was a Barnes & Noble nearby. 'Of course,' he said, 'there's a Starbucks and a Barnes & Noble on every corner. Do you know how to get onto Fifth Avenue from here? Good. Then walk along the Fifth, and there's one between forty-five and forty-six.'

Lilia couldn't have figured out the way to Fifth Avenue if the man hadn't pointed it out while giving her directions, but now she walked towards it. This was a typical sunny yet chilly New York day. She soon realised that she'd forgotten just how cold the island could get. A strong wind blowing through the air corridors created by the tall buildings cut through her lungs. As she walked, she held on tightly to the collar of the purple coat she'd bought from the Disabled Veterans charity shop. Still, she felt the breeze coming in through the sleeves since it was two sizes too large for her. She didn't have a hat or gloves and she was sure that this wind was going to leave her with a headache later that night. When she saw the huge library across the street, she realised that she'd reached Fifth Avenue. She hadn't forgotten this place, at least. Just as in the past, the library stairs were full of people having their lunch, despite the cold. She had also sat on those stairs once. In fact, she had met Arnie on the sixth step. At that moment, Lilia finally admitted to herself that she hadn't set foot in the city for six years. It had been difficult for her to count the years and so instead she'd kept saying to herself, 'Three or four.' It was impossible not to notice how well dressed everybody was. She couldn't help eying up every woman who passed her from head to toe. She kept touching her hair and clumsily tried to stick a lock of it behind her ear. Her coat was making her more uncomfortable with every passing minute. She didn't even want to think how bad the dress inside the coat must look. When she finally saw a woman who looked as bad as she did she relaxed a little, before realising that it was her own reflection in the window of Barnes & Noble. She pushed the revolving door with all her strength and walked into the shop, trying to forget this disturbing image.

Tired of the walking, the crowds and her own emotions, she went up to the café on the first floor and got herself a cup of coffee. The people at the other tables had buried themselves in the magazines and books they had piled in front of them and didn't even seem to realise that other people existed. Lilia, on the other hand, examined them all carefully and enjoyed her first decent cup of coffee in a very long time. The carafe of their coffee maker had broken three years ago and they'd been using a saucepan ever since, which meant that the coffee was never really hot. As she was the least experienced customer in the queue, she'd made the girl behind the counter wait until she'd made up her mind, ignoring the irritated sighs of the customers behind her. It had been around ten years since she'd last had coffee from Starbucks and they had a whole range of different types on the menu now. After she'd spent five minutes looking into every possible option – from caramel macchiato to skimmed mocha – and asked how much each one of them cost, she'd finally decided on a regular coffee. Making sense of the different sizes of the coffee cups had been another challenge altogether. She didn't know what to make of the sizes they called 'tall', 'venti' and 'grande'. She knew that 'venti' meant twenty in Italian, 'grande' meant large in Spanish and 'tall' meant tall in English, and so she simply couldn't work out which was which. It was the employee behind the counter who finally gave up and asked Lilia if she wanted small, medium or large. She replied, 'Small.'

After everything she'd gone through to get a cup of coffee, she held it with pride and felt that every sip was worth the money it had cost her. The coffee made her feel better, and even gave her a sense of being part of this city, and so she soon started wandering among the aisles. While she was only browsing around, not knowing what to look at, a particular section caught her eye: cookbooks. It had been a long time since Lilia had last cooked something using a book. As a matter of fact, she didn't even know where the first and only book she'd ever bought had got to. It was easy to look up some of the recipes she was curious about online, but after reading them once she usually lost the notes that she jotted down on small pieces of paper around the house. Lilia remembered how much she'd envied her mother as she watched her using a cookbook and how lovely she'd looked as she followed the lines with the tip of her finger. She'd dreamed that she would cook from one just like her when she had a family of her own, and she would sing as she did so. After all these years, she finally realised that even her least significant dream had never come true.

She stood in front of the five shelves full of cookbooks and gazed at them, dreamily. She wasn't looking for anything in particular, but she hoped that one of them would grab her attention, captivate her, make her read it and change her life. As it turned out, a book on the top shelf was the one and it found her in the end. She stood up on the tips of her toes as much as she possibly could and tilted her head to one side so that she could read the title better. Who would have thought she'd smile on a difficult day like this? But she did.

Marc's first attempt to make pasta went better than he'd expected – not counting a couple of small incidents. Instead of making any executive decisions, he simply followed the steps written on the box: he boiled the water, added some salt, cooked the pasta for eleven to thirteen minutes and drained it. He didn't try anything radical. Even though he had a real craving for the mushroom sauce Clara used to make, he decided to simply mix the pasta with butter and put cheese on top. Unfortunately, when it was time to grate the cheese he realised that he'd got rid of the grater and hadn't bought a new one. This meant he had to slice the cheese thinly instead with the help of his new knife. Afterwards, he opened the small notebook he'd left on the kitchen table and wrote down one word: 'grater.'

The total cooking time should have been just twenty minutes at the most, but it took Marc almost an hour. He came across his first problem when he covered the pan after putting the pasta in to cook. When the boiling water spilt over onto the stove and put the flame out, he transferred the pan to another flame and started cleaning up the mess. Although it hurt a little at the time, he would only realise how seriously he had burnt a couple of his fingers when he was washing up later on. When he had finished wiping the stove, he realised that the pasta was already tender – maybe too tender – and so he came across his second problem. Draining the pasta was no simple task. When some little pieces of spaghetti slipped through the holes and clogged up the sink, the water flowed back into the colander. When he tried to hold it in the air with one hand so he could clean the sink strainer with the other, he burnt the rest of his fingers with the hot water. And when he stepped on the bin pedal to get rid of the spaghetti in his hand, he saw that he hadn't put a bag in it. Since both his hands were full and he had no other choice, he left the dripping pasta at the side of the sink and held the colander under the running water. When he finally put the spaghetti back in the pan to mix it with butter, he felt as if he'd just come home from a very long day at work.

He cleaned everything up before he started eating. He washed every utensil he had used, turned on the TV and sat down. He tried hard not to feel too proud of himself, but he couldn't help smiling. His first meal wasn't bad at all. It might not be the most complicated type of food to make, but it looked as if he wasn't completely useless after all. He realised that as long as he followed the instructions, he wouldn't make too many mistakes; apart from the practical ones, anyway. Of course, he was going to need a cookbook. He'd hesitated for a while about whether or not to give Clara's books away, but had finally decided that he couldn't bear seeing her handwritten notes on the pages. He'd never realised that Clara had made notes about every single recipe and even added lines of her own instructions. If the book said, 'Cook at 180 degrees', Clara had added that 175 degrees worked better. Over the years she had written everything down – whatever she thought was missing or excessive – and in the end she'd made a whole new book of her own. Marc was sure that whoever was going to buy those books would love those notes. They would probably find them funny and wonder about the woman who had made them. Clara's sincerity could be seen in her 'l's, 'g's and even the 'v's, which was usually such a cold letter. That was what Marc couldn't handle: missing Clara's warmth. Maybe one day his wife's memory would make him happy, but right now that day didn't even seem close.

Later that night, Marc was just thinking how much he'd like some dessert when he heard a familiar sound on the TV. One of the Jacques Tati films that he'd seen so many times before was starting, and so he lifted his gaze from the comic book he'd been reading and looked at the screen. This was the one of his favourites: *Mon Oncle*. Although he knew there was nothing in the fridge, he got up, opened its door and looked inside.

He had finally realised what an achievement it had been for Clara to keep the fridge fully stocked at all times. It was a real luxury to be able to find anything he felt like waiting there for him and it took a lot of work. Trying to fight his urge to eat something sweet, he went back to the table. As he listened to Jacques Tati's mumbling voice, he opened a new page in his small notebook. He started a shopping list with a couple of essential items of food that came to mind. Since almost nowhere was open on Sundays in Paris, he was going to have to do that shopping on Monday. Still, he couldn't think of a better day to buy a cookbook than the last day of the week.

With every passing minute, he understood a little better how his new muse, *la cuisine,* could govern someone's life. She helped him to divide his week into days. She stood behind him, pushing him to start living again, like a good old friend. She didn't let him pity himself. The kitchen didn't have time to stop, to think, to cry. People would always return to her arms when the time was right. They would ask for her help, rest on her chest and wash their faces with the water she gave them. And so, she had to be ready; she had to wait, safe and sound, prepared to give her children a piece of bread when they came home. The kitchen was your mother's bosom, the hands of a loved one and the centre of the universe.

Early the next morning, Marc walked through the empty streets of Paris to the Odéon district, which was the only place nearby where he could find somewhere to have breakfast. Nowhere opened before twelve o'clock in his own neighbourhood. The desolate streets of the early morning would come to life later in the day, making even the people who had lived there all their lives fall in love with the city all over again. Delicious smells of food would rise up from the market at the corner of Rue Monge and St Germain, and Marc, like many others, would stand in the queue to buy a couple of slices of bread with garlic cheese and salami on top. People who didn't even know each other would gather around the barrels, drink wine and maybe talk about their adventures the night before – but not just yet.

When he entered La Crêperie des Pêcheurs by tingling the bell on the door, there was only one customer inside: an American. The man's face had turned red from the effort of trying to order his breakfast – emphasising the 'r's instead of rolling them – and he obviously felt exhausted. The waitress, on the other hand, didn't even try to understand the American and greeted Marc with a smile and a nod. She knew she didn't have to worry about him. Marc was going to sit at the furthest corner of the bar, order his usual crêpe with ham and cheese and bury his face in his comic book. The waitress wouldn't notice that her customer hadn't brought a book with him this time and instead simply sat there, examining the crêpe. After he'd finished his breakfast, he ordered another cup of coffee and waited impatiently for the bookshops to open. He knew it was time to go when the bells of Notre-Dame could be heard from a distance, chiming ten times.

Unsurprisingly, he was Fnac's first customer of the day. The staff still looked sleepy, as if they'd just got out of bed. Since he didn't know exactly what kind of cookbook he was looking for, he tried to find his own way around, wandering among the shelves. He didn't stop in front of the books he had always been interested in before; in fact, he walked right past them. He finally found the cookbooks on the second floor and was astonished to see that there was a huge room reserved just for them. He slowed down, trying to take everything in. There were books that explained which type of food could be cooked in which dish. He never would have guessed that somebody could write a 100-page book about the history of casseroles. While one volume explained which dishes could be cooked on the heat of a car's engine, another offered delicious recipes for food made from insects. One of them even explained how to cook animals that had been accidentally killed on the road. After losing himself among these strange titles for a while, Marc finally found what he was looking for. It was a book offering very basic recipes: *La Cuisine de Ta Maman.* Your mother's kitchen. The recipes he saw as he flicked through it were exactly what he needed. The only thing that worried him was the ingredients. He had never realised how rare some of them were and even the simplest ones were a mystery to him.

He sat down in a corner with the book in his hand. Maybe what he needed to do was to pick a recipe every day and cook that one. Instead of starting at the beginning, he closed his eyes and opened a page at random. *Papillotes de Poulet et Tapenade.* The ingredients: four chicken breasts, 200 grams pitted black olives, two garlic cloves, two spoonfuls of capers, fifteen milligrams of olive oil, a pinch of salt and pepper. The recipe: peel and crush the garlic. Mix it with crushed olives and capers. Add two-thirds of the olives to the mixture. Add the pepper … Marc took out his notebook, wrote down the ingredients and folded back the corner of that page. He could probably find everything he needed at the open market on his way home. Just as he was about to make his way to the cashier with the book tucked under his arm, he caught a glimpse of the shelves reserved especially for desserts. He remembered how Clara used to complain all the time about how difficult it was to make a good pudding. Every time she baked a cake, she would watch it anxiously through the glass to see if it had risen enough and she never let her hopes get too high. She had come to accept the fact that despite how much the cake rose, it could always just collapse once it was taken out of the oven. Adding a spoonful of baking powder was out of the question. If she wasn't good enough to bake it naturally, then she was going to have to make do with the desserts her husband brought home from the pâtisserie. Marc looked at the books full of dessert recipes and smiled. He wasn't going to try to make one before he could even cook. Still, it didn't stop him from reaching out for one book he saw among the others.

'Mum, have you tried the pasta with artichokes yet?'

'Yes, darling, and it turned out pretty well. But I couldn't remember if I was supposed to thinly slice the garlic cloves or crush them. I didn't write that part down.'

'Thinly sliced. They're supposed to be caramelised. Did grandma have some?'

'Oh, Öykü, don't mention her.'

'Why, what has she done now?'

'Let's not talk about it, darling.'

'Why? Tell me!'

'She's just not herself any more. One minute she's as sharp as a knife, the next minute she's living in another world. Hold on, honey, she's saying something.'

She covered the speaker with her hand, extended the cord and looked into Mrs Nesibe's room before calling out, 'Yes, mum ... OK, one minute, I'm coming.'

Then she went back to talking to her daughter.

'I have to go, darling. She needs me. Again. Her bowels are the problem now. We're dealing with that all the time at the moment. As if we have nothing else to do.'

She went to her mother's room dragging her feet, uncharacteristically for her. This was something she had never done, not even as a teenager.

'Ferda, help me use the bedpan. I want to try again.'

'Mum, you don't have to. Your bowels don't work as much as they used to because you don't move. The doctor says the same thing. Let me move your legs a little. That'll help.'

'Don't you understand, child? I can't move my legs. I'm crippled.'

'Mother, the doctor came and said himself that you aren't paralysed. You can even walk if you want to. And you don't have to do anything, let me move them.'

'That doctor doesn't know about anything below the belly. He's probably a chest doctor.'

'God! Mum, I think you've finally lost it. Why would I bring a chest doctor here?'

'All right, all right, it doesn't matter. Help me use the bedpan.'

'You have no sympathy for me whatsoever, do you? We're dealing with this all day long, do you realise that?'

'It's too bad I'm old. One day you're going to get old, too, and I wonder what your daughter will be like. I pray to God she'll do the same things for you.'

'What do I do to you? I don't know what else I can do for you. I hope my daughter will take care of me as well as I take care of you.'

After she had given her mother the bedpan, Ferda left her alone in her room and ran to the kitchen. She could feel the pressure of the tears welling up in her eyes spreading all over her face. She had always missed her father, but she missed him even more now. She'd had to say goodbye to her childhood and grow up at a very early age, what with his death and the illnesses that her mother allegedly suffered. She had never known whose arms to cry in at difficult times. She had wiped her own nose when she was sick and dressed the wound on her knee whenever she fell. She had never felt like her mother's child; she had always been her companion. She'd had to learn motherhood long before she became a mother herself.

There was no powder left in the pantry to make *salep* with, just as there wasn't any rose hip or lime blossom tea. In the end, she had to reach right to the back of the cupboard for the posh tea box, which had been a gift from one of her daughter's friends. This expensive twenty-four-bag tealeaf set had been left there for almost a year, unopened. She had been saving it as a gift to give to someone else in an emergency – just as she'd done with every other expensive gift she'd ever received. After hesitating for a couple of minutes, she finally tore off the plastic wrapping and opened the box. She had no idea what it said on the tea bags, which were packaged as individual pyramids. She only understood that two of them were green teas, but even though she understood the literal meaning of both of the words on the 'caffeine free' label, she didn't quite understand what it meant. Did it have caffeine in it, or not? When she unwrapped the paper around the one with purple writing, the smell of the tealeaves in a silk bag filled the whole kitchen. She gently held the end of the string and went to the china cabinet to pick a cup from there. An elaborate tea bag like that deserved a dignified teacup. She picked one that had belonged to her grandmother and rested the tea bag inside it. As she waited for the water to boil, she tried to ignore the sounds coming from her mother's room. Fortunately, the whistling of the kettle on the stove was powerful enough to drown out everything else. Once it had boiled, she poured the water carefully over the bag and waited until the steam touched her face.

While she was sipping her tea, her mother had tired herself out and finally fallen asleep. This was one of Ferda's rare chances to leave the apartment. She was lucky; Istanbul was being generous with the sun that day. The constant rain had stopped at last. Ferda started wandering through the streets, regretting the fact that she'd missed the autumn, which was her favourite season. She'd never confessed to anyone how much she had always liked stepping on dry leaves, ever since she was a little girl. This was just one of the pleasures she kept from others. She hadn't even realised that it was already February and that she'd lost track of time while taking care of her mother. What's more, nobody had reminded her. Everybody close to her was trying to get on with things without paying too much attention to Ferda, anyway. They were all playing at the three monkeys: see no evil, hear no evil, speak no evil. She didn't dig too deeply into her own feelings, either; she was going through the motions, almost like a sleepwalker, without even realising what she was doing. She was too scared to touch her own heart, in case it would break into pieces. That was why she hadn't gone to see a counsellor, in spite of what all the doctors and professional articles recommended. The last thing she needed right now was to start analysing her own emotions. She could deal with the tears sweeping across her cheeks every once in a while, but any more than that would mean having to judge her whole life.

Ferda walked slowly through the streets, not knowing that at the other end of the world a woman couldn't recognise herself in a shop window and a man in Paris was trying desperately to pull himself out of the depths of his sorrow. She wasn't selfish enough not to realise that other people suffered, too, but there couldn't be a better time than this to feel sorry for herself. She only noticed how the cold weather was biting her ankles when she stopped off at a bookshop on her way. The employees of D&R, who had been lined up against the window to warm their backs, greeted her with smiles. She continued walking, looking around her, stopping every now and again to glance at a book. Ferda had always felt uncomfortable around books, just as she felt in museums. Anything to do with art gave her pain as well as pleasure. They made her feel that she'd thrown her life away and given up on her own creativity. Even though she knew she'd never been given the chance to do anything else, she couldn't help herself thinking that she'd led an empty life. She couldn't help being envious of Jane Austen – whose books she'd often read when she was young – or the paintings of Adélaïde Labille-Guiard, which she'd seen at the Louvre. When these women had lived so far ahead of their times, how could she stay so far behind hers? During the late 1960s, when the world's youth was going through such a drastic upheaval and ended up changing the world, she had again been taking care of her mother, and living her life as flatly as could be.

Feeling disappointed in herself, she walked towards the cookbook section. She had read somewhere: 'If we hadn't failed ourselves, how were we to know what our real expectations and hopes were?' Although this statement made sense to her, discovering her real expectations hadn't helped Ferda at all. Facing up to her failures had done nothing but break her heart. Her mind slipped away from these sad thoughts and she began to calm down when she started looking at the cookbooks. Once again, she was somewhere where she felt safe. Her thoughts had climbed out of the sinkhole of her emotions and come back to normal life. *World Cuisine with Simple Recipes* was the closest to what she was looking for. After glancing through the pages to make sure she wouldn't have to go to Istanbul's most expensive gourmet markets to find the ingredients, she decided to buy the book. Before turning her back to the shelves, the cover of a book caught her eye. She picked it up without hesitating, not knowing that a tired woman and a sad man had reached out to the same book on the same day, somewhere else. The title was

Soufflé. Underneath, it said in small letters, 'The Biggest Disappointment'. Ferda looked around her, surprised. Even though she had witnessed before how life sometimes intersected exactly with her own thoughts, she was stunned to see it happening once again. She blushed. She wanted to tell someone about the miracle, but instead she went to the cashier and paid for both of the books.

Six

Lilia had never imagined that there could be so many different types of soufflé: prawn soufflé, cheese soufflé, lobster soufflé, cheese and bacon soufflé, caramel soufflé, ice cream soufflé, courgette soufflé, peach soufflé, mocha soufflé, spinach soufflé, coffee soufflé, fig soufflé. With every page, the recipes got harder. Even though she thought of herself as a very experienced cook, she didn't dare start from the middle of the book, let alone the final pages. She knew how hard it was to make a good soufflé, even though she'd never tried it before. No chef ever attempted to make one on a TV show. Even the chefs at the highest calibre restaurants were alarmed when somebody ordered this legendary food or dessert. There was a reason why Grimod, the forefather of modern food writers, was depicted with a serving of soufflé in a nineteenth century painting hung at the Carnavalet Museum in Paris. A food critic always ordered this infamous dish to decide whether to praise a restaurant or destroy it. There was no middle road, because there was no such thing as an average soufflé.

Someone who had never heard of the dish's bad reputation wouldn't understand what the big deal was about by simply looking at the recipe. He'd think he would be safe if he used all of the right ingredients, was careful to mix the egg whites and yolks in separate bowls and then mix them together very cautiously. An ignorant, arrogant amateur cook would follow the recipe word for word, cook it at the exact temperature, watch it rise through the glass with a knowing smile and then think to himself, 'That wasn't so hard after all.' Once he'd removed it from the oven, however, he'd have to face the unpleasant truth and wouldn't know what had hit him. In this case, he'd check the recipe again, trying to understand where he went wrong, and he wouldn't know who to blame, since he'd done everything correctly. Maybe then he'd talk to someone who knew better and learn that the centre of the soufflé tends to collapse no matter what, even if the oven door is opened just five seconds earlier or later than necessary. A soufflé was like a beautiful, capricious woman; nobody could predict her mood. No book held the secret to it. No one could say: take it out of the oven at the thirtieth second of the twenty-fifth minute; no oven ever reached the right temperature. Every cook found his or her best recipe by making it over and over again. Each one made the best soufflé only after using their bowls and oven dozens of times; after wearing them out and finally restraining them at the end of a long and exhausting battle.

Maybe this wasn't a battle that Lilia needed at that precise moment in her life. On the other hand, maybe it was exactly the kind of sweet quarrel that could help her to forget about her more serious struggles. How disappointed could she get over a failed recipe? Could it really be the 'biggest disappointment'? Her life had become a sweater with a tear in the yarn. Every day another knot came loose. Every emotion she thought she'd kept hidden deep inside her surfaced, one after another. It was like a game of 'whack-a-mole'. As she hit each one of them with all her strength, another popped up from a different hole. She pitied herself so much that she had no time to feel sorry for her husband. Whenever she heard him grumbling in his room, she wrapped her arms around herself instead of comforting him. She pitied him, but that didn't necessarily mean she really cared. That small kiss they gave each other every night had also disappeared. This was partly because of Arnie's dry lips, caused by his medication. Having to wipe her husband clean after he used the bathroom every day didn't bring them any closer, either. A complete lack of privacy wasn't the same as intimacy. In fact, they'd never felt this distant before. They couldn't even look each other in the face while they were speaking. When their eyes met acciden-tally, both of them saw a thick, grey wall standing between them, impossible to cross.

Just like Lilia, Arnie only felt pity for himself. He didn't care that his sixty-two-year-old wife had to take care of him, clean him or wake up in the middle of the night to answer his never-ending string of demands. He didn't dare confess this to himself, but he knew deep inside that he pushed her so hard just to take revenge. While he racked his brain thinking how he was going to get out of this situation – imprisoned in his tiny room – he couldn't bear to hear her chatting away with other people in the kitchen, ignoring him completely, with a flirtatious tone in her voice.

Although she knew how much the smell of food bothered him, she still cooked from the early hours of the day until late in the afternoon, and that made her think of herself as a woman of the world. He didn't care for Georgian food or bread made from corn flour. Now he was being forced to discover Spanish cuisine, as if it wasn't enough that he'd had to eat Filipino food for most of his life. He was perfectly aware of his wife's attraction to that young man, Flavio. Every time she heard his voice, she almost ran to the kitchen. Arnie wasn't jealous of him. In fact, he found it rather funny; tragicomic, indeed. What was she thinking? That a man like that was going to find her attractive despite her messy, greasy hair, dirty apron and tasteless outfits? This little world she thought she'd created for herself was nothing but a small balloon that was going to pop at the most unexpected moment. Destruction would come out of nowhere, just like that blood clot in his brain. Now, just when he was thinking the same things all over again, the sound of a cup falling onto the kitchen floor interrupted his thoughts. He had no idea that Lilia was getting ready to try her first soufflé that day.

Lilia started the recipe by following each step in order, despite her usual habit of improvising. After turning on the oven, she greased the middle-sized soufflé bowl and sprinkled Parmesan cheese inside it. When it was time to separate the egg yolks from their whites, she remembered how much she'd longed to do this when she was a little girl. She'd always thought people would consider her a good cook as long as she could keep the yolk free of its white by transferring it from one half of the broken shell to the other. While she kept going back and forth between her past and present – just like the yolk of the egg – she tried to ignore the sounds coming from Arnie's room. They clearly showed that he wasn't happy about something. She had a tough recipe ahead of her, which required unswerving devotion, and there was no way she could take a break. Every minute counted. The six egg whites had to be beaten until they formed soft peaks – no less, no more. Trying to draw some strength from the sound that the metal beater made every time it hit the bowl, she did her best to close her ears to her husband's grunting. It sounded like Arnie was annoyed about something again. He'd spent most of his life getting annoyed at things, anyway; at everything and nothing. A split rubbish bag, a broken lighter, spilt candle wax or the folded corner of the rug was enough to get on his nerves. Arnie paid no attention to the things that really should have irritated him, but trivial episodes like that drove him completely mad. According to Lilia, he had no idea how much time he spent huffing and puffing each day. In his eyes, whatever went wrong was his wife's fault: the rubbish bags split because she'd bought the cheapest quality ones, or she forgot to throw out the lighter when it ran out of fluid. She hadn't thought of adjusting the folded end of the rug and she'd spilt the candle wax because she carried the candles so carelessly. Finally, she heard him calling out to her with an exhausted voice.

'Arnie, I can't leave what I'm doing right now. What is it? Is it anything that can't wait?'

'My computer's frozen. You have to unplug it.'

'Can't it wait a little longer?'

'Are you cooking for the royal family? Can't you come in here for two minutes?'

Lilia put the bowl down and walked quickly to the next room. Without saying anything or even looking at her husband, she unplugged the cord and plugged it back in. Arnie didn't thank her any more for the things she did, either. He must just see all these things as chores she had to take care of.

When she went back to the kitchen, she couldn't start where she'd left off. She put her palms on the counter, her arms wide apart, and stared at the surface. She tried to figure out which ingredients would do the trick. Red pepper, ground nutmeg, salt. She mixed some flour with a little water and moulded this simple dough mixture into a human form. Then she laid the tiny figure on the counter and said these words, while she sprinkled the mixture over it:

'I've salted everything you've sent me, I've seasoned everything you've sent me, I protect myself from all kinds of evil you want for me. You can't harm me and you'll never harm me.'

She put a small piece of the statue in the mixture for the soufflé and continued where she'd left off. After she was sure she'd done everything right, she put the bowl in the oven. She had never dreamed of serving her first soufflé to Arnie, but if she wanted the magic to work that was exactly what she had to do. She'd imagined her new friends tasting her soufflé and wanted to include them in this experience until she'd perfected herself, turning it all into a bit of a game. She not only expected her first attempts to fail, but almost hoped that they would. This was more than cooking for her. This was an experience that contained life inside it, and – just like other important experiences – it had to make her stumble first before bringing her slowly to excellence. It looked as if fate had decided to include Arnie in this experience too, and Lilia had never resisted her fate. Maybe they were going to learn something through this, just as they'd forgotten many things together.

It was Ulla who came home first, ten minutes before the alarm on the oven went off. She clasped her hands together excitedly when Lilia told her it was a soufflé in there. She knew all about the book her landlady had bought and her small project. That was why she looked so surprised when Lilia told her the food was only for Arnie. Just as Lilia was thinking of an excuse, Kano walked in. He pointed at the oven and asked, 'Is that what I think it is?' As Lilia started telling Kano it was only for her husband, Flavio and Natalie came in. She had no time left to explain at that moment, as she needed to concentrate on the soufflé and take it out just at the right time. She took a step forward and stopped in front of the oven. When the alarm went off, she held her arm out behind her and waved to the group, urging them to be quiet without knowing exactly what she expected from a complete silence. Everybody stepped back a little and watched their landlady's movements closely. Lilia carefully opened the oven door, balanced the ceramic bowl in her hands and took a couple of steps backwards, without turning around. The minute she turned to face her audience with the bowl held close to her bosom and surprise in her eyes, the centre of the dish collapsed. A big smile spread across her face. Who else would be this proud about failing at their first attempt at a soufflé?

Instead of going to the gallery, Marc picked up the shopping bags he'd just bought and went to the farmers' market. The people behind the stands greeted him with anxious yet happy nods and gave him their condolences. After Clara had disappeared, one of them couldn't wait any longer and had gone to the pâtisserie to see if they knew anything about her. That was when they'd learned that she'd died suddenly and that her husband was hiding away from everybody. Marc would never know about this, but Clara's farmer friends had arranged a small ceremony in her name and said their goodbyes, raising their glasses of wine in toasts to their lost friend. They'd been waiting for Marc ever since. His face, which was easily forgettable under normal circumstances, had a deeper meaning for them now. He'd become a kind of keepsake for them. That was why Madame Dilard smiled more widely than ever when he shyly approached the vegetable stand. Marc was peering at his list and trying to work out which was which among the greens, reds and oranges. Just when he'd gathered enough courage to ask which one was a celery root, Madame Dilard asked if she could see the list. After she had taken a look at it, she walked around the stand and stood beside him. It looked as if Marc couldn't even tell one kind of pepper from the others. Only time would tell if he would ever be able to decipher which vegetable was which. He looked like a blind man who had just regained his sight. He picked everything up, rolled it in his hand, smelled it and tried to understand what its essence was.

Although he was having a very hard time now, a day would come when he would know which vegetables went well together just by smelling them. He was going to discover that lemon complemented leeks and carrot blended really well with cumin. Until then, Madame Dilard and the others were going to help him. After buying the vegetables, he found himself standing in front of the cheese stand. A French man who didn't know anything about cheese was as strange as a fish that couldn't swim in the eyes of many of his compatriots. He didn't know the names of his favourite cheeses, but he could tell a little from the way they looked. Thank goodness that the cheese man, known as Louis le Gros in the market, loved his job and didn't mind spending forty-five minutes offering Marc small pieces of cheese on the tip of his knife. Louis – who had been given the same nickname as Louis VI because of his big belly, which barely fit behind the counter – had asked Clara to run away with him many times even though he was married and knew that she was, too. Clara would always ward off this loud proposal with a smile and say, 'Maybe in another life.'

After all his help, Marc felt bad and asked Le Gros to wrap up a couple of the cheeses he'd tried before telling him the name of the cheese he was actually looking for, glancing at his list again. 'Ohhhh, Comté,' said Le Gros, 'why didn't you say so? How do you like it? Aged or not?'

'What's the difference?'

'*Alors*, the young cheese has a buttery flavour and tastes almost like hazelnuts. It becomes more intense, more earthy, as it ages.'

And so Marc learned that Le Gros didn't stop talking easily once he'd got started – especially when he came across someone like Marc, who knew almost nothing about the subject but was willing to learn. He wanted to explain the full history of Comté, such as why it had tiny holes in it, when was the best time to eat it, and particularly how it differed from the Swiss Gruyère. If anyone ever wanted to buy Gruyère from him, he just suggested loudly that they should go to Switzerland. After he'd finished his lecture, he asked:

'Are you going to use this in a recipe?'

'Yes.'

'Which one?'

'*Tarte au Fromage.*'

'Then you want the young one.'

Marc had picked two recipes from his new book for the next two days and had written down all their ingredients in his list. He wasn't going to eat just whatever he found in the neighbourhood that Sunday, or buy a roasted chicken and new potatoes from Mouffetard. After he'd made sure he had everything he needed, he nodded goodbye to everybody and crossed the street. His first farmers' market experience hadn't gone as badly as he'd imagined. Even though everybody there knew who he was, nobody had talked about Clara or tried to console him. Marc still couldn't remember his wife without feeling pain. He still couldn't stand hearing his own lonely footsteps in the apartment. The emptiness at the other side of the bed broke his heart every morning and night, and one fork made so much more noise than two. Sometimes he felt that his mourning would never end. He felt as if he could only be happy again if he could completely forget that someone named Clara had ever existed.

He'd stayed away from his friends for a long time now. He hadn't accepted any of their invitations and had tried to keep the phone conversations short. Whenever they stopped by the gallery he always found an excuse to get away. He wasn't unhappy every minute of the day. On the contrary, he'd been finding peace in his solitude lately and he was proud of this development. But these were very short moments that ended as soon as he remembered his wife. He didn't know how long it would be, but he knew that he needed more time. He wasn't one of those wise old souls who had come into this world knowing every feeling without having to experience them. He was learning to deal with life one step at a time.

After he'd put everything in the fridge, Mark made himself an espresso. He turned on the TV as he prepared his pen and paper, which he kept ready on the table at all times. He tried to catch episodes of *Escapade Gourmande* on Saturdays now as well as late on week nights. He didn't care much about the recipes, to be honest. He scribbled them down and tried to keep up with them as much as he could, but what he really liked was the conversations between the two men who hosted the show. Marc had never been that close to any of his friends. Clara had filled every little hole when it came to friendship and intimacy. He'd never imagined that allowing his life to revolve around just one person could cause such a deep emptiness one day. But now, those two men who, he didn't know and probably never would, had become his best friends. He went wherever they went and felt as if he was standing behind them and eavesdropping on every word. Those two men represented the concept of friendship to him.

He was also intrigued by the simplicity of their recipes. The only problem was trying to follow everything they said. Sometimes he couldn't read the notes he took later on and had to throw them out. There was also no way he could understand the measurements that were given in every recipe. One teaspoon didn't mean anything to him and neither did one tablespoon. He remembered that some of those gadgets had been among the things he'd thrown out, but until now he hadn't known what they were for. He jotted them down on his shopping list, right under 'Grater', before he forgot. He had to go to Tout le Marché again that day. He'd realised that French cuisine simply couldn't survive without a grater. He wondered if the young woman who had helped him the last time would be there. If Sabina hadn't come to his rescue on his first trip, he would probably have just given up by now. Marc had found something peaceful in the girl's straight hair, plain face and fine lashes. He'd felt safe walking with her among the aisles. Even the murmur of the store and the sound of the music had faded away.

After the show had ended, he washed his espresso cup and put it on the dish rack. He turned on the light over the oven, left the TV on, went into the living room to light the standing lamp and left the apartment. He couldn't stand entering a dark, silent house now that he'd started living alone. That was why he always left the radio on during the week and the TV on at the weekends before leaving the building, and the lights stayed on almost all of the time. The faces of the French TV presenters, who had been there for ever, became even more familiar to him now. He wouldn't be surprised if they said hello to him when he came back to his apartment one day.

He was unaware of the fact that his neighbour, who lived across the hall, put her ear to his door every day just to hear these voices. It wasn't that she wanted to pry into his life, but because she knew exactly what this young man was going thorough. When she'd lost her husband several years ago, Clara had been the one who'd helped her the most. She'd knock on the door some afternoons with a plate of biscuits and they'd drink tea together. Clara would listen very attentively to everything Madame Beaumont had to say, almost as if she wanted to record every word in her brain. She'd really tried to understand the pain and her eyes would well up with tears at the end. Madame Beaumont knew that this young woman was imagining herself in her place and that it made her sad to think she might go through the same kind of sorrows one day. When Madame Beaumont lifted her ear from the door and walked back to her apartment, shaking her head, she was thinking how unprepared Marc had been for that amount of sorrow. She heard him go in and out most of the time, but never opened her door even if she was going out herself, just to avoid making him feel uncomfortable, and so she usually let him leave the building first. He obviously didn't want to be consoled. All the same, she'd realised that Marc had started coming home at more normal times recently. He stayed at home at the weekends and didn't just run out of his apartment without looking back. He'd thrown away bags full of stuff and come home with new ones, she assumed. These days, the sound of pots and pans accompanied the voices on TV every now and then. Madame Beaumont knew exactly how hopeless Marc was in the kitchen. Clara had told her many times – joyfully – how he couldn't tell the difference between okra and beans. Did he know that he could knock on her door if he was ever missing an ingredient, or when he needed help? Did he realise that she and Clara had become as close as mother and daughter over the years and that she also missed her terribly? It looked as if Marc had pushed everybody in his life away. Nobody came to their apartment any more, which had once always been filled with people so that it warmed the heart just to see it. But time would heal everything. When the right time came, he would take out all of the memories, like old pictures from a buried box, look at them one last time and then become free again.

Marc knew where to go this time as he climbed up the escalator. Although he only had two items on his list and remembered exactly what they were, he took out the piece of paper and glanced at it one more time. Did he really have to come all the way here just to get a grater and some measuring cups? He knew he could find practically anything he needed in that Chinese shop in his own neighbourhood – but he didn't have time to analyse his actions any deeper as he was concentrating on not falling over the last step of the escalator. The place was packed, just like the last time. Dozens of people stood in front of the shelves, picking things up and examining them carefully. The digital sound coming from the tills mixed with the voices of customers. There was a huge queue in one corner of the store. Men and women were reading books as they waited. While he was trying to understand what was happening, someone spoke behind him:

'Gordon Ramsay.'

When he turned around he found Sabina standing there. At that moment he realised that he'd wanted to see her again. Now he was sure that he felt comfortable around her. When Sabina realised that Marc was looking confused, she started to explain:

'I helped you when you came in a couple of weeks ago.'

Showing him the name tag on her collar, she continued: 'Sabina.'

'I remember. I'm sorry, I was just thinking about something else. But I recognised you the moment I saw you.'

'Those people are waiting to get an autograph from Gordon Ramsay.'

'Gordon Ramsay?'

'The famous British chef. Well, he's Scottish I think, but he's British. He does shows like *Hell's Kitchen*, *Ramsay's Kitchen Nightmares*. Haven't you heard of them?'

'No. I haven't.'

'Maybe it's better not to know. They're horrific. They're nightmares, just like their names. He changes the menus of some restaurants and supposedly helps them to become better places. What kind of help is that though? He yells at the restaurant's chef, or the owners, and humiliates everybody. Sometimes they even cry. Besides, they aren't always small places. Some of them are really good restaurants that make a lot of money. One of his books has just been translated into French. That's why he's here.'

'People seem to like him.'

'I think a lot of them are here to see if he's really as mean as he is on TV.'

'Is he?'

'He's a real English gentleman. They wanted me to bring some paper to his table and when I went there he stood up. I think he's playing another character in his shows.'

Marc hadn't had a conversation like this with anyone in a very long time. He talked to Amou at the gallery, but only about work and it never lasted for more than five minutes. Amou was also the one who took care of their customers. Marc only ever left the office at the back of the gallery when he was absolutely needed. Actually, he hadn't been all that different before Clara passed away. The only person he liked to talk to was his wife and he'd always listened very attentively to any detail she had to give on any subject, even the ones he wasn't all that interested in. He'd always been the quietest person at their friends' gatherings and parties. He'd always known that his wife would fill in any gaps he left in a conversation and so he'd never come across as irritating, despite being a bit antisocial. And now Sabina was driving the conversation; she was the one who would decide where it might lead and where it would stop.

'Anyway, I don't want to take up any more of your time. How may I help you today?'

'I need a grater and some measuring cups.'

'OK. Let's take a look at the grater first. What kind of a grater would you like?'

'What do you mean?'

As Sabina told Marc about all the different kinds of graters, Marc wondered for the first time if this was the young woman's main job. Was she someone who only sold kitchenware? Or was she working here temporarily, just to earn some extra money? Whichever it was, since she talked so enthusiastically about graters she must be loving her job. He didn't understand a word she was saying, so he finally decided on the simplest one: the grater that looked exactly like the one in his grandmother's kitchen. Sabina smiled and said:

'Of course, it's a classic. Old-fashioned, but always the best choice.'

It was easier to pick the measuring cups. He only had to decide on how big a set he wanted. Bigger was better for Marc. He'd even be able to find out how much a gram was. When Sabina asked if he wanted anything else, he thanked her:

'I'm sure I need a lot of things, but I don't know which ones yet. I think I'll come and get them one by one.'

'That's the best way to build a kitchen, anyway. Slowly but surely. See you later, then, I guess?'

'Yes, I hope so. See you later.'

'Bye. Good luck.'

As he walked towards the cashiers, Marc turned around and saw that Sabina was still watching him, smiling. He waved goodbye, smiling back. He felt slightly sweaty under his arms. Without letting himself wonder whether it was because he was excited or because of the heat in the store, he paid for his items and left. He didn't realise he was smiling, but he was definitely craving some dessert.

Since she'd woken up very early that morning to an eventful day, her eyes were still heavy with sleep. She'd already had two cups of Turkish coffee – something that was very out of character for her – and yet she still felt exhausted.

Ferda had opened her eyes to the sound of her mother's screams: 'Police! Police!' First she'd woken up her husband, shaking him wildly before tearing the earplugs from his ears.

After sitting up in bed, terrified, for a couple of seconds, they'd acted together as one person. Sinan had gone to get one of the wooden coat hangers from their old walnut cupboard, trying hard not make any noise as he opened its door, while Ferda called the police from her mobile phone, which she left switched on at all times on her bedside table in case her daughter or son called for an emergency in the middle of the night. She'd followed her husband to the bedroom door while she told the operator her address, and right before they stepped out onto the landing she'd picked up one of the perfumes that had stood there for years and had already gone bad from lack of use and placed her index finger on the nozzle. She took no notice of the gestures her husband made, which meant, 'Stay behind.' She wasn't about to wait in her room while a thief or murderer choked her mother to death. Besides, what could Sinan do with one coat hanger? When they finally reached Mrs Nesibe's room – without any kind of plan – and nervously stuck their heads around the door, they saw the old woman lying on the bed, waving her arms wildly and yelling into empty space. Sinan had pushed the door right back to make sure there was no one behind it, and when he was sure they were alone he'd gone into the room and turned on the light. As Ferda tried to calm her mother down, he'd walked into the living room, turning on all the lights in the house. The three locks on the main door were secured and all the windows and balcony doors were closed. It was clear that there had been no intruders. He still heard his mother-in-law yelling as he drank a glass of water to slow down his pulse. Now she was saying, 'Please don't strangle me.' His wife was begging her: 'Mum, it's me Ferda. Please don't scream. Look, it's me. You must have had a nightmare. Look, it's me, your daughter. I'm not strangling you. Please open your mouth, take this pill.'

Even though Sinan had wanted to go in there and help his wife, the pain in his chest wouldn't let him move. He'd sat down on one of the chairs around the kitchen table and waited for the pain to go away. This didn't seem like one of the heart attacks he'd had before; maybe it was a small spasm. Just at that moment, Ferda had realised that her husband was unusually quiet and she'd run to the kitchen, leaving her mother alone. When she saw her husband's pale face with beads of sweat dripping from it, she'd run to the medicine cabinet, her hands shaking. In the meantime, she asked, 'Sinan, can you breath? Can you breath?' With great difficulty, he'd replied, 'Yes. It's not a heart attack.' Ferda had put the small pill under her husband's tongue, helped him to swallow it and run to the phone, this time to call the ambulance. Just when she'd finished telling them what was wrong among her mother's screams, the doorbell had rung. 'Police!' said the voice coming from outside. She'd completely forgotten to call the police to let them know that it was a false alarm. They'd entered the building by buzzing on her neighbours' doors, so now everybody knew something was happening. Some of them had already been woken up by Mrs Nesibe's screams anyway and they'd been waiting for events to unfold. Ferda had opened the door and let the police in while explaining to her neighbours that nothing was going on. She shouldn't have bothered; the ambulance's sirens would wake the building's residents up again just five minutes later. As the police tried to understand what was happening, the paramedics had walked in, carrying a stretcher. The neighbours were at their doors again, trying to work out what was going on. Ferda had cut it all short, telling them that Sinan was having a spasm before closing the door. She knew what everybody was going to say behind closed doors: 'That poor guy was going to die because of his crazy mother-in-law. What would Ferda do then?' By the time the paramedics walked in, Sinan had already recovered. The colour in his face was back and he could talk again. As he told the paramedics he felt fine and that he was going to go and see his doctor right away, the police were leaning on the counter between the kitchen and the living room, waiting for them to finish so that they could continue with their interrogation. The paramedics had left after taking Sinan's blood pressure and wishing him well. Now it was the police's turn. Ferda explained in one breath that they'd woken up to her mother's screams, immediately thought that somebody had broken into their apartment, called the police, found out that there was no one in the apartment, but forgot to call the police because this time her husband was having a spasm. Mrs Nesibe had stopped screaming in the meantime, but she was still groaning. Ferda had mentioned that her mother was confined to bed and got confused once in a while. The police didn't seem all that willing to leave despite everything they'd heard. They said they wanted to talk to the old lady and went into her room. It was still dark outside and Mrs Nesibe's eyes looked even smaller now as she stared at the light on the ceiling.

'Good morning, ma'am. Can you tell us what happened?'
'These people torture me. They beat me.'

'Who?'

'These ones.'

'Your daughter and son-in-law?'

'She's not my daughter. And he's not her husband. This man sells this woman for money and he wants to sell me, too. When I refuse, they both beat me.'

When Ferda heard what her mother was saying, her eyes had almost popped out of their sockets and she blushed. She was in such a state of shock that instead of crying, her tears seemed to fall in her stomach like fireballs. Sinan was standing right behind her, shaking his head, incredulously. Ferda was scared that her husband might have another spasm, and so she turned to him and said, 'Go to bed, honey.' Unfortunately, the police weren't so keen on sending Sinan back to bed.

'Wait a moment, ma'am. We'll need to talk to your husband. You can go and wait in the kitchen.'

'What are you saying, officer? My mum doesn't know what she's talking about right now.'

'She says she's not your mother.'

'Please. Let me bring her ID, and mine and my husband's. You can also look at our marriage certificate. But please, let's talk in the kitchen. I don't want her to get any more agitated than she already is. I'll give her a tranquilliser.'

'Please go and get all of those documents first. Let's make sure who's who first, then you can give her a tranquilliser.'

When Ferda came back five minutes later with their IDs and marriage certificate, one of the officers had looked from the picture of the woman in the ID to the old lady for a very long time. Ferda knew that the picture on her mother's identification card looked nothing like her now. Her mother had insisted on keeping a picture from her younger days on her ID. Especially now, with her completely white hair and her hollowed cheeks, she looked like someone else altogether. In the end, the officers decided it was good enough for them and moved their investigation to the kitchen. One of them turned to Sinan and grinned, a little too obviously:

'The old lady's a bit confused, I guess.'

'My mother-in-law's started forgetting things recently. Her health is good one day and bad another. We don't know what she's going to say next.'

'I guess there's no truth in what she said.'

'Officer, please. How can there be? You can't start listening to everyone with dementia. Besides, why would we call the police if there was any truth in it? When we heard her screaming we thought someone was in the apartment, hurting her.'

'So … you have a heart condition, huh?'

'Yes, I need to see my doctor today.'

'Well, OK then. Hope she gets better. Sorry about all the questions.'

'No problem. Thank you very much for coming. Have a good day.'

Ferda had closed the door behind them and pointed in the direction of their room, telling him: 'Go ahead, sleep a little. I'll call Dr Kemal, so you can see him today. Don't go to work, OK?'

'Aren't you going to sleep?'

'No, I don't feel like sleeping at all.'

'Is your mother asleep?'

'No. I gave her some pills. She'll probably go to sleep in a little while. She doesn't know who I am. She didn't make a fuss about taking the pills because the officers were here. She's obsessed with you now. She asked if they'd taken you away.'

'What did you say?'

'I said they're going to put you in prison.'

'What's going to happen when she sees me again?'

'What's going to happen is she won't remember what's happened. She'll go back to normal, I guess. I'll call her doctor today too and tell him the situation.'

'There must be a solution to this, right? We can't live like this. All the neighbours woke up because of us, too.'

'What can we do, Sinan? We can't just get rid of her, can we? It's something that could happen to anyone.'

'How could it happen to anyone, Ferda? Is there anyone as crazy as Mrs Nesibe? She was like this when she was young too, wasn't she?'

'Please, Sinan, she wasn't like this. Please, I feel terrible already.'

'OK, I'm sorry. Are you hungry?'

'No, are you?'

'A little. Maybe I should eat something before I go to sleep.'

'I can't believe it, you're always thinking about food! OK, sit down, I'll fix you something.'

Ferda had put some slices of bread in the toaster, mumbling to herself, 'How come all the nutcases find me?' The tears she'd been expecting started tumbling through her eyelashes while she peeled the skin off a tomato. Her headache, which was always waiting for an opportunity to surface, had started making its presence felt. It would start to drill, slyly, at one side of her head whenever she felt happy, sad or excited. Back in the day, she'd wait for the pain to take control of her whole head, almost her whole body, and then close herself away in the darkness of her room and could only be convinced to take a dose of Novalgin on the third day, when there was nothing left in her stomach to throw up. Now, she'd popped two painkillers onto her tongue before she even knew what she was doing. She didn't even have time for her migraine any more; her mother had claimed those three days she spent by herself behind closed curtains. It wasn't that she enjoyed the pain – which sometimes even made her think about taking her own life – but at least that time belonged only to her. It was her pain and her problem, no one else's. There was a kind of bond between her migraine and herself. If she didn't have an attack for a while, she would wonder where it had been. Even though she'd feel relieved, her balance would be completely off.

She'd made her first coffee after sending Sinan to bed. Even when she drank the second cup hours later, she still couldn't get rid of the heaviness behind her eyes. Her mind was far too active to go to sleep, and yet her headache wouldn't let her wake up fully, either. She'd sat quietly at the kitchen table, trying not to wake either Sinan or her mother, and had watched the dawn breaking while she browsed through the book she'd bought. She was surprised to find out that the first edition of the soufflé book had been printed in 1841. She hadn't known that this dish was so old, just as she hadn't known how difficult it was to make it. She'd had a soufflé a couple of times before with Öykü at a café on Istiklal Street, but she'd never realised that those were failures since their centres had already collapsed by the time they arrived at the table.

According to the book's introduction, this was why soufflé was the biggest disappointment. It didn't matter how disciplined you were or how well you followed the instructions, the tiniest mistake could ruin all of your efforts. Ferda found the recipe for chocolate soufflé among the pages and started reading it. It looked really simple. A little bit of sugar, some chocolate, three egg yolks, six egg whites. The book explained how to mix each of them in great detail. So, what was so difficult about it? Ferda had to find that out for herself. She folded down a tiny triangle at the top of the page and closed the book when she heard her mother calling her. After taking a deep breath, she stood up and walked to Mrs Nesibe's room, not knowing which dimension of her mother she was going to have to face.

'Ferda, what time is it?'

'Half past eight.'

'What's wrong? What happened to you? Do you have a headache?'

'A little.'

'Why?'

'Don't you remember anything from this morning?'

'What do you mean this morning? It's morning now. Have you gone crazy?'

'Don't you remember waking up before dawn?'

'I think you must have been dreaming. I just woke up.'

'You started screaming very early in the morning, we thought there was someone in the house attacking you, we called the police, they came. You accused Sinan of selling us to men, and they questioned Sinan.'

'God forbid! Have you lost your mind? You must have had a nightmare. This is what happens if you don't have anything to eat.'

Ferda knew that it would be pointless to try to explain things any further, as her mother wasn't going to remember any of the things she'd done. She didn't even realise the damage she caused when she was completely conscious, let alone when she didn't even know who she was.

'Ferda? You're lost in thought again. You were like this when you were a little girl, too. You used to sleep on your feet. Can you please change me? You know, the nappy. God, I'm so embarrassed. Look what I've become. I wouldn't wish this kind of illness on anybody. Being crippled is the worst punishment.'

'Mum, you're not crippled. You think you are and that's why you can't move. But the worst thing is, you really can't move any more. There's no muscle left in your legs. Are you happy now? I really don't understand why you chose to live like this. You're torturing yourself and me.'

'I know I'm a burden to you. But don't worry, I'm not going to be around for much longer. Your father is waiting for me on the other side. I always see him in my dreams now, and he says it's time. You know, you're going to get old one day and you don't know what's in store for you.'

'OK, mum, OK. I didn't say a thing. Please don't start again. Hold on to my shoulder and try to lift yourself a little. I'll put another pillow behind you. Mum, not on my neck, please, on my shoulder.'

When her mother had fallen asleep again later that afternoon and Sinan had gone to see his doctor, Ferda tried her first soufflé. She used the chocolates which she normally kept for her grandchildren's visits, put them in a metal bowl and placed it on top of a pan of boiling water. She stirred them gently until the steam had melted them. She whisked the three egg yolks in a cup and mixed them with the chocolate. Then she whisked six egg whites with a pinch of salt until they'd formed tiny peaks. She continued stirring the mixture while slowly adding the sugar. Then she sped up and continued stirring until the mixture became really firm. She took almost a cup of it and mixed it with the chocolate and egg yolks. After she had blended them together really well, she added the whole mixture to the remaining egg whites and sugar. She'd already warmed up the oven. For successful results, the oven should always be preheated. After she'd buttered the soufflé mould and sprinkled sugar inside it, she poured in the batter and wiped the rim with her thumb. Then she put it in the oven and got ready to wait for twenty-four to twenty-six minutes. She made herself some linden tea in the meantime and took too big a sip while staring inside the oven. She badly burnt her tongue and this really annoyed her. Now she wasn't going to be able to taste her first soufflé properly.

She sat in front of the oven and watched the soufflé in the dim light through the glass door. When the batter started to rise, she held her breath. She reached for the book from where she sat and looked at the photograph to get an idea of how the dessert should look. She heard her mother begin to moan in the twenty-fourth minute. Mrs Nesibe was like a baby: she woke up in stages and loved making noises while she did so. Ferda didn't care; she waited. By the twenty-sixth minute, her soufflé looked exactly like the one in the book. She put on her oven gloves and carefully opened the oven door, ignoring her mother's cries of 'Fusun! Fusun!' The centre of the dessert collapsed even before she took it out. She put the tray on the counter and went to look after her mother.

Seven

On her birthday, Lilia woke up to the same life as always. While she tried to banish the number 'sixty-three' from her mind, she went downstairs as the creaking of her knees mixed with the creaking of the steps. As she accompanied Arnie to the bathroom, she thought how she was even going to be deprived of the flowers he got her every year. The kids hadn't called to wish her a happy birthday in years and they wouldn't this time, either. She knew that her siblings would call. They always did. She was going to mark the end of another year with a five-minute phone call with each of them. Lilia acted like it didn't matter, but however old she got she couldn't help caring about the day she was born. What else did she have to care about? She'd never understood people who forgot their birthdays, who said, 'Oh, is it my birthday today?' whenever you called to congratulate them. She wished she could have been one of them. That way the calls that weren't made, the kisses that weren't given and the words that weren't said wouldn't hurt so much.

Arnie looked weaker today. His pale face had become almost translucent and the lines around his eyes had deepened. He didn't have the strength to hold on to his cane and he'd lost his determination, too. It looked as if he'd lost almost ten pounds in one night. After they'd finished with the bathroom duties, she put her husband to bed and went to the kitchen. She watched Kano from the window as she prepared the coffee. He was almost done with his prayers. After a few minutes, he'd come in and ask, '*Nanika atta?*' and Lilia would answer, 'Not bad', trying not to show that she'd lost her spark of energy and that she simply wasn't happy. She'd always said 'good' before, whenever people asked her how she was. 'Good', 'very good', or 'pretty good'. Still, over the years she'd finally learned to say 'not bad'. like other people. And, as a matter of fact, she felt bad. Pretty bad. Just as she'd expected, Kano walked in.

'*Nanika atta?*'

'Not bad. *Nanika atta?*'

'I'm good. I have an exam today, to pass to the next level.'

'I'm sure you'll pass.'

'Thank you. What are your plans for today?'

'Same as every day.'

'So, you'll be home?'

'Yes.'

Lilia found this last question quite strange. She wondered if Kano knew it was her birthday. Maybe she'd mentioned it before in a conversation. She decided not to ask or say anything about it. She wasn't one of those people who wanted to find out about surprises before they happened. She liked being surprised. She already felt better, though, and so she tried to change the subject.

'I'm going to try the courgette soufflé today.'

'How were the others?'

'This will be the fourth one. The second one collapsed like the first one. The third one stood up for twenty-two seconds longer. Let's see how today's one will turn out.'

'How about trying the same one until you master it?'

'Actually, they're all the same recipe. The additional ingredients aren't that important, I guess; the problem is getting the basics right. Especially the eggs. You get used to it the more you do it. I think it even matters how quickly you whisk the eggs. Or how you use your wrist.'

'*Nana korobi ya oki.*'

'Meaning?'

'Don't give up if you can't get it right the first time. An old Japanese proverb.'

'That isn't a proverb. There's no metaphor. It's more like a suggestion.'

'True. How is Arnie, by the way? He doesn't look so good these days.'

'I just thought the same thing today. It looks like he's letting himself go, and he gets tired very quickly.'

'Was he always like this?'

'Like what?'

'Very tense but polite.'

'*Ang taong walang kibo, nasa loob ang kulo.* An old Filipino proverb.'

'Meaning?'

'Anger builds up in someone who always looks calm.'

'There's no metaphor in this one, either.'

'No, unfortunately.'

As she was getting dressed in her room later that morning, she could hear everybody leaving one by one by listening to their footsteps: Ulla's quiet rustle, Flavio's heavy and determined steps, Natalie's hurried rattling. Ed was nowhere to be seen lately. Maybe he'd finally found himself a girlfriend. He'd started getting irritated by the new tenants after he'd lost interest in Ulla. He'd become almost like a spoiled child over the years he'd spent in their house. He was used to having the whole floor to himself, but now he had to share it with Flavio and Natalie. His complaints about the use of the bathroom were never-ending.

Lilia suspected that something was going on between Flavio and Natalie based on their comings and goings at the same times of the day, the way they finished each other's sentences and the noises coming from upstairs late at night. Even though she'd tried to find out what was happening from Natalie a couple of times, she hadn't been able to. Jealousy was swimming in her stomach. Even after coming to terms with the age difference between herself and Flavio and the young man's obvious indifference to her, her feelings hadn't changed. The tumour in her body continued to grow. In fact, it was almost as if she wanted it to grow. She was trying to hold on to a feeling that helped her to go on with her life. Maybe those feelings would go away if she let them, but she didn't want them to. And so she carried on living in a chaos of thoughts, which didn't add up to any answers.

She received the first phone call from her youngest sibling right before she left her room. The others soon followed. She was sure that one of them had reminded the others. That was probably why they all called in a row every year. She walked into Arnie's room before hanging up on the last call, and laughed a little bit louder and acted a little bit happier than she actually was so that her husband would hear her. All the same, she could tell from Arnie's blank expression that he wasn't following the conversation. It looked as if he was having trouble keeping his eyes open and was almost falling asleep again.

'Arnie … Arnie …'

Her husband replied with difficulty:

'Yes?'

'Are you OK?'

'I'm tired. I want to sleep.'

'You just woke up. You don't look well. Should I call the doctor?'

'No. I'm OK. I'm just a little tired.'

'Are you sure?'

'Yes, I am. I'm going to sleep a bit more. Please pull the blind down.'

Lilia pulled it down and left the room. Even though she had a feeling that he wasn't all right, she decided to wait for Tamia to come later that afternoon before making any decisions. Maybe he really was just tired. Maybe making such an effort with the physiotherapy was wearing him down. He was only two years younger than Lilia and so it was quite normal really for him to feel exhausted after having to deal with this kind of an illness. Then, all of a sudden, another thought swept through her mind. Maybe he was doing it on purpose. Maybe he was acting sicker than he actually was because he knew it was her birthday. She saw the hateful looks he gave her most of the time now. It was impossible not to notice the distance in his eyes and the anger in his voice. Maybe he was angry because he couldn't control his wife the way he had done for so many years. Maybe he resented her because she didn't care any more or because she spent her dinnertimes chatting with the others instead of keeping her mouth shut. Could he have noticed the feelings she had for Flavio? She decided it was impossible. They'd never talked in front of him. Besides, Arnie had only seen Flavio once, when he'd moved into the house, and that was months ago. That was the only time. Arnie preferred to control his needs whenever there was anyone in the kitchen. He always waited until everyone had gone before leaving his room. Maybe he was just punishing her for trying to live a relatively happy life by not remembering her birthday, pretending not to hear the phone conversation she'd had with her sister, refusing to say a single nice word to her and reminding her of everything she had to do for him, and of his own existence. By blocking her escape. She tried to shake away these thoughts, waving her hand in the air as if she was shooing flies. She wasn't going to ruin the rest of her day by analysing the same tired things all over again. She had no reason to give up on her new age. Actually, despite all the weariness she felt and the confused turmoil of her thoughts, she still felt spiritually strong from time to time. Change was a little like thin air; no one realised when they were breathing it in. It quietly filled people's lungs, changing the maps of their brains, and nobody even realised until the moment when they finally woke up. She knew that everything she was experiencing, everything that happened and didn't happen, her expectations and disappointments, was leading her somewhere else. One day she would realise that she'd finally come to the last step of a long ladder and she would sit on the throne that was meant for her. Her surrender wasn't a sign of fatalism; it was more like a type of empiricism. As far as she was concerned, not a minute of life was wasted. Everything a person lived through was chained to something else and, just as the Hindus believed, the soul renewed itself many times. All the same, contrary to the Hindu philosophy, it started a new life not in another lifetime, but in this one. If Lilia had given up on her hope for the future she would have taken her own life years ago, as her disappointments had started very early on.

She put on her reading glasses and opened the book that was lying on the counter. She repeated the name of the recipe a couple of times, trying to read it properly. She had never liked the way in which Americans stretched the French words ending with an accent. She hated to hear them say 'clichey' instead of *cliché* and 'souffley' instead of *soufflé*. She hoped she would never become so American that she would start destroying French words like that. Before she started to cook, she poured herself a cup of coffee and turned her back to the winter sun that was coming in through the window. If it wasn't for these precious moments, she didn't know when she would be happy in this life. Without moving or looking at the time, she stood there, sipped her coffee and waited for her back to warm up; until the warmth had spread from her back to her heart. Then she finished her coffee, took her reading glasses off the top of her head and put them back on.

Since the recipes were always designed for four people, she only used a quarter of the ingredients. When she'd first started she'd planned to include her tenants in this project, but over time it had turned into a private ceremony that belonged only to her. She was discovering that her ability evolved each time she made the recipe and had realised that she'd been wrong to think she'd got it right before. She'd made peace with the fact that she was going to have to say, 'So I shouldn't have done it like this, then', every time she made this dish. Now she understood why they said soufflé was one of the hardest recipes to perfect: because it always had the potential to get better. Maybe there was no such thing as an ultimate soufflé. The egg whites could form better peaks every time they were beaten. The consistency of the mixture became more mature each time, encouraging people to find a way to improve.

She started making her soufflé without realising that the most important lesson of her life was flowing from those pages to her mind. She let herself beat the eggs for a long time, allowing all sorts of ideas to run through her head without interruption. Then she carefully mixed the yolks with the whites. When it was all done, she put her porcelain soufflé dish in the oven, ready to be taken out at exactly the twenty-fourth minute. Not a second earlier or later. At that moment, whoever was at the door would have to wait and all calls should go through to voicemail; Arnie mustn't need anything and Lilia should concentrate on her food. Some things in life should be done on time, and opening that oven door was at the top of her list. While the soufflé was cooking, she walked around the house for the first fifteen minutes and tidied the place up a little. She dropped the umbrella into its place and organised a pile of envelopes, stacking them neatly on the table. She picked up one of the cushions that had been left on the floor for God knows how long and fluffed it up. Then she went back to the kitchen, trying to ignore the dust that covered the whole house. She started to wait in front of the oven with the gloves already on her hands, having learned from the previous times. She opened the door on time and tried to take out the dish without shaking it too much. Just after she'd put it on the counter, she heard the doorbell ringing. It must be Tamia. The centre of the soufflé still hadn't collapsed at the thirtieth second. If it didn't fall for another twenty-three seconds, she was going to break her own record. The doorbell rang one more time. Lilia shouted out, hoping to be heard from outside, 'I'm coming!' Nonetheless, she wasn't surprised to see Tamia walking in through the kitchen door, since it was -8 degrees outside. Once she'd climbed up the stairs, still trembling from the cold, she found Lilia staring at the soufflé and at the old watch on her wrist.

'Lilia?'

'Shhhh.'

While Tamia stared at her, thinking she'd finally lost her mind, Lilia started to scream: 'Fifty-three, fifty-four, fifty-five, fifty-six, fifty-seven, fifty-eight … ohhh!'

Finally, she turned to Tamia and said:

'Hi. Sorry I couldn't come to the door.'

'H-hi … What's that?'

'Soufflé. I mentioned it before, I think.'

'Yes, you did. Why did it collapse like that?'

'That's the whole point. That's why I couldn't come to the door. I wanted to see how long it would stand up for today.'

'So, it did for fifty-eight seconds?'

'Yes.'

'How long should it stand up for, usually?'

'Normally it shouldn't collapse at all.'

'Hmmm. So what happened?'

'I'm not doing too badly, actually. It collapsed right away the first time. And my record was fifty-two seconds until now. Maybe I'll manage it one day.'

'Good luck. How's Arnie?'

'He's been sleeping since this morning. He couldn't wake up at all. Well, I haven't checked on him in the last hour, but since he hasn't called me he must still be sleeping.'

Tamia ran straight to Arnie's room as soon as she heard this. Her patient's head had flopped to the right and his drool had formed a big, damp circle on his pillow. She took his head in her hands and straightened it out. Arnie opened his eyes a little and looked at his therapist. He was having a hard time opening them completely. He felt as if he was carrying years' worth of sleep on his shoulders. He'd never felt this tired before in his life. His mind didn't want to wake up and he didn't want to push it. When he tried to stay awake for only a couple of minutes, he felt like his brain was swimming in water. When he said, 'I'm sleepy', Tamia ignored him and tried to make him talk.

'Arnie … Arnie … Can you open your eyes?'

'I want to sleep.'

'Try a little. Try to look at me.'

'I'm so tired.'

Tamia turned to Lilia and told her to call the hospital.

'Has he been like this all day?'

'Yes.'

'You should have called the hospital hours ago.'

'But he just looks tired. Isn't it normal?'

'He can't even talk. You think that's normal?'

Lilia did what she was told without saying or asking anything else, and tried to ignore the sharp tone in the therapist's voice. It looked like she was going to spend yet another day – her birthday – in the hospital corridors. On top of this, if anything happened to Arnie, everybody was going to blame her. They were going to think she'd been irresponsible; that she'd done nothing even though she knew something was wrong. She didn't even want to think about how Dung would react in that situation. It would finally give her a reason not to see Lilia ever again for the rest of her life. In reality, she didn't have a leg to stand on since she'd only visited her father three times in the last five months, but as always she'd end up blaming everybody but herself. She wasn't the one who took Arnie to the bathroom five times a day. She didn't have to clean his stinking body (caused by all that medication), cook for him, take care of his every need and deal with his ill temper every single day. If Lilia couldn't have some time for herself on her birthday, when was she going to have it? She listed everything she was going to say to her daughter in her mind, as if something had already happened and they were facing one another right now. If it wasn't for Tamia's voice she'd have continued with her monologue, but the therapist was calling her for help. It looked like Arnie hadn't realised that he had to go to the bathroom in his deep sleep, and so he'd wet himself. They would have to clean and change him before the ambulance arrived. Lilia brought clean underwear and clothes from upstairs and changed Arnie with Tamia's help. Arnie was trying to open his eyes a little so that he could help the women, but the sleep was much more powerful than his own will. It was heavier than anything he'd ever known, even his embarrassment. They lifted him up with difficulty and sat him on the armchair. Before Lilia had time to change the sheets, they heard the sound of the paramedics, who had just arrived. Before leaving the room to open the door, she turned to Tamia and said, 'Today is my birthday', without knowing why. She didn't wait for an answer and went straight to the front door.

The doctor told Lilia that there'd been another couple of blood clots in Arnie's brain. That was why he'd been sleeping all day long. Even though Lilia tried to understand what was being explained to her, she only heard a string of words following one another, nothing else. There was something about brain parts switching to sleep mode. They couldn't localise the blood clots. He might or might not go back to normal in time, and since he'd had more than three blood clots in the last five months they could expect him to have others. They couldn't know where this would end, but the blood clots would definitely affect his life depending on their size, intensity and location. There wasn't much they could do, other than wait. They didn't have any reason to keep him at the hospital, because they couldn't do anything, anyway. They simply prescribed bigger doses of blood thinners.

Lilia didn't know how to take Arnie back home. The nurse was going put him in a wheelchair and help him out of the hospital, but then they would be on their own. Lilia couldn't work out how she was going to manage to put him in a cab, then take him out of it, walk him to the house and carry him to his bed. She thought about calling one of the tenants, but decided not to pursue that thought. She didn't want to scare them away or introduce illness into their lives. She went to the information desk at the entrance and asked for the number of the taxi company they used. Maybe they'd agree to help her if she offered to pay them a bit more. She dialled the number and tried to explain what she needed to the first person she spoke to. Unfortunately, the man on the other end of the line didn't speak very good English and wasn't making much of an effort to do anything about it. Instead, he kept giving Lilia useless advice in his heavy Pakistani accent. If the patient wasn't conscious then he should stay at the hospital, he said, why was she trying to take him home? No, nobody at the taxi company would take responsibility for carrying a sick man. If they dropped him by accident, for example, God forbid, they'd be sued, wouldn't they? Lilia hung up the phone fuming with anger, unable to understand how the subject of a legal procedure had come up in the first place. How could a person end up feeling so lonely in such a populated country? She had memories of people helping each other back in the Philippines; people who helped each other without worrying about being accused of anything. Once again, she tried to remember why she'd come to the United States. Why did she stay here when she'd already realised that she wasn't going to achieve any of the things she'd dreamed about? She didn't need to call another taxi company; she knew that the answer would be the same. After looking grudgingly at the phone in her hand for a couple of minutes, she finally called Giang. Her son sounded reluctant, as if he didn't want to take this call.

'Is everything all right, Lilia?'

'No, we're at the hospital again. Arnie had a new blood clot in his brain. It looks like he's all right in general, but he can't stay awake for some reason. Still, they don't want him in the hospital. They say there's nothing they can do. But I can't take him home all by myself.'

'Did you call a taxi? They might help if you give them a good tip.'

Lilia couldn't stop the tears welling up. She didn't know what to feel saddest about: because she had to call her son, who hadn't even remembered her birthday, because she had to beg him for help or because he didn't want anything to do with her and her husband?

Lilia had looked deep into her heart many times to see whether she'd ever done the things her children blamed her for, or if she'd ever even considered doing any of those things. The answer was always 'no'. Lilia had adopted Dung and Giang purely because she'd wanted to, because she'd wanted to make a difference to somebody else's life outside of her own self. She'd only ever had good intentions and had never even thought about getting help from the government or any other kind of profit. If she'd ever suspected herself of having bad intentions then she wouldn't feel this heartbroken now and would simply say, 'What you give is what you get.' All the same, even at her darkest moments, when she felt the least proud of herself, she couldn't find herself guilty. She didn't know why she put up with all of the insults and hatred that came from her adopted children. Did saving someone's life mean having to protect it unconditionally for a whole lifetime? Was she going to feel responsible for them for ever, no matter what? She was struggling to stand up at the hospital entrance since her legs were shaking so much. So many emotions were passing through her mind at once, compressing every vein that led to her heart. She felt short of breath. That stranger who she called her son waited, silently, on the other end of the line, seeming to enjoy every minute of the tension that hung in the air. Finally, Lilia collected all of her strength and began to talk:

'You know what, Giang? Just forget it. Forget what I said. I'm never going to call you again and I don't want you to call me, either. I never want to see either of you ever again. You can tell this to your sister.'

And she hung up the phone. She was going to call their lawyer the next day, first thing in the morning. She would have them both removed from her will. It was time for this part of her life to come to an end; at least then she'd have control of one thing in her life. She wasn't going to let them linger at the corner of her thoughts, keeping her from sleeping at nights and injecting their venom into her heart every single day. Just as people in the old days used to drain dirty blood from their bodies to get rid of their illnesses, she should now stretch out her arm and give her own blood.

By the time they arrived home at the end of the day – with Tamia's help – it was already night-time. She might as well admit it; she'd hoped to find her tenants in the kitchen, crowding around a cake with candles on it. She couldn't deny that she'd thought the lights were off in the house because they were all going to shout 'Happy Birthday' as soon as she came in. She still hadn't given up hope when they walked into the kitchen. But it was no good. The house was dark because there was no one there. There wasn't a cake on the counter or waiting for her in the fridge. However long she waited, this day wasn't going to turn into a better one. As if she could only do one favour a day, Tamia didn't even say 'Happy Birthday' as she left, after getting paid for helping Lilia to bring Arnie home. In fact, Lilia had thought they'd become quite close after sharing a cup of coffee and brownies around the kitchen counter most days of the week. She'd thought there was some kind of a bond between them that could turn into friendship. When she went back to the kitchen after watching Tamia leave for a while, she saw the soufflé she'd left there that morning. It had been waiting on the same spot for her to come home. She walked to the storeroom, opened one of the cupboard doors and found the candles she'd put there years ago, looking as new as the day she'd bought them. She took one of them back to the kitchen, pressed it into the collapsed centre of the soufflé and lit it. She closed her eyes, held tightly onto the edge of the counter, made a wish and blew it out. After she'd eaten it all, she wrote a note on a big piece of paper listing all the food in the fridge, left it in the same spot as always and climbed up the stairs to her room. She wouldn't remember Arnie's dirty sheet until the next day: the second day of her sixty-third year.

Marc held his bleeding finger under the cold water, and waited. His hands had almost changed shape since he'd started cooking. If he didn't cut one of his fingers two or three times a week, he'd burn it with oil from the frying pan. He'd come to realise how important it was to put on an apron and why he couldn't work in a jumper with baggy sleeves. First he'd thought that he could just clean the stove once a week, but he'd soon realised that it was much harder to get the spots out that way, and so he'd started scraping away at the surface every day after washing the dishes.

After making sure that the bleeding had stopped, he turned off the water and put one of the plasters he kept in the basket on the table over his new cut. He went back to his cooking, his ear tuning in to the TV. He'd started leaving the gallery earlier in the evenings now. He needed time to do some grocery shopping and to cook whatever it was he'd bought. He was spending most of his time in the kitchen again, just like in the old days. Only, this time he had his own routines; different to the ones he'd had with Clara. As he carried on dicing the tomatoes, he tried to pay a little more attention to what he was doing. Six people on the show *On a Tout Essayé* were talking about new books, CDs and films, just as they did every day. He was beginning to realise that he'd never really followed what was going on before. It had always been Clara who had let him know about new things. He'd lived in his own little bubble for years and preferred to only hear about the things he was interested in. Cooking was changing the way he lived; quietly, without forcing or smothering him. He was gladly taking on a new shape in this new life. Now he wondered about the new singers. He realised that he'd started recognising some of the new songs and even whistling along to them. Only in recent months had he started thinking about what kind of a husband he'd been. What did Clara think about his detachment from everyday life? She couldn't have cared much since she'd never complained, but had she ever wished he was a different kind of man?

Just as he was about to cut his finger again, he saved it in the nick of time. This must be happening so often because the knife was so sharp. It was going to get blunt at some point, and maybe then he'd stop butchering himself. He added the chopped tomatoes to the lightly fried onions and garlic and mixed them all together. Now it was time for the mushrooms, squash, aubergine and peppers. He looked at the open page of the book at his side to see how he had to cut them. They should be in cubes; small cubes. Realising that it was going to take longer than he'd thought, he turned the heat right down on the stove. There was no way he could chop all that in such a short time. Maybe somebody else could, but not him. Today's dish, Ratatouille, came from the South. It was originally a dish made of leftover vegetables, especially in the summer. There was nothing special about it. Even the verb meant 'to mix together'. All the same, it had become really popular recently, especially after that animated film became so famous all over the world. According to the book, mushrooms had only been added to the dish in later versions.

Marc remembered that mushrooms hadn't been so common when he was a little boy. There was always the question of whether they were poisonous or not. There used to be announcements on the radio all the time, and then there were the lists and photographs of the poisonous kinds that used to hang on the walls of the town hall. All the same,

Marc used to feel scared every time he saw mushrooms on his plate and wondered if he was going to die while eating them. His mum would understand his fear and tell him where she'd got them and everything else he needed to know. But nobody thought about that any more. Just like everything else, mushrooms were standardised these days.

When he'd finished chopping all of the ingredients, he saw that the other ones in the pot weren't burnt and felt genuinely proud of himself. It looked like he was going to be able to cook this type of food without any accidents. If he didn't count his finger, that is. As well as the burns and cuts on his limbs, he'd caused the fire alarm to go off before. How was he supposed to know that the oil would burn so quickly? He was learning something new every day. He tried mixing all of the ingredients together, just like it said in the recipe, without them jumping out of the pot. The aubergine would start letting out its natural water in a couple of minutes, the book said, and the other vegetables would benefit from that. He kept mixing them together, trying not to mush the squash that had already softened up. He did this while listening to the song playing on the TV and remembering his childhood.

He hadn't thought much about his childhood before Clara died. Maybe that was because those years hadn't really come to an end. But now he found himself thinking about his mother and father at the strangest moments, without even realising it. He remembered the round table where they used to eat their dinner, the sofa they all used to sit down on together and the comic books they used to buy from the stands next to the Seine. He couldn't understand how he hadn't missed his parents or remembered those times more often before, even though he had such great memories. But now, as he listened to this song in this kitchen, trying not to mush the squash, he missed them. He missed all of them. He was learning how to miss. Tears welled up in his eyes despite the steam from the food that was hitting his forehead, with the beautiful song playing in the background, just when he was convinced that he'd managed to start life all over again. Once again he thought that he couldn't take it; that he couldn't go on living. He had no hesitations about talking to himself. He said to the kitchen's misty windows: 'I'll never be able to forget Clara. I'll never recover. I'll never be happy again.'

He also tried his first soufflé that night. He knew he wasn't going to be able to sleep until much later on. This was one of those days when he couldn't stop thinking about the past and he'd learned that there was no sleep for him on nights like that. He'd wanted to try the chocolate soufflé ever since the day he'd bought the book. He found the page for that recipe and took a look at it one more time. He took out all of the ingredients and put them on the table. At first glance, the soufflé recipe looked easier than many other desserts. So, how come it was one of the hardest to make? It was going to take him months to understand the reason for this. Over those months, he would try making chocolate soufflé over and over again, along with his other daily recipes. He was going to feel an emptiness in his chest every time the soufflé collapsed, but he wasn't going to give up; just as he continued living despite everything that had happened. On those days, when Marc worked late into the night, his pots and pans clinking and clanking around him, the residents of the apartments on the same landing couldn't help themselves taking a quick peek. They couldn't ignore the sounds coming from his window, which he kept ajar to let the air in. Through the open curtains, they witnessed how he slowly learned to put on an apron, how he sometimes danced to a song while cooking, how he cried from time to time as he stirred the food in the pot and how angry he got with the salt shaker when it poured out too much salt because of a problem with the hole. They witnessed how this quiet man, who had lived in his wife's shadow for so long, was building a new life for himself. While the men thought it was about time for Marc to bring a new woman back to the apartment, the women came to the window nervously, worrying that they might see someone new standing there. They'd always thought of Clara as a lucky woman, but they'd never imagined that they'd still think she was lucky after her death. Who else would mourn a woman this beautifully? Who else would shed this many tears?

Realising that he didn't have a mixer or a hand beater didn't stop Marc from trying the soufflé recipe. He only remembered now how his mother had beaten the mixture for the most delicious cakes using just a fork. He didn't know where all these images and memories had been hidden for so many years, but whenever he was in the kitchen he remembered something new from the past. Everything good or bad in his life had happened in that kitchen, ever since he was a very young boy. He remembered how his parents used to fight there sometimes. Then his father would come and hug his mother from behind; his mother would carry on stirring the food, keeping her cool, but then she she'd smile, which meant she forgave him.

He realised now that he'd lived his whole life in the same place, and it had revolved around the events that took place there; he'd never seen that before. Maybe he'd never cooked before but it looked as if he'd recorded both his mother's and Clara's movements somewhere at the back of his mind. Pausing for a couple of seconds, he added the mixer and hand beater to his ever-growing list and continued to beat the eggs with the fork. In this case, Marc's soufflé wouldn't even have the chance to rise, let alone collapse. If those eggs could speak, they'd tell him that he couldn't just stop beating them like that, go away and then come back. What's more, the speed and intensity of every beat of the fork was supposed to be exactly the same.

Marc decided that it was time to stop beating when he felt a cramp in his arm. He didn't know yet that he'd feel the same pain the next day. Even though he tried using his left hand for a couple of seconds, he soon gave up after making a big mess around him. As he poured the batter into his only soufflé mould and put it in the oven, he didn't hope for much. At the same time, he hadn't expected it to turn out quite that badly. The alarm on the oven went off while he was in the bathroom, and since he'd read that it was very important to take it out just at the right moment, he ran back to the kitchen with his hand on the fly of his trousers. In the end he didn't manage either to close his fly or to take the soufflé out on time. He was going to think this was the only mistake he'd made until the second attempt. But the next time he was going to open the oven door at exactly the moment he was told, and then he would finally understand that making soufflés was a lot harder than he'd thought.

Even though his attempt to make a soufflé had been a disaster, it had calmed Marc down, taken his mind off his sorrow and tired him out. After he'd waited long enough to take one bite from his dessert, Marc saw that it tasted as bad as it looked. Still, he was in no shape to care at that time of the night. He hung his apron on the back of the chair and went into the bedroom. He tasted the last bits of chocolate that were stuck to his palate and quickly fell asleep.

Sabina was helping a woman who was trying to find a new compact food processor to replace her old one which had broken. It looked like the woman had built some kind of personal relationship with the machine and couldn't forget their happy days together. Sabina couldn't convince her to try another one, even after explaining that the company didn't sell the same model any more but they had a newer version from the same brand and its performance was supposedly three times better than the old one. It wasn't as if she didn't understand how the woman felt. There were times when she'd grown so attached to her furniture or appliances that it was as if they were alive. Besides, she also found it hard to understand why companies felt like they had to stop producing a perfectly good product and release an updated version that didn't work quite like the old one. She had the same approach to almost everything in her life. If she liked a hand lotion, she'd hoard tons of it in her cupboard, she bought cases full of her favourite deodorant – since she knew they'd cancel it one day – and she took really good care of every last one of her dishes. She'd also had a food processor back in the day that she'd been smitten with, and when it broke she'd felt like she'd lost a cat. That was right before she moved from Lyon to Paris. It was almost as if all of her belongings had broken up with her, sensing that she was going to leave them. Her fridge had started shaking violently one day and then stopped working altogether. Her microwave had stopped heating anything for more than five seconds and the lever on her toaster had broken. Obviously, they'd all decided to dump her instead of being dumped. That's why she knew just how hard it would be to convince her customer. She saw Marc out of the corner of her eye just as she was telling the woman which food processor might be as good as the old one. She watched him standing still for a couple of minutes, rubbing his hands together, before walking towards one of the shelves and standing there without moving. The customer had sensed that her attention had wandered. She followed Sabina's eyes and turned in the direction in which she was looking. She knew how hard it was to find someone to help her in this huge place, especially someone as attentive as this young woman. Afraid of losing her, she finally decided on one of the processors. Could they check if it worked OK? She didn't want to have to come back if it didn't. She didn't live close by. Sabina agreed, happily, but kept following Marc with her eyes. She was scared that he'd leave.

Marc wasn't going anywhere. He was standing in front of the mixers, trying to understand how they were different from one another. He was going to wait patiently for Sabina to finish with her other customer. Picking one of those items was as hard as understanding quantum physics for him.

As Sabina took her time with the woman, he carried on wandering among the shelves. He saw so many things and he couldn't understand for the life of him what they were all for. There were some objects that he didn't recognise in the slightest. An egg-shaped bottle opener, an olive oil container which he thought was for sugar, a salt and pepper shaker which worked in some mysterious way that he couldn't figure out, a 'spork' which he didn't know what to do with, a teaspoon with an S-shaped handle, an eggcup which Marc wouldn't know was an eggcup if it didn't say so on the price tag. Just as he was examining a knife with big holes in it, he heard Sabina's voice behind him:

'That's a cheese knife.'

'Why does it have holes in it?'

'It's for soft cheeses. You know how soft cheeses stick to the knife when you cut them, and you have to scrape it off? Well, it's to stop that happening. The cheese comes out of the holes.'

'Hmm. I don't know how Clara missed this detail.'

Even though Marc had said the last sentence to himself, Sabina couldn't help but hear it. The young woman looked carefully at her customer, who was playing with the knife in his hand. She hesitated at first, but then she asked all the same:

'Is Clara your wife?'

This was the first time Marc had heard somebody else say his wife's name in months. He didn't know how to answer the question. Well, he knew, of course, but he couldn't bring himself to say it. He hadn't talked to anyone about Clara since she'd died. He hadn't had to say 'my ex-wife' to anybody yet. Or 'my deceased wife'. Whenever these words formed in his mind, he tried to push them back out. He wasn't denying the fact that Clara had died; he just wanted to forget that a woman called Clara had ever existed, or that she'd been his wife. He would never have expected to have to utter those words he'd been running away from for so long in the middle of a shopping centre – while he was holding a knife with holes in it and was surrounded by kitchen appliances. Sabina guessed from that long pause that she'd asked the wrong question. She was still curious, but she apologised and said that he didn't have to answer.

'No … It's OK … Clara … was my wife. We lost her five months ago.'

'I apologise, I shouldn't have asked. I'm so sorry for your loss.'

'Thank you.'

They stood there for a while, unable to say anything else or even look each other in the eyes. Sabina was fiddling with her hands while Marc was still playing with the knife. He was waiting for the knot in his throat to unravel so that he could speak again. Just as he was getting really desperate, Sabina spoke:

'What did you want to buy today?'

'A mixer.'

'There are so many kinds, right?'

'A lot. Why is that? If you didn't help me I couldn't buy anything.'

'I'm so happy that I can help.'

As Sabina told Marc which mixers would be best for him, she wondered if it would be too much to invite him out for a coffee. She didn't want to fall in love or be fallen in love with, but maybe she could take refuge in Marc's friendship in Paris, where she felt very lonely. She was going on her break soon and would go to the café around the corner to take a look at the newspapers left on the table by a previous customer, just as she always did. It was a very simple offer and completely unplanned, but she still couldn't find the courage to do it. She didn't want to have to deal with that strange silence again. Marc was clearly a gentleman who couldn't refuse a woman's offer, but she didn't want him to accept it just for that reason. Maybe later, she thought; maybe next time. She picked the mixer which best suited his needs and gave it to him. Meanwhile, Marc had picked up on Sabina's anxiety. Maybe she still felt bad about the question she'd asked. He wanted to say, 'It's not important', even though it was. He thought that this young woman, who made people feel good just by existing, shouldn't have to feel bad about anything. Marc really wanted to tell her how grateful he was, but he couldn't. Finally, he took his mixer and started walking towards the cashier so that he could put an end to this epic awkward moment, even if it meant giving up on the other things he wanted to buy. Before he turned away from her, he said:

'Thank you for your help. That's all I need for today. See you later.'

'See you later.'

Although she wanted to say more, she just waved as he walked away. She was already wondering when he would come back.

When Ferda couldn't take her mother's craziness any more, she would give her a couple more sleeping pills and take some time off. She'd soon got over the feeling of guilt she'd felt after the first couple of times she did this. Mrs Nesibe rarely knew what year it was, she didn't recognise her daughter or her son-in-law, she complained about them to everyone who came to visit and disturbed the neighbours with her screaming and shouting. After seeing her great-grandmother in that state, Naz had grown scared of her and had stopped visiting her beloved grandmother. One thing Ferda couldn't stand was not having her grandchildren around. Her grandson didn't understand what was happening but her granddaughter had a pretty good understanding of events. At one moment when her great-grandmother had lost her mind, Naz had asked Ferda what 'whore' meant.

'It's a very bad word, my darling. Don't ever use it.'

'But nana said it. She said you were a whore. What does that mean?'

'Don't even learn that word, honey, it's a bad word.'

'Are you a whore?'

'What did I just tell you? Didn't I just tell you not to use that word? I don't want to hear it again.'

'But what does it mean?'

'It means a bad woman.'

'How?'

Ferda really resented having to explain this word to Naz. This wasn't the kind of thing a grandmother wanted to teach her granddaughter.

'Well … like … there are some women … and those women … those women spend time with men for money.'

'To walk around with them?'

'Uhm … to walk around with them and … to … to … You know how men and women make babies together? You know that, right?'

'Yes, my mum told me. It's not only kissing. They lie down together and then –'

'Yes, darling, I know the rest. You don't need to tell me. Well, some women do that with some men they don't know for money.'

'Is that a bad thing?'

'Yes, it's a bad thing. Something they shouldn't do. Please forget about it now, OK?'

'So, did you do that?'

'Of course not, honey.'

'Then why did nana call you a whore?'

'Can you please forget that word, my little princess? Your nana can't think straight. She mixes everybody up. She doesn't know who we are sometimes.'

'She doesn't know who I am, either?'

'No.'

'But she really loves me. She gave me chocolate.'

'But she's very sick now.'

'Are you going to be sick like that? You're old, too.'

'I'm not that old yet. I hope I won't be like that, honey.'

'I'll take care of you, grandma.'

'I'm sure you will, honey. But I promise I won't be sick like this.'

God knows why, but whenever Mrs Nesibe fell outside of reality she accused her daughter of being a prostitute and her son-in-law of selling Ferda. She almost never called her daughter by her real name; sometimes she thought she was Fusun, and most of the time she blamed her for killing Fusun, who had died before Ferda was born. Knowing the truth didn't stop Ferda from having nightmares. On the nights when she didn't wake up to the sound of her mother screaming, she woke up breathless because of her terrifying dreams.

In many of them she slept with men she didn't know, and sometimes she choked a baby girl. It looked like her mother was going to drive her crazy, just as she'd done with herself. Ferda's face looked very tired, with deep lines that hadn't been there just a couple of months earlier. Back in the day, she used to look in the mirror and see the wrinkles around her eyes and lips as proof of her personal growth, and had even thought they made her more beautiful. Now, the deep vertical lines on her face made her look uglier. Every time she looked in the mirror, she realised that it had been a mistake to cut her hair short. She'd thought it would be easier to take care of, since there was no time for vanity any more. Unfortunately, her curly hair had no chance against the humidity of Istanbul and had puffed up in a most unstylish way.

She couldn't share any of her feelings with her husband. Sinan looked as if he was nearing the end of his patience. The only reason why he didn't say much about it was because he spent most of his time outside of the apartment. As for her son, he had his own life to deal with. Even though she wanted to talk to him to help her relax a little, she didn't want to bore him, either. Besides, didn't they say: 'Your son is your son until he gets married, but your daughter is your daughter until death do you part?' She knew that she'd live a happier life if she just accepted this fact. After all, one of the reasons for her mother's emotional collapse was this same thing: didn't she feel like she'd been abandoned by her precious son? Ferda's brother came to visit their mother once in a while, but he always had work to do, always had other responsibilities. One day he'd said: 'She doesn't even recognise us any more, so what's the difference?' Ferda couldn't believe her ears. She'd said: 'You have to come here for yourself. You need to see your mother, the woman who gave birth to you, as much as possible before she dies. It doesn't matter if she knows who you are or not. You know who she is.' Ferda knew there was no point in pushing it. Nothing she said could reach her brother. He was a pragmatic man. He'd become his job and approached every issue mathematically. Hadn't her mother been delighted when he'd got the job as a maths professor at the Istanbul Technical University? Well, now she was living with the consequences.

Although Ferda had really wanted to continue with her studies, she'd had to give up her dreams after secondary school. She'd taken care of her mother throughout her childhood and she'd been a mother to her younger brother during all those times when their mother was lying in bed. That's why she'd never been a good student at school and had realised at an early age that she had no chance of going to university. Getting married to Sinan was the best she could do. At least she'd married a man who loved her at a time when girls married not for love but because their parents wanted them to. She'd carried on taking care of her mother after she was married and even supported both Mrs Nesibe and her brother financially. She'd done everything in her power to help her brother go to university and stood by him so that he could have all the things she couldn't. Even though she sometimes wished that she'd been as determined for her own education as for her brother's, she was still proud of having chosen the best possible direction for herself.

That was why she'd never stood in the way of her own daughter. She thought that Öykü should do whatever she wanted in this life. And she did. Although her heart had broken when Öykü told her she was moving abroad, she hadn't objected or tried to change her mind. Maybe she'd suffered for months afterwards, but her daughter was happy and that was the most important thing. Öykü had told her she was coming to visit them very soon in their last conversation. Although Ferda wanted to see her daughter and needed her support, she didn't want her to have to see her grandmother like that. She shouldn't have to wake up in the middle of the night to the sound of screams or see the ugliness in this house. All the same, there was nothing she could do to stop her from coming. She preferred to focus on the positive and look forward to seeing her daughter rather than thinking about the bad things that might happen.

She'd already started thinking about the menu. She always made sure she had everything Öykü liked on the day she arrived. In the days before Öykü came home, she spent hours working in the kitchen and had everything ready from *borek* to strawberry shortcake, from artichoke hearts to stuffed vine leaves. Watching her children wolfing down her food was maybe one of the things she enjoyed most in this life. Thank

God they loved food. Not even a burnt rice *pilaf* had ever been wasted in their house.

She picked up the crystal Benedictine bottle, which usually stayed on the console table at all times, and poured some into one of the tiny matching glasses. She hadn't even had a sip of it in a very long time. In fact, she'd learned to deprive herself of many of the world's delicacies. It had been a while since she'd touched a piece of chocolate, had some creamy Turkish Feta or drunk a glass of wine. She picked up her glass of Benedictine and sat at the kitchen table. She opened her notepad, turned to a blank page and started writing. Seasoned cranberry beans, stuffed vine leaves, artichoke, courgette pâté, cinnamon lamb stew, stuffed peppers, aubergine *borek*, strawberry shortcake. 'Or maybe chocolate soufflé,' she said to herself. She knew how much Öykü would like it. First she considered crossing out the strawberry shortcake with her pencil, but then she decided not to. Her daughter always said that she'd never had a cake as delicious as hers, although once she'd come close to it in New York at one of the most famous cafés in the city. Ferda couldn't ignore this compliment. She'd have to bake them both. As she turned her back to the last rays of sunlight, she thought how much she missed the serenity of her former life. In fact, it was a part of a lifelong longing for peace. She'd never experienced absolute freedom, never known what it was like to live without responsibilities. She'd always thought that she'd have more time for herself when her children were grown up. She'd always imagined that her mother would die of old age in her sleep, and that she'd cry for a little while but then get on with her own life. Instead, her mother's plans had come first, as always. For a couple of seconds, she pictured the day of Mrs Nesibe's death. Even though she felt awfully guilty about it, she'd been catching herself dreaming about that day more and more often lately. She was fifty-eight years old and liked to think she could have her sixties and the rest of her life all to herself.

She knew that her mother would wake up very soon. She'd probably be hungry and accuse her of trying to kill her by starving her to death. Before that could happen, she put some water in the pan for some pasta. Pasta with cheese always had a calming effect on Mrs Nesibe.

Ferda had managed to prepare everything on her list despite all the trouble her mother had caused. She kept going back to the kitchen every five minutes and checked time and time again that she hadn't forgotten anything. The *borek* was already in the oven. It was going to be at the perfect temperature when Öykü got home. The strawberry shortcake had been in the fridge since the night before, just as she'd planned. The vine leaves had soaked up the olive oil beautifully and now took their place on the kitchen counter. At almost the last minute, she'd decided to stuff some artichoke leaves as well as the hearts, even though it had meant spending an extra hour on her feet. She was sure that Cem was going to drool over them. Since her grandchildren loved it like that, she'd let the edges of the courgette pâté fry a little longer than usual, and had told the butcher to leave the fat on the lamb to make Sinan happy. Mrs Nesibe had followed the frantic preparations in the house when she hadn't cut her ties with reality and kept making sarcastic remarks. 'Oh, go on, get ready for your daughter. They're going to give you a medal.' Ferda found this very hurtful, because she knew this was her mother's way of saying that she herself had never got a medal for the things she'd done. 'Did you make artichoke leaves for your son, too? Yes, yes do it. You're going to get the elbow from him one of these days.' Ferda had never liked this peculiar gesture her mother sometimes made. She held her right wrist with her left hand and stuck her right elbow out to the audience. Mrs Nesibe thought that everybody was going to be betrayed one day, and she called this 'to get the elbow'. Sinan was the only person she didn't criticise when she was in her right mind. Sinan was her hero. Her best investment, her best decision. Her son-in-law had never given her the elbow. But if Ferda carried on walking around with hair like that, she was going to get it from her husband. She kept giving her daughter advice, saying, 'Take care of yourself a little, be beautiful for your husband', but seemed to forget that Ferda spent most of her time changing adult nappies.

Mrs Nesibe was shockingly and completely herself the day Öykü was due to arrive. Maybe she'd forced herself to be on her best behaviour since her granddaughter was coming to see her from so far away. Ferda had always envied that special relationship between them. Her mother and daughter would shut themselves away in a room together, speaking quietly and giggling for hours on end. Ferda had always been curious about where Öykü found that sense of humour in her grandmother; something that Ferda could never spot. She wanted to know exactly what was funny about her mother. Öykü called her grandmother 'rare Indian fabric'. Hearing this, Ferda wanted to say, 'You don't say. She's definitely one of a kind.' Every ten minutes, Mrs Nesibe called out to Ferda from her room:

'Ferda! Isn't she here yet?'

'No, mum, you'd know about it if she was here.'

'So the plane hasn't landed yet? You should call her.'

'I called her a minute ago. Her mobile's still switched off. Maybe there was a delay.'

'I hope she gets here safely. Didn't a plane crash a couple of weeks ago in Diyarbakir?'

'For God's sake, mum! You're like an owl, always bringing bad news. How can you say such a thing at a time like this?'

They'd got used to shouting from one room to another like that. When they didn't understand each other because another voice was interrupting theirs they simply carried on yelling, but this usually annoyed them and then they ended up really shouting at each other. When Sinan was at home, he was usually glued to the TV in the living room at the back of the apartment with the big Bose earphones on his head – a treat Cem had got for his father on a recent trip to the United States – and he didn't hear a thing.

'So, what did you make?'

'Oh, you know, everything Öykü likes. And Cem's artichokes.'

'What did you make for me?'

'Mum, you eat whatever we eat, right? But I made the cinnamon lamb, just the way you like it.'

'I hope you didn't make the butcher clean off the fat.'

'No, I didn't.'

'Good. How did you cook it? Tell me.'

'Same as every time I make it.'

'So, you sautéed the meat with onions first …'

'Yes.'

'Then you added the cinnamon.'

'No, I put the potatoes in first, and I added the cinnamon after that.'

'You did it wrong then.'

Suddenly furious, Ferda found herself standing at her mother's door. Mrs Nesibe always found something to criticise about her daughter's cooking. Either the ingredients or the time or the amount was always wrong. And whenever anybody – including her daughter – asked her for a recipe, she always left out one of the ingredients. She never wanted anyone to be able to cook like her.

'Mum, haven't we been cooking this recipe like this for years?'

'I don't cook it like that. I guess you've been doing it wrong all along.'

'Really? That's strange, because you eat it every time without complaining.'

'Well, I didn't say it wasn't delicious. Only the method is wrong. Did you make rice *pilaf*?'

'No, I'm going to make it right at the end. But I put the rice in water.'

'Well, cook it now, so it can rest a little before we eat. It tastes better that way.'

'It looks like you're feeling yourself today, mum.'

'What does that mean?'

'Nothing. I'm happy for you.'

Her mother's comments always got under her skin. Despite much she tried not to notice and not to care, she did. Even though she knew her mother was crazy, she still wanted her approval. A simple remark from her could bother Ferda for hours, sometimes days. She dialled Cem's number and waited for him to answer.

'Yes, mum.'

'Cem, can you check online to see if Öykü's plane has landed? Is there a delay? Take a look, and then call me back.'

'Hold on, don't hang up. I'm at my desk, I'll check it right away. When was her flight?'

'Half past one from there.'

'There was no delay. But it doesn't show whether it's landed yet or not.'

'But then it must have landed.'

'That's true. Maybe it has.'

'Well, I've been calling her but she isn't answering.'

'Maybe they're waiting on the runway.'

'OK. I'll call the airport.'

'Why are you worrying? Just relax, she'll be here soon. I'm going to leave the office soon, too. I'll go home, pick everybody up and come over to yours. We'll be there in two hours.'

'OK, darling, see you soon.'

'What did you cook?'

'You'll see when you get here.'

'Are there artichokes?'

'Hmm, I don't know about that … '

Ferda dialled the airport as soon as she'd hung up with her son. When she reached 'arrivals/departures' by pressing the numbers as instructed by a mechanical voice, she couldn't find out any more than she already knew. The voice said the arrival was scheduled for half past five that evening, but didn't say if it had landed or not. It was now a quarter to six. Öykü should have left the airport by now. She waited until the end of the recording and started to dial again, trying to reach customer services. The music that was playing while she waited – as the second customer in a queue – reminded her of the old days of television. It was the same tune that used to play between programmes while an image of a pitcher filled the screen. Sinan must have been worried too, as he'd finally taken off his earphones and come to stand next to Ferda.

'Who are you calling?'

'The airport.'

'Has it landed?'

'I don't know. I'm waiting for a customer representative. Try calling Öykü again.'

Sinan dialled his daughter's number from his mobile and waited. After the voicemail greeting in both French and Turkish, he left a message saying, 'Call us as soon as you can.' He was trying to hide his anxiety to stop his wife from getting more nervous than she already was. With his hands in his pockets and his eyes on Ferda, he stood next to his wife. It wasn't possible to ignore the rumbling sound coming from Ferda's stomach. Her bowels always reacted very quickly to any kind of worry. After waiting for a couple more minutes, writhing in pain, she finally passed the phone to Sinan and ran to the bathroom. It had been more than the estimated waiting time and there was still no sign of a customer representative. Mrs Nesibe was following all of the phone calls that were happening right outside her room from where she lay in her bed.

'The plane hasn't landed yet?'

'I don't know. Nobody's picked up the phone yet.'

'What time was it supposed to arrive?'

'At five.'

'It's gone half past now.'

'Let's wait and see.'

'Where's Ferda?'

'In the bathroom.'

'Is it her bowels again?'

'Yes.'

'I'm sure she'll get a migraine attack, too.'

Before he could answer his mother-in-law, Sinan heard a human voice on the other end of the line. The flight from Paris hadn't landed yet. No, there hadn't been a delay. They didn't know why yet. They could help him if he called back a little bit later. Sinan couldn't help raising his voice and saying that he didn't want to have to hold for that long again when he called back ten minutes later. There was nothing they could do, said the voice. They apologised for any inconvenience they had caused, but they couldn't help him just yet. Sinan hung up the phone, angrily, not knowing how he was going to explain this to his wife. Ferda had run out of the bathroom and was looking curiously at Sinan, her hand still on the fly of her trousers. Her mother started talking before she could say a word:

'What did they say?'

'They don't know anything.'

'So the plane hasn't landed?'

Sinan looked at his wife, nervously, wishing that his mother-in-law would stop talking. His wife nodded at him, waiting for an answer.

'No, it hasn't landed.'

'Was there a delay on departure?'

'No, it left on time.'

Ferda steadied herself on the door frame, as if she was about to faint. Sinan acted quickly, putting his wife's arm around his shoulder and holding her before she collapsed. He tried to explain the situation both to himself and to the women of the house, saying: 'They probably kept it circling in the air because of the traffic.' All the same, he couldn't figure out why the customer representative wouldn't give him this type of information. Ferda almost had a heart attack when Mrs Nesibe said, sobbing: 'What if terrorists hijacked the plane? Please watch over our daughter, God.' Sinan knew what he had to do. He ran to the kitchen, mixed together some yoghurt, water and salt, grabbed a bottle of club soda and ran back to the corridor where his wife was sitting. He helped her drink the *ayran* first, and then the soda. As he waited for her to recover, with her head resting on his knee, he tried to ignore the pain in his heart.

The mystery of Öykü's flight would only be solved later that evening, when TV crews arrived at the airport and started following the TK 4 flight, which was still circling in the air. Ferda had sat in an armchair in front of the TV and was looking in disbelief at the plane in which her daughter was flying, with one hand to her mouth and tears on her cheeks. Her husband had stabilised her blood pressure with his quick intervention, but she still looked like a wreck. Sinan wasn't in much better shape. He had secretly popped a pill under his tongue and was trying to look calm. Mrs Nesibe was following the news on the TV in her room. Cem was glued to the screen with his wife and children at home, watching the report as he held the phone with his mother on the other end of the line. He kept repeating that there was nothing to be afraid of, that they would jump out with parachutes in the worst-case scenario. 'I don't know about the others,' he said, 'but I'm sure Öykü could manage it.' When he realised that these words were scaring his mother more than comforting her, he tried another tactic: 'But don't worry, mum, nobody will have to jump. The pilots will land this plane.' Mrs Nesibe was saying, 'What a pity! What a pity!' over and over again. When Ferda couldn't take it any more, she yelled at her mother, 'Mum, stop it! Please stop moaning, for God's sake!'

'Oh God … oh God … do I have to see this before I die? My only granddaughter. Send her back to me in one piece, please God.'

Ferda dug her nails into her face and slid them down her cheeks. Her sadness was vying with her anger, but she didn't even want to leave the screen for two seconds to go to her mother's room. She didn't want to take her eyes off that plane, not for one second. Right at that moment, the screen divided into two and a TV presenter appeared on its right-hand side. They had finally received some new information from the Turkish Airlines authorities. According to their original statement, the front wheels of the Boeing 737 were unable to come down and therefore the airport was trying to secure the runway for an emergency landing. However, the new information clarified that only two of the plane's three wheels would come down – the one at the front and the one on the right – and the pilots were going to attempt to land on them. Precautions were being taken on the runway and first aid officers were on standby. The plane had been circling for an hour in order to secure the area and arrange the air traffic accordingly. A flight expert, an old air force pilot, was explaining how difficult this type of landing really was. If they'd had to land the plane using only the back wheels it wouldn't be so hard, but a landing depending only on the front and one side wheel could potentially cause all kinds of accidents since it could easily throw the plane off balance. The wind level also had an important role to play.

Ferda started sobbing. Cem had sunken into silence on the phone and couldn't find anything to say. He was trying so hard to deal with his own feelings that he couldn't think how to calm his mother down. Sinan went to the kitchen to pop another pill under his tongue, trying to hide his ever-paler face. As he walked back to the living room with a glass of water in his hand, he stopped to check on his mother-in-law. Mrs Nesibe was trying to dry the tears on her cheeks. Sinan kept on walking and gave the water to Ferda. 'Don't worry, they're going to land this plane,' he said. 'Get a hold of yourself. I think we should go to the airport.'

Ferda had thought they should go to the airport from the beginning, but now she couldn't drag herself away from the TV. She had to see her daughter reach the ground, safe and sound, with her own eyes. 'Cem, go and pick up your sister,' she said on the phone and continued, 'I can't go anywhere and I can't send your father, either.' Cem already had his car keys in his hand. He hung up the phone, after telling his mother to stay calm one more time.

Ferda had moved from where she'd been sitting and was now on the floor, closer to the TV. She felt as if the closer she got to the screen, the more effective her prayers would be. The cameras showed the ambulances and fire engines waiting at the side of the runway. When they went back to the plane, they showed that it had left the circle it had been drawing and had started flying away. The cameras zoomed in to get a better idea of what was happening. Then the plane made a U-turn, swerving to the left, and started heading back towards the cameras. Now they were face to face with it. As it came closer to the screen, another camera took over and shot it from the side. After describing all of these small manoeuvres, the presenter went completely silent and watched, as millions of people were doing in front of their TV screens. When the plane began its descent, the old air force pilot made his final comment: 'Now there's nothing else we can do. Let's all pray.' The landing gear opened: one in the front, one on the right. When it came very close to the runway, Ferda held her breath. She touched the plane on the screen for a second and then pulled her hand back quickly. When the wheels touched the ground, the left wing almost hit the runway too. This must have been the balance issue the expert had been talking about. The minute the captain understood it wasn't going to work, he raised the nose of the plane again. After hopping on the wheels a couple of times, it took off once more. Ferda was terrified, because until that moment she'd been hopeful and hadn't realised quite how dangerous this really was. The expert started talking again. He was telling the audience that the pilot was going to circle one more time and then try again. 'This was the difficulty I was talking about,' he said. 'If the left wing had low friction with the ground, this could start a fire and cause serious damage. Alternatively, the plane could lose its balance and flip over on its side.' Finally, the presenter realised that the passengers' families might be watching and warned the expert not to cause any panic. Ferda was already on the brink of losing her mind. Sinan, on the other hand, kept pacing between the window and the balcony door. They had all forgotten about each other in the apartment. The cameras started following the plane closely as it made its way towards the runway once again. Ferda was rocking back and forth where she sat, hanging on to the last scraps of her sanity. Now the wheels touched the ground. Since the pilot had tilted the plane to the right a little before landing, the left wing didn't come as close to the ground as it had before, but still it lurched wildly. Instead of rising up again, the pilot reduced the speed and tried to draw the plane to a halt despite the sparks caused by the friction. The fire engines which were driving parallel to the plane backed up when it started hurtling along the ground. When it finally stopped diagonally on the runway, four fire engines drove quickly towards it and started foaming the area. Two minutes later, the doors of the plane opened and all of the passengers exited using the evacuation slides. Öykü was one of them. Instead of running like all the others did, she turned to the cameras she'd spotted and waved. She didn't know if they could see who it was from that far away, but still she waved with tears running down her cheeks and a big smile on her face. The cameras, of course, were not about to miss this shot. Ferda knew that it was her daughter despite the blurry image. As she cried and laughed at the same time, she heard her mother's voice:

'Ferda! Isn't that Öykü waving?'

'Yes, mum.'

'She's a nutcase.'

Driving home in her brother's car, Öykü kept wondering how she was going to break the news to her family. She'd forgotten the speech she'd prepared during the flight thanks to all that commotion. Her concentration level had been pretty low at that particular moment. Even though she hadn't been overly scared, she couldn't stop shaking. She was glad that it was only her brother who had come to pick her up. This bought her some time. Cem, on the other hand, thought it must be the trauma that was causing his sister to be so unusually silent and couldn't begin to guess what she was thinking.

'Smoke a cigarette if you want.'

'Why?'

'I don't know. It's supposed to calm you down.'

'I'm calm already. Anyway, it makes me nauseous.'

She felt herself relax as she spoke. Whenever she came back to Turkey, she realised what a pressure it was not to be able to speak in her mother tongue most of the time. People couldn't argue properly in other languages if they weren't native speakers. They couldn't stand up for the things they usually would, couldn't show enough love or sympathy and couldn't even swear properly. She'd only recently got used to speaking without using adjectives of endearment. In Turkish, the simple addition of the letters '-cim' or '-cum' to names showed just how dearly people were loved. It was painful for her not to be able to address the man she loved in that way. Another word she loved was 'brother'. In their language, people called their elder brothers and sisters not by their first names but using the words 'brother' and 'sister'. She pitied the French, who didn't know how intimate that feeling was. Could they really be so close to each other without having these words in their lives?

'How's grandma?'

'Not good. I hope mum won't lose it before she dies.'

'That bad, huh?'

'The other day the next-door neighbour visits mum, right? She says she wants to say hi to grandma. The nutcase starts screaming. She says, "You whore, aren't you ashamed to be the mistress of a married man?" She thinks grandpa is cheating on her with the next-door neighbour. She tells the whole story, too. How she caught them in bed together. How the neighbour sweet-talked grandpa, how she wrote letters to seduce him. She says he pays her. He actually rented her apartment for her. The neighbour leaves so fast that mum doesn't even see her go. But mum relaxed a bit after that. She says at least now they'll understand that grandma makes everything up. Because you know she tells everybody that dad is mum's pimp.'

'She's always been crazy. But have you noticed that she only comes up with these obscene fantasies?'

'I know. It looks like her subconscious is pretty pulp fiction. Prostitution, theft, murder ... everything's there. Our very own Agatha Christie. I tell mum not to care and to try to ignore it.'

'Yeah, right, because she can really do that. She threw a whole pot of *asure* away just because grandma said it wasn't good enough. You know what, forget I said this. Every woman becomes their mother in the end.'

'You aren't like mum.'

'Mothers are like time bombs inside their daughters. They're going to blow up sooner or later.'

Cem laughed, while his sister gazed at the streets outside the window.

'God, this neighbourhood looks awful.'

'Well, it's not Paris.'

The moment she saw her daughter at the door, Ferda started crying again. Öykü couldn't react much since she wouldn't fully understand how big an incident it had been until she'd seen the landing repeated many times on TV. The only thing she knew for sure was that there couldn't have been a better time for her to say what she'd come there to say. Everybody was so happy to see her alive and well that they wouldn't care about anything else. The dining table in the living room and the counter that separated the kitchen from the living room were covered with all kinds of food. Before even taking off her coat, she popped one of the stuffed vine leaves into her mouth. A piece of *borek* followed it. Ferda was glad to see that her daughter hadn't lost her appetite. In fact, she seemed to love food more than ever, because she wolfed down another piece of *borek* before she'd even finished the first. Mrs Nesibe started sobbing as soon as she saw her granddaughter appear at her bedroom door. She said that she'd been scared and sad and she didn't want her to go back to France. She wanted her to stay there with them and take care of her grandmother. Hadn't she promised when she was a little girl that she would take care of her grandma? Öykü sat on the floor, right next to her grandmother's bed, and listened patiently to every detail of every little pain in her body as she ate the food her mother had given her on a plate. All the other members of the family had piled into the tiny room, too, and the ones who didn't fit stood outside the door. It was Naz who couldn't wait any longer and finally asked, 'Tell us, aunt, what happened in the plane?' Öykü started telling the story from the beginning. When she described the applause in the plane at the moment when it finally stopped, the kids started applauding frantically, too. As they all moved to the living room to start the dinner, Öykü felt that the time was coming. She could wait until the next day, but it would be better when everybody was there and the air was filled with festivity. Just when her father was about to fill the wine glass in front of her, Öykü put her hand over it. Sinan looked at his daughter, surprised. She'd never said no to wine before. Öykü started talking in a slightly louder voice than usual, trying to catch everybody's attention: 'I'd prefer not to drink wine today, dad.' She continued hesitantly, 'Because ...'

Ferda knew why. She'd known it the moment her daughter had walked in, the moment she'd had the first stuffed vine leaf. She knew it from the glow on Öykü's face despite everything she'd gone through. She was sure. Even though she hoped not to hear what she expected, she was sure of what the following sentence would be. Praying that Sinan's heart could take one more blow on top of all the excitement it had experienced that day, she waited for her daughter to complete her sentence.

Öykü cleared her throat and continued: 'Because I'm pregnant.' Realising that only her father seemed surprised, she turned to him and said: 'I've been seeing a guy for the last year. His name is Duval. We've been thinking about getting serious. Actually, I was going to bring him here to introduce him to you. But I found out that I'm pregnant in the meantime. We want to get married right away. After you've met him, of course.' When nobody reacted one way or another, she continued, anxiously: 'He was going to come with me, but I decided that I should tell you alone. That's why he didn't come this time.' This news, which would be welcomed joyfully under normal circumstances, buried the whole dining table in silence. Everybody waited to see what Sinan's reaction was going to be. Sinan had known all along that his daughter was going to end up marrying a French man and he had no objection to that. Still, that didn't mean he'd never wondered what he was going to do with a son-in-law whom he couldn't talk to, play backgammon with or sit with at a *raki* table for hours. As for the pregnancy, he couldn't do anything about it, could he? It didn't matter whether he was angry or not; his daughter was pregnant. Under these circumstances, it helped that Öykü lived in France. It meant that they wouldn't have to explain anything to anybody. That was, of course, if they got married right away. After collecting his thoughts, he asked, 'When are you going to get married, exactly?' The calm in his voice surprised everybody. Even though Öykü was taken aback that she hadn't been congratulated by anyone yet, she decided to deal with her disappointment another time, since things were actually going better than she'd expected.

'Right away.'

'Where?'

'Well, I thought it wouldn't matter whether it's here or

there. We'll just get married at a town hall. I don't want to make a big deal out of it.'

Ferda suddenly cut in, almost shouting: 'That won't work! I only have one daughter and I want to see her in a wedding gown. Why should we be embarrassed?'

Öykü couldn't help a big smile spreading across her face. Seeing her daughter smiling like that, Ferda once again couldn't fight back the tears, and stood up to hug her. Cem broke the silence that had lasted far too long, and stretched out his hand with a glass of *raki* in it, making a toast: 'To my new brother, Duval, and the new grandchild, then.' As they all drank to celebrate, they heard Mrs Nesibe's voice from inside her room, saying: 'What's going on in there? Who's the new brother and the new grandchild?'

Eight

Each time the centre of the soufflé collapsed, Lilia saw her own life falling apart. No matter how much she tried to go on living, the centre of her soul would collapse all of a sudden and her life fall to pieces around her. Her own ups and downs weren't so different from those of this legendary dessert. Whenever she felt just a tiny bit happier, sorrow came knocking on her door again. And whenever she felt that she couldn't go on, she found a new strength – which came out of nowhere – to fight back. A single event could cause her to feel many different things in one day. She pitied Arnie one moment and then hated him the next. She was inspired by a look from Flavio and then fell into complete despair. One minute she thought her life wasn't so different from other people's, but then she thought it was more dramatic that anybody else's the next.

Although she'd almost mastered the ability to break the promises she made to herself, she'd called their lawyer the day after bringing Arnie home and made an appointment to talk about a very important issue. When she went to Manhattan two days later, she was in much better shape than she had been the previous time. She'd combed her hair very carefully, ironed her outfit and hadn't forgotten to put on her pearls. She looked at herself carefully in the window of Rite Aid in Grand Central Station when she got off the train. She only kept on walking when she was convinced that she didn't look too bad. Their lawyer's office was on the twenty-second floor of a high rise building at the corner of twenty-eight and Park Avenue South. Everything looked too industrial, the employees' suits were way too sharp and the receptionist was a little too rude. She hadn't been here since the days when she used to come with Arnie many years ago. After a while, she'd simply signed the papers Arnie brought home with him whenever her signature was needed and had been glad that she wasn't expected to go to the city any more. The power of attorney she'd given to Arnie had helped her live her life without having to take care of those things. The truth was, Lilia had known that she wouldn't end up going to see the lawyer if they didn't give her an appointment right away, as she knew her anger would just vanish in time. That's why she'd struggled with her feelings while she'd waited on the phone for the secretary to give her an appointment. She'd hoped they would give her one soon on the one hand, but also hoped to get one much later on the other.

She was thinking that she'd done well as she flicked through one of the magazines she'd picked up from the fan-shaped design on the coffee table. It must have been the right decision since neither her son or daughter had called to say they were sorry after what had happened. This was because they knew Lilia very well. Giang had called his sister right after hanging up with Lilia and told her all about their conversation, using her exact words. He'd asked Dung for advice, since he knew she was always cool-headed and knew how to approach subjects with a much-needed distance. Dung smiled and asked her brother: 'Do you really believe Lilia won't talk to us ever again? She'll forget what she got cross about after a couple of days. Besides, what else does she have in her life? Who else is there? She should be happy that we go there once a year.' All the same, there was something else on Giang's mind. He didn't know how often his sister asked Arnie and Lilia for money, but he'd always found a cheque in the post box whenever he needed help. He was worried that they'd stop doing this, what with Arnie being sick and everything. Whenever he felt under pressure thinking about his responsibilities – a house, two cars, the loans he'd taken out in order to have the kind of life he'd built for his family – the idea of inheriting some money from Lilia and Arnie always calmed him down. With some hesitation, he raised this issue: 'What if they write us out of their will?' Dung had laughed at this, too, saying: 'Giang, you really take Lilia far too seriously. First of all, she's so lazy that she'll never get round to taking care of those things. And second of all, Arnie would never let her.' Giang thought his sister was right, as always. There was no way that Lilia would act on their short conversation. Besides, she couldn't do anything as long as Arnie didn't give his permission. And when he died, they would divide everything in three ways. Even though Giang didn't really think that Arnie and Lilia had adopted them to get money from the government as Dung did, they'd talked about this subject so many times and with so much conviction that he'd made himself believe it in the end. That was why his anger towards the couple had grown sharper every time Dung had said: 'They saved the money they made from us in their bank account.' Besides, if there was no truth in their allegations, would they really be so forgiving? Would they really keep sending money to them after everything that had happened?

Just when Lilia had finished reading about the very messy divorce of a very famous couple in *US Weekly*, their lawyer came out to greet her. She was surprised to see how young that man still looked after so many years. There wasn't a trace of those twenty years on Benjamin's clean-shaven face. Only the hair above his ears had got a little greyer and his forehead had widened slightly. Apart from that, it was obvious that he'd followed a healthy diet and exercised regularly. Benjamin, on the other hand, was shocked to see how this woman – who had once mesmerised everyone with her exotic beauty – had aged so badly. She looked like one of those women who let themselves go with the flow of life outside the city. He was sure she'd spruced herself up before coming to Manhattan, but she just didn't have that spark of vanity any more, which she'd carried so successfully back in the day.

Their lawyer didn't know anything about the events of the last five months. He didn't know that Arnie had experienced internal bleeding, that they'd ended up at the hospital several times, that Arnie now lived a very limited life, or that Lilia had been taking care of him. Benjamin listened to that story with genuine grief. Even though he hadn't always supported the decisions they'd made, he'd always respected Arnie and Lilia for their courage. They'd been the first followers of the adoption rush. According to his records, the couple owned two houses, which were worth around $500,000 in total. They should still have savings of $12,000 thanks to Arnie's monthly salary of $6,000. Their children had grown up and shouldn't need their support any more. But, of course, according to what Lilia was telling him this was no longer the case. Their savings had been wiped out thanks to Arnie's hospital expenses. His pension was less than half of what he'd made before and most of it was spent on the physiotherapy he received three days a week. The estate tax payment was just around the corner and Lilia didn't know how they were going to deal with that just yet. They had rented five rooms in their house, and they made $400 from each of them, which was tax-free. That made $2,000 a month, but most of that money went on groceries and other basic needs. Just as Benjamin could tell her that they needed an accountant instead of a lawyer, his client explained why she was there. She wanted their adopted children to be taken out of their will. She didn't want them to get a single penny after they died.

Benjamin leaned back in his chair and crossed his legs. He brought his index fingers together and drew them to his lips. He didn't know whether to be glad to see that he'd been right in his predictions. Most of all he was wondering how he was going to explain the situation to this woman without hurting her even more.

'Lilia, I really understand your concern, but we need to know what Arnie thinks about this first and foremost. What does he think?'

'I think you know Arnie more or less by now. He doesn't think there's a problem. He thinks it's fine that they come to visit us once a year, never call and hurt and blame me every chance they get. But he doesn't realise what's been going on since he's been sick. We don't get any support from these people whom we call our children. Don't get me wrong, I'm not talking about financial support.'

Lilia felt like she had to tell her lawyer about the last conversation she'd had with her son.

'Arnie doesn't know anything about this conversation. He isn't in any condition either to listen to it or understand it at the moment, anyway. But I'm pretty sure he'd react differently to me if he knew. He thinks that people have separate lives and nobody has to do anyone any favours. But he's missing the point. I'm sixty-three years old and I'm the one who does everything in that house. I know that Arnie wouldn't agree to leave them out of our will. But at least I don't want to give them my part.'

'What do you mean, your part?'

'My part. Since we share the assets. I don't want them to have my part of it.'

'Lilia, you don't share your assets.'

'What do you mean?'

'Both of your houses and the money in the bank – well, you've spent that already – belong to Arnie. And, according to the contract signed by yourself, you don't get anything, for example, in the case of a divorce. And in the case of Arnie's death, the three of you share everything equally.'

'According to the contract I signed?'

'Yes.'

'When?'

'Uhm … give me a minute.'

Benjamin flicked through some pages in the file he had in front of him and said:

'Thirteen years ago.'

'What contract? I don't remember such a thing. I signed some papers from time to time but I don't remember anything like that.'

Benjamin looked at Lilia, sadly. He was surprised once more to see how old she looked.

Lilia had a very hard time walking back to the train station. The brightness of the sun blinded her and blurred her thinking. It had been a long time since she'd last seen the brighter face of Manhattan. Whenever the sun shined like that, the city's flaws became much more visible.

When she arrived at Grand Central, she bought herself a cup of coffee from Starbucks and sunk into one of the leather armchairs downstairs instead of taking the first train home. She knew that she had to go home as soon as possible. Arnie shouldn't be left alone any longer than he already had. Arnie – who had no hesitation in taking everything she had away from her. Why had he made a plan like this, and when? The lawyer had said that everything Arnie was going to inherit from his mother was also included in that agreement. Eighty-eight-year-old Daniela Nied lived in Florida and didn't know about her son's condition. Arnie had talked to his mother a couple of times and complained about how busy he was with work. Mrs Nied was just like her son. She didn't think Arnie should go and visit her. When they saw each other – once a year or maybe even once every two years – they always hugged very loosely and usually kissed the air over each other's shoulders instead of their cheeks. Even though Lilia had found this way of showing affection very strange, she'd got used to it in time. Daniela Nied was going to leave her son a house and some money in the bank and now Lilia knew that she wasn't a part of that, either. She thought about all the cards she'd sent to her mother-in-law on Christmases, Thanksgivings, Mother's Days and her birthdays every year. She'd thought that Arnie had appreciated the effort she'd made. She must have been wrong about her husband in every way. Even though she knew it was impossible, she still tried to remember the day when she'd signed those papers thirteen years ago. Their lawyer had given her the exact day: 9 September. Thirteen years ago, Dung was twenty-six, and Giang was twenty-seven years old. They'd been long gone from home by then; they'd finished university and had already started working. When she forced herself to try harder to recollect her memories, she realised that it was around the time when things had got worse between them and when Dung had started blaming them the way she had. Could it have been the year after that Thanksgiving? She took another sip of coffee and narrowed her eyes, as if to help her focus better. Was that the year? Giang had met his wife right after that Thanksgiving and had got married the following summer. As Lilia had written out a fat cheque to contribute to their big white wedding, she'd remembered what their children had said to them and told Arnie that she didn't actually feel like giving him any money. She remembered that day very well, because she'd still felt the pain from months before.

Arnie had made her sign the papers in September 1995. Lilia couldn't remember the day she signed it, what Arnie had told her, or why she didn't read them, but now she understood why Arnie had done such a thing. He must have thought it was the ethical thing to do. He'd probably assumed that his wife wouldn't give anything to their children if he died first and wanted to guarantee that everything would be divided between the three of them in that case. No matter how hard she tried, she couldn't remember how he'd stopped her from reading the papers. Well, Lilia had never really been a fan of reading any papers that were put in front of her. Trusting her husband came naturally to her; it suited her idea of what a marriage should be.

Did Arnie realise what kind of a position he'd put her in? If he died now, the children would get two-thirds of both houses. If and when they wanted to sell them, Lilia would have nowhere to live. She was going to have some money, but how long would that last? In the best-case scenario, it would be $100,000 after tax. She needed to guarantee her whole life with that amount. How was she expected to find herself a place to live, take care of her expenses and continue to live on that kind of money? She'd better give up her travel plans for those later years. She'd be lucky if she didn't end up dying on the streets.

She took her last sip of cold coffee and stood up. She went upstairs and bought a ticket for the train, which would be leaving ten minutes later. She found herself a window seat and went back to thinking. She needed to decide what to do very soon. Was she going to take care of Arnie and be left with some money that wouldn't even compensate her for the amount of work she did now when he died? Or was she going to stop the physiotherapy and save that money

241

for herself? She considered divorce for the first time in her life. She wished that she could leave him, just like that. If he could let her down like this after so many years of marriage, why shouldn't she do the same? It didn't take her long to find the answer: because she couldn't. She'd signed that contract which said she'd walk out empty-handed in the case of a divorce.

For the first time in years, she thought about going back to the Philippines. Maybe the only good thing about being an immigrant was being able to go back when things didn't work out. She knew that the money she'd get when Arnie died would be enough to live on there. She could buy herself a nice, cosy house with a garden in the village where she was born and live happily with hired help until the day she died. Nobody could say that she'd failed in America. They couldn't say that she hadn't been able to make it there and that was why she'd come back. She'd already passed that point in her life. She might not even find people from her past when she went back there. If so, she could start a brand new life. She remembered a line from a book she'd read once: 'One can begin so many things with a new person! Even begin to be a better man.'

When Lilia got home, Arnie was asleep again. Maybe he hadn't even noticed that she'd left. Although he tried to concentrate during the limited time when he was awake, he simply couldn't do it. He was aware that they'd been to the hospital, that they'd had a hard time coming home and that his wife had changed his sheets and clothes a couple of times, but he didn't know in which time slot those things had happened or for how long they had lasted. He could tell that his wife was more aggressive now, though. She turned him on his side clumsily, and if he couldn't stop his head from falling to one side she didn't fix it and usually grumbled something, angrily. He could say a lot of things about Lilia – lazy, untidy, clumsy – but he'd never thought she was a bad person. She'd always been kind and thoughtful to people. She'd always stayed away from conflicts and knew how to calm down a fight between other people. She'd stayed polite to him, too, despite spending so many years in the same house. But now she flipped his body around carelessly, making him feel like an empty sack, and didn't even stroke his cheek kindly like she used to in the old days whenever he got sick.

Seeing that he was asleep, Lilia left him alone and escaped to her room. That invisible needle had come once again and pierced her endurance. Maybe because she'd never had to look for an exit so quickly in her life before, she'd never encountered so many closed doors. She'd been going with the flow of whatever life brought her for so many years and now she was really struggling to change the current of the river.

The silence in the house told her that nobody was home. She'd thought she'd found the family she'd been looking for for all these years when the tenants had first moved into their house. They'd eaten together and talked about their days, and that way Lilia had managed to forget about her miserable life. Sadly, their existence had soon become a routine and Lilia had gone back to being nothing but a cook, someone who was always at home when the others came back and was always there when they needed her. Of course, they didn't know how many hours a day she spent in the kitchen just so that they could eat the food they liked and were used to. For them, the food was just a part of the rent they paid, not a feast they looked forward to impatiently. They didn't come home at dinnertime any more and just ate their food quickly, on their feet, without even warming it up. They'd come to know the city well and knew how to survive in it. They preferred to go out and see it for themselves instead of learning about it from Lilia. All the same, Lilia had fantasised about taking her children out of their will and leaving some money to Ulla, even though she didn't need it. Just as a token of her appreciation.

Her interest in Flavio had slowly faded and finally disappeared. Of course, if the young man had ever looked in her direction as much as he looked in Natalie's, her love for him could have flourished, but she only had to listen to the sounds coming from the second floor to understand what was going on between those two. Although Lilia had felt jealous in the beginning, the wound in her heart had healed fairly quickly.

She knew that Arnie was one of the reasons why her tenants didn't want to spend much time at home. They didn't see him very often, but it still must have been depressing for them to know that there was a man in their house who was struggling with death. None of them had mentioned anything of the sort, but Lilia was actually right in her assumption. Flavio and Natalie had talked about it several times, for example. They were both happy to be living on the second floor, as far away from the illness as possible. Natalie even said she could smell medicine whenever she went into the kitchen. Although Flavio insisted that the smell was purely psychological, he'd also admitted that he didn't like spending time in the kitchen. Ulla, on the other hand, had a hard time understanding why a woman like Lilia chose to put up with such a rude and unloving man, and Kano also felt bad that their landlady had to take care of everything by herself. All the same, despite how bad they felt for Lilia and however much happiness they wished her, it wasn't enough to make them stay at home.

Lilia still wished they would stay on in the United States. She didn't see them as much as she used to, but she'd got used to them being in the house. At least the footsteps on the stairs or short chats in the kitchen reminded her that there was some sort of life in her home. She was happy just to be able to say 'Good morning' once a day.

After she'd freshened up, she changed her outfit and went back to the kitchen. She turned on one of the news channels just to get rid of the silence. Although election day was still six months away, the TV presenters and commentators were talking about it excitedly all the time now. It didn't look like the competition between Barack Obama and Hillary Clinton was about to come to an end just yet, and the real excitement would only get going after one of them became the Democratic candidate. Since Lilia knew that they were just going to talk about the same things all over again, she changed the channel. Someone was accusing somebody else of betraying her in one of those never-ending soap operas. It looked like these people would never stop crying. Asking herself if anybody really lived like that, she clicked the button on the remote again. Martha Stewart was talking about a recipe in her green and yellow kitchen with some of her hair tucked behind her ear, as always. Lilia had never mentioned this to anyone, but she'd made her kitchen curtains by following Martha's example on one of her shows. She put the remote on the counter and went into the storeroom. She peered inside the freezer, checking what was there. For her, this was the most valuable appliance in the house. She was proud of being able to keep it filled with all kinds of different products at all times. She took out a big pork shoulder, went back to the kitchen and put it on a large plate. She crammed it into the microwave, set the timer to defrost and – just when she was about to take a look at the TV show again – she heard Arnie's voice. He hadn't talked in days. He'd been sleeping almost all the time lately and even when he didn't he couldn't fully wake up. Actually, Lilia was much happier this way. After all, they didn't have anything to say to each other even when he could speak. It had been a very long time since they'd last said anything meaningful to one another. Since he was calling her by her name now, he must be feeling better. She didn't move for a couple of minutes and simply waited. When he spoke again, his voice was angry and impatient. 'It doesn't matter how many times he escapes from death, how many times Azrael lets him go, he never learns,' Lilia said to herself.

Arnie was impatient because he felt clear headed for the first time in days. He was so thirsty that he felt like he was going to die if he didn't have a glass of water right away. He didn't know how long he'd been out like that. 'It looks like Lilia hasn't given me a drop of water for days,' he thought. She must have just left him to die. He didn't remember how Lilia had tried to feed him during the rare moments when he could stay awake. He knew that his wife was in the kitchen – he'd just heard the microwave door closing – but still she didn't come to his room. 'She wants to torture me,' he said to himself. Well, he was going to get better one of these days and then she was going to have to pay for her actions. He'd be able to divorce her easily when he told the judge how she'd mistreated him when he was sick. What was she going to do then? She had no clue that she didn't have any money of her own. She could go back to the Philippines and live on the top of a tree as far as he was concerned. Wasn't she used to that anyway? Living barefoot in nature, surrounded by genies and all kinds of paranormal creatures?

Even though he was a little bit tired, his mind felt even clearer than it had before. It was almost like his brain had been renewed during the hours he'd spent sleeping. He shouted out to Lilia for the third time. When she finally came into the room, she stood next to the door and watched him, coldly. She had her apron tied around her waist, as always. She must have been cooking one of her famous dishes. Her tenants were going to give her a *cordon bleu* one of these days. After adjusting his voice with a couple of coughs, trying not to sound too rude, he said, 'May I have a glass of water?' He wasn't going to question her; that would just give her an opportunity to vent her emotions. Besides, he needed her help after all. Lilia came back two minutes later with a glass of water. The expression on her face hadn't changed. Arnie thought: 'She must have been studying this sour expression in front of a mirror.' He couldn't even imagine how heartbroken his wife really was. His voice didn't change, either; he sounded flat. He said 'thank you' without looking her in the face.

'You're welcome. How are you feeling?'

'I'm good, thank you.'

'You're not sleepy any more?'

'No.'

'Do you want something to eat?'

'I'm not hungry. Can you turn on the lights?'

'Sure.'

'Do we have a newspaper?'

'No. Do you want the remote for your TV?'

'Please. By the way, what did the doctors say? I can't remember.'

'You had several blood clots in your brain, that's why you've been sleeping like this. They said it would make no difference if you stayed at the hospital. They said that you might recover or you might not.'

'So I could've just carried on sleeping like that?'

'Yes.'

After waiting for a couple more minutes, Lilia gathered that their conversation was over and turned to walk out the door. As she left, Arnie said, 'Can you close the door, please?'

Arnie hadn't felt the need to thank Lilia for everything she'd done, or ask how she'd managed to bring him home from the hospital by herself. Lilia couldn't understand how her husband had woken up all of a sudden and had no idea where this whole episode was going. They might have to live like this for years and Lilia didn't know how long they could carry on pretending to be nice to each other. She'd actually wanted to tell her husband what she'd found out that day the minute he woke up: that she knew how he'd betrayed her. That was why she hadn't gone to his room the second she'd heard him calling out to her. She'd waited until she'd got her nerves under control. If she told Arnie what Giang had said on the phone, would that change anything? Or would he say, 'He doesn't have to come and pick me up.'

Now Lilia understood that she'd played all the wrong cards over the years. She'd always been much more open than she should have been and she regretted putting so much trust in people now. She wasn't going to say anything to Arnie this time, not until she knew what she was going to do. She'd found out more about what kind of a person her husband was in the last five months than she had in all the years they'd been together. Now she saw that their relationship was just like one in a play. It looked like all of the times when she'd opened up to Arnie had meant nothing to him. He'd listened to her quietly, not because he was a quiet man, but because he simply didn't care. She'd only shared a house with that man, when she'd thought that they'd shared a life.

She went back to the kitchen feeling glad that she hadn't said anything. After stroking the pork that she'd laid on the cutting board for a while, she picked up her cleaver. She knew by rule of thumb that she could slice it into six pieces. She was going to make small cuts in each piece with the tip of a sharp knife, fill them with crushed garlic, rosemary, salt and pepper purée and then rub the meat with olive oil and yet more garlic. The smell of the meat was going to spread throughout the house, but especially to Arnie's room, which was right next to the kitchen. She knew perfectly well that he was going to hate the rest of his life. Would it comfort him to know that he wasn't alone?

Marc carried on living, but he couldn't say that he was happy or that he woke up smiling in the mornings. He just didn't run out of breath like he had done in the first weeks after Clara's death and he didn't think he was going to die any more. He wasn't scared now of going to the farmers' market three days a week or to the places where he'd gone shopping with Clara. He knew how to find his way around the market and could tell parsley from coriander. All the same, he still needed time to learn about the differences between ginger and sunroot. He understood now why his wife used to go to the market with presents in her hands at Christmas and why she came back with gifts, too. The whole farmers' market was like one big family. A family that watched out for each other.

It was almost as if he'd begun to understand the city better since he'd taken up cooking. He'd started going to places where he'd had no reason to go to in the past to buy a particular ingredient and then he'd find himself in a completely different neighbourhood, and therefore a completely different world. He was only just beginning to realise that the whole city was talking about food. He couldn't help overhearing a recipe for leek soup while waiting in a queue behind two women in a supermarket. Every Sunday he started the day by walking to the market at St Germain, then onwards along Rue Mouffetard, stopping off at almost every shop along the way. Sometimes he stood and drank one or two glasses of champagne before turning down one of the side streets to avoid being seen by the dancers who waltzed at the end of Mouffetard, since most of them knew Clara.

He'd run into some familiar faces in recent months but he'd ignored them if he could, or if not he would quickly ask how they were and then run away before his wife's name could come up, saying he was in a hurry. He found this kind of behaviour very childish, but he still didn't have the strength to go back to his old friends.

That was why he wasn't exactly delighted to see Odette standing in his gallery all of a sudden. After trying to contact Marc a couple of times, she'd realised that she couldn't reach him and had decided to leave him alone. It wasn't easy for her to see him, either. The mere thought of him was enough to make her furious most of the time and she didn't even know why. Maybe it was because she considered herself more loyal to her friend than Marc was. She knew that he was going to find someone else sooner or later and forget all about Clara. She, on the other hand, was never going to be able to put someone else in her friend's place. Despite all of these theories and her unexplained anger, she didn't feel too good about abandoning Marc. She felt as if she'd neglected a needy child. She'd seen Clara in her dreams a couple of times and her best friend had asked after her husband. When she eventually started thinking about him all day long, Odette decided that it was time to go and see him. It would be pointless to call him or invite him over for dinner. That wasn't going to happen. The best way was just to go and see him.

Now, as she stood right in front of him, she saw that Marc didn't know what to say, or where to put his hands. So, she took him by the shoulders and placed two kisses on his cheeks. He looked much better than he had before. He'd gained the weight he'd lost and got rid of the dark circles under his eyes. The feeling of jealousy started to fill her heart again. It looked like he had another woman. After standing face to face for a while, Marc realised that Odette wasn't planning to leave after a couple of minutes. The one thing he wanted the least was about to happen: they were going to have to talk. He didn't want to have to tell her how he was. He didn't know how he was any more, anyway. It felt as if his body was missing his soul; he just kept on breathing in and out. He'd never been someone who could easily say what was in his mind and heart. In fact, whenever he'd wanted to say what he thought before Clara died, he'd found that he couldn't do it; Clara always had to say it for him. Then Marc would say, 'Exactly like that. I feel just like that.' Unfortunately, Odette wasn't Clara; nobody was Clara and nobody knew that he couldn't explain how he felt, even though he wanted to.

It was Odette who finally broke the silence, saying, 'Let's go get a cup of coffee.' How could he refuse? What could he say? He checked his watch and saw that it was almost time to close up. He put on his jacket and said to Amou: 'I'm leaving now. It's time to close, anyway. See you tomorrow.' Odette looked at Marc, suspiciously. She'd heard from their other friends that Marc had been going to the gallery earlier in the mornings and closing later at night ever since Clara had passed away. Since he was closing before five now, he must have gone back to his usual schedule. Where did he go afterwards? It was very early, too. What did he do? He probably met his girlfriend and went out to eat somewhere. Maybe they went to the cinema afterwards, before going back to one of their apartments. Odette's heart began to ache even more.

Maybe Marc left the gallery and went straight home, where his new girlfriend was waiting for him. Anything was possible. Maybe she even cooked there, using Clara's pots and pans. Odette thought, 'Impossible', and then: 'The second women are always lazier. I'm sure the new one will spend every cent that Clara saved.' She turned towards Marc and looked him up and down. She searched for a sense of style – any sign that he might be trying to impress a young woman – in his trousers, hair and jacket; but she couldn't find one. Marc was still Marc. That jumper was probably one of the ones that Clara had picked out for him.

They sat at one of the cafés on Rue St André des Arts and ordered two glasses of wine. Although they'd spent the last fifteen minutes together, they hadn't said more than a couple of words. Just when Odette was about to begin her monologue, Marc started talking, which was very unusual for him.

'How's Henri?'

'Good ... good. As always. He's working a lot.'

'And the kids?'

'They're well. You know, we don't see them much any more. They're doing exactly the same thing that we did to our parents. But I guess you don't know: Celine is pregnant.'

'Congratulations! Do you know if it's a boy or a girl?'

'No, not yet. They're not planning to find out. They want it to be a surprise. Can you believe I'm going to be a grandmother? When did we get so old?'

She didn't find the silence strange; she knew that Marc wasn't one of those men who said things like, 'You're not old at all' or 'You married young, that's why.' If someone wasn't ready to accept the truth they shouldn't say it to Marc, because he was never going to object unless it wasn't true. Now it was her turn to ask questions.

'And how are you?'

'I'm good.'

'I've heard that you're spending very long hours at the gallery.'

'I did for a while.'

'And now?'

'I'm back to my normal hours.'

Odette knew that she had to ask about it now if she wanted to get the truth out of him, but she didn't know how to.

'Of course, you have to go back to your normal life. So, do you eat out a lot?'

'Rarely.'

Odette raised her eyebrows unintentionally, fixing her questioning eyes on Marc's and tilting her head to one side. When she realised that Marc wasn't going to continue, she rearranged the question.

'OK, so you order in?'

'No. I make a couple of things myself.'

Odette couldn't believe what she'd just heard. Although she wanted to laugh out loud, her anger was stronger than her sense of humour. His new girlfriend must have taken over the task of cooking. She knew as well as anybody that Marc couldn't tell sugar from salt. He couldn't even press two pieces of bread together, let alone cook. But how could she say that to him? She'd been slightly nervous at the beginning, but now her rage had turned into a ball of fire inside her. She had to hold herself back so that she wouldn't start hurling insults at him. The snake that writhed on the tip of her tongue was ready to bite. Just as she was about to open her mouth after taking a big gulp of wine, Marc held out a folded piece of paper which he'd taken out of his pocket. Odette held the piece of paper as far away from her eyes as possible so that she could see what was written on it, and read the ingredients that were listed there one after another. Mussels, red onions, cream. She turned her curious eyes back to Marc.

'It's the ingredients for the recipe I'm going to cook today.'
'*Moules à la crème?*'
'Yes!'
'You're going to make it?'
'Yes …'
'Marc, you can't even tell mussels from oysters.'

'Well, I can't, but the guy at the fishmonger's can. Besides, I've started learning. I bought myself a couple of cookbooks. I try one new recipe every day. They're very simple ones. The kind of recipes our mothers used to cook. They usually turn out not so good, but sometimes I do OK.'

Odette felt her heart melting away. She couldn't stop the tears from welling up. She had to stop herself from getting up and hugging that man who was sitting across from her. She imagined Marc in the kitchen, in front of the stove. Maybe he put on an apron, too. At that moment, she saw the plaster on Marc's left thumb for the first time. She put her hand on it and caressed it, softly. Marc smiled, saying, 'I often have accidents.' Odette broke into tears. With her hands on Marc's and her forehead pressed against the table, she sat there and cried.

When she'd pulled herself together enough to talk again a few minutes later, Odette didn't say anything else about it despite all the questions in her mind; and Marc didn't tell her anything else. This man was just like a little boy and he preferred to deal with his pain alone. Odette had misjudged him, thinking that he was going to find healing in another woman's arms. Instead, Marc had given himself up to the emptiness that Clara had left behind her. Again, something related to Clara. There was a poetic loneliness in the kind of life Marc had chosen to live; a loneliness that should be respected and appreciated. Now that she was aware of it, Odette asked shyly, 'May I taste your food one day?' Marc smiled, embarrassed. His food was nowhere near ready to be served to other people. There were even times when he could barely eat his food himself, and he threw away the rest of it after filling his stomach. The prawn casserole he'd made the week before had been a complete disaster, for example.

Everything had looked fine before he'd put the casserole in the oven. He'd followed every step of the recipe carefully, and put it in to bake feeling sure of himself. Now he understood why Clara had made notes in her cookbooks. There was always something missing or excessive in the recipes. Maybe he should start adding notes in his book too, he thought. The biscuits should be baked not for twenty-two minutes but for thirty-two; he shouldn't put one and a half cups of water in the prawn casserole, but only half a cup. That way he wouldn't have to clean up all that mess again.

He'd sat in his chair after setting the oven timer and started looking at one of the new comic books he'd bought. It was a book by Gipi, an Italian artist. He'd discovered him in recent years and always waited for his new work to come out. He was one of the artists he most wanted to add to his clientele. While he was completely absorbed by the drawings, he suddenly heard the fire alarm ringing, loudly. And when he turned around, he saw smoke escaping through the sides of the oven door. Since he'd experienced a similar situation before, he knew exactly what to do; he ran to the corridor and turned the head of the fan that stood there towards the fire alarm. It should stop ringing in fifteen seconds at the most. Then he ran back to the oven and opened the door, and as he did so the smoke hit him flat in the face. The water in the casserole was bubbling furiously and drops were bouncing off the walls and bottom of the oven, burning at 200 degrees. The whole oven was covered in grease. According to the recipe, the food needed another fifteen minutes. He was supposed to sprinkle the cheese he'd grated on top of it after eight minutes and then wait for another seven until it had a crust on top. On the other hand, he didn't want the oven to get even dirtier and it was obvious that even cheese couldn't save that dish, and so he took out the casserole and almost threw it down on the worktop.

The ingredients were swimming in water. The green peppers hadn't browned and the prawns hadn't caramelised like in the picture in the book. After he'd blown on a spoonful of pepper, tomatoes and prawns, he put it in his mouth. He'd been burning his tongue so often lately when tasting his food that he wasn't even sure if he'd be able to taste it any more. As it turned out, he couldn't taste it but that had nothing to do with his burnt tongue; the prawn casserole had simply been incredibly unsuccessful. After throwing the whole thing in the bin, he put a pot of water on the stove for some pasta, which he'd become very good at. He opened the oven door one more time to assess the damage. It was covered in big spots of grease. When he tried to wipe some of it away with a damp cloth, smoke rose from it again. It looked as if he'd have to wait and clean it once it had cooled off. It would take him one more day to find out just how hard and boring it was to get rid of grease once it had dried. And that was how he first met Mr Propre.

Marc didn't feel like telling Odette about any of these things. These were the daily trivia of his simple life. What's more, they were details that showed up just how empty his life really was. It broke his heart to see how lonely and miserable he was now when he looked back on those days. He missed Clara even more when he thought of himself in the kitchen, trying so unsuccessfully to cook. He'd never been the kind of man who pitied himself before. After all, he'd had a beautiful life. But now, whenever he looked at himself from the outside he wanted to cry. Hoping Odette hadn't guessed from his face that he'd been feeling sorry for himself, he smiled weakly and said, 'Believe me, you don't want to taste my food.' All the same, it was impossible for Odette not to pick up on the cracking sound in his voice. In fact, she'd been imagining this man all alone in his kitchen at that same moment and the image almost broke her heart. Although she'd promised herself not to mention Clara's name in this conversation, she couldn't help it, and said, 'I'm sure Clara would be proud of you.' When Marc didn't say anything back, she tried to lighten the mood with a joke: 'Maybe not of your food, but at least of how hard you're trying.' The teardrop that had been waiting at the edge of Marc's eye decided not to fall. When he had made sure that his eyes were no longer wet, he raised his head and smiled at Odette, saying:

'She definitely wouldn't be proud of my food.'

'Let me decide that, OK?'

'Not now, but I promise I'll let you taste it when I'm ready.'

'OK. Which cream are you going to use tonight for the *Moules à la crème*? Don't forget that it's very important which one you choose.'

Before paying the bill and leaving, Marc noted down Odette's suggestion on his list: Madame Eloise. Maybe he should introduce the Madame to Mr Propre. The day after the prawn casserole catastrophe, Marc had stopped by the supermarket on his way home from work and met Mr Propre, who would become one of his best friends for the rest of his life. It hadn't been hard to pick out this bottle with its picture of a bald man with big arms, a white t-shirt, one earring and big white eyebrows among the others on the shelf. This image must have been engraved in his visual memory after seeing it millions of times on television, the metro and billboards over the years. He looked at the picture on the bottle he held in his hand. Why was this man so big? Why did he have only one earring? Why were his eyebrows so white? Marc didn't know it, but these same questions had been asked many times before and there were all kinds of speculations about them. Some people said that Mr Propre was a genie in a bottle. He came out of the bottle when women needed him the most and solved all their problems. Some said he was a legendary American navy man. If Mark had followed the news carefully he would know that one year earlier the European Parliament had declared Mr Propre inappropriate, since its brand suggested that only huge, powerful men were capable of cleaning. If he'd paid more attention to his environment in the other countries he'd been to on his travels, he would also have realised that the Monsieur was extremely popular. He had a different name in every country: Don Limpio in Spain, Maestro Limpio in Mexico, Meister Proper in Germany, Mastro Lindo in Italy and Mister Clean in the United States. This had been the most popular cleaning product all over the world since 1958 and the Monsieur was definitely a revolutionary character, judging from all the improvements he'd gone through over the years. Completely oblivious to all of these deeper meanings behind the product and just because the face looked familiar, Marc bought that bottle. But it wasn't until he saw just how well it cleaned the oven that Marc really began to respect the Monsieur.

Since this discovery the week before, Marc had started cleaning obsessively, wiping every greasy corner of the kitchen. He'd gone out and bought the Monsieur's other products for various different purposes and had got rid of every stray particle of dirt in the apartment. He was developing an unhealthy love of cleaning materials. The next step would be to start raving about Vileda's self-twist mops.

He walked slowly up Rue Monge after saying goodbye to Odette. The changing season not only looked but also smelled different. If this was any other day, he'd be walking home thinking of Clara with this smell in his nose. But it wasn't, and now he thought about what he'd cook if Odette and the others came over for dinner. It wasn't that he was planning to give a dinner party any time soon; he just liked playing with the idea. He thought about the dishes he'd cooked so far and tried to decide which of them had been the most successful, which ones he could serve to his friends. He stopped in the middle of the pavement, his hands in his pockets, and shook his head: the answer was none of them. He was so occupied with his own thoughts that he didn't even realise that the man walking past him had given him a dirty look, because he'd almost walked into Marc when he'd stopped so abruptly. Maybe he would have to review the cookbook from the beginning once again, choose a couple of things he could do well enough and work on them for a while. The reason he'd got so excited all of a sudden about the idea of a dinner party wasn't because of a new feeling of kinship he'd developed towards Odette or his other friends; it was the sense of a challenge, a desire to prove himself to others as well as to himself. Of course, his subconscious had something to do with that, too. Finding something new to think about whenever he was about to remember Clara was just another way of trying to forget her. As he arrived at the fishmonger's, he decided that he wasn't ready to give a dinner party just yet. Pierre greeted his customer as loudly as ever. He was very good at talking to everyone simultaneously. While he asked Marc how he was, he kept on talking to the other customers who were already in the shop. When it was Marc's turn to order, Pierre almost convinced him to buy fish instead of mussels. After a fifteen-minute struggle, Marc left with a bag of mussels, feeling proud of himself. Pierre, on the other hand, was still yelling behind him: 'If you change your mind, I'll take the mussels back.' Now it was time to fetch Madame Eloise. On his way to the supermarket, he nodded at everyone he'd got to know in the other shops before finally getting the cream and going home.

As soon as he got back to the apartment, he turned off the radio, turned on the TV, put on his apron and got to work. He opened the page for that day's recipe. He put the mussels in a pot to boil first. In the meantime, he sliced one medium-sized red onion, put it in a pan with a splash of olive oil and butter, caramelised it and then added some red cooking wine. When the sauce began to bubble, he poured in some cream and turned the heat down as low as possible. The mussels had already opened up, which meant it was time to add them to the sauce and blend them with it thoroughly using a spoon. Just before he put the mussels in, he remembered to add some salt. The book said one pinch, but Marc had learned from his previous experiences that one pinch was never enough. He also knew that adding salt to the food at the table never tasted as good.

Just fifteen minutes later, his dish was ready to taste. He hadn't cut or burnt any of his body parts this time. He began by breaking off a piece of bread and dipping it in the sauce. He wasn't disappointed. He separated one of the mussels from its shell and rolled it in his mouth. He smiled to himself. He raised his glass of wine to the hosts of *On a Tout Essayé*. He'd finally found one dish he could put on his list for the dinner party.

Öykü and Ferda had to find some time to spend alone so that Ferda could enjoy her daughter's pregnancy. At the beginning of the week, when Sinan was at work and Mrs Nesibe had dozed off a little more deeply than usual because of the increased amount of sleeping pills Ferda had given her, mother and daughter sat opposite each other at the kitchen table and had their emotional moment without hiding any of their feelings. The glow on her daughter's face told Ferda that Öykü was going to be a happy mother. She was only two months pregnant, but had already put on some weight. Her appetite was just fine and she didn't feel nauseated or tired. She took some short naps now and again, which was something she'd hated all her life; but that was it. Ferda had made the soufflé while Öykü was taking one of those naps. She'd put it in the oven close to the time when Öykü was going to wake up and let the smell cover the whole house. She knew that her daughter would come into the kitchen with her nose held high, sniffing the air. As Öykü tried to shake off the drowsiness, Ferda took out the soufflé moulds and put them on the table, one for each of them. When they saw that the centres still hadn't collapsed after five minutes, they were both almost shocked. Öykü clapped her hands and chirped, 'Bravo! Bravo, Mrs Ferda!' This was only her second attempt. Nevertheless, she'd gone over the recipe in her mind and mentally practised it so many times that she'd felt really comfortable melting the chocolate, mixing the egg whites and adding the yolks. It tasted great and the touch of cream in the middle made it even more delicious.

Ferda needed to put the dessert aside after just two bites, of course. She had to live life in small doses like that if she didn't want to lose her battle with her migraine. It wasn't a problem, though; after finishing hers, Öykü started on her mother's. In the presence of this delicacy, mother and daughter talked about Öykü's future for the first time. Ferda opened the subject by talking about her own pregnancies. The first one had been hard. She'd experienced all of the disadvantages of being young and unprepared. She hadn't been able to breastfeed Cem no matter how hard she'd tried and she still felt guilty about that. During her second pregnancy she'd been much more knowledgeable; still, she'd suffered terribly from nausea and fatigue. She'd breastfed Öykü, though. Breastfeeding was very important, more important than anything else, and she shouldn't forget that.

While Öykü listened carefully to her mother, she scraped the bottom of the soufflé mould with her index finger. She'd scraped so many bowls, pots and pans over the years that Ferda was sure that her daughter was going to get married on a very rainy day, as the old saying went. When there was nothing left at the bottom of the soufflé mould, Öykü got up, went to the fridge and looked inside for a long time, leaning on the door. It was filled with a lot of delicious things, as it always was, but she didn't know exactly what it was that she was craving. The only thing that stopped her from reaching for the stuffed vine leaves was the two bowls of dessert she'd just wolfed down. After looking at the shelves for a little bit longer, she finally closed it and turned to her mother:

'Do we still have some of that *borek*?'

'Yes, my dear. It's in the small oven.'

Öykü sat opposite her mother again and started munching on the *borek*. She knew that she was going to look like an elephant by the end of this pregnancy. She guessed that her doctor was going to put her on a diet in a couple of months and start to limit what she could eat. She'd already made up her mind to eat anything she wanted until she reached that point. She didn't care how many pounds she was going to gain. She'd never been so deliciously hungry in her life before and had never enjoyed food this much. She'd always had a good appetite, but this was something completely different. She felt as if there was a button in her brain that made her happy whenever it was pressed, and it was activated with each bite she ate. What's more, she wasn't about to pass up on her mother's delicious food while she was still allowed to enjoy it. One of the things she liked most in this life was to eat whatever was cooked in that kitchen.

Ferda didn't mind her daughter eating like that – in fact, she was very happy that her cooking was being appreciated – but there was an issue they had to take care of before she got any bigger. Ferda already knew that every woman who would attend the wedding was going to realise that Öykü was pregnant the moment they saw her. Then they would go home and say to their husbands: 'That girl is pregnant. That's why she's in such a hurry to get married.' Their husbands would say: 'No, where did you get that idea? Didn't you see how skinny she is?' The women would protest, saying, 'Come on, her face was glowing like a rose, didn't you see that?' So, Ferda didn't want her daughter to put on any more weight on top of this to make it even more obvious. If she got married right away, when she looked like this, at least people couldn't be sure.

'My dear, what's the French custom? What's the wedding party going to be like?'

'Mum, what wedding party?'

'Excuse me? Don't you remember what I said? I want to see my daughter in a wedding gown and I want to enjoy that day.'

'Well, I can put on a gown, but we can just get married at the town hall.'

'The town hall?'

'Yes.'

'No. I only have one daughter. How can I enjoy it if you just put on the gown for ten minutes and have done with it?'

'All right, so what should we do then?'

'I don't know. What kind of a wedding do you want? That's why I asked what their custom is. Does the groom's side take care of the wedding like they do here? Besides, what kind of a family does he have? Are they close to their son? Do they have money?'

'Duval and I are going to take care of the expenses ourselves, OK? The weather is going to get better in a couple of weeks; we can have it in a small garden. With a small group of people. Maybe forty or fifty.'

'Forty or fifty people is not possible. Let me tell you this now, OK? Say eighty, at least. I guess the groom will have some relatives coming over. Or maybe not. Will he?'

'Let's say sixty, mum.'

'OK. Then we're going to take care of your wedding gown. And they'll take care of Duval's suit. That's not something heard of in our culture, but it's OK.'

'OK.'

266

'When's it going to be? The 6th of April?'

'In three weeks?'

'Yes. The sooner the better.'

Ferda looked pointedly at Öykü's belly. Even though she'd always imagined having her daughter's wedding dress custom-made, it looked like they were going to have to buy one. She'd already planned every detail. Lying awake in bed while everybody else was sleeping, she'd decided on where to have the wedding party, where to go for the gown and even what kind of food they were going to have. Her brother's wife held a senior position at the City Hall, and she could take care of booking a date at such short notice. The names on the guest list exceeded sixty even when she thought about it without writing them down. If the number came to seventy or seventy-five, she was going to have to sacrifice some of her savings.

If Öykü carried on eating like that, there was no doubt that she was going to put on at least fourteen or fifteen pounds in three weeks. She was a skinny girl, so even that might not make her look too big, but there was no one in that shortlist of guests who wasn't close enough to the family to notice the difference. She took another sip of the rosehip tea she'd made for herself and said:

'Make sure you don't overeat in the next three weeks, all right, my dear? I'm not saying don't eat, just be careful.'

Öykü shook her head back and forth with a piece of *borek* sticking out of her mouth. She didn't know how she was going to resist all this food, but she'd do her best. She had to go back to Paris in two days' time. It was going to be hard to stop herself from eating Duval's delicious food and the various delicacies of the Parisian bakeries. And there was going to be another tough thing for her to do on her wedding day: going to the bathroom with her gown on. She'd found herself in the bathroom every fifteen minutes ever since she'd got pregnant. She hadn't moved from her spot for the last hour so that she wouldn't interrupt her mother and to fill the last empty corner of her stomach, but she couldn't hold it any longer. As she ran up the hallway, Ferda had already started thinking about the style of the gown. There was no way they could go with a long veil.

Mrs Nesibe understood what was going on in the house whenever she was in her right mind, but she invented her own versions of events on the days when she wasn't. According to those versions, Ferda was sometimes the housekeeper. She stole all of the family's valuables. That was why Mrs Nesibe had become poor: she'd lost it all to the housekeeper. What's more, that bitch had also seduced her husband. She often said: 'I curse every penny I gave you. I bought you holiday gifts, notebooks and pens for your children every year. I even bought your daughter's wedding gown. I curse it all. Aren't you ashamed of flirting with a man who's old enough to be your father?' Sometimes Ferda was Mrs Nesibe's mother. On those days, Mrs Nesibe thought she was in bed because she was pregnant and thanked her mother a million times for coming to take care of her. What would she do without her? That man she called her husband had already started going out every night since she'd got pregnant. He left her alone at home in that condition. He was the reason why Fusun had died, anyway. He hadn't given her any money to buy food for their child, and in the end she'd died. She wasn't going to let him kill this new baby, too. She begged her mother: 'You're not going to let him do that again, are you, mum? We'll take care of the baby together, won't we?' Then she fell out with her mother and accused her of all sorts of things. She'd always loved that Devil more than she loved her, hadn't she? Ferda knew that the 'Devil' was her uncle, who they all used to call Devil. Since she'd also called her uncle Devil all her life just like everybody else, she didn't even know his real name. Uncle Devil was known for being a very smart man. He'd always known how to take care of things and he always played tricks to get what he wanted. According to the stories, he'd tricked his sister, Mrs Nesibe, many times. He'd disappeared for ages after their father had passed away and only came home when he'd run out of money. Then he took whatever their mother had put aside and even confiscated the amount that had been saved for Mrs Nesibe's dowry. Despite all this, their mother had always praised him and never let anyone say a bad word about him. That was why Mrs Nesibe now asked: 'You always liked Devil more than me, didn't you?' Even though she'd always been a good daughter, she'd never received the same kind of affection from her mother.

Ferda was particularly shocked whenever her mother confused her with herself. Even her looks changed during those moments. She would shout:

'Nesibeeeee! Girls were queuing up to marry my son, so why did he pick you? You're too old for him. You put a spell on him, I know, otherwise why would he want you? You're older than him. And you're a liar. You say you're twenty-two. I'll be damned if you're twenty-two, I'll slash my wrists if you aren't at least twenty-eight. Even your boobs are sagging. Why don't you say something? Cat got your tongue? I'm sure your blood pressure will drop now. You're going to faint, aren't you?'

Ferda stuttered, not knowing what to say at those times. Was it possible that her mother was already famous for her fainting fits even when she was that young? And sometimes Mrs Nesibe became Ferda's grandmother and gave advice to the young Nesibe, 'Look, Nesibe, listen carefully. Things happened, but you're not going to tell anyone about them, OK? What can we do? It was her faith. You won't make the same mistakes next time. If your mother-in-law tries to make you talk, make sure you don't say anything. You're not going to give her a reason. She's the devil herself, you'll see how she'll try to trick you into talking. You'd better keep your mouth shut.'

Ferda couldn't help wondering what all of this meant. Even though she was tired of her mother's many personalities, she was also desperate for some sort of secret or family mystery that had been kept hidden for years to finally surface. What was this mysterious thing that shouldn't be told to anyone? What were those mistakes which mustn't be repeated? Did her father's mother really insult her mother like that? Did she really accuse her of putting a spell on her grandfather? She'd also thought before that her mother might be older than she said she was. This woman who lay in front of her looked older than eighty-five. She looked closer to eighty-eight or eighty-nine.

What was this story about her father not giving her any money to buy food for the baby? Her father had always been very kind to her and her brother. In fact, she'd always been closer to him than to her mother. Just like the people in their neighbourhood said, Ferda had also thought many times that her mother was the reason why her father had died at such a young age. In most of her early childhood memories, she saw her mother being sick in bed and her father making dinner for them. That was one reason why Ferda had started working in the kitchen at a very early age. She had a much stronger motive than just wanting to feed herself and her brother; it was to stop their father from running away. Whenever he saw her in the kitchen with an apron on, he'd gently stroke her hair and always complimented her on the food she'd cooked. That was why Ferda simply couldn't imagine him torturing the child who was born before her. On the other hand, she knew for a fact that the story of her father cheating on her mother with the housemaid was a total lie. She didn't remember them ever having a housemaid, for one thing. That must have been one of Mrs Nesibe's extravagant dreams.

Now her mother watched her running around from where she lay in bed and interfered with things if she was feeling more like herself. First of all, wasn't this Duval going to come and ask for Öykü's hand? She didn't care if he was French. This was their custom and he had to do whatever they wanted. Although she was doing millions of things at the same time, Ferda felt obliged to answer her mother's questions. Duval was going to come. He was coming with Öykü to meet them one week before the wedding. Mrs Nesibe kept saying: 'This is unheard of. How can you get to know a man in one week? Who is his family? What kind of people are they? They have

271

to stay engaged for some time before getting married. Where is Öykü's gondola?' Although Ferda had already asked herself some of these questions, she couldn't help but laugh at the gondola remark. She didn't think that the French would know that they should bring the bride chocolates in a silver gondola when they came to ask for her hand.

Öykü had never kept any secrets from her grandmother and so she'd wanted to tell her about the pregnancy, but Ferda had stepped in to convince her not to do this. She told her daughter that Mrs Nesibe couldn't think straight any longer and could say anything in front of anybody. Öykü accepted this argument, unwillingly. All the same Mrs Nesibe hadn't entirely cut her ties with the outside world. After Ferda spoke to her sister-in-law on the phone and found out that everything had been arranged with the wedding official, Mrs Nesibe took up the subject before letting her daughter get away: 'Of course, that pickle has a pea in the pod, that's the reason for all this hurry.' After standing in shock beside the phone for a while, Ferda walked into her mother's room.

'Where did you get that idea?'

'I guessed, since she's getting married in such a rush.'

'Don't you know your granddaughter? She never does anything the normal way, does she?'

'Come on. I realised it the night she arrived. You all went silent, then Sinan mumbled something. Everybody was acting strangely. Her face is like a full moon, anyway. She's even more beautiful now. It suits her. She's going to have a boy.'

'How do you know that?'

'If it was a girl, she'd get uglier. When I first became pregnant with Fusun, my whole skin was a mess. Then I had you.

It got even worse. That was right before your father started cheating on me.'

'God, mum! How did we end up here again?'

'All right, all right. But you hurt my feelings. Why did you hide it from me?'

Ferda answered by saying, 'We thought you might not approve', avoiding the subject of her memory loss. She'd tried to tell her mother before how she lost track of reality sometimes and didn't know what she was saying, but had never been able to convince her. Mrs Nesibe knew nothing about those times. In fact, if she ate anything when she was out of it and then came back to reality, she usually didn't remember that she'd had something to eat and asked Ferda why she hadn't given her any food. That way she usually ended up having two meals at a time.

Since that answer seemed to satisfy her, Mrs Nesibe dropped the subject. Nevertheless, she wasn't finished with her questions yet. Where were they going to have the party? How many people were going to be there? What kind of food were they going to serve? What kind of cake were they going to have? Were they going to have the wedding dress custom-made or were they going to buy it? She said: 'Take my advice, and buy the gown one size up. What if she doesn't fit in it at the last minute?'

And, of course, she came to the main subject in the end. What were they going to do about her on the day of the wedding? She had to be there as the grandmother of the bride. Oh, how she'd dreamed of dancing on that day for so many years; it was too bad that wasn't going to happen. How was she going to go to the wedding when she was bedridden like this? Ferda had been trying to convince her mother to sit in a wheelchair for months. When the problem of her going to the bathroom had first come up, Ferda's neighbour, Mrs Hanife, had offered to give them her late father's wheelchair to make things easier. It was no good, though; they couldn't convince Mrs Nesibe to sit in it. She was crippled. How was she going to manage to keep her balance in the wheelchair? Besides, how could she sit in it every day? No, she couldn't lift herself using her arms. Did she have any strength in her arms? Ferda wouldn't be able to lift her up and down by herself, would she? So who was going to do that, then? The nappies were just fine. Was Ferda disgusted by her own mother? She'd changed Ferda's nappies when she was a baby, hadn't she?

Now she was feeling more positive about the idea of using a wheelchair, at least just for one day. She was ready to endure anything for that pickle of a granddaughter. 'Take all my suits out,' she ordered Ferda. They would have to dry clean whichever one she was going to wear. Where were her flower-shaped brooches? Who had stolen the pink one? Had Ferda stolen it? She stole everything that belonged to her, anyway. Hadn't she caught her trying to steal her money from under the pillow the other day? And all of a sudden Ferda had become the housemaid they'd never had once again.

Nine

As spring turned into a humid summer, nothing changed despite all of the many ups and downs in Lilia's daily life. Arnie had been back to the hospital two more times in the last three months, but had been sent home each time since there was nothing they could do. The blood clots that had appeared in different areas of his brain affected different parts of his body, and while some of them healed, some stayed where they were. He was tired of this constant uncertainty in his life. Most of all, he was afraid of being paralysed and having to live like a piece of furniture in his own house rather than dying. His wife was careful to take care of all of his needs, but didn't show him any sympathy whatsoever. The look in her eyes was almost icy. They had never been particularly close, Arnie knew that, but they had never been this distant, either. They hadn't talked in such a long time now that they couldn't find a word to say to each other when they were in the same room any more. Lilia didn't spend any more time there than was strictly necessary to bring food, clean the room and take care of Arnie's bodily needs, anyway. He'd got used to the clinking and clanking sounds coming from the kitchen. He could guess which cupboard door Lilia had opened, which pot or pan she had used and, surprisingly enough, which type of food she was cooking from where he lay in his bed. He still hated the smell of food that covered his room, pyjamas, sheets and pillow, but didn't dare say anything about it any more. He'd finally realised that the smell got even stronger on the days when he irritated Lilia.

The tenants didn't gather in the kitchen very often any more, and that made the house a lot quieter, too. As far as he could tell, two of the tenants had moved out and new ones had moved in. They hadn't bothered to meet him and he didn't want to know them, either. As for the ones who'd left, they hadn't even said goodbye. On those days of change, Lilia's colour had become even darker and she hadn't even tried to hide her red eyes. She's so stupid, he thought. What had she expected? That they would end up living with her for the rest of their lives?

Of course, Lilia knew that her tenants wouldn't stay there for ever, but she still had a very hard time holding back the tears when Flavio told her that he was moving out. He and Natalie had found an apartment in Manhattan and wanted to stay there until their visas expired. They planned to go to Spain afterwards and get married there. Lilia did her best to smile and said, 'Of course. It's a wonderful plan.' Although she'd stopped fantasising about Flavio a long time ago, whatever was left over from those dreams still broke her heart.

She'd gone back to the school the next day to put up a new ad for tenants and had soon found one for each room. Flavio and Natalie left, promising to visit her again in the future. Where else could they eat such delicious food? Nobody else made a casserole like hers. Of course, they were going to miss her biscuits, too, but they were going to see each other very soon, weren't they? In reality, Flavio and Natalie were never going to visit Lilia again. They were going to talk about her from time to time as a sweet, kind woman, but however guilty they'd feel about it they were never going to find the time to visit her. Only years later, when they came back to New York from Spain for their anniversary, would they finally want to see the house where they'd first met. They'd stand outside 102 Clinton Road and realise that somebody else lived there now, and so they wouldn't knock on the door. Then they would go and have coffee at some diner and wonder what had happened to her.

'Do you think she's dead?'

'I don't know.'

'She was really in love with you, poor thing.'

'Don't remind me.'

It didn't take Lilia long to get used to her new tenants. Like the others had once done, they hung out in the kitchen most of the time during their first weeks in the house and eventually came to understand their way of life there. Lilia slowly injected them with American culture, just as she'd done with the others. They should never go to anybody's home without calling, never stare at people, never fight with anyone on the street. If someone invited them over for dinner, they should email them the next day and thank them for the lovely dinner. What's more, the members of the family who lived two houses away weren't black, they were African American. Lilia had learned from her previous experience: Eyal from Israel and Alex from Serbia were going to start living their own lives after a certain point. With this in mind, she found joy in their presence but didn't expect it to last.

She had to make some changes to her cooking with Eyal's arrival. Living with a Jewish person didn't only mean giving up pork. Everything had to be kosher to begin with: meat, milk, bread, salt, vegetables, wine, grape juice, cheese. What's more, the meat shouldn't be mixed with the cheese. Not only that, but they couldn't be in a sandwich together, or even on the same plate. She shouldn't even cut them with the same knife. Lobster, prawns, crab, mussels and all that kind of thing were on the non-edible list. Eyal couldn't eat meat and fish during the same meal.

Lilia had to sit in front of her computer and read about this for hours in order to get a sense of the culture. She printed out various rules and put them somewhere easy to reach in the kitchen. If there was one kitchen that wasn't kosher, it was hers. First of all, she had to change almost all of her bowls. Any bowls that had previously contained pork or anything non-kosher couldn't be used any more. Not only that, but a bowl which she'd used to make something with milk in it before couldn't have meat in it now, or vice versa. She had to use a different serving spoon for every dish and make sure that they didn't touch each other. Even the spoon holder next to the stove had an important role to play. The spoons for two different dishes mustn't touch each other and therefore shouldn't be placed in the same part of the holder. These were very difficult rules to follow for someone who'd cooked pork all her life and had no idea about any of them, but Lilia wasn't about to let her tenant starve. Despite all of these restrictions, she still carried on with her soufflé experiments, trying to follow one recipe at a time. She knew the basic recipe by heart now, and only had to look at the book for the particular ingredients for the kind of soufflé she was making. The centre sometimes collapsed very quickly, and sometimes stayed up for longer. She'd become completely hooked both on the taste and on the experiment. She'd read on one web site that she could use starch to make the soufflé rise higher, but she didn't want to try that. The excitement of waiting for that moment – and the disappointment or happiness that came with it – usually gave her the sweetest moments of her meaningless days. Just as Eyal lit a candle eighteen minutes before sunset on Friday nights, Kano prayed towards the sunrise and Ulla meditated with her hands on her knees, Lilia found her solace in these private moments.

She'd decided not to ask Arnie anything about the will. She knew he wasn't going to change his mind whatever she might say and didn't respect her opinions at all. She'd started putting aside the money she saved from her grocery shopping and household budget and was trying to secure her entire future with a couple of thousand dollars. Dung and Giang had only called Arnie once in months and hadn't felt any need to visit. Lilia didn't ask, 'What did they say? Why aren't they coming?' as she used to in the past. She didn't want to know what they talked about, or what Arnie thought about it. She felt too tired to say a word or ask a single question. It didn't matter how hopeful she felt when she woke up in the mornings; before going to bed each night she found herself right back in the arms of her own dark thoughts. Arnie's life had to come to an end so that she could continue living hers and have a life of her own. Most nights she dreamed that Arnie was dead and woke up with a sense of total happiness. She'd also given up being ashamed of her thoughts. If this was the only piece of driftwood she could cling onto in the middle of an ocean, she was going to cling onto it. On the mornings after those nights, she went downstairs slowly and walked into Arnie's room feeling hopeful. If her husband was still asleep, she would watch him carefully to see whether he was still breathing, and if she wasn't sure she would stand next to him and put her face close to his. A couple of times Arnie had opened his eyes just at that moment and almost given her a heart attack. He hadn't been able to stop himself from smiling. He'd said 'Good morning' each time, like a kind of revenge, asking innocently, 'Is anything the matter?'

Lilia was only just becoming aware of the path she'd drawn for herself throughout her life. She'd always lived other people's lives when she'd thought she'd been living her own, and she'd built her life around them. She couldn't blame anyone else for that. Every decision she'd made was hers and no one else's. In fact, she'd waved away the warnings of some of her friends before marrying Arnie, and only believed what she could see with her own eyes. She'd also chosen not to listen to what her siblings had to say before adopting Dung and Giang. Now she vaguely remembered a conversation she'd had with a friend on the subway in Manhattan. She'd recently stopped working and had decided to dedicate herself completely to the children they were going to adopt. Her friend had said: 'I hope you won't regret this one day, Lilia.

A woman has to make her own money.' But Lilia had always been too full of hope to look as far as the next step.

Worst of all, she was still doing the same thing. She was still basing her life around other people. The continuation of her pathetic existence depended on making sure that the other people in her life lived theirs the way they wanted to. They had to eat so that Lilia had a reason to live during the day. Arnie had to go to the bathroom under her supervision so that she had a reason to wake up in the morning. She realised this hurtful truth about her life one day when she was stirring the food in the pot one last time and lowering the heat. She felt dizzy for a second. She'd never felt this shaken by any other moment of self-awareness. She pulled over one of the stools and sat down on it. She'd been sure that she was going to achieve something when she'd first come to this continent from so many miles away. But in the end she'd even failed at loving someone, let alone at being loved. She'd finally reached the point when every day was simply a time frame in which she breathed in and out. They had no importance, no cause and no consequence. She wouldn't have to go to the supermarket to buy groceries if she didn't have to cook for her tenants, and she had no idea how she would spend those empty hours.

All the emotions she'd been storing up for years appeared clearly in her mind as she sat on that stool. She felt incredibly helpless. She didn't know how she could turn her life around, where to start and if she even had the time to do that. The worst thing was realising that she'd wasted a whole life. She tried to imagine how many millions of people did no more than fill the space they lived in. How many millions of people carried on living just because they'd been born and simply stole from other people's happiness, success and wealth? She remembered a Canadian man a couple of days ago on TV saying that every human being had the right to use thirteen gallons of water a day, and now she saw the subject from a completely different point of view. What about people like herself, who didn't know what they were living for and did nothing but suck energy out of the earth and steal from those people who knew why they were alive?

Lilia's mind grew clearer with every passing minute, but at the same time her heart darkened. She didn't remember ever feeling so meaningless before. She would never have imagined years ago, as she sat on a stool in her mother's kitchen in the Philippines and watched her cooking, that years later she'd consider giving up on her own existence. Her mother used to cook and talk her daughter through the different steps at the same time, just like the women who gave recipes on TV nowadays. 'Now we add a cup of flour, a cup of corn starch.' If she realised that she was missing one of the ingredients, she would never get angry but would instead turn calmly to Lilia and say: 'Don't forget, there's a substitute for every ingredient. The most important thing is not to panic.' Lilia had always kept that advice in a corner of her mind while she was cooking. Maybe now she had to apply it to her own life, too.

When she was a little girl, like almost all Filipinos Lilia believed in the existence of spirits who lived outside of this world. They came to visit humans once in a while, brought them news from the other world, showed them a path and changed people's destiny for the worse if they did something to upset them. Since a lot of strange incidents had happened around her, and because her family was believed to hold a very strong power, her senses had been more open than many other people's ever since she was a baby. She'd always enjoyed talking about her dreams and having them interpreted by the elders, and even thought that she could heal sick people by closing her eyes really tightly. Most importantly, she'd thought that she would always have that power. She'd never imagined that a person who was born with a gift like that could ever be deprived of it. Her great aunt had never mentioned the importance of practice, because she hadn't known any other way of living herself. What's more, she'd never imagined that somebody with that kind of a gift wouldn't use it.

When Lilia came to the United States it was the mid sixties. She'd been exposed to American culture before – this 'Far West civilisation' had spent a long time in her country, after all. All the same, when she found herself in New York during the most intense time of political and cultural change in the history of the world, everything she'd known had been turned upside down. The American way of living she'd seen in her own country looked like a cheap imitation of the real thing. They'd learned how to dress and eat like Americans, but having the American mentality was something else altogether. This beautiful young woman who had come from so far away, carried traces of many cultures and spoke English, Spanish and Filipino had easily been able to find a place for herself in the arts, fashion and intellectual world of New York. While those New Yorkers who had come to the city from small towns in the United States tried to emphasise Lilia's exotic quality, Lilia tried to strip herself of it. This had been her main reason for changing her name, in fact, rather than having it pronounced the wrong way. The more Americans had tried to make her Filipino, the more American she'd become.

That was why she only kissed her friends on one cheek now and didn't stand up to see them out at the end of their visit. It was also why she asked people about their jobs even though she had no interest in them. In the beginning she'd had to stop herself from turning her plate upside down whenever somebody left the table early, as according to Filipino culture this would prevent famine from finding the house. In the end, she'd managed to get rid of all of her superstitions. Even though she'd wanted to warn her friends against dumping their leftover rice in the bin, explaining that this would make them poor, she hadn't done it. In time she'd come to see that nobody became poor in America for throwing away rice, there was no evil eye, virgins didn't have to marry old men just because they sang while they were cooking, and women didn't have twins because they'd eaten bananas during their pregnancy. She'd decided that those spirits they believed in didn't exist in this continent. She would wonder about this throughout her life, and would only talk about it years later over dinner with her sisters when they were telling stories from the old country. Then her niece, who was born in the United States but was more Filipino than any of them, would say: 'The spirits from the old world couldn't cross the ocean, because they were scared of the water. That's why this continent is so empty.'

By the time Lilia recognised the beauty of believing in something other than her own existence, it was too late. She would never have thought that those beliefs, prayers and even spells that had been buried for so many years could gather dust, be forgotten and finally weaken. That was why when she'd mixed some flour with water many years later, turned it into a mini sculpture, put it on the counter, sprinkled it with red pepper, nutmeg and salt and prayed, it hadn't worked. The moment she'd said, 'You can't do anything to me, and you'll never be able to' was exactly the moment when the spirits had finally closed their ears. She'd tried the spells she remembered from the past a couple more times after that. She'd put a fish's eye in Arnie's soup, a drop of morning dew in his cheese, said prayers to the rice in the *pilaf*, made sure she put only odd numbers of chickpeas in his food and added black pepper to the honey she served with his tea. All the same, nothing had worked and her wishes hadn't been granted. Her beliefs must have turned their back on her, just as she'd once turned her back on them. No matter how much Manggagaway wanted it to happen, however tightly she closed her eyes, she couldn't heal her own sorrow. She possessed no power, either for good or for evil. The first twenty years of her life had been swept away by the last forty. She stopped trying after a while. Her mother must have been wrong. She couldn't save a whole life just as she could save a dish of food. There was no substitute for life's missing ingredients. She couldn't reach the satisfaction she wished for, no matter how much starch she used. There was no egg white to stick things back together in real life. The tastes didn't blend together; they couldn't create an ultimate, single delicacy. The spice of life was always either too much or too little. The universe was terrible at knowing how much a pinch was.

She came back to reality with the smell of burnt food. She turned around, still sitting on the stool, and looked at the pot on the stove. It took her some time to remember where she was; in which year, in what lifetime. She pulled herself together a couple of minutes later and remembered the food she was supposed to be cooking. Without lifting the lid, she could already tell how burnt it was. She stood up, turned off the heat, lifted the lid and added a glass of hot water. At least this would help her to salvage the bottom of the food.

As he looked at himself in the mirror, Marc realised just how much he'd changed in the last nine months. His hair, which he'd always carefully kept short before, had grown longer, the beard and moustache he'd decided to keep had artfully covered the signs of age on his face and there were small rings under his eyes, which were the sign of a late-found love rather than exhaustion. This new love was Marc's love of life. He'd always thought he'd been very happy before his wife died. Still, it was only after her death – when he'd started struggling with life for the first time – that he'd finally realised how much of it he'd missed and that he could have been much happier. Cooking had become a passion for him. He compared everything he ate in restaurants with what he cooked at home and corrected whatever was lacking. He would keep on cooking a dish he knew well many times in a row, until both the knowledge and the habit had settled in his system.

The kitchen had become the door to a new life for him. He could even smell all kinds of things he couldn't have done before. It was almost as if he'd finally started using all of his senses since he'd taken up cooking, while he'd only used a couple of them before. He wasn't only attracted by the smell or taste of fruits and vegetables any more; he could also feel their texture. When he saw how the change of season was reflected clearly at the farmers' market, he understood for the first time that the whole world was a complete work of art. Only now could his mind comprehend that appreciating art by reading books or looking at tableaus in museums was just a very small part of a much bigger picture. He'd had to learn which part of the veal provided the best steak to understand that Annibale Carracci hadn't been inspired by other paintings, but by the raw visual of a hunk of veal hanging in a butcher's window. He only understood the true depth of Clara's personality now that he'd been left without her. It wasn't that Marc had forgotten his wife; he'd simply accepted her absence and got used to this new life. He still thought about her every day, and pictured one of her facial expressions or gestures, but he'd finally learned that he had to go on living like this: living in longing all of the time.

He still went to Tout le Marché almost once a week. He'd never imagined how long it would take him to build a new kitchen when he'd got rid of everything he had there. That must have been why Clara felt so attached to each and every item. She must have seen them all as new additions to their family over the years. Marc tried to go to the store on the days when Sabina was working. He'd got used to seeing the same face each week for several months. The young woman, of course, had made it easy for him to build up the habit. Her hair never changed, and neither did her ever-plain face, the uniform she wore for work or, most importantly, the smile on her face, which never faded; this all made Marc feel more secure. He saw her as an unforgettable part of the most important era of his life. They'd never met outside the store or had long conversations, but still he felt that his new friend already knew everything he wanted to say and everything he wanted to tell her. They'd mentioned Clara a couple more times, only because they'd had to refer to something in particular; they hadn't touched on anything deeper than that. Sabina also found some security in Marc's friendship. She'd become certain that there was a special bond between them when Marc told her that he preferred coming to the store on the days when she was working and therefore wanted to know which days they were. She wasn't in love with this older man – she didn't imagine being in his arms – but she'd already confessed to herself that she'd rather be with him than other people. She'd been tempted to invite him for a cup of coffee during her break a couple of times, but she'd always changed her mind at the last minute. Marc was clearly going to invite her out for coffee when he felt ready. Until then, they could just walk among the pots and pans, spend a few minutes in front of the new knife sets and talk about all kinds of things while staring at the graters. Neither of them understood how they could start off talking about any little thing and end up having a meaningful, absorbing conversation. All the same, they were never surprised to find themselves talking about the Italian Renaissance in the company of a colander, for example. Sabina's manager was, of course, aware of the amount of time that she spent with this particular customer; still, he couldn't really say anything when he calculated the total amount this man had spent so far.

As Marc got ready in front of the mirror in his apartment, he toyed with the idea of asking Sabina out for a cup of coffee for the first time. He was sure that this young woman wouldn't misunderstand him. He wasn't in love with Sabina; he knew that. In fact, he'd wished he was in love with her from time to time. He was more comfortable with her than he'd ever been with anybody apart from Clara. He also guessed that Sabina didn't have feelings for him. In that case, it wouldn't hurt to ask her out for a drink. Besides, he felt like he owed her. He knew that he couldn't have built his new life without Sabina's help. The young woman knew her job very well. She'd never made him buy anything he'd regret later on. In fact, she'd stopped him from buying some things he'd wanted to get, just because he'd seen them in a magazine and thought they might be useful. She'd said, 'You don't need an electric rice cooker to make rice *pilaf*', or 'Remember the colander you got last month? You can use that for this recipe, too', and had ended up saving him some money. Yes, he had to buy her a cup of coffee. Maybe he should even wait until her break and buy her lunch. After looking at himself one more time in the mirror, he sprayed some aftershave inside his collar for the first time in months and went to the kitchen. He put the list he'd prepared in his pocket and turned up the volume of the radio on the window sill. He didn't have to turn on the light. Summer hadn't only brought heat, but also longer days. After he'd made sure that the stove and the oven were switched off, he left his apartment to go to Tout le Marché.

He waited for Sabina, playing with the apple peeler in his hand. He realised that she didn't treat him any differently from the other customers, judging from the attention she paid to each one of them. She was always very gentle, respectful and attentive to everyone. She didn't look at all bothered by having to show a woman all sorts of nutcrackers, explaining how they were different from one another. Marc thought that a sophisticated woman like her, who not only knew everything there was to know about kitchen appliances but also a lot about art and literature, shouldn't be working in a place like that. He'd never heard her complain or say that she was tired or bored, but this was clearly a sign of her maturity, which she'd reached at a very young age. Today he wanted to ask her the question he'd been thinking about for months. What did she want from life? What were her plans? There must have been some higher goal she'd set for herself.

This new interest he had in other people's lives really surprised him. Maybe he'd never wondered about them before because his own life had been so well organised. His and his wife's place in this world had been fixed, and that had been enough for him. He'd never wanted to know about those people they called their friends, or Amou, or his neighbour across the hall, who even closed the door of the lift slowly so she wouldn't make any noise, and he'd never shown any interest in knowing how these people lived. He'd known Odette for years, but he'd never thought of sticking his nose into her life to see what was really happening there. Odette had a happy marriage, didn't she? She had two kids. She was going to be a grandmother soon. What did she enjoy in life, and what didn't she like?

The neighbour across the hall had lost her husband, hadn't she? She must have felt so alone. Did she have any children?

Did they come to visit her? Now, when he thought about her, he realised that she had a hump in her back. She always walked hunched over. Did her back hurt? He was sure that Clara had known all the answers to those questions. She must have known even more. Maybe she even knew Amou better than he did. Hadn't she brought lentil soup to the gallery for him, saying it was his favourite? When had she found out about that? How come she'd made that soup, put it in small containers and carried them to the gallery? Hadn't she also brought flu medicine for Amou a couple of times? How had she known he was sick? He hadn't even realised that himself.

But now, he wondered why Sabina worked at the store. Had she graduated from university? She must have. What had she studied? Arts? Literature? Why wasn't she doing something related to her degree? Where was she from? She must come from the South – he'd gathered that much from her accent – but where, exactly? He didn't need to ask why she'd come to Paris. Everybody wanted to come to Paris in the end. The whole world wanted to be there. Marc couldn't understand how this city accommodated so many people. Why did all those people cram themselves into such small apartments? He'd never paid any rent in his life, thanks to his parents, but he'd heard that people paid ridiculous amounts for those tiny spaces. How did all these people make that kind of money? Where did Sabina live? Maybe in the twentieth arrondissement. Or maybe on the outskirts of the eighteenth. Could he ask her all of these questions? Should he? Or would that be too personal? Before he could reach a conclusion, Sabina walked over.

Marc looked different today. Sabina was witnessing the changes in this man's life, a man that she didn't know at all and helped only as a customer. His hair had grown; it was flopping over to the left at the front. There were as many reds as greys in his ever-growing moustache and beard. His hair, on the other hand, had no hint of red. No, the sorrow on his face hadn't vanished, but it looked calm rather than depressing now. While he hadn't been able to look up at all during his first visits to the store, he'd started looking around him more curiously lately. He could find something to say, too, instead of just listening. Sabina smelled a hint of aftershave. It was a smell she knew; something fresh. The smell of the sea. Had he bought it recently? Or had he had it for a long time, waiting in a corner, and finally found the courage to put it on for the first time in months? Maybe this was the scent his wife liked on him. Maybe he'd kept it hidden away for months because it reminded him of her.

Sabina had thought Marc might kill himself the first time she saw him. He was so unhappy, so hopeless. He couldn't stand anything that reminded him of his wife, and that mainly meant himself. If he didn't show up for a couple of weeks, Sabina would think, 'He did it, he committed suicide.' Didn't Marc have any friends? She didn't know. Family? Siblings? Cousins? Even though she really wanted to know the answers to these questions, she didn't have the courage to ask. Instead, they always talked about daily events whenever they saw each other and let themselves go wherever the subject took them. Nothing they'd talked about had carried them to their private lives so far. Sabina didn't mind about that. There were many details she wouldn't like to share about her own life, anyway.

Maybe that was why she hadn't asked Marc to have a drink with her, although she'd thought about it a lot. If he asked questions about her life, she wouldn't want to lie; she liked to be honest with people. That was why she never engaged in long conversations with anybody, and never allowed the subject to come up. She could talk about other things for hours, such as politics, art, books or kitchen appliances, as long as she didn't have to talk about herself. She was already ashamed of only describing one part of her life to her family, whom she'd left behind in the South; that made her feel like a liar. She didn't want to have to carry a heavier weight than that.

Despite all of these feelings, she couldn't say 'no' to Marc when he asked if she wanted to have lunch with him that day, after he'd put everything he needed in his basket and had started walking towards the cashier. When she left the store half an hour later as they'd arranged, she found him standing in front of the Hôtel de Ville, watching the skaters. The roller skaters in their short, colourful leggings had started filling the area where people went ice skating during the winter. Marc had tried ice skating a couple of times when he was a little boy when his mother had insisted, but he couldn't even imagine himself on wheels. Sabina, on the other hand, had never tried either of these things. 'Ice skating is all right, but doesn't roller skating belong in the eighties?' she said to Marc. They started talking about how bad almost everything had looked in that era, despite the age difference between them. Sabina confessed that she'd backcombed her hair just like everybody else. Marc didn't even know what that meant. This was the first time he'd ever heard the name of that style, which had made his wife's hair look ridiculous. Of course, he couldn't help knowing about shoulder pads. Who hadn't been a victim of that crime against fashion? Or of those jackets with the rolled up sleeves?

They both knew that if there had been any chemistry, any kind of sexual attraction between them, they couldn't have talked about things this easily. Comfortable in their lack of love, they walked towards the nearby café. They picked a table where they could watch the roller skaters and sat down. Sabina had only half an hour left; they would have to order quickly. Then she had four more hours of standing up ahead of her. Marc almost asked her, 'Why don't you find another job?' but decided not to at the last minute. Maybe next time, he thought. Instead, they talked about how the nineties were the real eighties. The nineties was a lost decade. Humanity had jumped straight from the eighties to the two thousands. The world had become very modern all of a sudden and technology had advanced so quickly. After Sabina had analysed the issue right up until the last minute and had stood up to get back to work on time, Marc also got to his feet. Although they'd known each other for months now, they kissed each other on both cheeks for the first time and said farewell until next week. Marc realised at that moment that this was the first friend he'd made by himself in years. He sat back down and ordered himself another cup of coffee. He took out the notepad he'd started carrying around with him wherever he went and opened it to a blank page.

He'd been playing with the idea that Odette had given him for a while now. They had talked on the phone a couple of times since they'd last seen each other and she'd been kinder to him than ever. Each time she'd asked if he needed any help. During one of those calls, Marc had mentioned what he was planning to cook that night, since the conversation had brought them to the subject, and Odette had once again had to hold back the tears and had given him some useful tips. She knew that Marc paid attention to her suggestions, because he'd asked her to wait a minute while he went to fetch a pen and paper, and took note of the things she said as he spelled them out: 'Sa-lt-one-si-de-fir-st-then-the-oth-er-side. Let-it-s-tand-for-ten-min-utes. OK.'

Marc had been slowly discovering just how useful it was to share knowledge about cooking. Even if the recipe was very detailed, there was always something else, something important that another cook could add. Clara used to talk to her mother once or twice a week before she'd died years ago and asked her about a recipe every time. She used to say that her mother was always a step ahead of her. She'd always complain that no matter how well she cooked, she could never be as good as her mother. She'd had to forget some tastes altogether after her mother died. She'd tried to make those things, but they never turned out the same way. Whenever that happened, Marc could never understand why his wife was crying. Was it because she missed her mother, or because she couldn't eat one of her dishes any more? Now he understood exactly what his wife was going through. There were some tastes that he just couldn't forget, which he craved for and desperately wanted one last time. They were the tastes of Clara's food; but he knew that he could never make them the same way or find the same tastes anywhere else.

Sometimes people at the farmers' market – maybe the butcher or the man at the fish counter – gave him tips that couldn't be found in his cookbook. Marc wrote them down if he could, depending on where he was, and if he had too many packages with him he would keep repeating them to himself until he got home and could fill in the empty spaces around the recipe in his book. When he flicked through the pages from the back to the front, he could see just how far he'd come. He thought he should go back to the beginning when he'd finished all of the recipes and start all over again. This time he would definitely take his notes into consideration, and maybe even add some new ones.

The soufflé book, on the other hand, was left on the shelf with many of its pages unopened. He'd tried a couple of recipes from it, failed each time worse than the time before and then decided to put the book away until he'd got better in the kitchen. He had no idea why he'd bought that book in the first place or how he'd ever thought he could make a soufflé so soon. Maybe he'd never be able to reach that level, even if he cooked for the rest of his life. There were some people who spent their whole lives in the kitchen and could still never manage to make a decent one. Unfortunately, he'd found this out from the hosts of *Escapade Gourmande* long after buying the book.

He listed some of the dishes he felt comfortable with on the new page he'd opened. The problem was, he didn't know which ones went well with one another. He wasn't even sure if he could serve them all on the same night. He added 'salad' at the end of the list. How wrong could he go if he simply mixed tomatoes, cucumbers and spring onions with the greens that came ready-washed in boxes? Still, there was always the vinaigrette to worry about. He hadn't been able to get a good sour taste in the salads he'd made for himself so far. He still hadn't thought of simply mixing a splash of lemon juice with vinegar.

He thought maybe he could ask which dishes went well together at the farmers' market. Maybe the guy at the fishmonger's could make some suggestions. Sabina must be a good cook, too, judging from their conversations about kitchen appliances. They hadn't had time to talk about food yet, but he was sure that the young woman would be able to give him some good ideas if he asked her. He decided he should invite her to lunch again next week when he went to Tout le Marché, so he could show her his list and ask her what she thought. Maybe he should even invite her to the dinner he wanted to give. He looked up from his list and stared at the roller skaters. The music playing for the skaters to dance to echoed off the buildings around them and every line was repeated twice. He'd heard this song on the TV the other day while he was cooking. It was a young woman who sang it. Olivia ... He couldn't remember her last name. There was no way he could remember the name of the song, but it was good enough for him to know that much. In the past he would have just carried on with his life without noticing any of those details.

He opened another page from his notepad and wrote down the names of the probable guests: Odette, Henri, Sylvie, Jacques, Suzanne and Daniel. This was an idea he'd been playing with ever since Odette had asked to taste his food. It had been almost a year since he'd lost Clara and since then he'd been avoiding the people who loved his wife the most. He knew they were hurting, too, and missed her as much as he did. Maybe they would like to come to the place where their friend had lived for so many years and connect with her there one last time. Not only Odette; they all had to be there for that dinner. Maybe it was time to say a decent farewell to Clara. Besides, these people who had been so close to him for so many years deserved to know how he was living now.

The list made seven people, including him. He added Sabina's name there, too, and tried to see how it looked on paper. She was the only friend he'd made without Clara's help. Of course, they were all going to think she was the new woman in his life. Maybe he should call Odette and tell her that she wasn't beforehand. Then she could let the others know. What would Sabina think? Would she feel like some kind of replacement for his dead wife? Would she understand that the invitation didn't mean anything when the dinner party was full of couples? He finally crossed the name out.

So far, Marc had prepared all of his dishes for just one person. He always divided the ingredients given in the recipe by four and cooked them accordingly. He didn't have a clue how to adapt the same recipes for seven people. First of all, he didn't even know if he could cook for seven people with his pots and pans. If the book said he should roast the meat at 190 degrees for two hours, he usually cooked just a quarter of it for only half an hour. If he decided to go with meat, then he'd have to be really careful about the timing. How long should it be in for? Naturally, it would be easier to cook for eight people. Then he would only have to multiply the recipe by two. There was nothing wrong with having one extra portion. In that case, he'd have to keep the meat dish he'd made for himself some time ago in the oven for four hours. He also had to marinate it for two hours beforehand, which meant that just one of the dishes on his menu would take six hours to cook. He would have to calculate every minute of that day very carefully and organise it all really well. He'd helped Clara at dinner parties before by carrying the plates to the table in the living room, but he didn't even know how to set a table by himself. All of a sudden he felt overwhelmed by it all and, thinking that he couldn't deal with his thoughts and all the things he was planning to do, gave up on the project altogether. The idea of bringing all of those dishes together at the same time, which had seemed very difficult to begin with, became even more complicated when he thought about cooking for so many people at once.

He closed his notepad and put it in his pocket along with his pencil. He paid the bill and stood up in a hurry. The sun that had calmed him before made him sweat now and the music he'd listened to so happily almost scratched his ears. He started walking towards St Germain at a brisk pace, all the way home. When he entered his apartment, the song he'd heard in the square was playing on the radio. He left whatever he had in his hands in the doorway and walked out as quickly as he'd come in. His heart couldn't fit in this apartment at that moment, just as it couldn't fit inside his rib cage.

Ferda had just had another very tough morning. Her mother had worn her out physically as well as psychologically over the last few months. Every bone that had been broken in her body in the past was aching now. The humidity, which had grown worse over the summer, wasn't helping either. Her wrist, which had knitted itself back together crookedly, was now swollen like a drum. While she was trying to help her mother to sit up using her own bandaged wrist, this image had triggered her mother's slippery mind and they'd had to go back to her dark past one more time. Ferda believed that there was some truth in all this nonsense. It looked as if Mrs Nesibe's memories, which she'd kept suppressed for years, were surfacing one by one now. There were secrets she'd never shared with anyone; her cruel thoughts about other people, her erotic dreams. Ferda felt ashamed of the things her mother said and couldn't even look Sinan in the face after hearing them. All the same, these clues from her mother's closed up life were helping her to define her own existence.

Ferda had always thought there must be some powerful reason that had caused her mother to be depressed all the time and to end up ignoring her own children; something much bigger than her father's death. She knew that some women who loved their husbands very much turned their backs on life after losing them and mourned them until they died, too. Still, her mother had never been able to enjoy life much, even when her husband was still living. Since Mrs Nesibe had also partially ruined Ferda's own life, she wanted to believe that some incredibly deep, sad event must have taken place to cause all of this sorrow. Ferda loved Sinan, especially because she knew how much he loved her. All the same, she hadn't married him because she'd been in love with him, or even because she'd really wanted to. She'd agreed to get married at such an early age because she knew it was necessary. She'd had to put her dreams aside and reclaim her future, which her mother had almost thrown away when she was far too young.

That was why she wanted to find out what that secret was before Mrs Nesibe died: so that she could forgive her mother. If not, she was scared that she wouldn't be able to remember her with any love. She'd been waiting for her to die for a while now and that feeling of guilt was eating her from the inside out. Still, she couldn't help but long for that day. As she lay down on her back each night and felt every inch of her spine fill with pain, she couldn't help closing her eyes and thinking about her mother's funeral. She often thought how free she was going to feel that day; her life would be peaceful again, perhaps even for the first time.

She felt the panic building whenever she thought about Öykü's nearing delivery date and simply couldn't find a solution to this problem. She had to be with her daughter when she had a baby so far away. She knew that Duval was a big support to Öykü – he'd already taken care of a lot of the household chores – but Ferda had been with her son and daughter-in-law during the birth of their two children and now she had to be with her daughter. Life mustn't let her mother steal this one away from her, too.

Mrs Nesibe started crying, 'Mum, hold me, I'm tired, I don't want to walk', as soon as she saw Ferda's bandaged wrist. Ferda had learned from previous experiences how to console her mother, adapting to one of her alter egos, instead of trying to explain things. She lowered her voice and cooed to her as she would with a baby. She added a third pillow under her mother's head and sat at the edge of the bed. She dried her mother's eyes as she caressed her hair. It looked like Mrs Nesibe had gone back to her own childhood. But which year exactly? Which country? Mrs Nesibe had been one of those children who'd come over from Salonika during the population exchange. She'd tried to pull out her memories from those times and describe them before, but she'd never fully remembered those events. She'd been very young when she'd come to Istanbul. She didn't remember either their arrival or what had happened afterwards.

Now she was crying, staring at the bandage on her daughter's wrist. Ferda asked her, as if talking to a little child:

'Do you want me to take off this bandage? Does it scare you?'

'I don't want to walk, hold me.'

'Where are we walking to, Nesibe?'

'That girl doesn't have a hand.'

'Which girl?'

'Hold me, I'm tired.'

'Which girl doesn't have a hand, Nesibe? Don't be afraid, tell me.'

'I'm tired, hold me.'

Ferda could see that she wasn't going to get anything out of her, so she stopped. Mrs Nesibe repeated the same sentence over and over again sometimes. Maybe she'd remember what that was about during one of those rare moments when she was feeling more like herself. It looked as if she'd seen someone without a hand when she was a child, maybe in Salonika. Maybe that chaos had left a deeper scar on her than they'd ever realised. Ferda was never going to find out that her mother had been taken to the hospital to get vaccinated when she was a little girl and seen a young woman without a hand there, who had been silently crying as she waited for her dressing to be changed. She'd never know that this incident had been tattooed on her mother's mind and caused her to be afraid of losing a limb for the rest of her life, or that little Nesibe had been tired at the end of that visit and cried out to her mother to be carried. Instead, Ferda preferred to think that her mother had gone through some painful times during the exchange, and that those memories had stuck in her subconscious and troubled her for the rest of her life. She knew from other exchange stories how some people had had to walk for hundreds of miles. She was going to place her mother within those stories and think that a little girl like that could never forget that kind of exhaustion.

Öykü's wedding had been a great success. When Ferda looked back at that day, she couldn't even find one little flaw. She had played a part in the catering and even checked that things were fine in the kitchen during the party. The venue they'd chosen was very beautiful and looked like a garden out of a fairy tale. The unpredictable Istanbul weather had also given a gift to the mother and daughter and granted them a beautiful day. Ferda had been really nervous the night before because of the heavy rain, but it had made way for a bright sky the next day. She'd done the right thing by listening to her mother and buying the wedding gown one size up. Öykü had turned out not to be able to stop eating and her breasts, belly and hips had rounded out even in such a short time.

All of the guests had guessed the reason for the urgency of the marriage. It was actually impossible not to notice that Öykü was pregnant just by looking at her. Everybody had spat twice and said, 'The gown looks gorgeous on her, her face is glowing', but they all knew what they really meant. They must have analysed the issue in depth among themselves. They must have been saying that Ferda had an infidel son-in-law now. Which religion was the baby going to belong to? How were the two families going to talk to one another? Despite all of these worrying questions, both Sinan and Ferda had found Duval's family very nice, polite and warm. They'd had a great time together, finding a middle way with the help of a very broken English on both sides and a lot of hand gestures. Ferda saw that they really loved Öykü, and so what else mattered?

As she pored over the wedding album on the kitchen table, she was surprised to see how quickly time had passed. It had already been two months since the wedding. In just four months' time she was going to be a grandmother again. She already loved her unborn grandchild, but felt sad that they were going to have to live apart. Could they really know and love each other that way? She was jealous of Duval's mother, who was going to be so close to the child. What's more, she was a very sweet woman. The baby was going to adore her. Just like herself, her grandchild was going to be one of those rare people who were closer to their paternal grandmothers. Ferda had always been the only one among her friends who loved her paternal grandmother more than her maternal one. The first time a girl at school had asked her which one she liked the most and she'd replied, 'My paternal grandmother', that child had almost lost her balance and fallen over. That wasn't the answer she'd been expecting. She'd called out to all the other little girls immediately and announced Ferda's strange response to her question. A cry of amazement had risen from the group: 'What?!' Of course, she'd felt the need to explain herself. Her maternal grandmother had died young, so she hadn't got to know her much, and she was sure she'd love her if she'd known her better. This explanation hadn't satisfied anybody. All that mattered was that a child had said she loved her paternal grandmother the most. Nobody did that. And now her French grandchild was going to say the same thing one day: 'I'm sure if I knew my maternal grandmother better, I'd love her even more than the other one.'

This was a problem that Ferda would have to deal with later in life. Now she had to plan how she could be with her daughter during the birth, in case her mother didn't die before then. Just like every other time she'd wanted to think about something in detail, she stood up first and put some water in the kettle. There was only one more tea bag left from her expensive set. Thanks to this tea set, Ferda had come to realise that some luxuries really did make people feel good, and she promised herself to use every gift she received from then on. She should let other people treat her when they wanted to do that.

She walked to the cupboard and picked out one of the delicate porcelain cups. She put the pyramid-shaped silk tea bag inside it and waited for the sound of the steam. Just before the kettle starting whistling, she turned off the stove and poured the water into the cup. She didn't want to take any risks, even though her mother was fast asleep, safely drugged by the medication. She only had a couple of hours during the day to spend alone. She felt like she'd lose her mind if she had to give them up, too. 'Let's think,' she said to herself. After three minutes, she removed the tea bag and took a sip of her tea. The taste and smell of the raspberry must have hit a crucial spot in her brain, because she calmed down instantly. Öykü had written on each tea bag to explain what they were before she'd left. Surprised and delighted to see that her mother had finally used a gift she'd been given, she'd said: 'Let me know when you've finished them all, I'll send you a new box.' Ferda wasn't a stranger to the idea of travelling for miles for some really special food. How many times had she carefully packed stuffed artichoke leaves into a parcel and asked Mrs Gulseren's daughter, who was an air hostess, to take them with her to Paris? Tulin hadn't only carried artichoke leaves for her, but also braided cheese, kasseri cheese, stuffed courgette flowers, leek pastries and lamb neck pudding. Usually Ferda wouldn't ask for this kind of a favour more than once, but Tulin had managed to convince her by insisting that it wasn't a problem. That was when Tulin had taught Ferda the concept of karma. It was basically the Sanskrit way of expressing the famous Turkish proverb: 'Whatever you plant, you'll harvest.' Tulin was sure that these good deeds would all come back to her one day. Still, even though Ferda knew all about the troubles people were prepared to go through for a certain taste, she wasn't about to call her daughter and ask her for new tea bags while Öykü was dealing with pregnancy and work at the same time. Instead, she was going to enjoy her last cup and then find some kind of substitute.

To her own embarrassment, once again she found herself thinking how convenient it would be if her mother could die within two and a half months. Then they would only have a month and a half left until the delivery date, which was just enough time for Ferda to take care of everything. 'Only if everything goes according to plan,' she thought. They couldn't plan everything, could they? 'God forbid, what if Öykü delivers early?' she asked herself. Trying to ignore that thought, she jotted down everything that would have to be done one by one in her mental notebook. Once Mrs Nesibe died, she'd have to take care of the seventh day prayer first and then the fortieth day prayer. If she really died within two and a half months, the earliest Ferda could make it to France would be just before the birth.

She tried to swallow these awful ideas with another sip of tea. Her grandmother sometimes used to say, 'Don't offend God.' This was exactly one of those cases. Trying to plan the death of one person and the birth of another might really offend God. She drank the rest of her tea in one mouthful, burning her throat as if she wanted to punish herself. Then she put the cup back on the table and raised both of her hands in the air. She turned her palms upwards and prayed: 'Forgive me, God. Send me good karma … Good karma.'

Ten

Lilia's days were always the same. She didn't even know which day she was living in most of the time and got confused about events. She thought that something that had happened the morning before had happened that day and couldn't see any difference between a night a week ago and a night this week. Since she did everything just like a clockwork robot, she couldn't even keep track of the things she'd done. When she walked into Arnie's room and said, 'We have to change your sheets', Arnie looked at his wife, worriedly, and had to remind her that they'd done that an hour ago. Her conversations with her tenants had been reduced to almost nothing and consisted only of repeated words: 'Hi.' 'Hi.' 'How was your day?' 'Good. How was yours?' 'Good.' 'This is really delicious, thank you,' 'Glad you enjoyed it.' 'Good night.' 'Good night.' Sometimes when she found herself saying the same words over again she would stop for a couple of minutes, think, look around her and try to find even the slightest difference from the previous day. She couldn't find anything to say to her siblings when she talked to them on the phone every once in a while. She had nothing to say about her tenants any more, Arnie was always the same and

Lilia was tired of her own complaining. When both voices on either end of the phone fell silent, they had nothing else to do but hang up, and then Lilia's siblings usually turned to their spouses and said, 'Poor Lilia.'

Lilia had finally given up hope, one thing she'd never imagined losing. She didn't expect anything either from the future or the day she was living in. She lived every minute and every hour just to be done with them and couldn't find anything special about them when she got to the end of the day. She wasn't conscious of her greasy hair, the dark circles around her eyes, or the holes in her socks. She didn't even know how she'd describe herself if she had to. She'd been someone who had wanted to paint once, a mother for only ten years, a wife who'd spent the last year as a housemaid and an optimist who'd managed to live this long without realising any of these things.

One day – all of a sudden – after giving Arnie his breakfast, she went to her room instead of going to the kitchen to prepare the day's menu. She took off her dress, which she hadn't done for days, even before going to bed. She went into the shower without examining her body in the mirror, as she'd usually done for a while over the last couple of months. When she'd made sure that she'd got rid of the dirt of the last ten days, she dried her hair with a towel. She fixed her thinning hair with the comb she hadn't touched for a while. After putting on another dress, which covered her body perfectly, she sat in front of the mirror and examined her face. She was startled by the emptiness in her own eyes.

Arnie had been concerned about Lilia for a while. Now he followed her movements as closely as possible and tried to understand what was going on. While Lilia was oblivious to the fact that she did everything automatically, Arnie saw how monotonous her life had become. His wife always came into his room after he'd finished his breakfast in the mornings, took his tray and went to the kitchen, where she started preparing the food for that day. Sometimes she talked to herself, but Arnie couldn't hear exactly what she was saying no matter how hard he tried. Today, however, she'd put the tray down on the counter and gone to her room without saying a word. When he heard the sounds coming from the pipes he realised that she was taking a shower. He carried on waiting, anxiously. He was dying to know what had managed to change Lilia's daily routine. Instead of turning on the TV and listening to the morning news, he listened to Lilia's footsteps. After twenty minutes he heard the door opening upstairs. He tried to work out whether or not she was coming to the kitchen by following the sound of her movements.

His wife went to the kitchen first, and after searching for something in a bowl for a while she picked something up. Then Arnie heard a clicking sound. That must be her handbag. Then the footsteps went to the front of the house. Now he heard his wife's voice. She was on the phone. She must be calling a taxi. After that he heard her walking around the house one more time and then the sound of the front door opening and closing. She must have gone outside. She hadn't felt like telling him where she was going. She hadn't said goodbye. All of a sudden, a fear rooted itself deep in his heart. Was she going to come back? Distressed, he shifted around in the bed. He'd never been the sort of person who listened to his sixth sense, since he'd never believed in that kind of thing, but now he felt something; something wasn't quite right. Lilia hadn't left the phone with him as she always did before leaving the house. Even though he could move around by himself with the help of his walker, he'd been scared to even stand up on his own since the last blood clot. He'd always pitied Lilia for being so completely dependent on him, but he was completely dependent on her now. And he hadn't shown her any gratitude. He carried on lying there, restlessly. It didn't matter how hard he thought about it, he wouldn't be able to find out what had happened until she told him. Thank goodness there were tenants in the house, he thought; he could ask them for help in the worst-case scenario. He turned on one of the news channels and watched the commentary on the upcoming election, trying to distract himself from his own dark thoughts.

Drowning in the wide seats of the taxi, Lilia was watching the empty streets outside. It was extremely unusual for anyone to walk around in this neighbourhood. It was frowned upon. People were suspicious of anyone who walked there. Nobody could enjoy the flowers planted in the small island in the middle of the road. 'Who was the last person to bend over and smell them?' she wondered.

When they reached the town centre, she told the driver to turn left on one of the side streets and stop in front of the only travel agency in the area. Asking him to come and pick her up in forty-five minutes, she got out of the car. The woman behind the desk welcomed her with a radiant smile. Women over sixty-five were their most valuable clientele.

They were mostly retired, with children who were already married and some money saved on the side, and they saw travelling almost as some kind of a job. A holiday was one of the bestselling gifts for anniversaries. It was also the perfect consolation for the recently widowed.

Lilia shook hands with the woman, who looked at least twenty years younger than her, and sat down on the chair that was offered to her. 'How can I help?' asked the woman. Lilia wanted to know about the cheapest available flight to the Philippines. No, it wasn't going to be a round trip. With her fingers on the keyboard, the woman looked at Lilia for a moment. She thought she must be one of those old people who wanted to go back to their own country to spend their old age. No, it was only her, not two people. This time the woman took a quick glance at Lilia's left hand to see if she was wearing a wedding ring. Yes, it was there. She must have lost her husband and probably didn't have any children. She clearly wanted to spend the rest of her life with her relatives in her own country.

The most convenient flights were in December. How did December 12 sound to her? Lilia took her credit card from her purse and held it out to the woman. After taking care of everything, the agent told Lilia to be at the airport two hours before the flight at half past six in the morning. And as soon as the customer had left, she comforted herself by saying that she was going to have a much better life when she was older. When Lilia left the travel agency, the taxi was already waiting for her outside. After telling the driver to take her back to where he'd picked her up, she turned to the window once again and lost herself in her thoughts. She was curious about all kinds of details she hadn't thought about in years. She had no idea how life had been in her country since she'd left. She'd only followed the presidential elections from time to time and had been proud of the fact that they'd elected a woman president twice. She wondered what life was like in her town these days. How developed was it now? Maybe it was much more modern than the last time she'd been there. Cantabon had been a poor, insignificant mountain village with no importance whatsoever until around twenty years ago. In the old days, Lilia never would have imagined that the Travel section of the *New York Times* would one day devote practically an entire issue to this small, forgotten village. Be that as it may, this unimaginable thing had actually happened after a spectacular new discovery.

Most of the article had talked about the Cantabon Cave. It explained that the cave had been discovered by foreign hunters in 1985 and that it was formed of dripstones measuring 300 metres long and 10 metres wide. Lilia had smiled to herself when she read it. Who would believe that she'd stolen eggs from birds' nests in that cave for her great aunt? How could she convince the writer of that article, who said it was dangerous to go into the cave without a helmet and a flashlight, that she'd walked around it just as she would anywhere else when she was a little girl? She'd also found out from that article that her village had become a popular tourist destination and that most of its inhabitants made money by working in that industry in one way or another. She knew that if she put a hot dog stand at the entrance of the cave she would be able to sell them in no time. If she made $5 a day, that would be fifty Filipino pesos. Not even a month's worth of water would cost that much. According to the article, living modestly in Cantabon would cost no more than $300 a month. If she could add more money to her savings over the next four months she might be able to live in a house in her own village for at least three years without having to do anything at all. Lilia hadn't been able to find happiness in the United States whatever she'd tried. The only expectation she had from then on was to live life only for herself.

As they got closer to home, the uncomfortable feeling came back. Even though she knew she only had a few months left, going back to the daily routines that she'd come to hate so much troubled her. After getting out of the car, she stood in front of this home she'd built with so many hopes back in the day and looked at it, closely. She'd learned that nothing in life happened the way people imagined and the universe followed its own course, but she wasn't about to give up without trying one last time. 'Four more months,' she thought to herself. 'Only four more months.' Holding on to the knowledge of the plane ticket in her handbag, she walked into the house. She didn't know that despite the distance between them, Arnie could still easily distinguish her footsteps from other people's. As soon as she walked in, he took a deep breath and closed his eyes.

Lilia spent the rest of the day in the kitchen, as she always did. She didn't say a word as she gave her husband his lunch and didn't return the looks he gave her. She didn't feel at all guilty knowing that she was going to be leaving in four months' time without saying a word, leaving her sick husband who needed her help behind. The only reason why she didn't look at her husband was because she couldn't stand seeing his greying eyes, which were getting smaller each day behind those thick glasses.

Although she'd always believed in the importance of living without harming anyone or any thing, she also accepted the cruelty she felt now for what it was; maybe because she knew that she'd have to give up on herself again if she wasn't cruel this time. In fact, she wished that Arnie would carry on being rude, brutal and disrespectful. She had a habit of weakening, of forgiving and forgetting the things that were done to her; she knew that forgetfulness was her weakest spot. That was why she needed life to be mean to her right now. As she waited outside the bathroom after seating Arnie on the toilet, she thought about the ticket she'd put in her dresser drawer and felt good. She was going to remember that ticket many times over the following days; whenever she felt down or distressed or like she couldn't go on, she would run to her room and take it in her hands.

She was going to have to stop herself from saying anything to anyone, despite how much she wanted to share her happiness. She'd come close to spilling the beans to her sisters on the phone a couple of times, but had managed to hold her tongue at the last minute. She didn't want anyone to try to stop her. She could more or less guess what people would say if they knew about her plans. They would say: 'Are you crazy? You can't set off on an adventure like that, not at your age. Whatever might have happened, Arnie has been your husband for so many years, you can't just leave him alone.' They were going to tell her to be loyal to her husband despite the fact that they'd never liked him or felt close to him themselves. They were going to load tons of guilt upon her. People always found something to say about any issue, even if they'd never thought about it before in their lives. The moment they were asked for their opinion, they found the courage to say whatever came into their minds as if they had a masters degree on the subject. It didn't matter how right or wrong they were, or whether they had any influence at all.

For all these reasons, Lilia was determined to keep her plans to herself. When the subject had coincidentally come to 'leaving' or 'going somewhere' while she was talking to Ulla a couple of times, she'd felt the excitement building. Her eyes had lit up and she'd wanted to show her tenant how courageous she was being, but she'd finally managed to cut off her feelings before it was too late. Instead, she'd broken off a big piece of bread, dipped it in the sauce and stuffed it into her mouth. By the time that bite had lingered on her palate and finally found its way to her stomach, she'd already calmed down. This was a way of eating she'd learned from Eyal. Americans never dipped bread in their food, either because they didn't have many saucy dishes or because they didn't have very good bread. They ate crackers with their soup instead. In Filipino cuisine, they almost never had bread with their food, either; they used rice as a substitute.

Eyal bought his bread from a Jewish store in Manhattan. Lilia had also started giving him money every three or four days and asked him to get some for her, too. It definitely tasted better than the sliced bread she bought from the supermarket. It was saltier and fuller and it tasted like food in its own right. She'd never thought that a bite of bread could make someone feel so much better. Unfortunately, if she wanted to save some more money over the next four months she'd have to give up on good bread as well as many other things. Alex and Ulla also liked this bread, which cost her five dollars and twenty-five cents each time. She couldn't simply afford to spend around $10 on bread each week.

Lilia had started cutting down on her grocery budget the day she bought her ticket to the Philippines. She actually had a storeroom full of food that would last her for months and it was about time she started using it. Over the years she'd become one of those Americans she'd found so strange when she first moved to New York. She filled her shopping trolley to the brim every time she went to the supermarket and usually forgot half of what she stored away afterwards. One day, shortly after buying the plane ticket, she picked up a pen and paper and went to her storeroom. There were almost ten cans of coconut milk on the shelves. She put them down on her list. Right next to them stood more than ten cans of corned beef. She could make any number of meals with them. Right next to the corned beef, there was a big pile of canned soup. Who would even notice if she put them in a pot and heated them up?

Her stock list was getting bigger by the minute. Next she climbed up the small ladder to see what was on the higher shelves. She had so many things that she actually had to check the expiry dates on some of them. She cleaned off the dust from every box she held in her hands and put it back looking as clean as possible. She was very surprised to find some bags of rice at the back of one shelf. They must have been there for a very long time. She put on the reading glasses that were dangling from her neck and tried to see if there were any worms in the bags. They looked OK. She also found some fine bulgur wheat right next to the rice. That must have been there for at least seven or eight years. The Turkish woman who had once stayed with them for a very short time had made them a salad by mixing the bulgur wheat with a lot of greens, tomato paste and onions. What was the name of that salad? Lilia tried to remember it in the weak light of the storeroom. She'd kept repeating the word over and over when she'd first learned it. The Turkish woman had laughed at her pronunciation and said that she adored it. Lilia couldn't remember either the name of the woman or the name of the dish. She held the plastic bag in her hand for a couple more minutes and thought about it; nothing came to mind. Then she raised it towards the light on the ceiling and lowered the glasses onto her nose so that she could see better. It looked like there was something in the bag. She carefully climbed down the ladder and went back to the kitchen. Now she could clearly see the worms in the bag. Her whole body started shaking. She opened the bin and threw the bulgur wheat away. Then she took the whole bin bag outside and left it there. She went back to the storeroom, with the hair on the back of her neck standing on end. At least all the other products were fine. She decided to ignore the tiny mice droppings on the shelves. There had to be some mice in a big house like this, surrounded by so much greenery. Everybody had them. It had been a very long time since she'd last cleaned the house properly. She didn't have the time or the energy for such a big job. She didn't have the money to pay for the Mexican lady who used to work for them, either.

That was why the whole place had turned into one big ball of dust. Who knew how long it had been since the shelves in that room had last been wiped? And she certainly wasn't about to start now. When Lilia left in four months' time, she wouldn't only be leaving behind a sick husband, five tenants and shocked relatives, but also a very messy house. A snarling laugh escaped from her throat. Giang and Dung would have to deal with all that chaos themselves. If they were going to deal with anything at all, of course. She wondered how Arnie would feel then about leaving everything he owned to those two ungrateful people. Lilia wanted to leave everything behind and never see those people again, but she also wished she could witness all the shock she was going to cause. If only she could see Arnie's face at that moment of realisation and hear him telling the kids what had happened. She was dying to know how Dung and Giang would react. They were going to be really pissed off.

When she'd listed everything in the storeroom, she finally realised that she could manage to survive on these things alone for a very long time. There was also plenty of frozen meat in the freezer, which meant that she wouldn't have to spend any money at all for around two months. After all, she was the one who insisted on cooking good food. Nobody else expected such a performance from her. Her tenants had told her many times that a sandwich would do. They spent most of their time out of the house, anyway. After sitting in containers in the fridge for days, the food usually ended up in the bin.

Her husband would be happiest of all just to have a sandwich for a change. Arnie was going to start observing Lilia's behaviour very closely from that day on. He'd noticed the change in his wife. He couldn't guess what it was, but he knew that Lilia was up to something. He'd listened to the murmurs coming from the storeroom as she'd spent hours in there and tried to guess what was going on; it was right next to his room, after all. What's more, he couldn't help noticing the change in the kitchen from that day forward. Even though Lilia still spent most of her time in the kitchen, she didn't do very much and kept making the same recipes over and over again. Arnie was glad that there wasn't much of a smell in the house any more and that he'd finally got to eat his simple sandwiches, but he'd feel a lot more secure if he knew the motivation behind that change. He'd thought about talking to his wife a couple of times to see if he could get anything out of her, but since she didn't even look him in the face any more he'd soon lost his nerve. After all, they rarely said more than five words to each other these days.

He was sure that Lilia must have left some trace of her secret somewhere in the house, but the only time he could take a look was when he left his room to go to the bathroom, glancing around for something different out of the corner of his eye. He usually listened carefully to the footsteps in the kitchen after eight o'clock and tried to eavesdrop on the conversations between his wife and the tenants. There was never anything important, though; they always talked about the same things.

One night he heard Ulla saying, 'I got the book you asked for', but he couldn't hear anything else since they'd kept their voices down after that. Lilia hadn't read anything apart from cookbooks for years, and he didn't think she was about to start now. He still wanted to know what it was, though. He called out to Lilia, not wanting to miss this chance. Lilia looked in the direction of Arnie's room, surprised. Ulla and Kano, who was getting some water from the fridge, were as stunned as she was. Arnie never said a word when there were tenants in the kitchen and always waited for them to leave before calling for his wife. Lilia excused herself and walked to her husband's room. She opened the door a crack and stuck her head around it, curiously. Could it be a new blood clot? 'I need to go to the bathroom,' said Arnie. In the meantime, both tenants had picked up whatever it was they needed and left the kitchen. The last face they wanted to see was their landlord's.

She helped him to stand up and walked beside him, quietly. When they left the room and stepped into the kitchen, Arnie said that he needed to take a break. No, he didn't want a stool. Leaning on the walker would be just fine. Lilia was used to the dizzy spells he suffered after getting out of bed and so she waited in silence. As he tried to hold himself together, Arnie looked up and examined his surroundings. He could see the book lying on the counter in the middle of the kitchen. It was a big, thick hardback with a shiny cover. He couldn't read the title because of the angle and the distance, but there were lots of different shades of green on the cover. There were some yellows and oranges mixed in there, too. It must be another cookbook. Maybe his wife had decided to adapt her cooking style and that was the reason for all that change. Judging from the cover, she must have decided on Mediterranean cuisine. As it turned out, Arnie's thick glasses were misleading him. If he'd been able to get any closer, he would have seen that it said 'The Philippines' on the cover.

●

Marc spent the whole week changing his mind. Each night after coming home from the gallery he'd sit at the kitchen table, right opposite the TV, and look over the two different lists he'd made. Adding a new item to the food list, then scratching it out and adding another one before getting rid of them all and starting all over again had become a kind of game for him. Reviewing old recipes was now as much fun as looking at Sempé's drawings. Having to go through such a big change in his life and then developing all these new interests was something that really surprised him. He couldn't deny that there was a certain amount of creativity in cooking his own food while in the past he'd just spent all his time looking at artwork created by other people. He was experiencing a feeling that he couldn't explain, that he'd be embarrassed to describe to anybody; both because the dishes he prepared were so simple and nothing like the ones he saw on TV and because some feelings could sound shallow when they were repeated to someone else.

He didn't think that making a new list, as he was doing at that moment, was a waste of time; he could tell that it was good for his soul. He hadn't made any decisions yet, even though he'd been working on a few recipes for a while. Still, he'd picked out a couple of dishes he was sure he could make and felt confident that the presentation would be good.

On the other hand, it looked as if he would never be able to decide whether or not to invite Sabina to the party. Every time he thought about it, he decided that Clara's friends wouldn't mind, but he still tried to convince himself that this was his real reason for not inviting her. Although he knew he didn't have any romantic feelings towards the young woman, he was scared that there was another driving force somewhere deep inside him. He felt like he had to make sure that he didn't have any hidden feelings for Sabina before he could finally get rid of all of the tension in his thoughts and act freely.

As Saturday approached, his indecisiveness increased and he felt the pressure mounting. He knew he didn't have to go to Tout le Marché, see Sabina or invite her out for coffee, but at the same time he felt that he had to do all of those things. He knew that the young woman's eyes would be looking out for him and he was worried that if he didn't go she'd interpret that the wrong way.

And so, the following Saturday he found himself walking down the street towards the shopping centre after having his breakfast and spending a couple of hours in the kitchen. Paris would be saying farewell to summer very soon, and then the rain was going to start. The colours in the Jardin du Luxembourg would soon begin to change, and the old men who enjoyed a game of *Pétanque* there were going to finish their summer tournaments. Marc loved the men who played it even more than the game itself, which he watched from the side lines every once in a while. He loved the cardigans they wore, the way they hung their jackets over the railings whenever there was a spring-like day in the middle of winter

323

and the way they teased each other as they played. Whenever he'd watched that game as a child, he'd imagined doing the same thing with his friends when he was older. As it turned out, he'd chosen to be a bystander and didn't know how to include himself in other people's lives.

The approach of autumn frightened Marc. It had taken him a long time to get his life back on track and now he was scared that everything would turn upside down once again with the first anniversary of his wife's death. What type of emotion could he take shelter in? He was tired of crying, but at the same time felt that he hadn't cried enough. He knew that there was much more pain inside him which was going to surface in time. Maybe the sorrow would get even more intense with every layer that was removed and then burn him one last time before letting him go. While all this happened, Marc was going to try to carry on living and would live the life of a refugee on the days when his heart wasn't aching.

He only managed to lose his dark thoughts when he reached the market at the corner of Rue Monge and St Germain. The colours were so lively and the smells were so stimulating that he felt as if he'd woken up from a deep dream. One of the men was holding a duck in the air and yelling: 'This was flesh and blood just this morning, but it's going to be resting in your belly tonight.' This line, which made French people hungry, terrified an American couple who happened to be standing there at that moment. Marc, on the other hand, paid no attention to them and walked straight towards the ducks. They really looked very fresh. This was the first time that he was going to cheat on his cookbook. Although he'd already prepared his list of ingredients for the day, he pointed at one of the ducks on impulse and told the seller to wrap it up for him. He knew that he was going to have a lot of trouble cooking it that night, but still he walked to Tout le Marché with the duck in his hand.

Sabina had happy memories of the previous Saturday. She was glad to have finally found the friend she'd wanted for so many years. Neither of them showed any interest in each other's lives and even if they did they chose not to talk about it. They didn't tend to bring every subject back to themselves, either. On the contrary, they talked about every issue on their own latitude and longitude and stayed far away from their meridians. Sabina had weighed up her feelings and finally decided that she wasn't in love with Marc and that she never would be. Love wasn't the only reason for sharing her life with someone, anyway. She'd been humiliated and torn to pieces for love before and she'd lost faith in herself. Those were the times she was most embarrassed about. The expression 'Being a slave for love' wasn't enough to describe her experience. When Sabina loved someone there was no limit to the pain she was prepared to suffer. When it came to loving someone she turned herself into a doormat, both physically and mentally, and in the end the other person always got exhausted by her strange behaviour and ended up leaving her in ruins.

That was how she could easily tell that she wasn't in love with Marc. Marc couldn't use her. He couldn't insult, humiliate or torture her. She hoped she was going to have lunch with Marc again that day. She was sure he'd come. He hadn't missed a Saturday in months. Besides, she knew that he wasn't making excuses to visit her; he really needed every one of the gadgets on his list. Marc wasn't reckless or passionate enough to come up with excuses. Just as she'd hoped, her most loyal customer appeared among the shelves with a bag in his hand around noon. He waited patiently for her as he walked among the aisles, just as he always did. Finally, a fork caught his attention. The handle looked just like a pen. It was made of red, rounded silicon and had a button on the end like a biro. When he pressed the button, the head of the fork started spinning. Not too fast and not too slow. While Marc looked at the fork, mesmerised, trying to work out what it was, he heard Sabina's voice:

'Made in America. It's a spaghetti fork.'

'Of course,' Marc thought. It made sense. But could human beings really be that lazy? After watching the spinning fork for a little while longer, he looked at Sabina:

'Has anybody bought it so far?'

'It's just arrived, so we haven't sold any yet. But I don't think any French person is likely to buy it.'

Once again, they found themselves talking about things they hadn't even thought about that day. At the same time, they starting filling Mark's basket with some of the small things he needed. What with everything he'd bought so far, Marc's kitchen had really improved. These days he bought some items not because he needed them, but because he liked them. He never would have imagined that a tablecloth or a salt and pepper shaker set could interest him that much before.

When they reached the cashier, they agreed to meet in fifteen minutes at the same café. While Marc thought how he only had fifteen minutes left to reach a final decision about

the dinner invitation, Sabina was wondering whether she'd
be able to invite him out one night after work.

Marc was glad to see that the table they'd sat at before was
free again. As summer was slowly turning into autumn, the
sun fell on their table from another angle this week. If they
sat at the same table every day at the same time, the world
around them would change and life would take on a different
shape, even if they didn't change a single thing in their own
lives. The thought that man had no real impact on life made
him shiver, despite the warmth in the air. Everything he'd
gone through in recent months had been enough to show
him that, anyway. He'd insisted on staying at the same point
in his life for years, but one day life had come along and
almost crushed him like a bulldozer. Even now, he still tried
to follow the same path. He had routines in his life once
again, only this time they were new ones. The flow of his life
might have changed, but it still flowed in a certain pattern.
The only difference was that he knew a little better now how
easily this, too, could be destroyed.

Despite all this, he sat fearlessly at the same table; in
fact, he sat in the same chair. Sabina, who walked towards
him just five minutes later, hadn't even considered finding
him in another spot, or even in a different chair. While
she sat down as if at the table of a very old friend, she said
casually: 'The sun isn't bothering us so much this week,
right?' After ordering, they started watching the people
roller skating in the same place as before and spotted faces
from the previous week. That girl was wearing the same
leggings and that man was still spinning that same girl.

Something was going to end up happening between those two, for sure. As they talked about these things, Marc took the menu he'd been carrying out of his pocket and put it on the table. He took his cue from Sabina's curious looks and started talking. He wanted to invite a group of friends, actually Clara's friends, to dinner. This would be the first time he was going to cook for someone other than himself. These were the dishes he thought he could handle. Did she think they went well together? Did he have enough variety, or not? The young woman started examining the piece of paper in front of her. She picked up the pen Marc had put on the table and put question marks next to some of the dishes. Did he have the recipes for them? Did he know how much he was going to make of each thing, or how long it was going to take? He would have to make sure he had all of the ingredients. They started talking about the details. What day was it going to be? He would have to decide which drinks to serve according to the weather that day. He should pick food with colours that complemented the season. Their conversation flowed so naturally and so quickly that soon it was already time for Sabina to leave. Marc allowed the question that had been rattling around in his brain for weeks to answer itself with the warmth of their conversation over the last hour:

'Would you like to come?'

Without thinking or fussing, but simply being her most natural self, Sabina answered, 'Gladly.' She stood up in a hurry once again, just like the week before, and started running back to work so she wouldn't be late. She was already half way there when she turned around and ran back. She pressed the wrinkled banknotes she'd been holding into Marc's hand and left before he could say anything. Marc carried on sitting there, watching the roller skaters. He'd actually hesitated about asking the question, even as the words had spilt from his mouth, but by then it was too late. There was something about Sabina that made everything seem so natural. Things that seemed difficult when she wasn't there looked easy whenever she was around. This explained why Marc felt good every time he went to the store, even though he felt so nervous beforehand.

As he asked for the bill, he looked at the duck lying in the shadow of the table. He picked up the bag by both handles and held it to his nose. One of his biggest fears in life was of getting poisoned. He always smelled the turkey slices he bought for his sandwiches before using them, but even then he could never be sure if they were still good. There had been a couple of times when he'd thrown away a sandwich after just one bite. He knew that he was going to end up having the same fear with the duck that night. If he couldn't tell whether it tasted funny or not, then he would make a note of the time when he ate it and wait for four hours to see if he started feeling sick. If he started feeling nauseated by then, or if his bowels started churning, he'd know that he had been poisoned. So far he'd experienced these symptoms a couple of times, but had decided they must have been psychological when nothing happened. Not wanting to go through the same nightmare again that night, he decided to stop by the market on his way home and ask the man who'd sold him the duck. He'd have to hurry, then. The markets in Paris opened early in the morning and disappeared early in the afternoon.

Nobody would guess they'd ever been there fifteen minutes after they'd left.

He ran across one of the bridges over the Seine and turned down a small side street that was connected to the main avenue. As he passed a comic book shop on the way, he turned towards the window as a reflex action, the result of many years' experience. The cover of a new book in the display grabbed his attention: it showed the silhouette of a young man standing on a dome, smoking a cigarette against a purple night sky. The title of the book told him that the minarets and buildings in the background were in Cairo. He looked at the bag in his hand one more time and then stepped into the store. It wouldn't take long to buy a book, after all.

Of course, it took him no less than half an hour to buy the book, along with a handful of others. When he checked his watch as he left the shop, he realised that he had no chance of catching the market people any more; but still, he ran. Once he'd reached the corner of Rue Monge and St Germain Boulevard, he saw that city workers were already cleaning up the spot where the market had been. He slowed down and took a deep breath. Maybe he'd have to take a risk with the duck after all.

Madame Beaumont had spent the summer in Sari-Solenzara, as she did every year. The glow on her face showed that she'd made the most of the sun's benefits. She'd told Clara many times about her small house and garden there and had often invited her and her husband to the house. Clara had said she'd really like that, but she'd postponed it every summer; maybe because she knew she'd never be able to convince Marc to go.

Madame Beaumont had come home just two days ago and she'd been following Marc's comings and goings ever since by listening to his footsteps and peering through the peephole in her front door. He looked much better than before; he had some colour in his cheeks, maybe because of the sun. She wondered if he'd found himself a new girlfriend. Had he made any progress with his cooking? She wanted to knock on his door and say hello. It looked as if he'd got over the initial shock and was carrying on with his life. Madame Beaumont didn't want him to think she didn't care; all she'd tried to do so far was to give him some space. Just as she was thinking about this, she bumped into him in front of the building. The young man had shopping bags in his hands, just as she did. They greeted each other, smiling. Marc remembered that this old woman had been important to his wife and he suddenly realised that keeping her at a distance for all those months might have hurt her. That was why he said 'Hello, Madame Beaumont' in his most sincere voice and grabbed hold of her bags, ignoring her protests. It was obvious that she was surprised by the sudden attention, but she didn't say anything; instead, she opened the door of the building, let Marc pass and followed him in. They walked up the stairs together, without waiting for the lift. She didn't want to miss this chance, so Madame Beaumont invited Marc in for a cup of tea. She'd already made the tea, in fact; she'd just gone out to get some biscuits. But, of course, just like every other time she'd ended up filling her shopping bag before she knew it. The tea must be really well stewed by now. Marc didn't turn down the offer. Instead, he told her that he was going to leave the bags at home and then come over. After taking the books out of the bag and putting them on the kitchen table, he took out the duck and opened the fridge. Just then, he realised that he could ask Madame Beaumont if the duck was still good. He knocked on her door, with the duck in his hand, still wrapped in the paper. He said, 'Before I come over, I need to ask you something', and held out the package, asking, 'Do you think this duck has gone bad?' The old woman stuck her nose into the meat and smelled it. She said that the meat smelled so fresh that she could tell it had been killed that morning. Marc thanked her and said he'd be right back. Five minutes later, as they dipped their *petit beurre* biscuits in their cups of tea, his neighbour told him how to cook the duck.

Her mother had lost a lot of weight. Mrs Nesibe, who had once made her presence felt wherever she went with her healthy looks and long legs, looked tiny now. Ferda could feel every bone in her body when she changed her clothes or washed her. Her once large breasts looked empty now and the skin on her arms was sagging. Ironically, while her mother thought she was crippled, her legs were the only part of her that looked as thick and strong as before. Ferda had never been away from her mother in her whole life. She had almost no memories which didn't include her. She'd been there in her childhood, in every step of her marriage, for the birth of their children, the birth of her grandchildren and every last minute of her life. She couldn't even imagine the emptiness her mother was going to leave behind her when she died. In some ways Ferda looked forward to that day, but at the same time she had no idea what life would be like without Mrs Nesibe. What's more, whenever she looked in the mirror she was amazed to see her own sunken eyes, deep wrinkles and the dark spots on her cheeks. While she'd been waiting for her mother to get old and leave her life, she'd ended up ageing herself. Looking at her own image in the mirror at half past seven in the morning, she realised that she looked older than fifty-eight. She remembered her daughter's advice and covered the dark spots with the face cream she'd bought for her in Paris. She had a long day ahead of her. She was having her school friends over that afternoon. The eight girls had never been separated. They saw each other regularly and met at one of their houses every other month. Now it was Ferda's turn. They'd said: 'It'll be too much for you. Let's meet at somebody else's house this time. You're doing far too much already.' Ignoring their protests, Ferda had insisted that they mustn't change their plans. Unfortunately, by this time of the day her mother had already sucked out all of her energy and she was regretting her decision. All the same, of course, she wasn't going to cancel. She hadn't slept all night and had a slight headache, but she was ready to go to the kitchen.

She'd already planned what she was going to make. She'd gone through every dish one by one in her head and had already baked a couple of them over the last couple of days, whenever she'd found the time. Now Mrs Nesibe was taking a nap, which meant she could finally prepare the dishes that were supposed to be freshly made. They'd had a very hard time the night before. Mrs Nesibe had woken up several times and made Ferda change her nappy. Sinan hadn't heard anything because of his earplugs and hadn't even noticed how many times his wife had woken up and lain back down with her eyes open, staring at the ceiling since she couldn't go back to sleep.

She wondered what her mother was going to blurt out in front of her friends. The girls knew Mrs Nesibe very well and they also knew that she'd never been mentally stable, even before the dementia. They'd come to visit her one by one in recent months, and often called so that she wouldn't feel lonely. Having said that, none of them had seen her in her latest condition.

Ferda went to the kitchen and tried to prepare things quietly, without making any clatter. She turned on the radio and listened to the news. They were talking about the presidential elections in the United States, which would be taking place in three months' time. They said that this election was going to change the course of events across the entire world. If this man called Obama was elected, he would be the country's first black president. Ferda had fantasised in the past about being born in another country, under different circumstances. She'd said to herself many times: 'If I was born in America, I could have been a different person; I could have had a different life.' She could have been a famous chef there, or improved her talent for drawing and become a painter, she thought. She would have gone to university, that was for sure. She wouldn't have ended up being this useless. Thinking about this once again, she mixed the dough for the profiteroles that her friends liked so much. She let it rest for a while before filling the pastry bag. Taking a break, she made herself her first cup of coffee of the day and sat down at the kitchen table. She hadn't even looked at the soufflé book since her daughter had left and hadn't tried any of the recipes. She picked up the book, put it in front of her and opened it randomly at one of the pages. She'd been thinking about making aubergine *borek* for her friends, so when she saw the recipe for aubergine soufflé in the open book in front of her she took that as a sign and changed her mind. Her friends were always ready to try new tastes in her house; she knew that they wouldn't be disappointed at all, even if her soufflé turned out to be a complete failure. If she could do it well, on the other hand, it would be a great success.

When she'd finished her coffee, she stood up and checked on the dough; it was ready to be squeezed onto the pastry sheet. When she'd finished and was washing her hands, she heard her mother calling out to her: 'Fusun!' She was glad she'd managed to get it done in time and was used to being called by a different name by now, and so she dried her hands and went to the small room. Just as her compassion could turn into hatred all of a sudden, her anger could easily turn into love, too. Since Ferda didn't know how to live with so many different emotions at the same time, she couldn't work out what she felt most of the time and spent hours each day trying hard to find the centre of her feelings. She had to prepare herself spiritually for every conversation with her mother by closing her eyes. Mrs Nesibe always had a surprise in store for her. With the help of this illness, her creativity had really reached its peak. When Ferda walked into the room, she saw that her mother had unbuttoned her pyjama top and taken one of her breasts out. What she saw didn't surprise her any more and neither did what she heard. Her mother was very rarely herself these days. She mostly lived in a world of her own imagination. Ready for a new battle, Ferda sat at the edge of her mother's bed. Explaining something to Mrs Nesibe was more difficult than with a child. Her mind hopped from one thing to another, never following any chain of logic.

'Mum, let's put your breast back in your pyjamas, OK?'

'Fusun, bring Ferda, I'm going to feed her.'

'Mum, Ferda is a big girl now. She doesn't need to be breastfed.'

With one hand under her breast, Mrs Nesibe stared at Ferda like she wanted to make sure she was telling her the truth.

'But I still have milk. Look.'

When she squeezed her breast and didn't see any milk, her eyes welled up with tears.

'I'm all dried up.'

'Yes, mum. But don't worry; Ferda is a big girl now. You don't need to breastfeed her, anyway. Let me help you get dressed. We have guests today. I'll clean you up after I've finished with all the preparations and you can put on some new pyjamas, all right? What do you think?'

Mrs Nesibe said, 'All right' without knowing what she was agreeing to. When had Ferda become so big that she didn't need breast milk? And Fusun looked much older than she was supposed to. She would have to get married soon or it would be too late. Time had flown away without her realising. As her daughter buttoned up her pyjama top, she fell asleep again. Ferda looked at her mother's toothless, open mouth as it flopped onto the pillow. Her mother had been a beautiful woman once. Lipstick had suited her lovely, shapely lips. How had she become this person? Tears welled up again in an unexpected flood of tears. What Ferda had been going through was like a very long fight; the kind that wore people out. She hated herself when she couldn't do anything to help but simply yelled at her mother and felt tremendously guilty whenever she saw her looking this fragile. Her heart had split in two and was fighting with itself. Sadly, this was a battle that neither side could win. She knew perfectly well that even though she felt sick to her stomach afterwards and promised herself to stop being that person, she wouldn't be able to help it. She fixed Mrs Nesibe's cotton bedcover and went back to the kitchen. After drying her tears and nose, she started to work again.

When Ferda cooked she never thought about anything else apart from her food and being able to concentrate like that always amazed her. When she did other things she always found herself thinking about something else; almost anything that troubled her, in fact. In the kitchen it was different; she became at one with whatever she was doing. Maybe that was why everything she cooked turned out so good and earned such high praise. When she added a teaspoonful of sugar to the leeks sautéed in olive oil, or when she was squeezing lemon juice onto the common bean, she focused on that one teaspoon or on that half lemon as if her whole life depended on it. That must explain why she was so attached to her kitchen; because it didn't let her think about anything else. It didn't allow her to question her life or herself, or to feel worried or sad.

That was how it usually worked, but this time when she made the pudding mixture for the profiteroles she went through the motions without putting her mind into it. She paid no attention to how much starch or sugar she used. She didn't even notice when she added the milk. She separated the egg yolk from its white with automatic movements and if she hadn't seen the empty shells she would never have known that she'd used them. Her mother had taken up all of the space in her mind, which she didn't seem to be able to pull together. It looked like Mrs Nesibe didn't have much time left. She might not even wake up from the sleep she'd just succumbed to, she looked that tired. Ferda left the pudding mixture bubbling on the stove and ran back to the bedroom. Mrs Nesibe was lying down, just as she'd left her. Ferda could only see her chest moving slightly up and down with every breath she took when she moved to take a closer look. She hurried back to the kitchen and stirred the pudding mixture more quickly to get rid of the thickness at the bottom of the pot. After turning off the heat, she did something that she never did; she scraped some of the mixture off the spoon with the tip of her finger and tasted it. It tasted just as it always did; exactly the same.

She was just about to take the tray out of the oven when the phone rang. Trying not to wake her mother, she ran so quickly that when she answered it she was out of breath.

'Mum, what's going on?'

'Hi, honey. Your grandmother's sleeping, so I ran for the phone.'

'Oh, so that's why you're whispering, too. Why don't you just get a new battery for that cordless phone? At least then you could move this phone somewhere else.'

'I know, I know. You're right, but we never get around to dealing with those things.'

She stuck her head into her mother's room with the phone in her hand; she was still sleeping peacefully.

'Don't worry. She didn't wake up. How are you, my darling? Is everything OK?'

'Yes … yes … but I wanted to ask you about something. The baby's due at the end of September or the beginning of October. It's almost time. What are we going to do?'

'You're asking if I can come, right? Well, we're going to figure something out. You'll see. I'll find a way.'

Ferda had comforted her daughter, but she didn't actually know what that way might be. Even if Sinan took some days off work, he couldn't possibly take care of Mrs Nesibe all by himself. Taking her mother to her brother's house would be even more difficult. They didn't have room for her there anyway, what with their two kids. Besides, her sister-in-law, Nazan, was very reluctant to look after Mrs Nesibe. They didn't even visit her, let alone plan to take care of her full-time. Öykü had told her mother at the beginning of her pregnancy that she didn't have to be there for the birth, but she'd started changing her mind as her belly got bigger. She had sounded worried in their last few phone conversations and was always asking questions. She'd bent over the other day without realising; would that harm the baby? She'd hit her belly on the corner of the counter; would anything bad happen? She'd had fish for dinner that evening and felt sick by midnight; could it be food poisoning? The phone calls, which had always only been on Fridays before, were happening almost every day now and could take place at any time. Ferda felt guilty, even though she knew there was nothing she could do. It troubled her not to be able to help her daughter when she was most needed. She often lost sleep over it and blamed her mother with a heart full of vengeance.

She felt even worse after hanging up the phone, and although it was only ten o'clock in the morning the day was already weighing heavily upon her. There was no way out, and she realised that now. She started filling the profiteroles with the pudding mixture, with automatic movements. When she'd finished covering them with chocolate sauce, she heard Mrs Nesibe's voice: 'Ferda!' She couldn't stop herself now and starting crying, her whole body shaking wildly. She didn't even care about getting a headache and red eyes, or that her friends were coming over. She carried on crying as her mother repeated her name over and over, resting her head on her hands covered with chocolate sauce.

The minute they walked in, Ferda's friends realised that she was having a very difficult day. She'd obviously been crying for hours, even though she'd tried to cover her swollen eyes and the red traces around her lips. They all knew how she felt since they'd all taken care of sick relatives one after another. They'd always guessed that their aunt Nesibe was going to be a handful when she got older. They'd been friends with Ferda since secondary school and witnessed how that poor girl had taken care of her mother during her childhood while they'd enjoyed theirs to the full. Ferda had spent her days either doing housework or waiting at the hospital while they sat around in cafés. She'd always taken care of the house, and been her mother's nurse. None of them remembered a day when their aunt Nesibe had said she felt good. Now she looked almost like a ghost. She was really sick this time. They'd listened to Ferda's stories from recent months, but now they saw that her mother didn't have much time left. It was hard to tell whether she was still with them or not when she was sleeping.

They closed her bedroom door and went into the living room, trying not to make much noise. Ferda kept warning them that her mother could say the weirdest things when she woke up and that they shouldn't take any of it seriously. Her mind tricked her all the time these days. They shouldn't be scared if she started screaming and shouldn't feel like they had to leave if she did. She'd got used to it, she told them. She'd stopped feeling embarrassed about it a long time ago. At first she'd felt uncomfortable, thinking that the neighbours might take the things she said seriously, but she really didn't care any more. 'Whatever will happen will happen, right?' she asked them.

If her friends had known what conditions Ferda had worked under all day long and how many times she'd had to travel back and forth between her mother's room and the kitchen, they'd definitely appreciate the food she'd made much more. Well, they all looked very satisfied anyway, their heads thrown backwards, their eyes closed, making delighted noises. They mashed each bite on their palates with the help of their tongues to get a real taste of it, rolled it one more time around their mouths and then swallowed it. The soufflé had turned out to be delicious, even though she'd had to make a lot of it and hadn't even noticed what she was doing. 'Well done, Ferda,' one of her friends said. 'I had no idea there was such a thing as an aubergine soufflé. How can you keep up with everything with all this going on? How do you find the time?' Another one commented: 'Well, her daughter lives in Paris. Of course, she knows all about European cuisine.' Another took up the subject and added: 'Why did you go to all that trouble just for us? You already have a lot to do. You could have just ordered something from the bakery. You know, I don't do anything, any more. I call Altinkek, and they bring everything I need to the house.'

They all knew how happy these comments made Ferda feel. She'd always found an escape route in the kitchen, ever since she was a little girl. She'd come to school with containers full of delicacies and loved to share the results of her talent with her friends. She'd always experimented with interesting recipes, even back then, and discovered tastes that the others had never tried before. All of her friends had eventually been served the same dishes in posh places on trips abroad or at very high-end restaurants and had been shocked to see that Ferda had done the same thing many years ago, as a child. Besides, back then she didn't have any fancy cookbooks or the Internet to give her inspiration. Even her presentation was elaborate. Her plates looked just like works of art. They all agreed that her talent had been wasted.

When her friends had left, Ferda was glad to have been able to forget about her problems, even just for a couple of hours. Her mother hadn't woken up during their visit because of the increased dose of tranquilliser Ferda had given her. Even though she'd hosted the same friends many times over the years, she'd still been excited as they tasted her food. She'd examined their faces especially closely as they ate the soufflé and tried to work out whether their compliments were real or not. It didn't matter to her who her guests were or how many times she'd cooked for them before. Every time was a new test for her, and she'd passed that day, too. She was proud of herself, even though she knew it was silly. As she collected all of the dirty plates and glasses, she felt happy despite her sore body and the headache that had been lingering at a corner of her brain all afternoon. Whenever they had people over for dinner, she could never get rid of the adrenalin she felt after they left, and while she cleaned everything up behind them she always wanted Sinan to tell her what he'd thought of each dish one by one, regardless of the time. Only after her husband had repeated for the third time how wonderful everything had been would she finally be convinced. All the same, this wouldn't stop her from asking out of the blue the next day: 'The walnut bread was really delicious, wasn't it?'

When she'd finally finished all the tidying and put her legs up on the coffee table, she heard Sinan's key in the door. Any minute now he was going to ask, 'What's for dinner?' And Ferda was going to give the same answer as always: 'Whatever God has given us.'

Eleven

Lilia had to push herself to get out of bed that August morning. She'd waited in vain all night long for the breeze to come in through her open window and had had a very hard time dealing with one of the hottest and most smothering nights of the summer. Drops of sweat had rolled down her forehead and the sweat on her neck had left a damp mark on the pillow. Although she'd slept for short periods of time during the night, she'd spent most of the time rolling around in her bed, trying to relax. And so, when she sat on the bed with her feet touching the floor and pushed herself to get up, she knew that it was going to be a tough day. She didn't have the strength to do anything at all; she didn't feel like going downstairs or taking Arnie to the bathroom. She felt as if she couldn't even make breakfast or put a single bite in her mouth. Like it or not, she didn't have an option. She wasn't alone; she had a husband to look after. There was a house to take care of and tenants to feed.

She walked to the bathroom with great difficulty and leaned on the sink, her elbows resting on the edge. She turned on the cold tap with her right hand and splashed some water onto her face. When she'd managed to straighten up and look at herself in the mirror, she realised just how tired she looked. She had big bags under her eyes, bigger than ever before. She wetted her hand again and pressed it against her neck. She reached back to her shoulders from inside the collar of her dress and cooled them off, too. It didn't look as if she'd be able to get cool at all that day, no matter what she did. Sweat was coming out of every pore in her body. She turned around and looked at the bathtub; could she force herself to take a shower? She didn't have the strength. She went back to her room, dragging her feet. She had to go downstairs. Arnie must have woken up by now and would be waiting for her to go to the bathroom. All the same, she couldn't find the energy to stand up. She sat back down on her bed and waited for the dizziness to go away. Her eyes closed as she sat there and the heaviness on her chest pulled her back to bed with a force more powerful than gravity. She lay back down on the bed once again. Maybe she'd feel better in ten minutes. Her left arm still felt heavy, even when she was lying down. Her fingertips must be tingling because she hadn't fully woken up yet. There was that sweat on her forehead again. The pressure on her heart was getting worse, too. She shut her eyes and took some deep breaths. Each time she inhaled, she felt a pain in her chest. She was too tired to even think about what it could be or to panic. The sleep that had evaded her the night before was back now. She couldn't open her eyes, despite how much she wanted to. Finally, she lost her battle with sleep.

When she woke up again, the sun had changed position and had left only the twinkle of its skirt behind it. Although she didn't feel the pressure on her chest any more and wasn't sweating, she still felt tired. She straightened herself out in the bed, moving in slow motion. She put her hands in the pit formed between her legs and tried to recover. It was after ten o'clock. Arnie must have woken up hours ago. He might have even tried to go to the bathroom on his own. Lilia had stopped using the baby monitor a long time ago. She'd switched the button off one night when she could no longer stand to listen to the wheezing sound coming from his chest or the sound of him fighting with his bed sheets.

She had thought that she'd loved her husband from a distance for years, but now even the noises he made irritated her. She knew he couldn't stand her, either. All the little things that they hadn't understood before had come to the surface one by one thanks to this illness. They had needed a tragedy like this one to help them to see the reality of their relationship. At last, they'd realised that the love they'd thought had gone rusty in recent years had, in fact, never been there in the first place.

Her body must have been exhausted, because she could only get up again after sitting there for ten more minutes. After splashing some more water onto her face, she finally left the room. Her movements were still slow and clumsy. Even if she'd wanted to move more quickly, her body wouldn't let her. She went downstairs, holding on to the bannister. There was not a sound in the house. Either everybody had already left or they were still in their rooms. She didn't know that Arnie was following her every move again from where he lay in bed. He'd been waiting, worried sick, since the early hours of the morning. He'd listened to the voices of the people who came into the kitchen and then left, but hadn't said a word or asked for their help, even though he'd been genuinely

346

concerned. He'd actually thought that something might have happened to Lilia. His wife was older than him; maybe she'd collapsed in her room, just as he had months ago, and was waiting for someone to find her. Despite this possibility, he hadn't told anybody to go up and check on her.

He'd tried to control his needs for the first half hour after waking up, before realising that he couldn't hold it any more. Then he'd tried to get up, leaning on his walker, but simply couldn't do it. Since he rarely moved at all these days, he felt dizzy even at the slightest movement; and even if he didn't, he still didn't want to take any risks out of fear of having another stroke. He didn't even want to walk to the door of his room without having Lilia at his side.

He hadn't left his room that morning for the same reason and had peed in the cup that always stood next to his bed. Although he'd managed to ignore the cramps in his bowels for a while, there had come a moment when he couldn't stand the pain. When it became clear that he couldn't hold it any longer, he'd taken all the papers out of a box, put it on his bed and did what he had to do, balancing himself as much as possible. He'd felt so tired at the end that he couldn't even cover the box, but had simply put it on the floor and almost thrown himself back into bed. The smell in the room was terrible; he couldn't have stayed there under normal circumstances, let alone sleep there. Still, he waited helplessly. He was very angry, but at the same time he was just as anxious. Lilia might not be the smartest or the most responsible woman in the world, but she wasn't a bad person, either. She wouldn't let him lie there like that for no reason. And so, when he finally heard his wife's footsteps on the stairs he was both relieved and exasperated. Why was she moving so slowly when she knew how late it was? He couldn't help but smile at the thought that she didn't know what was waiting for her in that room. Didn't she realise that Arnie had missed his pills that morning and was starving by now? Still, he waited, not saying a word. This was their new way of communicating: both of them guessed what the other one was thinking without either of them opening their mouths. He could tell from the sounds coming from the kitchen that Lilia had put the coffee on, taken the bread out of the fridge and put some slices in the toaster. Arnie could wait for a little while longer. If the only action he had left to enjoy in his secluded life was the shock Lilia was going to have very soon, then he could wait a bit longer. Now he was ready for her to come into his room. But the footsteps had stopped. Maybe she was standing by the kitchen counter, waiting for the bread to toast. They both hated that old appliance, but they hadn't bought a new one for years. This had to be the slowest toaster in the world. It took seven minutes to toast just two slices of bread. Arnie had been waiting for almost three and a half hours, so what was an extra seven minutes?

It was almost as if every second and every millisecond of that seven minutes had divided into small particles, each of them had split into years, the sun had collided with a black hole in the milky way and time had stopped throughout the universe. There was absolute silence in the house. There was not one sound in the whole neighbourhood, which was full of families with young children. Where was everybody? Why didn't the kids in those houses go out and ride their bicycles up and down the street? Why didn't they play tag, screaming their lungs out until a grownup told them to stop? Where were the hoses that belonged to those houses? Why didn't those naughty children play with water and give each other a soaking? The only noise he could hear in all this silence was the sound of the birds. They were the only ones who felt chatty, who wanted to sing and flirt. If it wasn't for the train that passed by the river and whistled every hour, nobody would ever know there was any life there at all. Arnie felt every moment of those seven minutes, one by one. He lay there without making a noise and waited for the sound that would be coming from the toaster very soon.

Finally, he heard the spring pushing the bread out. But that was all. Wherever Lilia had been standing, she hadn't walked to the toaster, taken the slices out, spread butter onto their crisp surfaces and put them on a plate. He could still only hear the birds outside. Arnie lay in his bed, and waited.

After walking into the kitchen, Lilia made the coffee and took the bread out of the fridge. Since she'd been careful with every cent she spent lately, she'd given up ordering the delicious bread Eyal bought and gone back to using the same old sliced bread in that yellow bag. She took out four slices, placed them in the toaster, leaned on the sink and started waiting. This toaster really took its time. She could tell that Arnie was furious; he hadn't said a word, even though he knew she was in the kitchen. However, Lilia didn't care that day. The heat had really got to her. She felt tired. She didn't even have the strength to turn on the tap and cool herself off a little. She took her slippers off and stepped, barefoot, onto the cool tiles. The cold spreading from the soles of her feet to the rest of her body helped a little. Then she lifted up her dress, holding it by the ends as she sat down on the tiles. It felt beautiful. She knew that the spot she was sitting on was going to warm up soon, but until then she could rest her head on the cupboard door and close her eyes. As she sat there with her eyes shut, she thought how seven minutes was a really long time. If people simply waited for the next minute to come like this without doing anything, instead of trying to fill them, life would be very long. Then people wouldn't even want to know where the years went. Seven minutes was a really long time. It was infinite. They shouldn't end. And they weren't going to.

Lilia never opened her eyes again, as she sat on the floor. She was never going to hear the sound of bread flipping out of a toaster ever again.

Mrs Nesibe looked at her daughter with bright eyes for the first time in days, maybe months. She looked like her younger self again. The firm way in which she held her head showed just how clear her mind was. Ferda, who didn't even have the energy to stand up any more after a series of very hard days, instantly understood that her mother was feeling more like herself. She felt a lump in her throat; tears welled up in her eyes. Even though she was exhausted and angry at her mother, she still missed her. Whenever Mrs Nesibe gained some level of consciousness Ferda wanted to talk to her about the old days, somehow trying to bring together all of the memories they shared before she died. Although there were many moments she'd like to forget, she found that she wanted to relive the days she'd spent with her mother.

Mrs Nesibe tapped the edge of her bed with her tiny hand. Maybe she, too, was trying to hold on to those precious moments when she felt fully herself. Ferda sat down gently and took her mother's thin hand in her own. Despite all the signs that Mrs Nesibe was in her right mind, she asked, hesitantly, 'Mum?' A smile mixed with sorrow appeared on her mother's thin lips. She was about to say, 'Yes, it's me', but then she changed her mind.

'Ferda, you've lost so much weight.'

'Yes, I have a little, but I'll put it back on.'

'Don't you dye your hair any more?'

'I don't have much time at the moment. Well, actually, I like these grey hairs. I'm thinking of leaving it like this.'

'No, don't do that. You're still a young woman. You'll drive your husband away.'

'Come on, mum.'

Ferda didn't want to talk about nonsense like that with her mother. They had other things to say to each other. More important, more emotional things. She didn't know if Mrs Nesibe would ever be able to talk like this again. That's why this conversation had to be all the more meaningful. All the same, she couldn't find the strength to dig any deeper.

'Don't you talk like that. You always have to look beautiful for your husband. Otherwise he'll go looking for other women, like your father did.'

No, no. Ferda didn't want to talk about her father. Her mother mustn't talk about pain and heartaches. They didn't have time to be shallow and talk about romantic nonsense all over again. That was why she decided to accept whatever her mother said and simply move on.

'OK. I'll dye my hair.'

'Put some make-up on, too.'

'I will.'

Her mother didn't understand that she had no time to do any of those things, and that the bags under her eyes were caused by sleepless nights. She didn't realise that Ferda took care of her both day and night and looked after the house as well. She couldn't even spend time with her grandchildren any more, let alone find time for the beauty parlour. She repeated all of these thoughts to herself once again, but didn't say anything out loud. Mrs Nesibe, on the other hand, was aware of the reality around her for the first time in months. She felt as if her mind had opened up at last and she could finally see everything clearly. She wanted to talk to her daughter about this, but since she didn't know how to approach the subject she kept beating about the bush. Then, at last, she found a way.

'Ferda, I'm so sorry for everything, for everything I've done. Please forgive me, my dear. My mind goes fuzzy all of a sudden and I don't know who I am any more. What do I say? What do I do? I don't even know. Please forgive me if I hurt you.'

The lump in Ferda's throat finally melted. Every feeling that had been accumulating there for months began to flow out in sobs and tears. These precious moments would soon be over and her mother would go back to being someone else. She was going to start shouting again and telling ridiculous stories.

Her mother must be able to tell from the way she looked now that she forgave her. They shouldn't need words at this point. Mrs Nesibe held her daughter's hand a little bit tighter; as tightly as she could. She let Ferda's tears fall until the last drop. She waited without saying a word. Maybe these were the most valuable moments that mother and daughter had spent together in years. Moments devoted solely to each other.

If it wasn't for the buzzing at the door, Ferda would have sat there with her mother's hand in hers for the rest of the day. She turned around and looked at her mother one last time before leaving the room. She had a smile on her tired face now. She felt as if the weight of many months had been lifted from her shoulders. She was peaceful now, as she hadn't been in a long time. Not one of her problems had been solved, but somehow she knew that she was going to be stronger from then on.

Among the envelopes the building administrator had brought them was a notice saying that they hadn't paid last month's electricity bill. She and Sinan had kept telling each other to pay it all month long and had ended up forgetting all about it. Although Ferda had insisted many times, Sinan had refused to start paying the bills automatically and wanted to see both the bill and the payment slip every month. Paying the bills hadn't been a problem for Ferda before – in fact, she liked taking care of things. Unfortunately, just like everything else, those little jobs had become a burden over the last few months. She'd have to go and take care of it that afternoon while she still remembered. She could go while her mother was having her nap.

She put the pile of envelopes on the kitchen table and opened the door of the fridge with a new sense of happiness. The night before, one of her neighbours had brought over three cups of Noah's Pudding, or *asure*, which she'd made in honour of her grandson's first tooth. Sinan had already eaten his share and stolen most of Ferda's, since he knew she wouldn't eat it, but he hadn't touched his mother-in-law's. Everybody knew how much Mrs Nesibe loved that dessert. She'd made the best one of all when she was healthy, everyone agreed about that. She'd used as many ingredients as possible, added the perfect amount of cinnamon and never liked anyone else's version as much as her own. In fact, the same thing could be said about every other type of dish. Although she'd been eating her daughter's food almost constantly in recent years, she always found something wrong with it. It either lacked oil or salt. It was either overcooked or underdone. She shouldn't cut beans like that, but like this. She shouldn't use anything but butter with rice *pilaf*. If it didn't look as if a cat had walked on it, the *pilaf* wasn't quite right. There shouldn't be any onion in pasta with ground beef, and cranberry beans shouldn't be cooked before being rubbed with lemon juice. If she ever liked the food Ferda cooked, it was usually because the ingredients were very fresh and extra good quality. While the rest of the world loved her daughter's cooking, Mrs Nesibe chose to say, 'Not bad.'

Ferda had offered her mother some Noah's Pudding the night before, but hadn't been able to convince her that it wasn't poisoned. When Mrs Nesibe wasn't herself, she refused to eat even her favourite meals and sometimes actually threw the plate of food on the floor. The carpet in her room was so filthy by now that they would have to get rid of it in the end.

She took the bowl of Noah's Pudding and went back to her mother's bedroom. She'd definitely want to eat it now. As soon as she entered the room, she saw something different in her mother's eyes. She still looked like herself – her eyes seemed completely awake – but there was something new in her expression that Ferda couldn't figure out. She looked around her, holding the bowl in one hand and the spoon in the other. At last, she focused on the bedside table right beside her mother's bed. The bottle of Passiflora, with its open cap, was completely empty. Ferda looked at her mother and at the bedside table one more time and then bent over and took a closer look at the things upon it. Both of the Luminal boxes were also empty. She'd only just bought them. In fact, she'd had a lot of trouble getting the prescription written. She looked at her mother again. Her mouth was shut and she kept swallowing. Ferda put the bowl and the spoon down on the bedside table and grabbed onto her mother's chin. She only realised a couple of minutes later that she'd been yelling, 'Mum, open your mouth!' By the time Mrs Nesibe finally opened it, she'd already swallowed all of the pills with the help of the Passiflora syrup. She unpeeled her daughter's hand from her chin and took it in both of her own. 'Sit down,' she said. Ferda sat down again in the space left on the bed next to her mother. This time both of them had tears in their eyes. Ferda pointed to the bedside table and said, weakly: 'I brought some *asure*, I know how much you like it.' Mrs Nesibe laid her head comfortably on the pillow. 'Will you feed me?' she asked. Ferda took the bowl in her hands. She folded one of her legs under her body and moved closer to her mother. She dipped the spoon slowly into the dessert and filled with it *asure*. Her hand was shaking as she held it out towards her mother's mouth. Mrs Nesibe, as always, took her time to enjoy the taste. She opened her mouth again and looked at her daughter. Ferda gave her another spoonful and watched her eat, slowly. After a couple of times, her hand wasn't shaking any more. She carried on feeding her mother, caressing her face every once in a while. Once they'd finished half of the bowl, Mrs Nesibe fell into a deep sleep. Ferda knew that she wasn't going to wake up again.

Marc opened his eyes a couple of minutes after sunrise without the help of the alarm clock, which was set to go off a little while later. The first light of the day lazily filled the room through the curtains he'd left open to make it easier for him to wake up. He'd had a hard time going to sleep the night before, and he hadn't been able to get a full night's sleep. This meant that his eyes were going to feel heavy all day long. Without caring how tired he'd be at the end of the day, he got up with a sense of excitement he remembered from his younger days and made his bed right away. Thank goodness he didn't look up and see himself in the mirror opposite the bed. If he had done, he'd have noticed the automatic movements of his body – those of a man used to living alone – and that would hurt him all over again. He'd tried denying the fact for a long time, but he'd got used to loneliness in the end. He was comfortable now in this life that he'd once found so strange.

He started the day by taking a shower, shaving and combing his hair carefully in front of the mirror. He'd expected to be sad that day, but instead he felt extremely excited. He'd thought about Clara for a couple of minutes since waking up, but at some point he'd got distracted by the ever-growing list of things he had to do before that evening.

After putting on his clothes, he stood in the middle of the living room and looked around him. He checked on the state of the cleaning he'd done the day before to avoid a big panic on the day of the dinner. There wasn't a single particle of dust to be seen on any of the shelves, books or the leaves of the plants. He'd even cleaned the dirt that had been stuck to the knick-knacks for the last year with the help of a damp cloth. He'd opened the drawers in the living room one by one and examined the table cloths that had been tucked away there for a long time and decided on a beige one. Nervously but carefully, he'd ironed out the cross-shaped lines on the cloth that had formed after being folded for so long and spread it out over one of the armchairs afterwards so that it wouldn't get ruined again. He'd also investigated the valuable Chinese dinner sets, which he hadn't touched once since the day Clara died, and picked out his favourite. He'd put eight dinner plates, eight matching side plates and eight salad bowls – which were to be placed above the side plates – on the table, but he hadn't put them in order yet. He'd also taken all of the necessary silverware out of the walnut box Clara had inherited from her grandmother and polished every piece, breathing on each one to add to the shine.

It was just the day to try out an idea he'd got from a catalogue he'd been given at Tout le Marché one day as he was leaving the store. All he had to do was to write everybody's names on rectangular pieces of paper and buy eight small pears. He was going to put the pears on the side plates and hang the pieces of paper on them using the small holes he would make in the corners, and that way everybody would know where to sit. He opened his little notepad to make sure he'd remembered to add the pears to his list. He checked everything on there one more time in case he'd forgotten something. He was already confused. Although he'd planned every last detail and had everything organised for the meal, the sauce and the salad he was going to prepare, he still began to panic because there were too many things to take care of.

He took a deep breath and looked out of the window. He could see the farmers' market being set up from where he stood. In fifteen minutes, all the stands would already be open. He decided to have his breakfast outside, to avoid creating any extra work in the kitchen. Just as he was about to leave the apartment, he realised that he was leaving a deep silence behind him. For the first time in months, he hadn't turned on the radio or the TV as soon as he'd woken up. He went back to the kitchen, turned on the radio on the window sill and left. This not only calmed him down, but also the neighbours, who had got used to hearing these sounds coming from the first floor.

He sat down at one of the tables next to the window at Le Citron and ordered a potato omelette with coffee. He needed a big breakfast to stop him from feeling hungry again later in the day. He couldn't let himself start stealing from the dishes he was going to cook. Now he understood why his mother had always got so annoyed when he used to steal bits of the food she'd prepared for her guests and smacked his hand with a wooden spoon. Every last piece of any given ingredient was essential. If there wasn't enough of any one of them, the whole meal could be ruined. He'd already ordered everything he needed from the butcher and calculated how many tomatoes and spring onions he would have to get, as well as how much milk and cream to buy. He had to go to the butcher's and the farmers' market before stopping off at the cheese stand and then heading to the wine shop to buy three bottles of Mouton Cadet. He checked the time and looked around him. Just as he was about to call out to the waiter, he showed up with his plate in his hand.

He left the café just twenty minutes later, feeling nicely full. He was going to take care of the market things first, then go to the butcher's. The people at the market greeted him, cheerfully. Of course, they were curious about why he needed more vegetables than usual today. Yes, for the first time he was going to cook for a group of people. What was he going to make? Sirloin steak with shallot sauce. Yes, he was going to add some red wine to the sauce. He was going to chop the shallots really small, sauté them with butter and olive oil and then add the wine and cream. Yes, he was going to use sea salt.

He was going to start by boiling the fingerling potatoes. Then he was going to sauté some dill, parsley and garlic with butter before adding the chopped potatoes. Madame Dilard spoke as she picked out the smallest and roundest potatoes for him: 'If you don't want the potatoes to get cold before the guests arrive, put them in the oven. They'll stay warm in there. And since they won't get cold, they won't lose any of their flavour, like they do if you reheat them.'

Since Marc had to explain what he was going to cook that night at every stand he went to, the shopping took much longer than he'd imagined. At the same time, he'd learned a couple of useful details that he never would have thought of by himself. After picking up the pears and some fruit for his yoghurt cocktail, he headed to his last stop, the cheese stand: 'Half a pound of blue cheese, half a pound of Cyprus Moon and some Brie, please. I like the Tour de Marzé one.'

After getting the cheese, he realised that he couldn't go to the butcher's or the wine shop with these bags after all. He didn't even have a spare finger left to carry one more bag with. The best thing would be to go home, leave them there and make another trip. When he opened the door, he heard a beeping sound coming from his answering machine every ten seconds. This was the first message anyone had left for him in a very long time. Actually, it was the first message since he'd reconnected the machine. He left the bags in the kitchen and pushed the flashing red button:

'You have one new message. First new message was left on Saturday, at ten thirty am: "Hi Marc, this is Odette. I guess you've started the day early, right? We're all very excited about the dinner tonight. I wanted to ask you if you needed anything. And also, I spoke to Sylvie and Suzanne like you asked me to and told them that you've invited a new friend of yours to the dinner, but you're not involved with her romantically. Even though your private life shouldn't be our business, we appreciate you sharing this information with us. I just wanted you to know that. We're looking forward to meeting Sabina. See you tonight. Ciao!" There are no more messages.'

Marc smiled as he deleted the message. It was true that his private life shouldn't be of any concern to Clara's friends, but he was still glad to have given them some kind of an explanation. At least he wasn't going to have to feel their eyes on him all night long. He knew that their husbands couldn't care less, but this way he could escape their meaningful looks, too.

He went to the kitchen, put the cheese in the fridge and left again. He was going to go to the butcher's and the wine shop, and then stop by the florist's to get a few flowers to bring some colour to the living room. Marc didn't know anything about flowers, either, but he was sure that Madame Paulette would help him with that. He'd run away from her at the beginning, just as he'd done with everybody else, but as he'd started going there to get some flowers he'd found himself becoming a part of this sweet woman's life, just as Clara had been once. Now they often sat in the chairs in front of the shop and drank their Benedictine or lemonade together. Cognac was only for the winter, of course.

After getting the wine, he went to the butcher's. Simon greeted him noisily, as he always did. He walked around the counter to see him, and as he handed him the bag of meat he slapped him on the back with his other hand. He was telling Mark that it would be impossible for him to find any other meat as good as that anywhere else. If he cooked it the way he'd told him before, it was going to taste just like a Turkish delight. He mustn't forget to make small cuts every two fingers on the cylinder of meat, dress them with bay leaves and then criss-cross the meat with the string that was already in the package. It would help to lock the flavour in. It would take two and a half hours to cook. He had to spoon the sauce over the meat in the last fifteen minutes and should never just dump it on all at once. Marc listened to the advice like a student, nodding his head. This wasn't the first time he'd heard this recipe, but he had no objection to being reminded of the important points again. With the wine in one hand and the meat in the other, he walked to the florist's. The front of the shop looked just like a garden. Madame Paulette was sitting in her chair as always, watching the people passing by and talking to the ones she knew. As soon as she saw Marc, she pointed to the chair beside her. Would he like some Benedictine? Marc couldn't help smiling. He wondered whether Madame Paulette realised that it was still very early in the day. He thanked her politely and said he had to be on his way since he had a lot to do. The old woman took the job more seriously than ever and thought deeply, her hands on her hips. Finally she prepared a huge bouquet of hydrangea in various different colours. She didn't think it was necessary to tell him that Clara had always bought these same flowers for her parties.

Only when Marc had gone home and put the flowers in a vase would this image start to look familiar. All of a sudden, he'd feel as if he was standing in the living room where Clara was setting things up; his legs would go numb and he'd feel lightheaded. He was going to end up experiencing the same feeling all day long, whenever he went in there to set the table, bring in the appetisers or put the name cards on the little pears.

Apart from those moments, Marc spent the rest of his day in the kitchen. Over the course of the next seven hours, he prepared everything with great care as he sang along occasionally to the songs coming from the radio and held his breath at some very crucial moments. Since he washed every cup, spoon and knife after he'd used them, there wasn't a clue left in the kitchen that he'd been cooking that day. Only the meat was still roasting in the oven; other than that, he was ready.

He stood in front of the table and looked at it once again. There was nothing missing, as far as he could tell. He checked the time. Ten to eight. The bakery at the corner was going to have fresh bread in ten minutes' time. Seconds after he came back with the bread, there would be a knock at the door and this apartment would soon be filled with people for the first time in almost a year. Sylvie, Odette, Suzanne, Henri, Jacques and Daniel were going to walk in slowly, looking closely at every piece of furniture in the living room as if they wanted to check they'd survived. No doubt, a wave of sorrow was going to sweep over their faces; but none of them was going to show any other sign of it, say a word about it or overshadow a night that this man had clearly put so much effort into planning. They were all going to watch Marc's excitement, hospitality and the way he ran between the kitchen and the living room with great sympathy. What's more, everybody in that crowd was going to find the bouquet of hydrangea very familiar and remember it from the old days.

They opened the first bottle of Mouton Cadet before Sabina arrived. While some of them talked about the events of the week, the others praised the table decorations, and they all agreed that Marc deserved a lot of credit for how clean the kitchen looked despite all that preparation. Just before nine o'clock, the doorbell buzzed again. With a sweet smile on her face and an unexaggerated shyness in her gestures, Sabina walked in. After giving a bottle of port to Marc, she introduced herself to the other guests. As this group of people tried to get to know the first new person to enter their private circle for many years, Marc took the meat out of the oven. When he put it on a special plate he'd already arranged and walked into the living room, everyone's attention changed direction. The meat looked great, and it was exactly the right colour. How had he made the sauce?

Now everybody was sitting around the table. They all admired the name cards. Where had he come across such an original idea? How had he managed to get all of the pears to be the same size? They all sat in the seats reserved for them and waited for the host to serve. Nobody could help noticing Marc's trembling hands. What they didn't know was that he was also trembling inside and his hands were ice cold despite the last heat of September. When all of the plates were finally served and the serviettes were placed on everybody's knees, a silence fell over the table. At that moment, with everybody knowing what the others were thinking, Odette held out her glass towards the middle of the table and broke the silence: 'To Marc.'